"City of Crime" and "Shadow Over Alcatraz"

TWO CLASSIC ADVENTURES OF

by Walter B. Gibson
writing as Maxwell Grant

Foreword by Edd Cartier

with new historical essays by
Will Murray and Anthony Tollin

Published by Sanctum Productions for
NOSTALGIA VENTURES, INC.
P.O. Box 231183; Encinitas, CA 92023-1183

Copyright © 1936, 1938 by Street & Smith Publications, Inc. Copyright © renewed 1963, 1965 by The Condé Nast Publications, Inc. All rights reserved.

The Shadow Volume 16 copyright © 2008 by Sanctum Productions.

The Shadow copyright © 2008 Advance Magazine Publishers Inc./The Condé Nast Publications. "The Shadow" and the phrase "Who knows what evil lurks in the hearts of men?" are registered trademarks of Advance Magazine Publishers Inc. d/b/a The Condé Nast Publications. The phrases "The Shadow Knows" and "The weed of crime bears bitter fruit" are trademarks owned by Advance Magazine Publishers Inc. d/b/a The Condé Nast Publications.

"The Shadows of My Past," Christmas card art and Cartier photos copyright © 2008 by Edd and Dean Cartier.
"Interlude" copyright © 2008 by Will Murray.
"The Mystery of the Vanishing Artist" and "The Man Who Cast The Shadow" copyright © 2008 by Anthony Tollin.
Detective Fiction Weekly cover by George Rozen reprinted by special arrangement with Argosy Communications, Inc. Copyright © 1938 by The Red Star News Company. Copyright renewed © 1966 and assigned to Argosy Communications, Inc. All Rights Reserved.

This Nostalgia Ventures edition is an unabridged republication of the text and illustrations of two stories from *The Shadow Magazine,* as originally published by Street & Smith Publications, Inc., N.Y.: *The City of Crime* from the October 1, 1936 issue, and *Shadow Over Alcatraz* from the December 1, 1938 issue. This is a work of its time. Consequently, the text is reprinted intact in its original historical form, including occasional out-of-date ethnic and cultural stereotyping. Typographical errors have been tacitly corrected in this edition.

International Standard Book Numbers:
ISBN 1-932806-88-1   13 DIGIT 978-1-932806-88-5

First printing: March 2008

Series editor/publisher: Anthony Tollin
P.O. Box 761474
San Antonio, TX 78245-1474
sanctumotr@earthlink.net

Consulting editor: Will Murray

Copy editor: Joseph Wrzos

Cover restoration: Michael Piper

The editor gratefully acknowledges the assistance of Joel Frieman, Tom Roberts and Geoffrey Wynkoop

Nostalgia Ventures, Inc.
P.O. Box 231183; Encinitas, CA 92023-1183

Visit The Shadow at www.shadowsanctum.com & www.nostalgiatown.com.

Volume 16

The entire contents of this book are protected by copyright, and must not be reprinted without the publisher's permission.

CONTENTS

Two Complete Novels From The Shadow's Private Annals As told to Maxwell Grant

Thrilling Tales and Features

FOREWORD: THE SHADOWS OF MY PAST
  by Edd Cartier 4

CITY OF CRIME by Walter B. Gibson
  (writing as "Maxwell Grant") 8

INTERLUDE by Will Murray 70

SHADOW OVER ALCATRAZ by Walter B. Gibson
  (writing as "Maxwell Grant") 72

THE MYSTERY OF THE VANISHING ARTIST
  by Anthony Tollin 127

THE MAN WHO CAST THE SHADOW 128

Cover art by George Rozen
Interior illustrations by Edd Cartier

The Shadows of My Past *by Edd Cartier*

More than seventy years have passed since I first began illustrating The Shadow's adventures, shortly after graduating from Pratt Institute.

I remember always wanting to be an artist, having drawn things since my childhood. My father owned a tavern, Cartier's Saloon. Even when I was in grade school, he let me paint Christmas pictures on its large plate glass windows. I later designed costumes for the school plays, and illustrated my 1933 high school yearbook.

When I was a kid, my friends and family told me I should be a cartoonist, because a lot of my art was humorous. In fact, I have been accused of putting *too much* humor in my illustrations.

As a teenager, I listened to cowboy music and practiced tricks with a lasso. I was fascinated by the Old West, especially the look of the era and the art of Frederic Remington and Charles Russell. I decided to become an illustrator specializing in Western art for books and magazines.

My professional art training began at Pratt in 1933. At the Institute's School of Fine and Applied Arts, I majored in pictorial illustration, and became close friends with a fellow student, Earl Mayan, who was also destined to become a pulp illustrator. My favorite instructors were Maitland Graves and Harold Winfield Scott. Graves taught figure drawing, and was instrumental in my ability to depict anatomy, both human—and not so human. Scott taught pictorial illustration, and through him I feel privileged to trace an unbroken chain of art instruction back to Howard Pyle, the "father of American illustration." The links are fairly close: Scott had studied under Dean Cornwell, a student of Harvey Dunn, who in turn studied with Pyle.

Harold Scott became my mentor and advisor. Later, after I began illustrating *The Shadow,* I received a letter from Norman Rockwell offering me a job as an assistant. I went to Harold and asked his opinion. "If you study with Norman Rockwell, you're just going to become another Norman Rockwell," Scott advised. "You'll be influenced entirely by him. You should remain on your own." So I turned down Rockwell's job offer, though I have regretted doing so ever since.

Harold was an acclaimed Western pulp artist, and I wanted to follow in his footsteps. But I got the chance to do my own professional Western art through another Pratt instructor, William James, who was also an art director at Street & Smith Publications. He liked my work and encouraged me to submit pen-and-ink drawings to the company's magazines. However, James insisted that I diversify and not limit myself to Western art. So I ended up doing illustrations for a number of magazines including Western, detective and romance.

I began by doing a single illustration per week for Street & Smith pulps like *Wild West Weekly, Movie Action* and *Detective Story Magazine* while still attending Pratt, and was paid eight dollars for each drawing. But they soon began giving me more assignments.

When I graduated in 1936, James offered me a steady assignment illustrating The Shadow's adventures. The regular artist, Tom Lovell, was moving on to pursue a painting career, so I alternated with him illustrating the twice-monthly novels. My first work for *The Shadow Magazine* accompanied *The Sledge-Hammer Crimes* in the August 1st, 1936 issue, coincidentally my twenty-second birthday. Initially, James wanted me to work in Tom's darkly shaded style. I was given a batch of his originals to use as a guide. I wish I had kept those illustrations, but I didn't even keep many of my own. At first, I felt quite inhibited imitating his style. However, no one complained when I later subtly started changing things and began illustrating in my own way.

City of Crime was my second Shadow story, and my illustrations were again intended to resemble Tom Lovell's work. By the time I illustrated *Shadow Over Alcatraz* in the latter months of 1938, Tom had been gone for a year and I was drawing The Shadow as I wanted to.

Shortly after graduation, Earl Mayan and I had leased a studio on the fourth floor of a brownstone located just west of New York's Central Park. Earl initially found little work, and moved out after a year. Six months later, feeling lonely in the city, I returned home to New Jersey and set up my second studio, above Cartier's Saloon in my hometown of North Bergen. I decorated it with Old West memorabilia, and used scrap lumber to build the drawing table which I have used to this day.

Although I continued to contribute drawings to the other Street & Smith pulps, *The Shadow Magazine* quickly became the focus of my career. My illustrations evolved with each new issue. I abandoned pen-and-ink, preferring to use a combination of brush, ink, tempera and lithographic pencil. I worked almost exclusively on the lightly-textured surface of illustration board, usually Bainbridge #80, roughing in my Shadow drawings on the board with a pencil, then outlining the illustration with brush and ink. Next came brush and tempera, combined with ink for the darker areas. Finally, I would erase my original penciling and finish up by adding shading with a lithographic pencil. Sometimes I added a bit of red ink to my originals, usually in the eyes or as dripping blood, the red ink reproducing as black on the printed

Edd Cartier at his original homemade drawing table

page. A typical drawing was usually one by one-and-a-half feet in size, or one-and-a-half by two feet, or sometimes larger, even though it might be reduced in the pulps to as small as a quarter of a page—or smaller still, as a spot illustration.

At the beginning of my career, I occasionally used fellow Pratt students, my youngest brother Vincent and my Uncle Dan as models, but I was always dissatisfied with the results. My later Shadow, fantasy, science fiction and adventure illustrations were all drawn entirely from my imagination. However, a few old bottles, jugs, lamps and chairs, which I still own, did appear in my work, along with The Shadow's big, black slouch hat that I have also preserved as a souvenir of the pulp era.

Many of The Shadow's adventures took place in New York City—often in Chinatown—and in the surrounding New Jersey countryside. Since I lived in New Jersey, just across the Hudson River from Manhattan, I actually knew the types of places where The Shadow's adventures were set.

The gritty atmosphere of The Shadow's relentless fight against crime gave me the opportunity to illustrate a weird and fantastic world. Much of the action took place in my stylized visions of urban locales: dark hallways, one-room flats, spooky mansions, dingy subways, dead-end alleys and fog-shrouded wharves. I especially liked doing full-throttle scenes of speeding boats, steam-belching locomotives, crashing cars and hovering autogyros.

Cloaked in black, his hawk-nosed face nearly concealed by the wide brim of his slouch hat, with a blazing .45 automatic in each hand, the mysterious Shadow was the dark nemesis of Depression-era villains. Walter B. Gibson, who authored most of The Shadow stories under the house name "Maxwell Grant," pounded out page after page of two-fisted, guns-ablaze action for the magazine. His novels allowed my illustrations to depict The Shadow in edge-of-death conflict with all sorts of nefarious spies, depraved murderers, criminal businessmen, lecherous kidnappers, Oriental megalomaniacs and mad scientists.

It was exciting stuff to draw, but I did find that The Shadow's black garb made him a somewhat lackluster subject to portray, except in action-filled scenes. I was able to put much more life and personality into the stories' other characters: The Shadow's agents, the victims, bystanders and especially the criminals. The drawings were almost always filled with grim or violent activities, which were reflected in story titles like *The Seven Drops of Blood*, *Brothers of Doom*, *Noose of Death* and *The Murder Master*.

Illustrating two Shadow novels each month kept me busy. As preparation for the work I read each story from beginning to end. I felt obligated to read every word because art editor William James had given me complete freedom to decide which scenes to illustrate. I often read manuscripts late into the night. One evening, I was so engrossed in The Shadow's adventure that I didn't notice a spider until it had draped strands of its web from the top of my head, down to my shoulder, and over to a nearby window frame!

Photo by Vincent Cartier

Edd Cartier circa 1939

Street & Smith's *Shadow Magazine* also chronicled the adventures of other fictional detectives. Among those I illustrated were some three dozen tales, written by Steve Fisher and Grant Lane, about a young, shoeshine-boy detective named Danny Garrett. I also illustrated the adventures of Hook McGuire, bowling detective, along with stories for a handful of Street & Smith's other mystery magazines including *The Whisperer, The Wizard* and *Detective Story Magazine.*

One of my first Shadow illustrations, from *The Sledge-Hammer Crimes* ...

In 1939, the editor of Street & Smith's *Astounding Science-Fiction* offered me the opportunity to illustrate an extraordinary new magazine he was launching to be titled *Unknown.* John W. Campbell, Jr., thought I would be ideally suited to illustrating fantasy. I always enjoyed drawing the weird and fantastic nature of The Shadow's adventures. And John said he had often admired that quality in my illustrations before he asked me to illustrate *Unknown.*

After I illustrated the lead story in the first issue of *Unknown*—with my former instructor Harold Scott providing the cover painting—William James asked me if I would mind having someone else take over *The Shadow* so I could concentrate on science fiction and fantasy. I said it was okay with me, since I also liked science fiction. When I was a kid, my brothers Alfred and Vincent read as much science fiction as they could get their hands on. They had Hugo Gernsback's magazines, and shared them with me. At first, I thought the stories were too fantastic. But I was soon hooked on the genre. After I became an illustrator, I knew it would be fascinating to do science fiction art, and I was pleased to move on to *Unknown* and, also, *Astounding Science Fiction.*

I gave up illustrating The Shadow's adventures in 1940, and the work was turned over to my former roommate Earl Mayan. However, after returning from military service, I regained the assignment in late 1946, and illustrated the final year of the post-war *Shadow* digest magazine.

In 1994, I was invited to attend the world premiere of *The Shadow* movie as a guest of Universal Pictures, and was thrilled to see the look of my old pulp illustrations come to life onscreen.

For decades, I have done a new drawing each year for our family Christmas card. I commemorated the 75th anniversary of The Shadow's debut by teaming him with Santa Claus for our 2005 card. It was the first time I had drawn The Shadow since 1948. Unfortunately, I developed a tremor in my drawing hand midway through inking the piece, and my son Dean had to help finish the drawing. I'm not certain, but my last piece of artwork may be that holiday illustration featuring the same legendary Master of Mystery who helped launch my career seven decades earlier.

Perhaps only The Shadow knows!

... and my 2005 Christmas card

Edd Cartier

with Dean Cartier
New Jersey, 2008

The Shadow enters a

CITY OF CRIME

to bring justice to a gangster-throttled community.

CHAPTER I
CROOKS IN AMBUSH

IT was gala night in the city of Westford. Streets were strung with brilliant lines of colored electric lights. Storefronts were illuminated, throwing their brightness upon festooned posts and displaying the elaborate decorations of their own windows. Tourists, driving through the main streets, gained the impressions that this city of two hundred thousand was engaged in celebration.

As the boosters phrased it, Westford was a "live town" that was definitely "on the map"; the city attracted visitors from every town within a hundred miles. Business was booming in Westford; it was predicted that good times were here to remain. Thanks for the prosperity belonged to Westford's "live wire mayor," Elvin Marclot. His administration was hailed as the greatest in the history of the city.

There was one man who viewed all this dourly, as he sat in a small ground-floor office that gave

From the private annals of The Shadow as told to

Maxwell Grant

Complete Book-length Novel

him a slanted view of the main street. He was a husky, square-jawed individual, with weather-beaten face and short-clipped hair that was well streaked with gray. He was attired in a blue uniform, that stretched tight as he sat erect. His insignia marked him as a lieutenant of police.

Nearly everyone in Westford knew James Maclare. A veteran police officer, he had gained a reputation for honest and efficient service. His record was one of blunt, painstaking toil, rather than that of brilliant exploit; yet no one had ever said that Lieutenant Maclare lacked brains.

Though slow to decision, Maclare invariably formed the right opinion. When matters perplexed him, he thought them over and waited until he had the answer. During that process he kept silence; when the time was ripe, he acted.

There was one man in whom Lieutenant Maclare placed confidence. That man was another officer, as straightforward as Maclare himself. He was Sergeant Cassley, Maclare's chief subordinate. Together, they had charge of the first precinct; and, of necessity, Maclare frequently told Cassley the trend of his half-formed plans. Cassley was Maclare's man Friday; never did he pass along a single word that he had heard from his superior.

TONIGHT, Cassley was sitting across the desk from Maclare, watching the lieutenant as he stared from the window of the precinct office. Though slow of thought, Cassley was positive that opinions were due. He was right. They came.

"This whole thing is the bunk!" announced Maclare suddenly, emphasizing his gruff statement with a ponderous punch upon the desk. "Look at those lights; all that tinsel! What do they mean to Westford? Nothing except trouble!"

Cassley looked puzzled. He was a bulky man; his wrinkled uniform made a contrast to Maclare's smooth blue coat. His beefy, flat-featured face displayed its bewilderment. The sergeant needed more statements, in order to grasp the full import of Maclare's objections. The lieutenant noted the fact and formed a wry smile.

"I know what you're thinking, Cassley," he told the sergeant. "You've fallen for the talk of business coming into town. Sure! Westford is prosperous. But what's come on with all this excitement? I'll tell you—a lot of riffraff who think that Westford is the right spot for any crooked game they can cook up!"

Cassley nodded slowly. He was tabulating a list of recent crimes. Maclare was right; there were crooks in Westford, plenty of them. But when Cassley thought further, his nod ended. He could not see just where the law had failed to battle crime.

"What about the Flying Squadron?" queried the sergeant. "It's been moving fast, Lieutenant, ever since Director Borman organized it. They were on the job quick, those fellows, after that last bank robbery."

"But the crooks got away," reminded Maclare. "Don't forget that, Cassley."

"You can't blame Director Borman for it."

"I'm blaming Kirk Borman for nothing," returned Maclare, leaning across the desk. "You know what I think of Kirk Borman. I say that he's the best police director this town ever had. Elvin Marclot, as mayor, made the best choice anyone could have, when he picked Kirk Borman for the job.

"But Borman hasn't stopped the rackets. He can't, even though he's got full charge of that Flying Squadron. The job rests with precincts, like ours here. We've got to raid the places where the crooks hang out. Clean them up before they have a chance to make trouble."

Sergeant Cassley sat silent. Lieutenant Maclare began to strum his desk; then spoke in rueful tone.

"We've drawn a blank everytime we've tackled the Club Adair," he admitted. "We know that Lance Gillick runs it as a gambling joint; but when we blow in, it's always an innocent-looking nightclub. We're going there again, though, Cassley. Only, first, I'm planning to hand Lance Gillick a jolt that he won't forget."

"How will you manage that, Lieutenant?"

MACLARE smiled at Cassley's question. Picking up a pencil, he indicated an inkwell that rested on his desk; drew an imaginary circle around it.

"That's Lance Gillick," stated Maclare. "Working inside his circle, the Club Adair. We know what his racket is, don't we?"

"Sure," nodded Cassley. "Gambling!"

"All right." Maclare began to tap all around the desk with his pencil. "Here's a lot of stores, poolrooms, flophouses—all through the city. They've got slot machines, punchboards; they're running the numbers racket on the q.t. The State has legalized a lot of that stuff; neither Mayor Marclot nor Director Borman can break it up. But it's gambling, isn't it?"

Cassley nodded.

"Agreed," added Maclare. "Therefore, it's a sure bet that Lance Gillick is behind it. He's the big shot in this town."

"Say!" exclaimed Cassley. "If you could hook all that on to Lance—"

"It wouldn't do a bit of good," interposed Maclare. "But I tell you what we *can* do. Since the rackets belong to Lance, all those fellows who collect on the machines and numbers must be working for him."

"That's sure enough," agreed Cassley. "They stick together, too. They all hang out down at the old Mississippi Hotel, near the railroad terminal. That hotel is running wide open, even though it's got no license."

"That's just it," chuckled Maclare. "So we're going to raid it, tonight. We'll make a roundup and bring in that whole bunch of hoodlums. The only fellow who could spring them will be Lance Gillick; and he won't dare do it, because it would show that he was behind the rackets."

Sergeant Cassley arose, grinning broadly. He queried:

"How soon do we start?"

"Get the squad ready," ordered Maclare, briskly. "Have the wagons come along with us. We'll go out the back way, keeping off the main streets. No one will know where we're bound until we get there."

As Cassley turned toward the door, Maclare picked up the telephone. He made a brief remark, before he lifted the receiver.

"It's a straight precinct job," asserted Maclare; "but we mustn't forget standing orders. I'm calling Director Borman, to let him know that we're starting out. He wants it that way, so he can have the Flying Squadron cover up afterward."

SERGEANT CASSLEY went out into the patrol room, closing the lieutenant's door behind him. He snapped orders to a group of bluecoats; paraded them and sent word to bring out the patrol wagons. Lieutenant Maclare arrived from his office; surveyed the dozen men who were standing at attention.

"We're raiding the Mississippi Hotel," announced Maclare. "Sergeant Cassley will enter from the front, with a detail of four men. We'll let them think it's a minor raid; whoever comes out by the back doors will find our main force.

"We'll have the wagons with us, to gather up the lot of them when they reach the backstreet. I'll be in charge of the main squad. Further orders when we're on the ground. All right, men. Ready for inspection."

Soon the entire squad was marching from the station house; Maclare, at the head, was leading the advance through dingy, poorly lighted alleys that had been neglected in Westford's campaign of bigger and brighter lights. As they reached a corner, Maclare gave the command to halt. Sergeant Cassley told off his four-man detail. Lieutenant Maclare gave him final orders.

"Don't get far inside the front door, Cassley," Maclare advised. "We want them to come through the back. Director Borman is sending the Flying Squadron. They'll show up about ten minutes after we strike. The Flying Squadron will roll up on the front street. After that, you can let anybody go out through the front door. Remember: put up a big show. We've got a right to arrest anyone who comes out the back while you're inside. We'll charge them with resisting arrest."

Cassley and his men marched away. Maclare moved the remainder through an alleyway; then along an ill-paved street that was flanked on the right by coalyards, with the railway tracks beyond. As he and his men stationed themselves in back of the decrepit Mississippi Hotel, two darkened patrol wagons coasted into view. Officers opened the doors of the black Marias; stood beside them, ready for the surge that was to come.

Tense minutes passed. A police whistle shrilled from the front street. Commotion began within the old hotel. Until that moment, it had been a quiet-looking frame structure, its dim windows silent except for the jerky music of an overloud player piano. But the whistle blast that marked the beginning of raid was like a spark igniting dynamite.

Shouts burst from the hotel. Tables clattered; lights blinked on and off. Gunfire sounded; heavy footsteps pounded. Doors ripped open at the back of the building; the vanguard of a horde of hoodlums appeared. As three men leaped from rickety steps. Lieutenant Maclare snapped a command to his main squad:

"Take them as they hit the street!" The bluecoats spread, fanwise. With Maclare in the center, they closed upon the back doors of the hotel. The first fugitives dropped against the steps, raising their arms in surrender. Footsteps told that more were coming; Maclare and his men were ready to bag them the instant that they arrived.

Then came the unexpected. From the low-roofed buildings of the coalyards, searchlights poured a sudden glare that made the street like day. Huge beams of light showed the entire squad of police, flat-footed on the sidewalk, against the paintless back wall of the hotel.

Maclare, swinging about, stood scowling from the center of his raiders.

Snarled oaths sounded from fences and roofs, delivered by thugs who were out of sight behind the searchlights. A harsh voice barked an order. Revolvers crackled from the darkness. There was a sharp rattle; the opening outburst of a machine gun. It ended almost instantly, for the trigger man had started it too soon.

That warning sound told how hopelessly the police were trapped. Crooks had surprised the raiders. Hidden in ambush, men of crime were equipped to wipe out Lieutenant Maclare and his entire squad at an instant's notice.

CHAPTER II
SCATTERED HORDES

THE menace of the situation was but partially grasped by Lieutenant James Maclare. He and his men had faced about; they were blinking at the blinding searchlights. None had been hit by the first revolver fire; the machine gun had stopped without delivering death.

It occurred to Maclare that ambushed crooks had intended no more than a warning; that they were afraid to deliver heavy fire because their own men were coming from the hotel. Looking about, Maclare saw that a dozen fugitives had arrived; but they were no longer in flight. They were a leering, contemptuous throng, massed upon the back steps of the hotel.

Like the thugs behind the searchlights, these crooks had the police covered. The inference seemed plain to Maclare. If the police stood by and let the crooks from the hotel make their getaway, there would be no massacre.

Maclare was partly right in this conclusion. He was to learn later just how far he was wrong. Sizing the situation, the lieutenant realized that he could not count on aid from Sergeant Cassley; he knew also that the Flying Squadron would not arrive for ten minutes. Much though he hated to see crooks gain their way, Maclare could not forget the welfare of his men. He saw no use in allowing the slaughter of his squad.

Scowling, the lieutenant lowered his revolver and stepped out into the middle of the street. His move was an order for his men to spread away and let the armed men from the hotel make a calm departure.

It was not until he had detached himself from his squad, that Maclare realized another purpose behind the ambush. Hardly was the lieutenant standing entirely alone before a rasped voice called from a low rooftop:

"Get Maclare!"

One man alone was marked to die; that was Maclare himself. Crooks wanted the raiding lieutenant dead; they were contemptuous of the policemen who formed the squad. Maclare, by his own action, had placed himself in the very spot that his enemies wanted.

Bluecoats, like crooks, heard the death order. The cry electrified them. They responded more quickly than the gloating thugs. They were loyal to Maclare; the danger that threatened him was to be theirs. Almost as one, the policemen raised their guns. Some aimed blindly for the coalyards, along with Maclare; others wheeled about, to fire at men whom they could see. Their targets were the massed thugs on the steps.

The scene was set for massacre. The street looked like the stage of a theater, beneath the glare of a spotlight. All eyes were focused upon Maclare, with the bluecoats clustering about him. The patrol wagons, standing deserted on either side, were like the wings of the stage. All was dim beyond those vehicles.

DURING these tense moments, an event had occurred offstage. Unseen, a figure had come up to the far side of a patrol wagon, almost beneath the shelter of a coalyard fence. Like an actor expecting his cue, this silent arrival had risen on the running board of a black Maria. His head and shoulders projected above the wagon top, where they were outlined dimly by the fringe of a searchlight's path.

That head was topped by a slouch hat. The shoulders were shrouded by a black cloak. Two black-gloved fists projected from the cloak; each gripped the heavy handle of a .45 automatic. Those guns were leveled at the instant the hidden crook shouted the word to get Maclare.

As policemen leaped to Maclare's side, ready to die with their leader, that strange marksman loosed the fire of one gun from atop the black Maria. His target was a large one; he picked the glass front of a blazing searchlight. As his trigger finger tugged, a bullet ripped to its mark. The searchlight vanished with a clatter of glass.

Crooks gazed toward the patrol wagon. They saw no one, for the marksman had picked the nearer searchlight and was no longer in the edge of the glare. But mobsters saw the next token that came from the blotted wagon top. It was another stab of flame, loosed from the second automatic.

Another crash marked the finish of the second searchlight. The street looked black; feeble lamplights and illumination from the hotel were pitiful at best. They were completely inadequate as an aftermath to the glare that had been so promptly extinguished.

From the sheltering patrol wagon came a sudden sound that belonged with darkness. It was the strident burst of a sinister, mocking laugh, that brought alarm to every thug who was straining his eyes to offset the gloom.

Men of crime knew that taunt. It was the laugh of The Shadow!

Black-clad master who battled evil, The Shadow was here in Westford, covering the very spot where slaughter had been ordered. His first coup had been to deprive crooks of their most important weapons: those searchlights on the coalyard roofs. With two strategic shots, The Shadow had equalized the battleground.

True, crooks outnumbered Maclare and his squad; they also had machine guns in readiness. But the law had gained an ally whose strength could offset a score of foemen. The Shadow was on hand, prepared for instant battle.

Again, the automatics spoke. From his vantage point, The Shadow fired along the fence top. Lieutenant Maclare shouted an order. Policemen dived everywhere, firing as they took to cover. Revolvers spat from the coalyard; machine guns began a hasty rattle. Thugs at the doorways of the Mississippi Hotel came leaping down the steps, cutting loose with their revolvers.

Those mobsters in ambush fired for the area where Maclare and his men had clustered. They fired uselessly, for the police had spread. Those coming from the hotel sizzled futile shots in the direction of the patrol wagon. They, too, were late. The Shadow had sprung to the fence; come up to the top and slugged down a lone thug who was stationed on the flank.

All that carried menace were the machine guns, for they began to spray their fire. There were two of them, clicking like typewriters from a rooftop midway along the fence. One rattling weapon ceased, as The Shadow blasted a fusillade at the gunners behind it. He had picked them by the spurting fire.

CROOKS fired for The Shadow; but their shots were wide. He had come up to a rooftop; there, he ripped another barrage, that settled the men who handled the second machine gun. Both weapons were silenced; everywhere, crooks were springing to the ground, to avoid the enfolding fire that The Shadow had begun.

By outflanking the foe, The Shadow had routed all but a few; they were the ones upon the very rooftop where he had so suddenly arrived.

Three in number, those crooks leaped forward with swinging revolvers, hoping to beat down the fighter whose shape was vague before their eyes. An automatic thudded against a skull; the other .45 spat its singeing flame between the eyes of an attacker. The third crook dived for the ground as his companions sprawled.

Meanwhile, Maclare and his squad had done gallant duty. Flattened in the street, some had aimed for the fence and rooftops, while others had delivered quick fire toward the open doors of the hotel. This choice had been a smart one; the officers who took it gained massed targets. Thugs who had wasted opening shots at the patrol wagon were caught against the framed light of doorways. Four sagged in quick succession.

Scattering crooks had paused to aim for the low roof where The Shadow had handled three foemen. They blazed for that darkened spot, again to no avail. The Shadow had dropped from the back of the roof; he was crossing the tracks of the railroad yard. His quick shots clipped two marksmen who were firing at the roof.

A hoarse voice shouted from between two buildings. It was the same leader who had issued the command to get Maclare. His new order was a command for flight. All thugs who were able, dashed for the street, crossed it and made off through alleys toward the front. Others sprang back into the hotel.

Lieutenant Maclare shouted for pursuit. Two of his eight men had fallen in the fight; leaving a pair to care for them, Maclare headed through the hotel, followed by the remaining four.

Inside, thugs were making for the front; Cassley and his detail let them go through. Loud-whining sirens were announcing the arrival of the Flying Squadron.

Crooks should have found a new trap; but when Lieutenant Maclare reached the front door of the hotel, he witnessed a wild getaway. The Flying Squadron, a score of men in pursuit cars and on motorcycles were coming in from the left. Scattered crooks had converged to the right; there they were boarding an assortment of automobiles that were parked beside an old brewery.

As the Flying Squadron pulled up, Maclare bellowed the news and pointed past the brewery. Promptly, the picked squadron took up the chase.

The brief delay had served the crooks. Cutting through to another street, a dozen of them made a getaway, in three cars that contained four men each. The three automobiles took different routes within the next few blocks, to split the pursuing squadron. Maclare, fuming at the door of the raided hotel, heard the sirens fade in the dim distance.

THERE was a fourth car that had fled; it had taken a route of its own. Rounding the brewery, this machine had followed a street that led across the railroad tracks, a block away from the Mississippi Hotel. Swinging past a freight siding, the crooks—three in number—were greeted by shots from the shelter of a steel freight car.

Wildly, they fired in return. Their bullets flattened on the steel wall of the freight car. The driver, clipped by a slug from darkness, lost control and swung from the crossing. His sedan jolted down a low embankment, slewed sidewise and crashed against a signal tower.

There was no stir within the car, when it halted. Distant policemen heard the crash. Footsteps racing upon sidewalks told that they were coming to witness the result. One carload of fugitives had been bagged, even though the other three had outraced the Flying Squadron.

Blackness moved from beside the freight car. The purple light of a switch signal glowed upward to show a shrouded form, tall in its guise of black. Gloved hands dipped mammoth automatics beneath the front of a flowing cloak. Unseen lips voiced a grim laugh from the muffling front of an upturned collar.

Weird, chilling tones betokened the final stroke of the night's victory. The sardonic mirth faded, as the cloaked figure passed from the purplish glow. The battle was ended; The Shadow had left the field to the law.

OUT of darkness, The Shadow had arrived to deal with crime in Westford. Into gloom, he had returned—after his efforts had saved the life of Lieutenant Maclare and a squad of officers. Yet the chill of his eerie laugh seemed to hover; for that spectral tone had carried a touch that seemed to concern the future.

Like Lieutenant Maclare, The Shadow had recognized the significance of tonight's episode. Fierce though the fray had been, it scarcely scratched the surface of the evil that lurked deep within this prosperous city.

Crime and death would be due again in Westford. Here, evil was organized far beyond the extent that Lieutenant Maclare had guessed.

There would be need for more and greater effort before crime and corruption could be banished.

The Shadow knew those facts. His appearance in tonight's battle was but proof that he had long been present in Westford, investigating the iniquity which held the city in its grip.

CHAPTER III
BEHIND THE SCENES

HALF an hour after the raid on the Mississippi Hotel, Lieutenant James Maclare arrived back at the first precinct station. Muffled oaths and dull clatter greeted Maclare when he crossed the patrol room. The sounds came from the cell room, where policemen had housed an assortment of hoodlums unloaded from the patrol wagons.

There had been many captures following the raid. Cornered riffraff had thrown away their guns, to surrender, denying that they had carried weapons. Practically all of these were men who had been inside the hotel at the beginning of the raid.

Lieutenant Maclare felt pleased as he took a seat at his desk and began to prepare a report. Armed resistance had made the case against the prisoners a stronger one. Maclare could see jail terms awaiting many of the participants. Maclare's pleasure increased, when Sergeant Cassley knocked at the door to announce a visitor. The arrival was none other than Kirk Borman, the police director.

Maclare was on his feet when Borman entered. Tall, heavy of build, the police director was as much a fighter as Maclare. Borman's face was sharp-featured; his lips showed a broad smile between his hooked nose and his pointed chin. Advancing to Maclare's desk, Borman thrust a congratulating hand across the top, to grip Maclare's hand in a solid shake.

"Fine work, Jim," commended Borman, in a short-clipped tone. "You cleaned out a nest of bad eggs. Carry on with it. Go after the gilt-edged places in this precinct."

"You mean the Club Adair?" queried Maclare. "That's one place I'd like to get, Kirk. Lance Gillick has a gambling joint somewhere in back of that fancy nightclub front."

"Go after it, tomorrow night," ordered Borman. "Telephone me first, though. I have two headquarters men watching things over there. I'm going to drop in there this evening and look the place over for myself."

"Lance Gillick will probably see you," remarked Maclare. "If he does, he'll pass you a lot of smooth talk."

"All the better," decided Borman. "If he thinks I'm the man he has to deal with, he won't be expecting you tomorrow."

Kirk Borman clapped his hand upon Lieutenant Maclare's shoulder; then turned about and strode from the office. Policemen saluted, as the director passed through the patrol room. Outside the station house, Borman stepped aboard an official limousine and told the chauffeur to take him to the Club Adair.

LOCATED just within the limits of the first precinct, the Club Adair fronted on one of Westford's main streets. The club itself was on the second floor, over a row of shops.

Alighting from his car, Kirk Borman entered a pretentious doorway and ascended a broad flight of thick-carpeted stairs. At the top, he left his hat and coat at a checkroom. Attired in tuxedo, the police director entered a glittering nightclub, where tobacco smoke clouded a thick throng of dancers who occupied the center of the floor.

An orchestra was producing strident music. Buzzed conversation, bursts of laughter sounded everywhere. The place was doing capacity business; a bowing headwaiter was apologetic when he ushered the police director to an obscure table, behind a pillar. It was one of the few tables that remained vacant.

A heavy-jowled man spied Borman immediately and came over to the director's table. He was one of the headquarters men; he reported in an undertone:

"They've been going through that door over there, a lot of 'em. Looks like the gambling joint's on the other side—"

Borman whispered an interruption. The headquarters man silenced as the headwaiter approached the table. Directly behind the headwaiter came a man in full evening clothes. The arrival was Lance Gillick.

The nightclub proprietor was tall and long-limbed. His manner was polished; his speech was suave. His features were handsome, despite their sallowness. His wavy black hair, his pointed mustache gave him a debonair air.

"Good evening, Director Borman," greeted Gillick, with a bow. "It is not often that I have the pleasure of meeting you here. I somewhat expected your arrival tonight"—Lance smiled, as he looked in the direction of the headquarters man—"because I saw two of your advance agents. This gentleman and the other, over by the wall."

Borman turned to the headquarters man.

"Go over there, Thompson," he ordered, "and bring Rhyne here. I want both of you to come along with me."

Lance Gillick arched his clipped eyebrows, as he heard Borman give the order. When the two headquarters men arrived at the table, Borman snapped brisk words to Lance:

"We're going through that far door, Gillick! You can conduct us there!"

"With pleasure," said Lance, with a bow. "Come at once, Director."

LANCE led the way to the door in question. He rapped a signal; the door opened. Borman and his men followed through into a large room, where some twenty people were seated at tables, laughing as they chatted and drank. All were well attired; the men in evening clothes, the women in evening gowns.

The room, itself, was magnificent. Its walls were adorned with huge oil paintings; the windows were covered by expensive velvet draperies. Lance conducted Borman and the others to a far door; he opened it, to show a small office with oak furniture and paneled walls to match.

"My private office," explained Lance. "The large room through which we came is simply an exclusive dining room for my more important guests."

"It passes muster," decided Borman. Then, eyeing the office: "I suppose you are very careful in your bookkeeping, Gillick?"

"I am," replied Lance, smoothly. "Perhaps you would like to see my books?"

"I would."

"Step into the office, Director."

Borman hesitated; then turned to the headquarters men, with an order:

"Go back to the nightclub proper. Take my table. I'll join you there."

Thompson and Rhyne departed, out through the door by which they had entered. Lance Gillick ushered Kirk Borman into the oak-paneled office. Closing the door, the nightclub proprietor grinned. He pressed a wall panel; it slid open, to reveal a darkened passage.

"Step in there, Kirk," chuckled Lance. "Take a look through the back of the big painting on the far wall."

Smiling, Borman followed directions. Looking through a peek hole, the director saw a quick transformation in progress.

Waiters were lifting the top of a huge buffet; as they rolled the bulky object forward, its sides fell away and it became a roulette table. Small tables were pushed in line; their covers whipped away. They produced the green board upon which players could place their bets.

Other waiters were bringing boxes loaded with playing chips, serving them to guests in return for credit slips. The chips began to click; a waiter took charge of the wheel and it began its spin. Director Borman stepped back into Lance Gillick's office. Lance closed the panel.

"They think it's hot," laughed Lance. "As soon as you're ready to go out, they'll see the lights blink. It will just be tables and drinks again, when you go through. A great setup, eh, Kirk?"

KIRK BORMAN nodded. Lance caught a troubled look on the director's face. Quickly, Lance questioned:

"Something went sour tonight?"

Borman nodded.

"What was it?" quizzed Lance. "Didn't they rub out Maclare?"

"Maclare made a cleanup," answered Borman. "He and his squad bumped off more than a half dozen of the mob. About the same number went to the hospital. Maclare hauled in pretty near twenty of the bunch that were in the Mississippi Hotel."

Lance glared sourly. "I can't figure why that outfit didn't get Maclare. As soon as you gave me the tip-off, Kirk, I phoned Beezer Dorsch and told him to be on the job. Beezer should have gotten Maclare."

"Smart work, using Beezer," commended Borman. "He's the one real mobster in town who's supposed to be at odds with you."

"Sure!" Lance laughed as he spoke. "That covers me perfect, in case Beezer gets recognized! Say, have you seen Maclare since the raid?"

Borman smiled; then nodded.

"I told him to blow in here tomorrow night," informed the director. "When he and his squad find nothing, they'll owe you an apology, Lance. Only, be ready to duck the roulette layout so deep that they'll never find it."

"I won't run the gambling joint tomorrow," stated Lance. "I'll tell the customers to stay away, on account of you being here tonight. Maclare and his crew of flatfeet won't even find a gambling chip. All the stuff will be out of the place."

Lance sat down at his desk, brought out a box of expensive cigars. Borman helped himself to one of the perfectos. Lance lighted up also.

"Let's forget Maclare," decided Borman. "There's something bigger to think about. We've got to worry about Prescott Dunson. If he runs for district attorney, we'll have a tough guy to deal with."

"Then it's up to Stephen Ruthley," decided Lance. "As the big reform champion of Westford, he can find fault with Dunson. No one has even guessed that you and I are working together; that Mayor Marclot is also with us. So how can they ever figure that Stephen Ruthley, the big philanthropist and reformer, is the man we all take orders from?"

KIRK BORMAN shook his head.

"A lot of reformers like Prescott Dunson," he

said. "Therefore, Ruthley can't move against him. Ruthley has to put up a bigger front than the rest of us. There's only one thing to do, Lance. Bump Dunson!"

"My specialty," laughed Lance. "Tip me off to where Dunson is. I'll do the rest. Say, though"—he stroked his chin ruefully—"I wish I'd kept Trig Callister here."

"Who is Trig Callister?"

"A bird who was here to see me last night. He's a one-man arsenal, that guy. Packs a couple of gats and knows how to use them. I let Trig go back to New York. I'll get hold of him again, though, before next week."

"We won't have to rub out Dunson before then. It will take a while to find him, too. You're right, though, Kirk. We've got to put Dunson on the spot. With him out, there'll be no opposition to Louis Wilderton running for re-election."

Borman chuckled at Lance's reference to Wilderton, the man who was, at present, district attorney.

"Wilderton is a babe in the woods," laughed the police director. "Any smart lawyer can tangle him into knots. But Wilderton means well.

"It also makes it easy for us," concluded Borman. "Wilderton is under Ruthley's thumb. Comes running to him for an opinion on everything. Like a kid visiting a department store Santa Claus, around Christmas time."

With this comment, Borman arose, as indication that he was ready to leave. Lance reached beneath his desk and pressed a hidden button, to blink the lights in the gaming room. Rising, he walked to the door with Borman, and stopped there for a few moments.

"Wait until they've had time to cover the wheel," reminded Lance. "Then put on your act when we go through the room. Don't forget about Prescott Dunson. Tip me off when you've located him."

"I'll have every copper in town on the lookout," returned Borman. "When I give the order, I'll state that it's for Dunson's own protection."

IN his office, the big-shot gambler grinned, as he took a long puff from his perfecto. Leagued with Mayor Elvin Marclot and Police Director Borman, Lance had little to fear from the law. Moreover, he knew that he could rely upon a leader more powerful than either of those two; namely, Stephen Ruthley, Westford's champion of reform.

The future looked rosy to Lance Gillick, despite the fact that crooks had failed tonight in their effort to slay Lieutenant James Maclare.

Lance Gillick had not yet learned that The Shadow's hand had been responsible for crime's failure.

CHAPTER IV
INTO THE SNARE

TWENTY-FOUR hours had passed since Westford had been stirred by the law's combat with crime. Lieutenant James Maclare had been heroized for his raid on the Mississippi Hotel. Westford's chief newspaper, the *Daily Banner,* had been loud in its acclaim. A great quiet had settled upon the city, as an aftermath to Maclare's exploit.

The newspaper headlines were of huge interest to a man in shirtsleeves, who sat in an easy chair, surrounded by the quiet of a modest parlor. The house which contained this room was a small suburban home in one of Westford's residential districts; but the man, himself, looked out of place in such an ordinary room.

His bulky frame; his huge, bulging forehead, denoted him as a man of action. His bushy eyebrows, with flashing eyes beneath, showed that he was tired of seclusion. This man was Prescott Dunson, long known as a challenger among political circles.

Across from Dunson sat a weary-faced, middle-aged woman, busy with her knitting. She looked up as she heard Dunson grumble aloud. She shook her head and sighed. Dunson mopped his huge forehead and smiled indulgently.

"It's too bad, Martha," he declared, in a booming tone, "that you had to marry a man who went in for politics; particularly in this rotten town. But I am determined to go through with what I started. I intend to be the next district attorney of this county. And Westford is nearly all the county."

"Is it worth the risk, Prescott?" inquired the woman.

"Yes! Westford is in the hands of rogues!" boomed Dunson. "Mayor Marclot is a smug pretender! Director Borman is a traitor, in league with criminals! I can prove those facts, Martha! And I have a suspicion there's a big shot above them all!"

Dunson's wife stared, amazed.

"As for Louis Wilderton," added Dunson, "he is a know-nothing. A puppet, acting as district attorney. What chance is there for justice, while he holds office?"

"I can't believe all that, Prescott," protested Mrs. Dunson. "It sounds incredible! If I won't believe it, how can others? They will say that you are a fanatic; they will laugh at your assertions."

Dunson thrust a big hand into his coat pocket; drew out a folded letter and held it aloft in his right hand.

"This came from a man who knows the truth," he announced. "A man whom I have never met; but who told me enough in his previous letters. He signs himself Theo D. Shaw; he has not only promised me more facts, he has offered to take me to a place of absolute security. With his aid, I can lift the lid. I cannot only tell the truth; I can prove it."

STOOPING, Dunson picked up the newspaper that he had dropped. He opened it to the editorial page; pointed to a paragraph.

"Look, Martha," he said. "Already, they state that they expect to hear from Prescott Dunson; that I have promised to throw light on hidden corruption; to name men who have bled this city. When I officially and publicly announce myself as candidate for district attorney, I shall wither the rogues whose names I mention. I shall—"

Dunson broke off. A telephone bell was ringing in the hall. With a nod to his wife, Dunson lowered his tone and ordered:

"Answer it."

The woman laid aside her knitting; she went to the telephone, held a brief conversation. She came back into the room, to whisper:

"Someone wishes to speak to you, Prescott. He says that his name is Shaw—"

Dunson bounded across the room. In the hall, he seized up the telephone, began a quick conversation.

"Yes, yes..." Mrs. Dunson heard all that her husband said. "Of course, Mr. Shaw... I knew that you would learn where I was living... Yes, I have my car here... The garage…? Right in back of the house… Certainly. I understand.…

"Twenty minutes..." Dunson nodded as he spoke. "Yes, I can make it in that time... Parking lot beside the Majestic Hotel... Up through the fire tower... Room 304... Very well, Mr. Shaw. I shall be there within a half hour."

Hanging up the receiver, Dunson came into the parlor. He told his wife the import of the call.

"Shaw wants me to meet him at the Majestic Hotel. I'm going straight up to his room. Pack my bag at once, Martha."

"Is it safe, Prescott?"

"Absolutely! I am to park my car by the side of the hotel, in that parking space that we've used so often. I'll go in by the side door; up the fire tower to Shaw's room. I'll call you, after I have talked with him."

Donning coat and vest, Dunson clapped a battered hat upon his head. He went out through the kitchen, while Mrs. Dunson started upstairs to pack the suitcase.

Five minutes later, Mrs. Dunson arrived downstairs, carrying a light bag. She heard the kitchen door slam; Dunson arrived, fuming incoherently. Taking the bag, he explained the reason for his annoyance.

"The battery is dead," he told his wife. "I'll take the trolley into town."

"Didn't Mr. Shaw tell you to drive in your car?"

"Yes. Probably because I said that I had one available."

"Perhaps you should call him at the hotel."

"No. That would be unnecessary."

Kissing his wife good-bye, Dunson stepped toward the door. He paused long enough to add a last assurance.

"The trolley stop is only one block from the Majestic Hotel," reminded Dunson. "That block is a quiet one. I can walk along the left side of the street, in front of Judge Benbrook's old house. When I get past there, I can cross over to the parking lot, and enter the hotel as Shaw suggested."

LEAVING, the house, Dunson took to a secluded sidewalk. The suburban street was deserted; Dunson felt secure as he paced in the direction of the car line. He reached the car stop; stood under the darkened shelter of a large tree. In a few minutes, a jouncy trolley car came along the street. Dunson stepped into the glow of its headlight and halted it.

There were only five passengers on the trolley car. None noted Dunson particularly. Setting his bag on the seat beside him, Dunson shoved his hat back from his bulgy forehead and stared from the window as the car rolled along.

After a few blocks, the car halted. A policeman stepped aboard the back platform, grunted a "hello" to the conductor. The car started on; the officer remained on the rear platform. The trolley had traveled another block before he happened to glance in through the door.

"Say!" exclaimed the bluecoat, to the conductor. "Isn't that Prescott Dunson, the fellow that's going to run for district attorney?"

"Guess it is," rejoined the conductor, peering through the door. "Looks like the pictures I've seen of him."

The cop whistled.

"We got orders tonight to watch for him," he informed. "On account of that battle last night, the police director's taking no chances. Guess he figures there'll be crooks looking for Dunson. Ring for a stop at the next corner. I'd better put in a call to the precinct."

"Want me to hold the car for you?"

"Naw! I'll take the next one. I wasn't told to go along with Dunson. Orders were to report if I saw him."

The conductor signaled the motorman. The trolley stopped long enough for the policeman to drop off; then resumed its jerky course. Coming into the heart of the city, it was halted frequently by traffic lights; but took on few passengers.

After ten minutes, the trolley neared the corner where Dunson intended to get off. The conductor, staring toward the street, noted that a touring car was loitering along beside the trolley; but he quickly forgot the fact. The trolley swung into a one-way street; Dunson arose and pressed a button. When the car stopped, the big man alighted at his corner.

DUNSON'S first move was to cross the street. This brought him to the left side of a short block. To his left was the looming bulk of an old-fashioned mansion, the residence of Judge Martin Benbrook, who was long retired from the bench. There were two gates in the iron picket fence that ran in front of the old house. One offered access to the front door; the other led to a side passage that ran to the rear of the house.

Just past Judge Benbrook's home, the remaining half of the block was composed of buildings with lighted fronts. Across from them was the Majestic Hotel, on the right side of the street. Nestled against the hotel were parked cars, scarcely discernible in the darkness of the parking lot.

Dunson strolled along at leisurely gait; he saw that he could easily cross the street unnoticed, after he had passed Judge Benbrook's.

It was when Dunson neared the second gate, that the first token of danger came. A touring car had swung the corner which the trolley had left. Its lights flashed suddenly from dim to bright. Dunson's walking figure was outlined in their glare. For an instant, the big man paused, hoping, the lights would swing away. They did, but in their place came the vivid glow of a spotlight.

Prescott Dunson was caught in full view, turned half toward the side gate in the picket fence. He was clutching his suitcase, blinking into the brilliance that had so plainly revealed him. To his startled ears came the sound of a rasped command, that delivered two words only:

"Give it!"

The suitcase dropped from Dunson's shaky hands. In that tense instant, the doomed man realized that he was on the spot.

Prescott Dunson had walked into the snare of death.

CHAPTER V
DEATH DELIVERED

OTHER eyes than Dunson's had seen the sudden glare of the revealing spotlight. They were eyes that were not blinded by the unexpected brilliance. Across the street, but beyond the spot where Dunson stood, a lurking figure was watching from the shelter of cars stationed in the parking lot.

To that observer, the spotlight told its story. He saw the helpless man caught in the path of light. With a quick spring, this watcher came from his place of security. Street lights showed him as a shrouded shape. The Shadow was again on hand to offset crime.

Before thugs could obey the command of their leader, The Shadow's fists came up. With quick fingers, he pulled the triggers of automatics; dispatched whining bullets straight for the death car that lay almost between him and Prescott Dunson. Cries came from the slowly moving touring car. The Shadow had scored hits upon human targets.

Those shots saved Dunson for the moment. They gave the doomed man a needed opportunity. Close beside Dunson was the gate to the side passage that led beyond Judge Benbrook's house. Had Dunson dropped his suitcase and pressed through the gate, he could have gained the shelter that would save him.

Instead, Dunson stood rooted. He seemed hypnotized by the light that blinded him. The death car veered, to escape The Shadow's bombardment. While the automatics still tongued, a clatter began from within the touring car. One crouching machine gunner had lain below The Shadow's fire, was pushing the muzzle of the death gun through the opening of a half-opened door, on Dunson's side of the street. That killer profited by Dunson's lack of motion. He let the doomed man have it.

The touring car sped forward, while bullets still streamed from its side. The driver was low behind the wheel; the machine gunner was crouched on the rear floor. Others were hanging from the side of the car while it ran the gantlet of The Shadow's fire. One in the front seat, the other in the rear, two thugs had stopped the bullets that had entered the right side of the car.

The Shadow boomed last shots at the driver. They failed to get him; for the rolling form of an intervening thug shielded the man at the wheel. As the touring car wheeled leftward to the main street, The Shadow put a bullet through the gasoline tank; but the automobile kept onward and disappeared from view.

THE SHADOW started across the street, to the darkness where Dunson's body lay. Before he arrived, he heard light, quick footsteps. As he came up in the darkness, he found a girl bending over the bullet-riddled man. The Shadow saw a white face in the darkness, as the girl listened to Dunson's last words.

"Tell—tell Shaw!" gasped Dunson. "I should—should have done as he—he said—"

The sentence ended with a sigh. Prescott Dunson was dead.

Bravely, the girl raised the man's head; felt it drop back from her grasp. At that instant, she sensed that someone was beside her. Looking up, the girl viewed a blackened figure almost at her elbow. She saw the burn of steady eyes. Frightened, bewildered, she tried to scream an accusation.

"You—you killed him!"

An approaching car had swung the corner. The Shadow saw it across the girl's shoulder. He knew that it was bringing a second crew of gunmen. Shoving one gun beneath his cloak, he seized the girl about the shoulders. Hurling his full weight against the gate, he rammed it open; then launched the struggling girl along the passage beside the house.

The Shadow performed this action with a complete spin that brought him again facing the street, a ready gun in hand. He had whirled the girl more than a dozen feet away; she was in a spot of safety. New battle was due; the *click* of an automobile spotlight foretold it. Standing at the gate, The Shadow was fully revealed by a stream of light.

Though spotted as Dunson had been, The Shadow was prepared. His laugh sounded its fierce challenge. Standing above the body of the murdered man, The Shadow loosed quick bullets from his single .45; though few, those shots were perfect. This time, The Shadow had the range he wanted.

His first bullet was straight for the rear door of the car. That door, like the previous one, was partly opened. The Shadow dropped the man who was behind it. His second bullet stabbed the spotlight, finishing its glare. As the driver gave the car the gas, The Shadow ripped a final bullet for the steering wheel. A cry told that he had clipped the hoodlum at the wheel.

The car zigzagged wildly. An unwounded thug managed to control it and yank it into the parking lot, where it sped through a path between parked cars.

The Shadow whipped forth the gun that he had stowed away; but he did not aim toward the car that had fled. He had a new target; this was a sedan that swung in from the other direction.

COMING from the main street, the sedan was plain against the lighted front of the Majestic Hotel. The Shadow saw a gun muzzle thrust from a rear window; he blasted away before the driver was ready to turn on a spotlight. Bullets that spat from darkness were too much for this crew. The driver wheeled the sedan to the left; took the route that the second car had followed, through the parking space.

Before The Shadow could make another move, he heard the whine of sirens. They came from both directions. The Flying Squadron was coming to the scene of battle. To others, that arrival signified the law. To The Shadow, it meant something else.

The Shadow knew the extent of crime in Westford; he knew that the Flying Squadron was a bluff. Crooks would make their getaway amid wild pursuit; the squadron would gain credit for prompt action. That was exactly what had happened last night, after Lieutenant Maclare's raid.

The Shadow knew more. He had guessed the personnel of the picked men who formed the Flying Squadron. He knew that they were as dangerous as crooks; otherwise, they would not be party to the fake pursuit that they so often staged.

Because of that, The Shadow saw danger in his own position. His guns were empty; he would have no chance to battle uniformed men who merely pretended to uphold the law. They, however, would be pleased at the opportunity to drill The Shadow.

Already, cars and motorcycles were swinging into view, converging toward the very spot where The Shadow stood; a fact that signified that they knew where to find Dunson's body. The Shadow had one lone path to safety. That was the passage past Judge Benbrook's house, the route along which he had sent the girl.

Turning, The Shadow swiftly entered the passage, swinging the gate shut behind him. Hardly had he started through the darkened space before he heard a siren stopping on the rear street. One of the Flying Squadron's cars had arrived there; Borman's men were coming through from the back.

Quickly, The Shadow swung into the shelter of an alcove at the side of the house. He stumbled down a short flight of steps; as he caught himself against the wall, he heard a whispered voice just above his head. The voice gave question:

"You—you're safe?"

It was the girl who spoke. She had taken this shelter ahead of The Shadow. She had guessed that the person stumbling in darkness was the one who had saved her from death. The Shadow gave quiet response.

"I am safe," he whispered. "Remain silent until everyone has gone."

"I have my key," began the girl. "If I could only unlock this door—"

Almost instantly, The Shadow blinked a tiny flashlight. By the glow, he saw the key that the girl was holding; her hand was shaking as she tried to fit it into the door. Quickly, The Shadow plucked the key with gloved fingers. He found the lock; opened the door and thrust the girl inward.

Following, The Shadow closed the door behind him, inserted the key from the inside and turned the lock.

LOOKING about, The Shadow found himself in an entry that led to a dimly lighted hall. The girl had gone through; she was staring back, trying to discern the man who had so promptly aided her with the door.

The Shadow stepped forward into the light. The girl gasped, as she saw his weird, cloaked figure. She silenced, as The Shadow gave a whisper. Fascinated, the girl met the gleam of The Shadow's burning eyes. She heard him speak; not a question, but a statement.

"You are Judge Benbrook's daughter?"

The girl nodded.

"Estelle Benbrook," stated The Shadow. "I have heard of you."

Though more amazed than ever, Estelle Benbrook found her voice. She thanked her rescuer.

"You saved my life," declared the girl. "You have my gratitude! But—but—"

The Shadow waited for the girl to continue. Estelle finally expressed her thoughts.

"But the police are now outside!" blurted the girl. "Why did we need to avoid them?"

"They are as dangerous as the others," replied The Shadow, calmly. "Criminals were ready to eliminate all who saw Prescott Dunson die. These police would willingly do the same."

Estelle Benbrook continued to watch The Shadow's eyes. When the girl spoke, her tone was one of conviction.

"I believe you," she declared, firmly. "I recognized Prescott Dunson, when I saw his body. My father has said that matters were wrong in Westford; but I have never repeated his statements. He is an old man; his mind seems tired. Yet I have known that he speaks the truth."

The girl paused; then added:

"I have never spoken this before; not even to Louis Wilderton. He would not believe me. He thinks that all is well in Westford. If Louis could only understand—"

"He will learn," interposed The Shadow, quietly, "when the right time arrives. Until then, you must remain silent."

"I promise," declared Estelle. "I shall say nothing of what I saw tonight. Terrible though it was, it has given me courage."

The Shadow stepped back into the passage. He listened at the side door; he heard the shuffle of departing feet. The members of the Flying Squadron had completed their search in the passage beside the house. They had gone forward to join the ones at the front.

The Shadow turned the key in the lock: Estelle saw the motion of his hand as she joined him in the passage. Anxiously, the girl queried:

"Are you sure that the way is safe?"

The Shadow's response was a whispered laugh; mirthless, it was scarcely audible in the darkness. It betokened ill for any who might block his path.

Estelle, as witness of The Shadow's mighty battle, understood the grim significance. As The Shadow drew the door inward, Estelle reached forward; she found the key and plucked it from the lock.

"Take this key," pleaded the girl. "I have another. Sometime, you may wish to return. Perhaps—perhaps there may be new danger, greater than that which you faced tonight."

Gloved fingers grasped the key. Estelle released it. She sensed that The Shadow had moved outward; but she expected him to speak again. It was not until half a minute later that she realized that The Shadow had departed. Silently, he had closed the door behind him. Estelle Benbrook stood alone.

SLOWLY, the girl went through the lighted hall. She reached a front room and turned on a desk lamp. The glow showed her well-formed face, attractive despite the paleness which dominated it. The darkness of her hair made her pallor seem more evident; for Estelle Benbrook was a pronounced brunette.

The girl had steadied since her ordeal. Her hand had no tremble, as it found another key in the desk. Steadily, Estelle returned to the side door and inserted the key. She found the door locked. The Shadow had silently attended to that detail from outside. Estelle managed a slight laugh, as she went into the hall and placed the key in her handbag.

A puzzled frown appeared upon her forehead. She would have liked to have learned more concerning this mysterious stranger from the night. She recalled rumors that she had heard this very day, concerning the raid made last night, by Lieutenant Maclare. There was talk of persons unknown, who had sided with the law.

Estelle believed that rumor; but she was convinced that one fighter, not a group, had been responsible for the aid that Maclare had received. Estelle could form that opinion from her own observation. She was still overwhelmed with admiration for The Shadow's prowess in tonight's battle.

As she closed the handbag, Estelle smiled. After all, The Shadow had taken the key that she had offered. That seemed more than courtesy. Sometime—soon, she hoped—the black-clad stranger might return.

In her thoughts, Estelle pictured this house as a real haven in the heart of Westford, should The Shadow need the refuge that it could afford. Such need seemed likely to Estelle, when she considered the odds that this lone fighter faced. Circumstances could arise to make The Shadow's return imperative.

Though Estelle Benbrook did not guess it, such circumstances were already in the making.

CHAPTER VI
CROOKS CONNIVE

NOT far from the center of Westford stood a large apartment house that fronted on a boulevard. This new and pretentious edifice had supplanted part of a row of old brick houses. The remnants of the row began at the side of the apartment house and continued to a corner. Deserted and dilapidated, they were ready for demolition.

The front windows on the second floor of the apartment house were heavily curtained, all in the same style. They gave the impression that they belonged to one apartment, which they did. That apartment was the residence of Stephen Ruthley, the wealthiest man in Westford.

Ruthley called the apartment his town home; and he considered an entire floor necessary for comfort, although his family seldom occupied the apartment with him. They preferred a country house, some miles from Westford. They lived there during the short intervals when they came home from Newport, Florida, or Europe.

Hence, Stephen Ruthley lived alone, except for a retinue of servants; and he liked this second floor apartment near the heart of Westford.

Recognized as the city's most prominent citizen, Ruthley enjoyed his prestige. He gained acclaim for his philanthropies and his constant stand for reform. His real pleasure, however, lay in the fact that never a whisper had passed concerning his actual capacity. None but his most trusted lieutenants knew that Stephen Ruthley was the real political boss of Westford.

Beginning with half a million dollars gained from honest enterprise, Ruthley had increased his fortune to ten times that amount by backing graft and crime. He had covered this procedure by expanding his legitimate businesses and making them look prosperous, though they cost him more than he gained. Ruthley considered this essential. As overlord of Westford, he maintained his security by keeping his real activities unknown.

There were two reasons why none of Ruthley's associates had ever dared to expose his game. First, because no one would have believed them; second, because they were in too deep. Ruthley took care of his tools; saw to it that they gained their share of the spoils. That kept them satisfied, and maintained their loyalty to their evil chief.

ON this night, soon after The Shadow had rescued Estelle Benbrook, Stephen Ruthley had a visitor. The caller was a stuffed-shirt henchman, who was at present Ruthley's most useful figurehead. He was Elvin Marclot, mayor of Westford, whom Ruthley had carried into office on a sweeping wave of so-called reform.

The pair were seated in Ruthley's den, a room that had windows only at the front, for it was the side of the apartment that was buttressed by the side wall of the first house in the row.

Ruthley's den was a cross between an office and a clubroom. It had a desk in the corner, along with a filing cabinet. Except for those articles of office equipment, it was furnished with deep-cushioned chairs and couches, thick rugs, ornate tables.

The side wall showed a pair of large bookcases, set apart; between them was a huge, life-sized painting that depicted Aramis, of the "Three Musketeers." The bottom of the full-length picture was less than two feet from the floor; the heavy mahogany frame was flush against the wall.

Ruthley was seated in an armchair, smoking an expensive cigar. Marclot was opposite him, watching him. In appearance, as well as manner, the two formed an absolute contrast.

Stephen Ruthley was elderly, yet active. His face was calm, pleasant, almost fatherly. His eyes, though searching, carried a twinkle; his gray hair added to his genial look. All this was a mask that Ruthley had worn for years; he seldom dropped it, even when he had no need for pretense. In fact, Ruthley prided himself upon the fact that when his temper rose, he could play his friendly, reassuring part to real perfection.

Elvin Marclot was portly, pompous and round-faced; serious of expression, he was ever ready to draw himself up and blubber in righteous indignation. He used that method to cover his crooked nature; it worked well in public, but it was useless in Ruthley's presence. The boss always had the mayor at a disadvantage; for Ruthley's calmness seemed natural, while Marclot's self-importance did not.

Tonight, if Ruthley chanced to be nervous, he did not show it. Marclot, however, was jittery, and could not cover the fact. He had already reported important news; all that he could do was repeat it.

"They've finished Dunson by this time, Steve," insisted Marclot, in a tone that was almost a whine. "Kirk Borman called me, like I told you. I thought I'd better be here when the news came—"

THE telephone bell rang. Marclot trembled as he reached for the telephone, which was on a mahogany table near the door. Ruthley stopped him.

"Let Haija answer it," ordered Ruthley. "He always does."

Marclot sank back in his chair, A Japanese house-man entered, picked up the telephone and spoke in mechanical fashion. He turned about and held the instrument toward Marclot, with the statement:

"Call for Honorable Mr. Mayor."

Marclot took the telephone shakily; gulped as he spoke. Ruthley listened intently to the conversation.

"Yes..." Marclot, always a faker, pretended to be astonished. "What is that, Director? A murder?... Not our friend Prescott Dunson?... This is terrible! Terrible!... Yes. It would be wise for you to come here at once..."

Haija took the telephone as soon as Marclot hung up. The Japanese replaced the instrument on the table and stalked from the room. Marclot spoke to Ruthley in a trembling tone.

"They got Dunson!" the mayor quivered. "Borman's on his way here."

"How soon will that be?"

"He said within five minutes."

Ruthley and Marclot dropped their conversation. Just as Ruthley flicked another length of ashes from his cigar, Haija entered to announce that the police director had arrived. Kirk Borman was ushered into the den. As soon as Haija was gone, the sharp-faced police director talked business.

"They chopped down Dunson in front of Judge Benbrook's house," stated Borman. "But there was a lot of fireworks afterward. Some sharpshooter began to pick off the men in Lance's cars; just like last night."

"Interesting," remarked Ruthley. He puffed at his cigar; then reached for a box and offered a smoke to Borman. Then he asked: "Did the Flying Squadron take care of the troublemaker?"

"They arrived too late to get him," returned Borman, in a rueful tone. "They had to fake a chase after the thugs; and it was tough to bluff it, for they were crippled pretty bad, the thugs were. I thought the whole game was going to be a cinch when Dunson was reported in that trolley; but it wasn't.

"Anyway, Dunson is done for. The Flying Squadron took his body over to the morgue. I saw him laid out there; and I found out something that's worth knowing. Wait until I show you the letter that was on Dunson's body."

Borman began to fumble in his pockets. Marclot took advantage of the lull.

"This will make trouble," insisted the mayor. "Maybe not for us; but suppose that public indignation seeks out Lance Gillick? He is one of us. We have to protect him."

"We shall," stated Ruthley, with a smile. "Quite easily."

"But how can we laugh off Dunson's charges?" continued Marclot. "He claimed that he could prove corruption in Westford."

"I shall handle the matter," returned Ruthley, still smiling. "Quite easily, Marclot."

Borman had found the letter. The police director was opening it. The paper was reddened at one corner; that stain had come from Prescott Dunson's blood. The fact did not annoy Borman; he was too anxious to divulge the contents of the letter.

"This was from a man named Shaw," he began. "Evidently the fellow had written to Dunson before—"

"Wait!"

STEPHEN Ruthley had heard a slight sound that came from behind the painting on the wall. He arose; went to the picture and pressed a hidden catch in the side of the frame. He swung the picture inward, in doorlike fashion.

Two men stepped over the sill, to join the conference in Ruthley's den.

The foremost was Lance Gillick, sleek in his evening attire. The big shot gambler indulged in one of his suave smiles. He stepped aside to let his companion enter. The other man was short and squatty; his leering face showed crossed scars on its left cheek. The man looked like a murderer; and he was.

Lance's companion was "Beezer" Dorsch, the mobleader who was supposed to be at odds with the sleek gambler. As Lance had mentioned to Borman the night before, the two were actually in league. Because of that, Lance had brought Beezer to this conference.

The ring of crime makers was complete. Stephen Ruthley, king of villainy, sat smiling as he viewed the faces of his four lieutenants. With Elvin Marclot to play the part of a pompous mayor; with Kirk Borman to pose as an efficient police director, Ruthley held two aces for a start.

This other pair were quite as essential to his schemes. Lance Gillick served as hidden lieutenant who commanded henchmen from the underworld, while Beezer Dorsch took charge of action in the field. In a sense, Lance and Beezer corresponded to Marclot and Borman. One pair represented the law; the other pair, crime.

The second duo of aces gave Stephen Ruthley the full hand that he wanted. All were his, to take his commands. Tonight's action had been the murder of Prescott Dunson. The kill had been made. Ruthley was prepared to order further measures to cover up the crime.

CHAPTER VII
THE FINGER POINTS

ELVIN MARCLOT and Kirk Borman were not at all annoyed by the arrival of Lance Gillick and Beezer Dorsch. The mayor and the police director had long since come to recognize those two as companions in arms. There was, in fact, a reason why both Marclot and Borman felt pleased when they learned that Ruthley had summoned his representatives in the underworld. Until tonight, neither Marclot nor Borman had made the actual acquaintance of Beezer Dorsch.

Nearly all contact between these pairs of lieutenants had been when Kirk Borman had visited Lance Gillick, on pretense that he was looking into the gambler's affairs. Marclot and Borman paid their own visits to Stephen Ruthley; but they always entered by the front door. When Ruthley needed to see Lance or Beezer, he had those outlaws come in through the secret entry.

The picture that served as a door covered a passage through the deserted house at the end of the row. Lance and Beezer reached it by entering the old house from a narrow, blind alley, well hidden from the lights of the front boulevard.

Tonight, it was apparent that Lance and Beezer had brought news. Therefore, Kirk Borman postponed his own report. He pocketed the letter that he had found on Dunson's body and settled back in his chair to listen. Lance Gillick picked out one of Ruthley's cigars, while Beezer Dorsch produced a cigarette and lighted it. Lance gave a nod.

"Spill it, Beezer," he ordered. "The boss will want to hear what went sour."

Beezer turned directly to Ruthley.

"I was going to tell you about last night," he began. "Only I got more dope to spring, the way things has happened. We muffed that Maclare job, on account of a guy who queered our setup. I was wise to who he was. He was The Shadow! And it was him again tonight!"

For an instant, Stephen Ruthley's eyes showed a hard glint. The boss had heard of The Shadow; for he had delved deeply into the lore of crime.

Ruthley turned to Borman.

"Too bad your Flying Squadron was slow," purred the boss. "They could handle this troublemaker, if they went after him."

"They'll have orders to bag The Shadow," returned Borman, grimly. "When I tell them to look for The Shadow, they'll find him!"

LANCE and Beezer smiled hopefully. Ruthley settled back in his chair to ponder over the facts that he had heard. During the lull, Mayor Marclot suddenly reverted to his former subject.

"We can't forget Dunson," pleaded Marclot. "Something has to be brought to light, to cover the stir he has made."

Ruthley smiled blandly. He arose and went to the filing cabinet in the corner. Opening a drawer, he produced a folder filled with papers. He brought them back to his chair; laid them upon a table. Motioning for silence, he spoke in calm, authoritative tone.

"Prescott Dunson is dead," announced Ruthley. "He was murdered because he threatened to make important revelations concerning graft and crime. The public will want facts; therefore, the public shall have facts. Those facts, however, will be to our own choice."

Smiling, Ruthley opened the folder and brought out the papers. As he spread them on the table, he spoke further.

"First," he declared, "some killer must be blamed for the crime. Very well; we shall name the man who is actually responsible. There he is"—Ruthley pointed to Beezer—"all ready to take the blame."

"Sure," snorted Beezer, "I'll be the fall guy. Great stuff, boss! Me and Lance is supposed to be on the outs. That'll cover him."

Lance chuckled.

"I already have an alibi," he remarked. "The best in the city. Just at the time when Beezer was rubbing out Dunson, who do you think dropped in to see me? I'll tell you. It was Lieutenant James Maclare. He wanted to see if I had any roulette wheels up my sleeve, so I showed him all around the joint. He drew a blank; wouldn't even take a cigar when I offered it to him. Maclare knows where I was when Dunson was chopped down. Being honest, he'll admit that I was right in my own nightclub."

Smiles of approval were exchanged throughout the group. Chuckles stilled as Ruthley resumed.

"Beezer will disappear," explained the boss. "The city will be scoured for him. A nationwide search will begin, with Beezer called a public enemy."

Beezer looked uneasy, until Ruthley added:

"All the while, Beezer will be comfortably located in the one place where no one—not even Lieutenant Maclare—will look for him. He will live in your apartment, Lance."

LANCE nodded his approval. The others joined with nods. They knew the location of Lance's apartment; off the passage that led from his private office. Since Maclare had raided the Club Adair and found no gambling devices, there would be no more raids.

Ruthley made a sweeping gesture with his right hand.

"The matter of a murderer is settled," he declared. "We must, however, consider the subject of corruption. Marclot"—he eyed the mayor steadily—"do you remember those contracts you signed for the proposed exposition buildings?"

"Certainly," nodded Marclot. "Adam Woodstock gained the contracts. He has already received a million dollars of city funds. He gave us our half of the money."

"That was a swell kickback," put in Lance, in an admiring tone. "I'll bet, though, that it doesn't show on Woodstock's books."

"Of course not," declared Marclot. "Woodstock was careful to cover the entire transaction."

"These papers," stated Ruthley, picking some from his stack, "give a comparison of the actual estimates and the false ones. Suppose that they were found in Woodstock's safe, along with other incriminating documents, such as letters signed by Beezer Dorsch—"

Elvin Marclot could not contain himself. Forgetting his pompous pose, the mayor exclaimed:

"People would think that Woodstock was the man higher up! The one who ordered Beezer to murder Dunson!"

"And the contracts?" queried Ruthley, smoothly. "What would happen with them?"

"I could cancel them," returned Marclot, "on claim of fraud perpetrated by Woodstock. His corporation would be held responsible for the funds that Woodstock received."

"Precisely," smiled Ruthley. "A million dollars would be returned to the city treasury; and half of it would be Woodstock's own money. You would then be able, Marclot, to let new contracts to another bidder quite as discreet as Woodstock."

"Meaning a new kickback," chuckled Lance. "Another easy half million!"

The perfection of Ruthley's scheme suited the bevy of plotters. They saw another half million already in the bag. One question came; it was from Kirk Borman.

"Woodstock will squawk," phrased the police director. "How will you handle that, Steve?"

"I shall attend to Woodstock," purred Ruthley. "He will never find an opportunity to raise objection. There is only one detail that must still be considered. That concerns Beezer. We must see to it that he is actually accepted as Dunson's murderer."

"I can fix that," returned Borman. "I'll have some of the boys in the Flying Squadron swear to it that they saw him knock off Dunson."

"That will help," mused Ruthley, "but it would be better if some disinterested witnesses could testify to Beezer's ability as a killer. Charges made by police are sometimes disregarded."

KIRK BORMAN stroked his chin. He was thinking hard; suddenly, he found an answer. Reaching into his pocket, he whipped out the letter.

"I have it!" exclaimed Borman. "This letter shows that Dunson was working with an investigator named Shaw. Chances are that Shaw knew as much as Dunson, maybe more."

"Therefore," pronounced Ruthley, "Shaw must be eliminated. Let me see that letter, Kirk."

Taking the letter, Ruthley noted that it was brief. Scrawled in a clumsy hand, it simply promised new revelations that would be as startling as those previously given. It reminded Dunson to destroy all correspondence that he had received to date. Ruthley pondered over the scrawled signature.

"Theo D. Shaw," he said, aloud. "Where can the fellow be found, Kirk?"

"Probably at the Majestic Hotel," returned Borman, promptly. "That's where we think Dunson was headed when Beezer overtook him."

Ruthley turned to Beezer.

"Get Shaw," he purred. "Take good men with you. Let yourself be seen. As for you, Kirk"—Ruthley swung to the police director—"have your men close on Beezer's heels. Afterward, produce this letter as proof that Dunson knew Shaw."

"That will pin it on me right," grunted Beezer. He seemed pleased by the prospect. "When I dive out, they'll think I'm on the lam for sure!"

STEPHEN RUTHLEY arose; his action signified that the conference was ended. Marclot and Borman prepared to leave by the front door; Lance and Beezer were ready for secret departure. It was Lance who voiced an afterthought.

"What about The Shadow, boss?" he queried. "Beezer is sure that he was the guy who mixed in the last two jobs."

"We can attend to The Shadow later," decided Ruthley, "after we have disposed of this informant, Shaw."

The decision showed that Stephen Ruthley was confident that new murder could be accomplished without The Shadow's interference. The overlord of crime felt sure that the lone fighter had been too hard pressed to rally for new effort; that The Shadow would not expect another murderous attempt so soon after Dunson's death.

Ruthley's four aces shared their chief's belief. Though they knew The Shadow's prowess, they could not credit him with the ability to be everywhere at once. Not even Beezer Dorsch would grant The Shadow that much, though Beezer himself had been the one to face the cloaked fighter in actual combat.

Beezer's leering face showed that he did not expect to meet The Shadow again tonight. The murderer anticipated no opposition when he went to handle the investigator, Shaw. Nor did Ruthley and the others; they were lulled by Beezer's confidence.

Had Stephen Ruthley and his lieutenants given more careful consideration to facts that they held in hand, they might have foreseen real trouble from The Shadow.

CHAPTER VIII
THE TRAP REVERSED

THERE had been excitement in the Majestic Hotel following the murder of Prescott Dunson, for the noise of gunfire, plus the arrival of the Flying Squadron, had been sufficient to create high alarm. Later, the lobby had quieted; but all about were little groups of men who discussed the new crime that had occurred in Westford.

The consensus of opinion showed approval for the police. It was known that crooks had eluded the Flying Squadron; but fully a dozen persons were prepared to testify that the law had reached the spot within five minutes after Dunson's death. Speedy flight by the murderers explained the getaway; no one could find cause to blame the Flying Squadron for failing in the chase.

One guest at the Majestic Hotel remained apart from the chatting groups. He was a tall, haggard-faced individual, whose eyes were restless, and who frequently took on a listening attitude as he roamed about the gaudy lobby. The clerk at the desk recognized him as a man named Shaw. He looked like one of the many guests who had come down from their rooms to learn the cause of the fray.

After a while, Shaw started for the coffee shop that adjoined the lobby. He stopped at the door, hesitated, then headed for the elevators. The clerk did not see Shaw go upstairs; but he remembered that the man had been in the lobby. He proved this later, when a stranger stopped at the desk and inquired gruffly:

"Where'll I find Mr. Shaw? Theodore D. Shaw is the guy's full name."

"He was here in the lobby, a short while ago," replied the clerk, while he sorted letters. Then, realizing the toughness of the questioner's tone, the clerk asked: "Why do you wish to see Mr. Shaw?"

As he asked the question, the clerk looked at the man who had approached the desk. He saw an ugly, scarred face that one who observed was not likely to forget. The clerk was looking at Beezer Dorsch.

"I'll tell Shaw what I want to see him about," informed Beezer. "Is he still here in the lobby?"

The clerk looked about and shook his head. Turning toward Beezer, he noted that the scarred man was accompanied by a pair of rowdies who matched him for toughness. One of them voiced a growl:

"Get the mug's room number, Beezer."

"A good idea," decided Beezer. "Say, you"—he glowered at the clerk—"where'll I find this guy Shaw?"

"His room number is 304," began the clerk. "Only, he may not be up there—"

The girl at the switchboard offered an interruption. She had heard the mention of Shaw's name; but had turned around to see Beezer and the others. She did not know that the clerk was trying to stall.

"Mr. Shaw just put in a call," stated the girl. "He ordered supper served in his room."

"That means he's up there," grunted Beezer. "All right. I'll go up and see him."

Followed by his pals, Beezer strode toward the elevator. Hardly had the door closed before a house detective approached the desk and inquired of the clerk:

"Did that tough guy give his name?"

"No," replied the clerk; "only one of the men with him called him 'Beezer.'"

"Then he's Beezer Dorsch, all right!" decided the dick. "We just got a call from police headquarters to flag him if we saw him. Where did he go?"

"To Room 304, to see a man named Shaw."

"I'll call headquarters!"

DURING this interim, Beezer and his two companions had reached the third floor. They found Room 304 near the inner end of a short corridor. Beezer tried the door cautiously, to discover that it was locked. He moved his companions out of the corridor.

"We got to figure some way of getting at the guy," decided Beezer. "Maybe there's a way of reaching a window—"

"Ps-s-s-t!" One of the thugs interrupted. "Scram, Beezer! There's an elevator door opening up!"

Beezer urged his companions into an alcove. They saw a waiter step from the elevator, bearing a tray. The attendant went to the door of 304 and knocked. Beezer saw the door open; he spied a haggard face inside the lighted room. The waiter entered; the door closed.

"I spotted Shaw, all right," whispered Beezer. "He's a sappy-looking guy. He'll be soft. Wait'll the waiter leaves."

Soon the waiter reappeared; he stopped in the hallway to nod, as he listened to a complaining voice from the room.

"I told you to bring lemon for my tea," Shaw was objecting. "Not cream. Do you understand?"

"Yes, sir."

"Very well. Return at once and bring the

lemon. The door will be unlocked. Knock, however, before you enter."

"Very well, sir."

The door closed; the waiter returned to the elevator. Beezer grinned and pulled a revolver from his hip pocket. He whispered instructions to his thugs.

"Stick close," he told them. "Stay outside the door. I'll handle this mug alone; if I want you, I'll call you. Keep an eye peeled for the waiter, or anybody else that shows up."

Creeping forward, Beezer reached the door of 304; waited until his followers were beside him. Imitating the waiter's knock, Beezer rapped upon the door. He heard an impatient voice:

"Who is it?"

"The waiter," replied Beezer, in a tone less gruff than usual. "Bringing the lemon you wanted."

Beezer grinned as he gestured with his revolver, for the benefit of his pals. He was bringing a lemon, all right; one that he fancied would prove more sour than any that Shaw had ever tasted.

"Come in," called the voice within the room. "Don't stand out there in the hall."

Beezer turned the knob with his left hand. He shouldered through the doorway, to find himself in a short passage that led to the main portion of the room. Shaw's table was out of sight beyond the corner; Beezer could hear the clatter of dishes. Carefully, he closed the door; then edged forward.

"Where are you, waiter?"

As Shaw's query came again, Beezer bounded forward. He passed the projecting corner, swung straight for the spot where he believed that the victim would be seated. Stopping short as he gripped his leveled gun, Beezer stared at a table by the wall. He saw the dishes and the food upon them; but the chair behind the table was vacant.

QUICKLY, Beezer looked toward the deeper corner at his left; it was toward the front of the room, a spot that he had passed as he hurried into Shaw's field of vision. As he turned, Beezer was quicker with his eyes than with his gun. As a consequence, he was forced to halt before he had a chance to aim.

Beezer Dorsch was staring squarely into the rounded mouth of an automatic—a massive weapon that he was viewing at closer range than ever before. That .45 was a living threat; for Beezer had heard it speak often during his recent career of crime.

Above the huge weapon were burning eyes, the only features that Beezer could see beneath the shading brim of a slouch hat. Below was blackness that formed a shrouded shape. Beezer saw cloaked shoulders; a thin-gloved fist that gripped the steadied gun.

Beezer's revolver slipped from his numbed fingers. It thudded the floor beside the dish-laden table. Slowly, his hands came up, while he stared at those eyes that seemed to paralyze him with their hypnotic spell. Through a confused whirl of thoughts, Beezer Dorsch grasped the situation.

There was no man named Shaw. Nor was there need to wonder why the person who used that name had learned so much of crime in Westford. Stephen Ruthley and his lieutenants had overlooked the obvious; they had failed to connect the supposed investigator, Shaw, with the one person whose presence they had actual cause to fear.

The supposed Shaw was The Shadow. The cloaked avenger was the being who faced Beezer Dorsch. The Shadow had awaited Prescott Dunson outside the hotel; that was why he had been on hand, to protect the man whom Beezer had murdered.

The Shadow had not forgotten the letter that Dunson held. He had foreseen that Dunson's killer might try to trap him. The Shadow had arranged for it. He had sprung a snare of his own.

The trap was reversed. The Shadow, archenemy of crime, had taken Beezer Dorsch into his toils!

CHAPTER IX
THE LAW INVADES

THE SHADOW had arranged his trap with consummate skill. Beezer recognized the fact, as he stared helpless. Between the table and the corner, The Shadow had placed a floor lamp; he had tilted the shade upward so that its glare was focused on the room.

In a sense, The Shadow had employed the device which Beezer had used on two successive nights. The lamp had the effect of a spotlight; the corner behind it, darkened in comparison, was The Shadow's lurking spot. The position of the lamp explained why Beezer had overlooked the corner when he passed it. The crook had not recognized The Shadow's ruse.

The lamp's glare outlined Beezer's face; and the sight was not pretty. It showed the mobleader's ugly profile; his scarred cheek and the knobby, ill-shaped nose that had won him his nickname. Beezer's features were yellowish in the glow; the snarl that came from his gritted teeth would have befitted a rat.

The Shadow had stepped close enough for Beezer to see him distinctly; that move had been essential to The Shadow's plan. His position enabled him to scrutinize Beezer closely; to form his own opinion of the ugly captive that he had snared. A few brief seconds convinced The Shadow that he held the actual murderer who had given death to Prescott Dunson.

Beezer's face showed it. So did his manner; for his attempt at bravado was a weak one. The yellowish tinge upon Beezer's face represented the closest that the murderer could come to actual paleness.

Perhaps The Shadow already knew of Beezer's part. The murderer could not tell; but he learned promptly that The Shadow had gained information concerning persons more important than this prisoner. That became apparent when The Shadow spoke; his tone was an uncanny whisper that produced a shudder in Beezer's squatty frame.

"State who sent you here!" ordered The Shadow. "Name all concerned in your present move!"

It was a command, not a question. Beezer realized the full significance of The Shadow's words. Chances were that The Shadow knew who had sent the killer here; Beezer could see trouble for himself if he lied. The crook tried to snarl an answer; his voice was incoherent. Quailing, he resorted to a whine.

"I didn't put the finger on you," he protested. "Honest, I wasn't sent to make no trouble! It was on account of—"

BEEZER stopped, knowing his whine to be useless. An interruption rescued him; the sound was a cautious rap at the door of the room. Beezer glanced nervously toward The Shadow. Hidden lips issued a command.

"Answer it!" ordered The Shadow, his whispered tone low. "Tell your pals to join you!"

Beezer gulped; then called hoarsely:

"Come in, you guys!"

"Move toward the table," ordered The Shadow. "Keep your arms high!"

Beezer obeyed while the door was opening. He saw The Shadow step back behind the focused lamp. Footsteps clumped inward from the door; one of Beezer's cronies questioned:

"Did you croak him, Beezer?" There was no reply from Beezer. The thugs stopped as they saw their leader, against the wall, his hands above his head. They swung about, looking for an enemy; their hands tightened on their guns, then loosened.

Beezer's pals had heard a sinister whisper. They stared toward the corner; like Beezer, they saw The Shadow. He had stepped into the light; both his fists were equipped with automatics. One .45 held Beezer motionless; the other covered the two thugs. They acted as Beezer had. Two revolvers thudded the carpet together.

Pointing with his guns, The Shadow huddled the three mobsters together at the end of the room. His unseen lips formed a mirthful whisper, as ominous as the strident laugh that crooks had heard earlier upon this night. The meaning broke suddenly upon Beezer Dorsch, as he saw The Shadow put away one gun. A telephone was in easy reach of The Shadow's free hand; his single automatic was sufficient to hold the clustered trio at bay.

"He's going to give us to Maclare!" gulped Beezer. "The guy we tried to croak last night! We're in Maclare's precinct; there ain't a chance for us when he gets us!"

As he gave this news, Beezer started forward. He halted at the threat of The Shadow's gun muzzle. Neither of Beezer's pals had nerve enough to back him in a break for safety. Beezer saw The Shadow reach for the telephone. A second interruption halted the gloved hand.

Another knock was sounding at the door. It became a violent pounding. The Shadow knew that it was not the waiter; so did Beezer. The murderer strained forward, itching to make a spring. A loud voice sounded from beyond the door:

"Open! In the name of the law!"

ONE part of Stephen Ruthley's game had, as yet, escaped The Shadow. That was the big shot's plan to make Beezer Dorsch a fugitive from justice. Hearing the voice from the corridor; noting the ugly triumph that suddenly appeared upon Beezer's face, The Shadow caught the idea.

He knew that the man who had shouted for entry was not an officer from Lieutenant Maclare's precinct. Outside were members of Kirk Borman's Flying Squadron, here to see that murder went through; prepared to cover the escape of Beezer Dorsch by pretense of a chase.

Instantly, The Shadow whipped out his second automatic. Turning his shoulder toward Beezer and the pair of thugs, The Shadow covered them with one gun, while he jabbed the other toward the door. Between two groups of enemies, he intended to hold unarmed men at bay, while he drove back invaders who would come with ready weapons.

As the door shoved inward, Beezer took a chance. He snarled a command to his pals; this time, they obeyed. Thinking that Beezer was with them, the two thugs made a desperate dive for The Shadow. Surging with full fury, they were upon him with a single bound.

The Shadow had only one course. Fading toward the door, he fired as he dropped. His bullets winged the thugs, sprawled them to the floor. Beezer dropped with them; but his fall was a foxy one. His pals had shielded him; Beezer still wanted them between himself and The Shadow.

That was scarcely necessary. The Shadow had no more time to deal with Beezer. Spinning toward the door, he whirled straight into a trio of policemen, who were clad in khaki, the distinguishing uniform of the Flying Squadron. Had there been a bluecoat in their midst, The Shadow would have let that man dive away. All, however, were khaki-clad. Director Borman had chosen those uniforms, that crooks might know their friends. The Shadow treated them alike.

His long arms were lashing; his heavy guns clipped heads beneath visored caps and sent the trio sagging. In the corridor, The Shadow ripped quick shots at three more members of the Flying Squadron; winged one and sent the others diving for cover. As The Shadow sprang past an elevator, the door clanged open; four members of the squadron saw him and charged. They swung their revolvers; this time, The Shadow was in the midst of a slugging throng.

BACK in The Shadow's room, a shot was fired. One of Beezer's wounded pals had taken a pot shot at Beezer himself. It was in payment for his cowardice, in letting his pals bear the brunt of The Shadow's quick defense.

That shot went wide; it was Beezer who fired the next ones. Savagely, the killer drilled both of his pals, sprawling them dead upon the floor, to leave no witnesses who might proclaim his treachery throughout the underworld.

Springing to the hall, Beezer arrived to see The Shadow wheeling away from four foemen. Beezer dived for a stairway; The Shadow paused to deliver halting shots. A khaki-clad foeman pounced upon him; knocked down his gun arm. The Shadow whirled away to avoid a clinch. Shaking off another attacker, he reached the door of a fire tower.

All along the hall were members of the Flying Squadron, coming to hands and knees, groggy from strokes that they had received. There were others who had dodged The Shadow's attack. They opened fire from corners of corridors. The Shadow saw the fire tower as a vantage point. He took it, slamming the door behind him. Hardly was he on the tower before he realized the value of his move.

Sirens were screeching from below. The entire squadron was out, surrounding the hotel. The Shadow knew what prolonged battle with these disguised thugs would produce. It would bring out the full police force; Lieutenant Maclare first, with the men who patrolled this precinct. They would side with the Flying Squadron. The Shadow wanted no battle with such loyal men.

To avoid that inevitable result, The Shadow hurried down the fire tower. He reached the bottom just in time to see Beezer Dorsch dash from a side door of the hotel. The Shadow had no time to aim for the murderer; Beezer was ducking behind an automobile, pointing to the fire tower as he dived for cover. Two squadron men saw him; they let Beezer go and headed for the tower.

The Shadow swung out upon them. As their guns came up, his came down in two long swings. One man took a blow upon the head; the other dodged, but received a glancing stroke that made him stumble. Hearing shouts from men who had rounded the front corner of the hotel, The Shadow sprang off between parked cars. Dodging back and forth, he reached a coupé and boarded it.

Another car had pulled away from the other side of the parking lot. The Shadow heard the whine of its gear and knew that Beezer had made his getaway. That flight was by arrangement with the law. The Shadow had no such pleasant prospect. Trouble began anew, as he sped his car toward the street.

A SQUADRON car shot in to block The Shadow's coupé. The Shadow tongued a quick blast from his automatic; to avoid the fire, the driver of the squadron car veered. The Shadow wheeled away from bright lights; as his coupé roared past Judge Benbrook's house, three khaki-clad men on motorcycles took up the chase.

The Shadow veered left at the trolley tracks; rounded the block, sped his car through an alleyway. A patrol car sighted him; it followed. Another block, two policemen in blue uniform saw the chase and commandeered a sedan to join the pursuit.

Again, The Shadow turned his course, headed back toward the city's center. Finding a side street, he took it, to avoid another squadron car that was coming straight toward him.

As The Shadow whizzed past a corner, he went by an automobile that had pulled up to the curb. The man behind the wheel of that car sat watching, as police cars and motorcycles sped by. When the wild parade had faded in the distance, that watcher slid from his car and shuffled toward an alleyway that offered direct access to the rear door of Lance Gillick's Club Adair.

A street lamp gave a momentary glimpse of the shuffler's ugly face. The man was Beezer Dorsch, grinning from ear to ear. He had expected a pursuit before he could head back to Lance's perfect hideout. With so many dumb cops in Westford, there was always a chance of trouble, as Beezer viewed it.

Circumstances had turned out well for Beezer Dorsch. He could forget the fact that he had failed to murder Shaw. After all, Shaw was The Shadow; and others could take the job of bagging him. As Beezer recalled it, Mayor Marclot and Police Director Borman had agreed to handle that particular task.

They had made a good beginning. The pursuit that Beezer had witnessed was a real one. The Shadow had put himself in wrong with the law. He had made Beezer's fake flight an easy one; and had given the Flying Squadron a real trail, for a change.

Beezer Dorsch was hopeful that the Flying Squadron would show its real ability tonight.

CHAPTER X
THE LOST TRAIL

THE chase that Beezer had witnessed was actually a hot one. The Shadow realized it as he sped toward the city limits, picking a course through the winding streets of one of Westford's suburbs. Pursuers had spread out, picking parallel streets. At every corner, The Shadow heard sirens that told of foemen on both sides.

Horns were honking from a hundred yards behind. They represented commandeered cars. More of the regular police had joined in the hunt. Like the members of the Flying Squadron, they would give The Shadow plenty, if they gained the opportunity. Questions and explanations would come afterward.

The Shadow's coupé was no speedier than the cars of the pursuers; but he knew this section of Westford. He had chosen it on that account. At intervals, The Shadow chose shortcuts, where angled streets afforded quick routes to other thoroughfares. These shifts put him farther ahead of the cars upon his trail.

Making a quick turn at a corner, The Shadow threaded through a maze of streets and gained a highway that led from the town. Speeding toward the open road, he saw the glare of two sets of headlights, coming straight toward him, side by side. Instantly, The Shadow knew that a radio call had been given. Patrol cars on the city's outskirts were heading in to block him.

Quickly, The Shadow chose the first side road that offered itself. The coupé jolted over bumpy paving; then came a muddy lane where a pair of ruts offered the only progress. Taking it at rapid speed, The Shadow saw the end of the road. He stopped the coupé on the very fringe of a small pond. Dropping to the ground, he looked back along the lane. He saw headlights bouncing as cars took the ruts. Half a dozen automobiles had neared this finish of the chase. One minute more would bring them to the spot where The Shadow stood.

High above, off to the right, The Shadow saw a glow of light. It came from the top of a huge water tower, its rounded bottom forming a bowl upon long, spindly struts. With long strides across scraggly ground, The Shadow covered the distance. He reached the bottom of the tower just as the police cars pulled up beside his abandoned coupé.

The glow from the tower came from lights beneath a projecting flange around the top. There, lights were concentrated to display a sign painted on the tower, stating that it belonged to the Westford Electric Co. A platform at the base of the tank itself cut off the light, so that all beneath was darkened.

Stopping by the first steel leg, The Shadow found that the support was equipped with a ladder. Without a moment's hesitation, he began an upward climb.

FORTY feet up, the ladder ended. In its place, The Shadow discovered a catwalk that led to the center of the tank, ending directly underneath it. Probing farther in the darkness, he discovered a side ladder that went to the top of the tank; but he chose the catwalk instead. His choice was a good one. Some of the pursuers had come over toward the tower and were flashing electric torches from the ground.

Reaching the end of the catwalk, The Shadow felt the bottom of the tank. He discovered supporting girders, shaped to the tank itself. Gripping the edges of a girder with his hands, The Shadow swung his feet upward and gained a toehold. Crawling face upward, he followed the outside of the huge bowl, until he was halfway to the platform that girded it. There, The Shadow paused; bracing his arms, he clung motionless.

Pursuers were coming up the ladder. Some reached the catwalk; followed its downward curve to the center of the tank. Others went around the platform. A few ascended the second ladder and flashed lights on the smooth surface of the conical top. The search took several minutes; it covered everywhere, except the under curve of the water tank, on The Shadow's side. No one suspected that a person could hide on that precarious portion of the tank.

Clangs from the ladder told that the police were making their descent. Slowly, The Shadow reversed his course along the girder. His arms and legs were tired, but the course was downward and required less effort than his climb. He reached the catwalk and settled to its surface.

From his high lookout, The Shadow watched the search along the ground. At least twenty men were beating the brush, as they circled the shores of the pond. Flashlights bobbed in the direction of a house, two hundred yards away. Lights appeared in the house itself. The Shadow knew that the police had roused the occupants, to make a search inside.

It was nearly an hour before the hunt ended. Even then, the terrain did not clear entirely; a few watchers were posted along the ground. None was near the tower; The Shadow moved along the catwalk and descended silently by the ladder. There, he waited in darkness, watching the blink of flashlights. Soon a pair came in his direction.

Sidling away from the tower, The Shadow listened while two men went up the ladder. They were choosing the very lookout that The Shadow had occupied, so that they could keep in contact with the men below. Evidently, the police intended to keep guard all night.

A clouded sky had rendered the darkness almost complete. That suited The Shadow. Silently, he made his way toward the house. He paused close beside the building while muffled feet tramped past him. A flashlight blinked, but did not turn in his direction. When the guard had passed, The Shadow crept to the wall of the house.

THE building was a frame structure; a trellis showed vaguely in the darkness. The Shadow used it as a ladder and made a quiet climb to a kitchen roof. He found a darkened window above; used it to reach a ledge. He was outside a third-story window; the shape of the roof indicated that this story of the house was an attic.

The window was a round one, on a pivot. The Shadow swung it to a horizontal position, using his cloak to muffle any sound. Headfirst, he wriggled through the half opening; came to the rough, unfinished floor of the attic. Using a tiny flashlight in guarded fashion, The Shadow studied the room, foot by foot.

The attic had been searched by the police. Pieces of old furniture had been shoved about; trunks had been pulled away from the wall. The Shadow reached a flight of steps; crept downward, to a door that was locked from the other side. This discovery pleased him. As long as that door remained locked, neither the house owners nor the law would bother with another search. This attic could be The Shadow's refuge as long as he chose.

Eventually, he would have the choice of two exits: the window by which he had entered; or the door at the foot of the stairs. Though the door was locked, The Shadow could easily open it. His picks, lock-opening instruments expertly handled, had overcome barriers that were far more formidable than that lower door.

Back in the attic, The Shadow made himself comfortable. He found an old couch that was thick-cushioned, despite its shabbiness. Opening a trunk, he discovered blankets. Rolling one as a pillow, he used the other for bedding; and stretched himself upon the couch.

From where he lay, The Shadow could see through the window. He watched the motion of flashlights through the darkness. They would continue until dawn; then there would be a search by day. That hunt would cover many places; but it would not reach this attic, except by some freak of chance. If the search came here, The Shadow would be ready. If not, he would remain in the attic throughout the day.

For The Shadow expected no more trouble in Westford until tomorrow night. His present policy was to let matters cool there. Word would go around that Beezer Dorsch had fled the city; the same would be said about The Shadow. Crooks would be bluffing when they spoke of Beezer; they would think that they told the truth, in the case of The Shadow.

Thus the stage would be set as The Shadow wanted it, when he returned. Again, he could thrust from darkness; meet crooks and stagger them. To date, The Shadow had steadily progressed. He had saved Lieutenant Maclare; only Prescott Dunson's own mistakes had spoiled The Shadow's efforts toward a second rescue.

Likewise, chance had favored Beezer Dorsch, when The Shadow had trapped the murderer. The same chance had driven The Shadow to this place of refuge; but he had not lost ground in his battle against crime. Every fight had crippled more foemen; always, The Shadow had come through unscathed, departing into darkness.

Tomorrow night, The Shadow's plans called for a greater thrust; a move to the very place where crime was fostered. His investigations in the city of Westford had given him close knowledge of all who were concerned in crime.

Unfortunately, The Shadow had not been present at that conference between Stephen Ruthley and his four associates. The Shadow's absence from that meeting had caused him trouble when he trapped Beezer Dorsch. It was due to provide him with more difficulties when he again went into Westford.

HAD The Shadow gained an inkling of the next move that Stephen Ruthley intended, he would not have considered it wise to remain in this secluded attic. His policy would have been to slip the cordon of watchers and return to Westford on this very night.

As yet, The Shadow had dealt only with those lieutenants who served the overlord of crime. He had not encountered Stephen Ruthley in action; nor did he expect to meet the master villain on the move. Ruthley, as The Shadow sized him, was a cunning brain who could sit back and let others follow his command. Past events had backed The Shadow's opinion. The future, however, could tell another story.

Stephen Ruthley, at this very moment, was completing a plan of crime that would give The Shadow new and different evidence of the master villain's ways.

CHAPTER XI
WITHIN THE LAIR

EARLY the next evening, an automobile stopped in front of Stephen Ruthley's big apartment house. The man who parked the car appeared to be a privileged person, for the curb where he pulled up bore the sign: "NO PARKING."

Entering the apartment house, this visitor walked up a broad flight of stairs to the second floor. He rang a bell, at the imposing door that formed the entrance to Ruthley's apartment. Haija answered the ring; the Jap bowed when he saw the visitor.

"Good evening, Honorable Mr. District Attorney," said Haija. "Honorable Master expect you."

The district attorney followed the houseman to Ruthley's den. Ruthley received him with outstretched hand; the gray-haired boss accompanied the gesture with his most genial smile.

"Good evening, Wilderton!" greeted Ruthley. "Sit down; have a cigar. Make yourself right at home."

Louis Wilderton took a chair opposite the portrait of Aramis. The glow of a floor lamp showed the prosecutor to be a man in his thirties; a serious chap who tried to appear older than he was. Wilderton was frail of build; light-haired and peaked of face. His pointed nose supported a pair of large spectacles that gave him an owlish expression.

"Trouble, Wilderton?" Ruthley purred the question in a fatherly tone. Wilderton nodded.

"Don't worry about Dunson's death," remarked Ruthley. He picked up a copy of the *Daily Banner* and pointed to the headlines. "It's up to the police to arrest this killer, Dorsch. When they once find him, you will have no trouble convicting him of murder."

"I know that," vouchsafed Wilderton. "It's something else that bothers me, Mr. Ruthley. Prescott Dunson intended to run against me, for district attorney. People haven't forgotten that."

"He would not have gained the support of the reform party," remarked Ruthley. "You have proven yourself competent, Wilderton."

"Thank you, Mr. Ruthley. Just the same, Dunson had many supporters, chiefly those who expected him to make startling revelations. That puts it up to me."

"To do what?"

"To disclose the facts that Dunson promised to reveal. I must find the man higher up; the one whom Dunson intended to attack."

Stephen Ruthley nodded in commending fashion. Approaching Wilderton's chair, he clapped the district attorney upon the shoulder.

"You have a great head, Louis," approved Ruthley. "I admire your foresight. Yes, you must make every effort to find the man who ordered Dunson's death."

LOUIS WILDERTON produced a sheet of paper and handed it to Ruthley. It bore a list of names, written in pencil.

"This is confidential," stated Wilderton, in a strained tone. "I have written down the names of a dozen men, any one of whom *might* have had reason to fear Dunson. I would like your opinion on it, Mr. Ruthley."

Ruthley studied the list solemnly. As he expected, his own name was absent; so were those of Elvin Marclot and Kirk Borman. Even Lance Gillick's name was missing; for, today, Lieutenant Maclare had openly testified that he had raided the Club Adair prior to Dunson's murder and that Gillick was there at the time the killing took place.

The names on the list were those of small-fry politicians; also a few local contractors. Ruthley suppressed a pleased smile as he noted the name of Adam Woodstock.

"Understand, Mr. Ruthley," remarked Wilderton, "I have no evidence whatever against any of these men. I have merely assumed that someone in Westford must have wanted Dunson to die."

"I understand." Ruthley placed the paper on his desk. "Wilderton, I think that the best course is to wait. This matter will smooth itself."

"How so?"

"If one of those men is responsible," returned Ruthley, indicating the list, "he will soon lose his nerve. Dunson's murder has raised a huge cry. The fact that the police so promptly identified Dorsch as the killer will make the man behind the murder feel uneasy. He will do something that will prove his part in crime. Your problem will be solved."

"I hope that you are right, Mr. Ruthley."

"I feel confident that I am right. Be tranquil, Louis. Sit tight—let us say for the next two days—and if nothing has occurred within that time, come to me again."

Wilderton arose. He smiled wanly; pleased by Ruthley's reassurance. Glancing at his watch, the prosecutor remembered an appointment. Ruthley showed him to the door.

AS soon as Wilderton was gone, Ruthley returned to his desk. He picked up the list; chuckled as he read it. The names were written on a sheet of paper that bore Wilderton's name, printed in the upper left corner. Ruthley turned the paper downward. He picked up the telephone; stroked his chin as he tried to remember a number. He put the telephone back on its table, picked up the directory instead.

Turning to the "W's," Ruthley found Woodstock's number. He repeated it aloud: "Marvin 6384." He was about to reach for the telephone when he heard a ring of the doorbell; Haija's prompt footsteps followed. Ruthley stepped to the desk, and made a notation on the back of Wilderton's paper. The memo that he wrote was: "Woodstock. Marvin 6384."

Haija appeared, to announce Kirk Borman. The police director entered. Ruthley leaned against the desk, to hear what he had to report. Borman was both prompt and brief.

"Just gave another interview to the *Daily Banner*," said the police director. "Stated that we are looking for Theo D. Shaw, as an accomplice of Beezer Dorsch. Our theory is that Shaw lured Dunson to the Majestic Hotel, so that Beezer could kill him on the way."

"Good business," approved Ruthley. "What else?"

"Finding Shaw's note on Dunson," continued Borman, "the police went to question the man. Found that Beezer Dorsch was there ahead. Surprised Beezer and Shaw in conference. Both made a getaway; but we bagged two of their accomplices."

"Fine!" chuckled Ruthley. "Beezer was wise to get rid of those fellows. Go on, Kirk."

"Still searching for Shaw out by the water tower. The Flying Squadron is watching for him, as well as for Beezer. They know that he is The Shadow; but they're keeping that to themselves."

"You've added more men to the squadron?"

"Yes. Lance Gillick brought in a new bunch today. We gave them the phony examination, to qualify them. It gives us a force of forty."

Another chuckle from Ruthley. One of the smartest moves in the master crook's game had been the formation of the Flying Squadron. To a man, that outfit was recruited from thugs whom Lance Gillick had called to Westford. All gave false addresses, pretending that they came from this locality.

Director Borman, in his call for "picked men," invariably gave these camouflaged thugs a high mark when he examined them. Other applicants were always rated low; thereby rejected.

"They'll chop down The Shadow, if they see him," declared Borman. "Too bad we didn't guess that he was Shaw, last night."

"We should have," purred Ruthley, his eyes showing a glint. "Look at this, Kirk."

STEPPING to his desk, Ruthley picked up a pencil. Beneath Woodstock's telephone number, he printed the name: "Theo D. Shaw." Crossing out letters in irregular fashion, he spelled the name: "The Shadow."

Kirk Borman whistled.

"I get it!" exclaimed the police director. "He faked that name for Dunson's benefit. So that if Dunson began to study it closely, he would catch on to the idea. No wonder Dunson trusted Shaw. He must have guessed that he was The Shadow."

"Just as we should have guessed it," returned Ruthley. He glanced at the paper. "Wait a minute, Kirk, while I call Adam Woodstock."

Noting the telephone number again, Ruthley made the call. He completed a brief conversation; crumpled the sheet of paper and tossed it into an empty wastebasket.

"Woodstock is waiting to see me," Ruthley told Borman. "I called him this afternoon; told him to stay at home tonight, and see to it that he was alone."

"Is he?"

"Yes. His family has gone out. By the way, did you get those notes I wanted?"

Borman nodded; he pulled folded papers from his pocket.

"I went to the Club Adair right after dinner," he stated. "My pretext was to make a final check on Lance's alibi. I gave him a clean bill of health. I saw Beezer, in Lance's office, while we were alone. He had the notes all ready."

Ruthley pocketed the notes. He nudged his thumb toward the door.

"You go out the front way, Kirk," he told Borman. "I intend to use the secret passage. I have a car parked in the back alley."

"Good luck to you, Steve. I'll be at my office in city hall, ready for any phone calls."

Kirk Borman departed, out through the front door. He descended the stairs and reached the street. He stepped aboard his official car. The chauffeur drove away.

THE front of the big apartment house was recessed and, therefore, dark, except at the door, where two lights glowed. Kirk Borman had glanced casually along the front wall, as his car rolled away; but he had noted nothing unusual. It was after the director's car had gone that the unusual occurred.

Blackness moved from the darkened building front. At a moment when no cars were passing on the boulevard, a shrouded figure stepped in front of the lights by the door. For one second only, a complete shape was revealed. The lights showed The Shadow, cloaked in his garb of black.

With quick glide, The Shadow entered the lower hallway of the apartment house. No attendant was on duty; even had one been present, he could easily have failed to spy the intruder. Though the large hall was lighted, its walls were dark-paneled and therefore dim. The Shadow's silent course was along the wall. He seemed no more than a mammoth blot, as he moved toward the stairs.

Reaching the second floor, The Shadow stopped by the door of Ruthley's apartment. He set to work with a pick; he performed his task with nicety, although it required several minutes to properly probe the lock. At last the door yielded; The Shadow stepped into the apartment and closed the barrier behind him.

Beyond a dim hallway, he saw the half-opened door of a lighted room. Advancing noiselessly, The Shadow reached that goal; he drew an automatic from beneath his cloak as he peered into Ruthley's lighted den. After a few moments, The Shadow stepped across the threshold.

The room was empty. The Shadow had reached Stephen Ruthley's lair, only to find that the master crook was absent.

CHAPTER XII
THE SHADOW'S CLUE

THOUGH The Shadow had anticipated a meeting with Stephen Ruthley, he was not disturbed to find the master villain gone. It merely meant that the meeting would be postponed; to a degree, that would prove to The Shadow's advantage.

Through various forms of investigation, The Shadow had labeled Ruthley as the master of crime in Westford. Until tonight, he had considered it good policy to wear down the forces at Ruthley's command; to weaken them, in preparation for a final conflict with Ruthley himself.

The death of Prescott Dunson had partly altered The Shadow's decision. He knew that other victims might be slated for the spot; therefore, it was no longer wise to hold back a final stroke. Moreover, The Shadow's own position had become precarious last night. Hunted by the law, he had needed his most stealthy tactics to leave the house by the water tower tonight.

Coming into Westford on foot, The Shadow had seen many signs of the increased Flying Squadron that was covering all portions of the city. He knew that the number of his enemies had been increased. Hence he had ventured onward, to strike directly at Ruthley, knowing that if he boxed the master of crime, the whole evil structure would collapse.

Since Ruthley was absent, The Shadow intended to remain until he returned. Meanwhile, he had an excellent opportunity to gain new facts regarding Ruthley, through an examination of the latter's papers. The desk and the filing cabinet offered possibilities, if searched. Stepping past an armchair, The Shadow reached the desk, to begin there.

As he placed his hand upon the handle of an upper drawer, The Shadow saw the wastebasket beside the desk. Conspicuous within the basket was a crumpled sheet of paper. Stooping, The Shadow picked out the paper and smoothed it. He saw immediately that he had made a find.

The paper was stationery from the office of Louis Wilderton; The Shadow recognized the district attorney's precise handwriting, for he had seen it on official documents. Studying the list of names, The Shadow understood their significance. These were persons whom Wilderton wanted to investigate. The prosecutor had come to Stephen Ruthley for advice on the matter.

Turning the paper over, The Shadow saw the penciled notations on the back. Again he recognized a handwriting that he had seen before: Stephen Ruthley's. The Shadow read the notation: "Woodstock. Marvin 6384." Below it, he saw the name, "Theo D. Shaw," with the letters crossed by lines. The Shadow's lips phrased an almost inaudible laugh. He had supposed that by this time Ruthley would have guessed the significance of the signature of Theo D. Shaw.

Most important was Ruthley's notation of Woodstock's name and telephone number. Knowing that graft was rampant in Westford, The Shadow had held suspicions of all persons who had undertaken city contracts. Woodstock's name, however, had been but one of several.

The Shadow had seen no reason to investigate the contractor, in preference to others. This notation, however, showed clearly that Ruthley intended contact with Woodstock. Since Ruthley was absent, it followed that he could have gone to Woodstock's home.

HAVING seen Kirk Borman leave the apartment house after a definite visit, The Shadow knew that Ruthley must have been at home while the police director was here. Therefore, Ruthley must have chosen another exit.

For the moment, The Shadow did not consider the large painting on the wall; for it seemed likely that Ruthley could have gone out by a back door of the apartment itself. The Shadow decided to look for such an exit. Before he did so, he went to the telephone, lifted the receiver and dialed Woodstock's number.

The only response was a busy signal. It meant either that Woodstock was talking over the telephone or that the contractor had taken his receiver from the hook. Hanging up, The Shadow went out through the hallway of the apartment, to begin a stealthy search for another outlet.

The Shadow had not proceeded far before he found reason to abandon his search. As he turned the corner of a hallway, he heard the creep of footsteps. Gliding through the doorway of a darkened room, The Shadow found another opening and reached the hall near Ruthley's den. Again, he heard a guarded creep.

Someone had heard the *click* of the telephone dial when The Shadow had used it. That person had visited the den following The Shadow's departure. His presence known, The Shadow had need of strategy. His best course was to return to the den, since the vigilant guard had already been there.

The Shadow crossed the hallway. His tall form threw a long silhouette upon the floor, almost to a corner beyond the door of the den. Gliding into the lighted room, The Shadow neared the desk, intending to pass beyond it. A sound made him wheel; he faced the doorway just as a wiry attacker sprang into view.

It was Haija. Almost as stealthy and as observant as The Shadow, the keen Japanese had spotted the silhouette upon the hallway floor. Coming from beyond the corner, he had reached the doorway of the den. Seeing The Shadow, Haija was leaping to prompt attack. The fact that The Shadow swung to meet him did not perturb the speedy Jap. Haija was grinning as he came.

With nimble hands, Haija caught The Shadow's right arm, as it swung toward the front of the black cloak. Haija thought that The Shadow was reaching for a gun. His guess was wrong. The Shadow had recognized a jujitsu thrust; his move was a bluff to counteract it.

As Haija performed a backspin, expecting to speed The Shadow over his shoulders, a gloved left hand hooked cross-arm, to clutch the Jap's neck. Haija jolted short. The Shadow whipped backward; his long arms were like tremendous levers, as they hoisted Haija from the floor. Releasing his grip, The Shadow let Haija hurtle over an armchair; shoulder foremost, the Japanese bashed against the side of the heavy framed painting that adorned the wall. The canvas quivered from the thud; instantly, The Shadow recognized that it served as a door.

HAIJA lay motionless on the floor, stunned by a bump his head had taken when he sprawled. The Shadow stepped to the telephone; again, he dialed Woodstock's number, to get another busy signal. Hardly had he finished with the dialing when he heard sounds from elsewhere in the apartment. Ruthley had servants beside Haija. They had heard the crash of the Jap's fall; they were coming to learn its cause.

For a moment The Shadow paused, ready to begin new fray. His gloved fingers, dipping beneath the cloak, crinkled the paper that he had placed there.

The Shadow changed his plan. Stepping over toward Haija's prone body, he tried the edge of the picture frame. He found the catch; shoved Haija aside with one foot as he drew the portrait toward himself. Listening, The Shadow noted that there were no approaching steps. Probably the servants were conferring among themselves, reluctant to advance until they knew more.

Leaving the big portrait ajar, The Shadow hurried from the den. He reached the hallway; gained the outer door and opened it, making a clatter as he did so. Giving the door a slam. The Shadow wheeled back toward the den. As he passed the unconscious form of Haija, he heard the pound of footsteps.

Servants knew at last that there was an intruder in the apartment. They thought that the unknown visitor had fled by the front door. With courage gained, they were making a pursuit. Calmly, The Shadow stepped through the opening behind the portrait; closed the doorlike painting and heard the catch *click* automatically.

Stephen Ruthley, when he returned, would never guess that The Shadow had found the secret exit. Haija would testify to a battle in the den; the other servants would swear that an invader had fled through the front door. As for the crumpled paper that he had gained, The Shadow doubted that Ruthley would even remember it. The master crook had considered it of no importance.

THE SHADOW, however, regarded the paper as valuable. He pocketed it securely, as he picked his way by flashlight through the interior of the vacant house. That paper was evidence of a sort that could be used, when the proper time arrived. There was a chance, though, that it might never prove necessary.

For The Shadow was taking a shortcut to reach Stephen Ruthley. He was convinced that the master crook had gone to the residence of Adam Woodstock. Knowing Ruthley's ways, The Shadow was positive that he would find the rogue engaged in secret parley with the contractor. If the two were hatching a new scheme of graft, it would be worth The Shadow's while to listen; then deal with Ruthley afterward.

Reaching the blind alley in back of the row of houses, The Shadow followed devious turns until he reached an obscure garage that was well away from brightly lighted streets. An attendant was

The Shadow ... hoisted Haija from the floor ... and hurried him over the armchair.

dozing in the office; he did not awaken when The Shadow entered a small roadster and coasted the car to the street.

This was a reserve automobile that The Shadow had purchased from a "used-car" lot in Westford. He was employing it to reach Adam Woodstock's home, on the other side of town. The Shadow knew the location of the contractor's residence; it was one of the largest houses in Westford.

All that disturbed The Shadow was the fact that it had taken him a dozen minutes to reach the garage where he had placed the old car. That interval had delayed his start to Woodstock's. There was a chance that the conference might be ended before The Shadow arrived at the contractor's home.

Had The Shadow learned the real purpose of Stephen Ruthley's visit to Adam Woodstock, he would have realized that the odds were badly against him. Though he was to profit by his present mission, The Shadow was faring into new and greater hazards than those that he had previously faced in Westford.

CHAPTER XIII
DEATH'S FALSE TALE

EVEN before The Shadow's combat with Haija, Stephen Ruthley had reached the home of Adam Woodstock. Admitted by the contractor himself, Ruthley had gone to a room on the second floor, there to confer with the man he had come to see.

Adam Woodstock was a dreary-faced individual; his bloodless countenance was almost as gray as the thin fringe of hair that surrounded his bald head. Seated at a desk in the room that he called his study, Woodstock assumed a listening attitude while Stephen Ruthley spoke. Woodstock had an odd habit of tilting his head to the right; Ruthley noticed it particularly tonight.

Across the desk from Woodstock, Ruthley was purring a persuasive story. It concerned the contract on which Woodstock had already paid back the half million dollars that had been required of him.

"There are several of us in this deal," confided Ruthley. "Marclot and I are not alone. That is why I have come to see you, Woodstock. These papers explain the situation."

Spreading the documents that he had brought from his own files, Ruthley chose one and passed it across the desk to Woodstock.

"This is the most important one," declared Ruthley. "It contains an itemized statement that you gave to Marclot. The bottom line lists five hundred thousand dollars under the head of excess profit."

"Quite right," returned Woodstock, in a drawly tone. "I listed my own profit as one hundred thousand; ten per cent of a million. The five hundred thousand represents the amount that I turned over to Marclot."

"We know that," nodded Ruthley, "but some of my associates have doubted the authenticity of the figures."

"But Marclot received the half million—"

"True. Nevertheless, we have only his word for it that your figures are correct."

Adam Woodstock blinked. In unbelieving tone, he questioned:

"Do you mean to say that someone has suggested that Marclot and I might have worked a side deal of our own?"

"Just that," replied Ruthley. "Of course, it sounds ridiculous. I said so myself. But the others did not think so. They had a reason for their doubts."

"What could that be?"

"The fact that you did not sign the statement."

Woodstock delivered a short laugh. Head still tilted, he reached for a pen that lay beside his desk telephone. Ruthley noted that the telephone was off its stand. He had suggested that Woodstock leave it so, in order not to be troubled by outside calls.

"I typed this statement myself," asserted Woodstock. "I have no objections to signing it."

Woodstock flourished the pen; he hesitated before applying his signature. His drawly tone was troubled as he remarked:

"This may be a mistake after all. I can't sign this statement, Ruthley. It would become an incriminating document if I did."

"Hardly," smiled Ruthley. "Not while it remains in my hands, Woodstock."

"I did not pay the money to you."

"You paid it to Marclot."

"The statement does not say so. It indicates that I could have retained the funds myself."

Ruthley reached for the statement. He studied it; nodded his agreement with Woodstock's opinion. Observing the contractor's typewriter on a table, Ruthley inserted the statement in the machine. At the bottom of the sheet, he typed two dotted lines, one an inch and a half below the other.

"Here." Ruthley spoke briskly, as he laid the paper on the table. "Let me have your pen, Woodstock. I shall sign the statement also, to give it my approval."

He took the pen; it slipped slightly between his fingers. Ruthley tightened his grip; signed his name on the lower line. He handed the pen to Woodstock, who placed a much-used blotter upon the signature; then prepared to sign his own name, by taking the pen from Ruthley's grasp.

In order to sign the lower line, Ruthley had come over beside the contractor. He stood there, one hand upon the table, while Woodstock signed the upper line.

Ruthley was on Woodstock's right. He thrust his hand into his right coat pocket as Woodstock was reaching for the blotter. His head still tilted to the right, Woodstock did not spy Ruthley's move. The contractor simply planked the blotter upon the statement; pressed it firmly with his fingers.

There was a glimmer as Ruthley's hand moved upward. Coming from cover was a .32 revolver. Taking advantage of Woodstock's tilted head, Ruthley jabbed the gun muzzle squarely against the contractor's temple and pulled the trigger. He stepped away as he felt the slight recoil of the weapon.

For a full second; Adam Woodstock's body remained rigid; blood seemed to hold back from the gaping wound that the bullet had blasted in his temple. Then the tilt of Woodstock's head began to overbalance him; he sagged in Ruthley's direction. Stone dead, Woodstock would have sprawled to the floor, had Ruthley not intervened.

WITH his left hand, Ruthley thrust Woodstock's right shoulder in a forward direction, so that the dead man slumped upon the desk. As Ruthley expected, Woodstock's right hand shoved out ahead of him. Ruthley waited until the motion had ended. In deliberate fashion, he placed the revolver in Woodstock's hand, carefully clamped the dead man's fingers about the weapon.

Ruthley was not disturbed by the noise that the gunshot had made. Woodstock's house was isolated; the windows of this room were closed. Nor did Ruthley bother about wiping the handle of the revolver to remove fingerprints. He knew that there were none of his own prints upon the gun.

This was explained when Ruthley held his hands palms upward in the light of the desk lamp, to give them brief examination. The glow made the murderer's fingertips look glassy.

Ruthley chuckled. Before beginning this expedition, he had taken the precaution to dip his fingers in collodion. That liquid had dried, leaving a smooth, gelatine surface upon the fingers. The presence of collodion explained why the pen had slipped slightly from Ruthley's grip. With larger objects, especially the revolver, the collodion did not matter.

Stepping to the far side of the desk, Ruthley reached across and whisked away the statement that he and Woodstock had signed. The paper slid easily from beneath Woodstock's left hand; but the blotter could not be so easily gained. It was beneath Woodstock's elbow.

Ruthley observed the projecting blotter edge; decided not to disturb it. The blotter was an old one, its upper surface showed enough ink smears to cover any recent marks.

Coming around beside Woodstock's body, Ruthley opened a desk drawer on the dead contractor's right. There he found objects that he wanted. The first was a long pair of scissors, that served as paper shears. Ruthley used these on the signed statement; he carefully clipped off the lower portion of the paper, just beneath the line that bore Woodstock's signature. Ruthley's own signature was removed with the clipped-off portion.

Crumpling the strip of paper, the master crook tucked it in his vest pocket.

From the desk drawer, Ruthley took a ring of keys. He walked across the room and stopped in front of a metal strongbox, where he knew that Woodstock kept important papers. Unlocking the box with the proper key, Ruthley found a suitable pigeonhole into which he tucked the signed statement.

Returning to the desk, Ruthley gathered other papers that he had brought with him. He pocketed some; carried others to the strongbox and placed them there. From another pocket, Ruthley drew a small wad of letters. Checking them over, he smiled as he noted Beezer Dorsch's signature. Choosing another pigeonhole, Ruthley planted the fake letters. He closed the door of the strongbox and locked it.

THE murderer's task was almost finished. Ruthley went back to the desk, replaced the scissors and the keys. He picked up the telephone and put it on its stand.

Ruthley looked around the room; smiled in pleased manner as he observed the drawn window shades. He made a last survey of Woodstock's position at the desk; in precise fashion, Ruthley shifted the dead man slightly, so that his position would better suit the killer's design.

The setup was perfect. Adam Woodstock looked as if he had braced himself for an ordeal; then pressed a revolver against his right temple. Assuming that Woodstock had been leaning forward, a bullet from his own hand would have produced the present result. It looked like a positive case of suicide.

Two details more; Ruthley attended to them. One was the matter of the pen, which had dropped from Woodstock's hand. Ruthley replaced it on the rack. The other was the drawer, that Ruthley had closed. Carefully, the murderer opened it again. From his pocket, he brought out a small box of cartridges, to match those in the death gun. He buried the cartridge box deep in the drawer.

Ruthley left the drawer open, to create the impression that Woodstock had reached into it for the gun. No other details were necessary. The suicide picture was complete; an examination of Woodstock's strongbox would fully support it. The signed statement; the letters from Beezer Dorsch would be as good as a written confession.

After a long, cold glance toward Woodstock's crumpled body, Ruthley turned and left the study. In a darkened hallway, he chose a flight of stairs that led to the back of the ground floor. Descending, Stephen Ruthley went out by a side door.

The master crook was deliberate, even in his departure. In fact, he had almost decided to linger a while longer upon the scene of his crime; for he was confident that no intruders would arrive until he wished them.

Though Stephen Ruthley did not guess it, luck favored him immensely when he made his chance decision to depart. Had he stayed two minutes longer, his false tale of death would have been rendered useless.

For Stephen Ruthley had unwittingly left a trail that led to this very house. The Shadow, master of vengeance, was close upon it.

CHAPTER XIV
ON THE SCENE OF CRIME

ADAM Woodstock's large house fronted upon a broad, but little-traveled, avenue. It stood well back from the street, and was almost surrounded by trees. Access to the house was gained through a broad driveway that began at the front avenue.

A small roadster had halted across from the entrance to the driveway. Keen eyes saw an empty lot, directly opposite Woodstock's house. Relaxing the clutch pedal slowly, the driver of the roadster urged his car between two trees; parked it in the lot and alighted.

All this was done in darkness, with the roadster's lights extinguished. As the arrival from the roadster crossed the avenue, he was silent and invisible. His feet did not even crunch the gravel when he entered Woodstock's driveway.

The Shadow had staged a perfect arrival at this house where crime had struck. Advancing on foot, he intended to make a stealthy entry; he was choosing the front door because it was nearest. It was not until he was almost to his objective that The Shadow halted.

He had heard the sound of a motor, throbbing on the other side of the house. It was followed by the muffled whine of a high-pitched second gear, a sound that faded almost instantly. For a moment, The Shadow expected to see an automobile come around the corner of the house; then he detected that the car had driven in an opposite direction.

Swiftly, The Shadow skirted the house. He glimmered a tiny flashlight upon the gravel of the driveway. The light showed that the driveway formed a circle; it was one that afforded two exits. In addition to the drive that came up from the avenue, there was another that led to a rear street. It was in that direction that the car had gone.

Noting a side door, The Shadow entered the house. There were no lights on the ground floor; but faint rays from a stairway indicated illumination on the second story. The Shadow ascended; arrived at the half-closed door of Woodstock's study. Peering inward, he saw the dead contractor slumped across the desk.

The Shadow entered, to examine the grim result of Ruthley's conference with Woodstock. Even to The Shadow, this outcome was something of a surprise; but its purpose dawned upon him the moment that he saw the scene of crime. The Shadow had foreseen that Stephen Ruthley would take measures to cover his own misdeeds; but he had not expected the master crook to deal in actual murder.

In fact, The Shadow had supposed that Ruthley had come here to ask Woodstock's aid in the important matter of quelling public sentiment regarding the death of Prescott Dunson. In a sense, Ruthley had done just that; but he had made Woodstock give aid without request. It did not take The Shadow long to recognize that Woodstock had become the scapegoat, upon whom would be placed the blame for Dunson's death.

CLOSE beside the desk, The Shadow studied the setup of Ruthley's perfect crime. It looked like suicide; it would pass as such. The opened desk drawer was an excellent touch. Any ordinary investigator would have decided that Adam Woodstock had reached into it to bring out his own revolver.

Keys shone from within the drawer. The Shadow plucked them up, examined them. He saw the strongbox; went to it and unlocked it. Stooped before the metal container, he began a search for planted evidence. He found it. The very items upon which Ruthley banked so heavily were the ones that won The Shadow's immediate suspicion.

The letters from Beezer Dorsch were pointed. They referred, in crudely veiled words, to a "job" that would be done as ordered. That meant the death of Dunson. One note spoke of "D," declaring that he would be no trouble. The Shadow left these letters where he found them.

Woodstock's signed statement explained still more. It gave The Shadow immediate knowledge of Ruthley's double-edged plan. The public would fall for the idea that the half million "excess profit" represented Woodstock's own harvest; but The Shadow knew its exact significance. That money was graft, paid back to Stephen Ruthley and the fake reformers who ran the present city administration.

Woodstock's corporation would have to disgorge the sum from its own funds. There would be a new contract; new graft, managed by Mayor Elvin Marclot who would raise his hands in amazed horror when he learned how Woodstock had tried to "swindle" the city of Westford.

One detail of the statement caught The Shadow's eye. The paper was slightly shorter than a usual typewriter page. Holding the paper to the light, The Shadow examined its texture; he saw its odd, wavy-lined watermark: the letter "W." It was a special bond paper, that Woodstock had evidently ordered direct from the manufacturers.

Approaching the desk, The Shadow found

It looked like suicide ... but it did not take The Shadow long to recognize that Woodstock had become the scapegoat.

other papers in the drawer. It was of the same bond; but the sheets were of normal length. Placing one blank sheet in Woodstock's typewriter, The Shadow tapped a few keys to observe the peculiarities of type and ribbon color. He saw at once that Woodstock's statement had been typed upon this machine.

Comparing the big shears with the statement, The Shadow saw how its lower edge had been clipped. He noted that the space was very slight below the line that bore Woodstock's signature. The Shadow laughed softly; he had gained an inkling of how Ruthley had induced Woodstock to sign the statement.

THE SHADOW replaced the statement in the strongbox; he locked the heavy door. He kept the sheet of paper that he had typed; placed it beneath his cloak. He dropped the paper shears into the desk drawer, along with the keys. Looking over the flattened shoulders of Woodstock's huddled body, The Shadow saw the much-used blotter that projected from beneath the dead man's arm.

Inch by inch, The Shadow worked the blotter free. He saw at once why Ruthley had left it on the desk. The blobby surface of the blotter could afford no clue. When The Shadow turned the blotter over, however, he made a simple discovery that had totally escaped Ruthley's notice.

The blotter was double surfaced. Woodstock, until tonight, had used the upper side. Tonight, he had begun with the blank side of the blotter. Its fresh surface showed only two marks. One was Woodstock's own signature, reversed; quite plain, for the contractor had pressed heavily with his pen. The other was lighter; but The Shadow recognized it. The second mark bore a distinct resemblance to Stephen Ruthley's signature.

The master crook had overlooked one small item in his arrangement of the suicide scene. Just as he had left evidence at his own apartment, indicating that he had gone to visit Woodstock, so had he left a clue which proved that he had actually come to the contractor's home. This blotter could nullify the evidence that Ruthley had planted in Woodstock's safe.

Ordinarily, The Shadow would have left the blotter on the desk. Circumstances caused him to do otherwise tonight. The Shadow had gauged Stephen Ruthley too well, to believe that the murderer would leave anything to chance. Though Ruthley thought his crime was perfect, he would certainly count upon the opinion of a man well qualified to judge.

This crime would be discovered. Police would arrive; with them, Police Director Borman. Knowing Ruthley to be the perpetrator of crime, Kirk Borman would be on the lookout for every minor detail. If Borman found the blotter, he would promptly dispose of it. As evidence, the blotter would never serve, if left upon the scene of crime. Therefore, The Shadow kept the blotter; he placed it beneath his cloak, along with other items that he had acquired upon this night of investigation.

The Shadow was ready for a return visit to Stephen Ruthley's apartment. He knew that he could enter there, through the secret passage, to surprise Ruthley in the latter's own den. Almost ready for departure, The Shadow paused on the far side of the desk, to lean across and make a last inspection of Woodstock's body. It was while The Shadow stood in this position that he heard a sound from somewhere in the house.

BOARDS were creaking, as though invaders were creeping up the front stairs. Wheeling from the desk, The Shadow crossed the room. He gained the hall and reached the top of the backstairs, to listen for sounds from the front. Audible whispers reached The Shadow.

"Maybe it was a crank call," came one comment. "The guy that phoned headquarters may have just thought he heard a shot."

"We can't take any chances, though" was the response. "Director Borman said to move in, soft-like, and investigate."

"Yeah. He's outside, too, waiting for us to report."

"That's why we'd better take a gander into that lighted room."

The approaching men were detectives from headquarters. A call had been made there, reporting a gunshot heard within Woodstock's house. Probably, Ruthley had made that call, soon after his departure. Kirk Borman had been at his office, expecting it. Since Borman was outside, it was likely that members of the Flying Squadron were with him.

The Shadow decided upon stealthy departure, in order to head for Ruthley's without trouble on the way.

The two detectives went past. As they neared the door of Woodstock's study, The Shadow began his descent of the backstairs. He was only halfway down when a shout came from above. The dicks had discovered Woodstock's body. They were pounding out into the hall, to raise a loud alarm.

Instantly, there was a response from below. Footsteps clattered near the bottom of the backstairs. There was a *click;* a flashlight gleamed upward; the light was furnished by another detective, who happened to be near the backstairs when he heard the shout. He, too, raised a cry.

The dick below had made a discovery of his own. Straight in the path of his upward glare, he saw The Shadow. The detective's shout was spontaneous. He told all, as he cried:

"There's a guy on the backstairs! Get him!"

More footsteps below, as new arrivals hurried to join the detective who held the light. Shouts from above, as the two who had found Woodstock's body reached the backstairs to see The Shadow against the brilliant glare.

The Shadow's chance of stealthy departure was

ended. Trapped between two forces, he was faced by a situation more pressing than the one he had encountered the night before.

CHAPTER XV
FOILED HOUNDS

ONE factor favored The Shadow. Though trapped, he had been found by men who were not of a criminal sort. Director Borman, knowing that Adam Woodstock's body was to be discovered, had used smart policy. He had sent ordinary detectives into the contractor's house; men who had long been on the Westford force. He had decided that their preliminary reports would be better than those of the outsiders who formed the Flying Squadron.

As yet, The Shadow had not clashed directly with any of the city's loyal police. Bluecoats had joined the khaki-clad squadron men in last night's chase; but The Shadow had been speeding away when the regular police took up the chase. Hence, he was an unknown factor to the real supporters of the law in Westford.

These headquarters men were like the police of Lieutenant Maclare's precinct. They were capable, but slow-witted. Director Borman preferred such officers. The Shadow knew that fact; he took advantage of it. Despite his trapped position, he saw chance for a quick getaway.

As usual, The Shadow did the unexpected. His natural course lay downward; but he spurned that route. His prompt decision was based on the fact that men were better prepared below; moreover, there was no way to guess instantly their number. Above were but two men; they were in the throes of a second surprise, for they had just found Woodstock's body. They did not expect The Shadow to come in their direction.

That direction, however, was the one that The Shadow chose; and he took his course with amazing speed. Wheeling on the stairway, he came upward with long bounds, swinging his arms high; each hand held an automatic. The detectives were drawing guns; but they ducked as The Shadow came upon them. Sweeping his arms sidewise, The Shadow carried the pair half across the hall.

He was clear of the light from below. The startled dicks were sprawled; despite the fact that The Shadow avoided damage with his sweeping blows. One headquarters man took the back of a gloved fist upon the chin. That swing, weighted with an automatic, was a knockout punch.

The other detective swung at The Shadow, missed him in the darkness and fired two wild shots at nothingness. A swinging forearm staggered him to the top of the backstairs, where he did a downward dive, into the arms of men who were dashing upward.

The Shadow sped down the front stairway, turning the landing just as the flashlight stabbed in his direction. A detective fired two useless rounds. The Shadow was gone before the fellow tugged the trigger.

THE SHADOW had made a perfect start; but he knew that it was but preliminary to the struggle that was to come. Revolver shots had been heard outside; shock troops were prepared to answer the alarm.

As The Shadow hurled the front door open, a spotlight glared full upon him. The shouts that went up were delivered by hoarse-voiced members of the Flying Squadron.

Nearly a third of that outfit was on hand. Those sharpshooting thugs were dangerous with their guns. Knowing it, The Shadow did not pause to fire at the focused light; instead, he sprang off toward a front corner of the house, getting away from the glare in an instant.

The light swung about; it did not show The Shadow. He had cut in back of thick, intervening shrubbery.

Guns began to bark; bullets whistled through foliage, thudded the house walls. A challenging laugh sounded from off beside the house. Raucous-voiced crooks shouted harsh epithets, as they heard The Shadow's weird mockery. They fired toward spots whence they thought the sinister mirth had issued. Their bullets were wide by yards.

No one could place The Shadow's laugh in blackness. Those who tried merely rendered their gunfire useless, as The Shadow wanted it. The real tokens of The Shadow's position came when automatics tongued streaks of flame, straight for men who had revealed themselves by the spurts from their own revolvers. Groans, not bullets, answered The Shadow. In four shots, he scored two hits.

The Shadow was on his way again, circling off through darkness while his enemies fired blindly. A loud command was issued; it was in Kirk Borman's voice. The police director recognized the futility of the tactics that his thugs had taken. He was ordering them to follow a better method.

Khaki-clad thugs spread away, toward the hedges that formed the boundaries of Woodstock's property. There were patrol cars in the avenue and on other streets. Each automobile served as a base; men with flashlights passed from car to car.

Borman joined the detectives inside the house; he put men on guard at each door. A few of the Flying Squadron lugged in the pair of wounded men

A swinging forearm staggered him to ... a downward dive into the arms of men who were dashing upward.

whom The Shadow had clipped; after that, they hurried to carry out Borman's latest orders. Those were instructions for the cordon to close inward.

SOMEWHERE in the darkness was The Shadow. He had paused, expecting the move that came. It suited him; for his intention was to find an opening and depart while his enemies made futile search. That was possible, if he moved at the right time.

Two minutes passed, while surrounding men crept closer; searchlights began to sweep from patrol cars, like a barrage above the heads of the advancing men.

Wisely, the men in the cars kept the lights high, hoping to disclose The Shadow without revealing the positions of the men who closed in upon the cloaked fighter. The Shadow saw his opportunity and took it; close to the ground, he moved rapidly outward, just before a flood of light came in his direction. He escaped the path of the gleam.

The cordon could not function fully until it tightened; the creeping men were expecting The Shadow to lurk until he neared them. One lone fighter, sought by many, would ordinarily have let the circle close about him. The Shadow's tactics were different. He was actually on a line with the closing men; beneath the gleaming lights, like themselves.

The Shadow, however, was moving in an outward direction. Moreover, he had chosen the simplest path as the one that would be least guarded. He was creeping along the driveway to the avenue.

The Shadow was almost to the gate before he was discovered; even then, he was noted by accident. Reinforcements had come up; among them, men on motorcycles. One of these was ordered to ride through to the house; to form new contact with the police director. Obeying instructions, the man on the motorcycle chugged for the driveway. As he took the curve, his headlamp threw a glare inward from the gate.

Squarely ahead, the rider saw The Shadow rising in his path. The man gave a shout; whipped a revolver from his holster as he applied the brake. He gained no chance to fire. The Shadow was launching forward; as the fake cop's gun came up, The Shadow hurdled the handlebars in a long plunge.

The Shadow's left arm clamped the man's shoulder; as the fellow spilled to the gravel, The Shadow came with him. The Shadow's right hand clutched a .45; it was poised for a swing, if the foeman made trouble. No blow was needed; the rider struck on the back of his head and rolled over, just away from his toppling cycle.

The Shadow sprang to his feet; he was just in time. The cry had been heard; searchlights were flooding toward the driveway. Men on the lawn heard shouts, as those in the cars spied The Shadow. All wheeled about to begin a barrage. Through sheer speed, The Shadow escaped them. He was leaping through the gate as the fusillade began.

Guns barked from the patrol cars; but the bullets were scattered. The men in the cars had the double task of keeping The Shadow spotted with light and continuing the fire until their companions arrived. They were not equal to the twofold effort. The Shadow was across the avenue before guns ripped away in earnest.

BOUNDING into his old roadster, The Shadow pressed the starter. The motor roared as he sped the car off between two houses. His lights blinked into view; the men from the cordon saw the roadster careen to another street, headed away to flight. Shouting, the khaki-clad thugs boarded their patrol cars and started in pursuit.

The Shadow reversed last night's procedure. Though pressed by swift cars and motorcycles, he headed into the city instead of making for the limits. The roadster lacked speed, but it was ideal for the tricky course that The Shadow took. He whizzed the small car around the sharpest corners; shot it through driveways, past houses, out through hedges. Three times he cut back upon his course, like a hare outrunning the hounds.

Shots ripped every time pursuers spied him; and The Shadow answered with bullets of his own. He crippled the driver of the closest patrol car and put that machine out of the chase. He picked another foeman from a motorcycle, just as the pursuer sped in from another street to block The Shadow's turn.

The Shadow knew that if he could outrun these foemen, he could reach the goal that he sought. If he arrived at Ruthley's to confront the master rogue, The Shadow could force the big shot to call off his hounds, under threat of instant death.

As the pursuit continued, The Shadow gained more distance; but new factors intervened to offset his purpose.

By heading toward the heart of Westford, The Shadow was running into new details of the Flying Squadron. Radio calls were humming through the ether. New units came in view at nearly every block. Sheer nerve was all that saved The Shadow from disaster; twice he ran the gauntlet of cars and motorcycles that sought to head him off, relying each time on quick stabs from his own guns to make the opposing marksmen falter.

Each time it worked; for the thugs who served as members of the Flying Squadron knew the identity of their dread foe. Drivers instinctively changed course when The Shadow's big guns tongued. Crooks could not fire accurately from their veering cars.

At last, a double circuit brought The Shadow to the railroad tracks. He sped the roadster across, planning a last dash in the direction of Ruthley's apartment house.

Then came the trouble that The Shadow had hoped to avoid. Shots flashed from a side street; to elude them, The Shadow drove into an alleyway. New guns barked from straight ahead. All came from men on foot. The Shadow had entered Maclare's precinct. The lieutenant and his bluecoats were answering the alarm that they had received just prior to The Shadow's arrival.

THE SHADOW jammed the roadster against the curb. He dropped from it; darted back into the street that he had just left. He saw an alleyway opposite; he took to it just as a burly man in uniform opened fire from beneath a streetlight. It was Lieutenant Maclare; The Shadow could easily have dropped him where he stood. But The Shadow's quarrel was not with loyal men.

Maclare bawled an order to his men. Though he did not realize it, the lieutenant was shouting for the death of the very fighter who had saved his own life two nights ago.

Bluecoats responded; they chased along the alley that The Shadow had taken. The Shadow had outrun them, but two police cars spotted him in the next street. Recognizing these as belonging to the Flying Squadron, The Shadow stopped to deal with them.

He halted the first car with well-directed bullets; but he could not stop the second. Bullets hailed from its windows; The Shadow gave a last volley, put away his emptied guns and dived for a space between two buildings. A bullet clipped him as he sprang. The thugs in the police car saw him falter. They leaped to the ground; chased into the alley where The Shadow had gone.

More of the Flying Squadron arrived; so did the regular police. Khaki uniforms mingled with blue; flashlights lighted space to show a blind alley that terminated in a high board fence, topped with barbed wire. There were boxes and packing cases stacked all about; any of them might conceal The Shadow.

Lieutenant Maclare arrived to shout an order for men to advance and rout out the fugitive. Before the order was obeyed, it was countermanded by a higher authority. Director Borman had arrived; in harsh tones, he ordered the police to riddle the boxes at the end of the blind alley.

While bluecoats hesitated at the murderous order, Borman's khaki-clad henchmen opened fire. Guns echoed between walls; bullets sprayed through boxes toppled stacks of them from in front of the fence.

With Maclare following, Borman strode forward. He knew that The Shadow had been wounded; he expected to find the cloaked fugitive dead. Nearing the fence, the director grabbed up the lowermost boxes and hurled them aside. He stared, as Maclare's flashlight showed a jagged hole in the corner of the fence.

The Shadow had dived beyond those boxes; with one good arm, he had bashed the decayed boards at the lower left corner of the fence. He had sledged those blows with an automatic; a few powerful strokes had done the necessary work. The Shadow had shouldered through, while his pursuers had massed at the entrance of the alley.

Blobs of blood stained the cement at the bottom of the fence. Those marks were new proof that The Shadow had been crippled. Kirk Borman restrained a snarl as he turned to his men; in booming tones, he gave an order for a prompt search throughout the district.

Eyeing the bloodstains once again, Kirk Borman indulged in a sharp smile of triumph. He was certain that The Shadow could not have traveled far; he knew also that the crippled fighter would not be able to put up a fight, when discovered.

Kirk Borman was sure that he would have good news for Stephen Ruthley tonight. News that the menace of The Shadow existed no longer.

CHAPTER XVI
NEW REFUGE

MORE than an hour after The Shadow's disappearance, the first show ended at the Criterion Theater, one of Westford's most elaborate motion picture houses. Among the throng that filed from the theater were Louis Wilderton and Estelle Benbrook. The district attorney was speaking apologetically, when they reached the sidewalk in front of the theater.

"I'm so sorry that we couldn't stay to the beginning of the feature picture," stated Wilderton, "but I am terribly rushed with work at the office, really, I shouldn't have come to the theater at all tonight."

"I understand," said Estelle. "I do not mind, Louis. Come; let us walk over to the house. You can leave me there and pick up your car."

As they walked along, Estelle added an afterthought:

"Your work is your most important duty, Louis. It will continue to be, until you have brought the murderer of Prescott Dunson to justice."

Wilderton blinked in owlish fashion; then formed a slight smile.

"You spoke like your father, Estelle," he remarked. "Do you know, people often speak of the fact that you so resemble him. They hold a high opinion of Judge Benbrook in this city."

The statement pleased Estelle; Wilderton saw it; he questioned suddenly:

"What is your father's real opinion of me? Does he favor my re-election? Or was he partial to Dunson's candidacy?"

"Father expressed no preference," replied Estelle, soberly. "He said, however, that Westford needs a man of courage in the office. A man who can do more than wish for results; one who can gain them."

Wilderton winced. The words were a criticism of his own ability, or lack of it, but he was aware that the statement was justified. When he spoke again Wilderton's tone was sincere.

"I could step aside for the right man," he declared. "I could not have dropped from the contest on Dunson's account; but if a man of greater prestige should run for the office—"

"Such as my father?"

"Yes, Estelle, a candidate of your father's caliber would help Westford. I would not run for re-election, if he sought to become district attorney."

"Unfortunately, Father cannot return to public life," remarked Estelle, ruefully. "He seems wearied; it takes a physician's care to preserve what strength he still has. I appreciate what you have said, Louis; so will Father, when I tell him."

"Your father was always a champion of reform," reminded Wilderton. "The name of Judge Martin Benbrook would sway the public. Such ardent reformers as Stephen Ruthley; such men as Mayor Marclot, Director Borman, and others of this fine administration—all would support Judge Benbrook's candidacy. I repeat again, Estelle; your father is one man for whom I would gladly postpone my ambition to remain as district attorney. If—"

WILDERTON paused. They were at the corner opposite the Majestic Hotel. People were halting at the sounds of sirens. A police car whizzed by; two motorcycles whirred and chugged as they swung the corner. Everywhere were the khaki uniforms that denoted Westford's Flying Squadron.

"It looks like a manhunt!" exclaimed Wilderton. "Possibly they have caught the trail of that murderer, Dorsch. Wait here, Estelle, while I inquire."

Two bluecoated policemen were searching doorways. Wilderton approached them; they recognized the district attorney and saluted. After a brief parley, Wilderton returned to where Estelle stood. He explained the situation while they continued toward the girl's home.

"Trouble at the home of Adam Woodstock," said Wilderton. "He was found dead, Woodstock was, apparently a suicide. The coroner is out there. When the police arrived however, they found someone in the house. They think that it was Shaw, the accomplice of Dorsch."

"Did they capture him?" inquired Estelle.

"No," returned Wilderton. "They say the fellow was rigged up in some kind of attire that helped him hide. He dashed away from Woodstock's. They pursued him into town; trapped him in a blind alley."

"He was cloaked in black?"

Wilderton looked puzzled as he heard Estelle's strained tone. Nodding, he replied:

"Yes, of course, he was in black. That was why he managed to escape. They riddled the blind alley with bullets—"

"To shoot him in cold blood?"

"Why not, Estelle? That was the way Dunson was slain. He never had a chance for life, poor chap."

Estelle tightened her lips, resolved to say no more. Wilderton concluded with the final information that he had gained from the policemen.

"Somehow, the fugitive managed to slip from the trap," declared Wilderton. "He was wounded, though; here and there, they found bloodstains on the sidewalk. The fellow must have been shrewd enough to stanch his wounds, at least temporarily. The trail of blood was lost. So they are making a general search."

Wilderton and Estelle had reached the girl's house. The young prosecutor started to accompany the judge's daughter through the side gate. Estelle stopped him; pointed to Wilderton's car, parked in front of the house.

"You have work to do, Louis," she reminded. "These new events may push you even more. You must hurry to the office. I have my key; I can enter the door without trouble. Good night, Louis."

As Wilderton headed for his car, Estelle hurried along the passage to the door. Her hand trembling, she tried to insert the key in the lock. It slipped from her fingers and clanked to the bottom of the steps.

Estelle leaned down to hunt for the key. Her fingers encountered moisture.

With a gasp, Estelle tugged a handkerchief from her handbag; placed it upon the cement and pressed it to absorb the stain that she felt sure was blood. She found the key during the process. Hurriedly, she put it in the lock, to find that it would not turn. The door was already unlocked.

Estelle opened it, stepped into the entry. She saw the dim light of the hall and was ready to start for it. Then she remembered to lock the door.

That done, Estelle moved toward the hall. She stumbled across something on the floor; caught herself as she tripped forward. There was a candlestick on a hall table, with a few matches beside it. Shakily, she lighted the candle and returned to the entry.

The long, wavering flame showed the sight that Estelle had dreaded. Huddled face downward on the floor was a black-cloaked figure, as silent as if dead. The rescuer of the other night had returned. Hunted by hordes who sought his life, he had found this last haven. Here, his strength had failed him.

Was The Shadow dead?

For the moment, the girl feared the worst. Then, bravely, she determined to learn. Estelle Benbrook was resourceful; she had proven that in the past, by caring for her invalid father without the aid of servants. Experience as a nurse had also brought her knowledge of how to aid the injured.

Estelle lifted The Shadow's head; his slouch hat fell away, to reveal a hawkish visage, pale despite its masklike contour. The Shadow's face was well-formed, distinguished in appearance. Yet Estelle scarcely observed it.

Her hands had found the blood-soaked shoulder of The Shadow's cloak. Easing away the black cloth folds. Estelle discovered the nature of the wound. A police bullet had winged The Shadow's left shoulder; but not badly enough to halt him. Loss of blood had overcome the wounded fighter, after he had gained this refuge. A wadded handkerchief showed that The Shadow had managed to stanch the flow; but only in temporary fashion.

THE SHADOW stirred as Estelle tried to lift him. His eyes opened wearily; he sensed his surroundings. With the girl's aid, he managed to come to his feet. Estelle supported him as he wavered, through the hallway, into a dim front room, where the girl guided him to a couch.

Estelle went out; she returned with scissors, bandages and a basin of water. Placing chair and table beside the couch, she set to work to attend The Shadow's wound.

The task was a painful one, although The Shadow gave no indication of the pangs that he suffered. When Estelle had finished the work, The Shadow's left shoulder formed a white-bandaged expanse. The girl had drawn away his cloak; she had cut apart the cloth beneath, in order to apply the bandage.

She noted that The Shadow's eyes were looking beyond her; that his thin, straight lips were about to move, as if to ask a question. Before The Shadow could speak, Estelle heard a footfall. She turned about, uttered a startled cry as her father stepped into the room.

Judge Martin Benbrook was a man of seventy. He stood square-shouldered and erect, despite the fact that he leaned his weight upon a heavy cane. His face was rugged; his features, though overlarge, were distinctive, for they were as firm as if chiseled by a sculptor. Flowing gray hair added to the judge's fine appearance.

He was dressed in attire that suited him well. An old-fashioned frock coat matched his cuffless trousers; his shirt was stiff-fronted, set off with a low-cut waistcoat. A large four-in-hand tie accompanied the wing-tipped collar beneath his smooth-shaven chin.

The judge's eyes were brilliant as they stared toward The Shadow. A responsive glint came from The Shadow's eyes. Those were flashes of mutual recognition; each was a fighter who could tell another of his kind. Estelle saw the exchange of silent greetings. A glad smile wreathed her face. Rising, she approached the judge.

"Father," said the girl, "this is the stranger whom I spoke about. The one who rescued me from death—"

"He is no stranger." Judge Benbrook pronounced the words as solemnly as he had given verdicts from the bench. "He is a person who stands for right. As such, he is our friend."

With slow but steady stride, the judge approached The Shadow. In his same solemn tone, he added:

"I have read beyond the headlines in these reports of crime. I have known that someone, here in Westford, stood for justice against overwhelming odds! You are wounded; but in whatever battle you fought, yours was the right cause!"

AS HE finished this pronouncement, Judge Benbrook began to sway. Estelle hurried to him; helped her father to the chair beside the couch. The judge smiled; gave a slight nod to indicate that the spell had passed.

"Stay here, Father," said Estelle. "I shall bring your medicine."

As the girl left, Judge Benbrook spoke quietly to The Shadow.

"You have seen the reason for my inactivity," he declared. "Each day, my strength seems to return. At evening, it fades. My malady perplexes me; I cannot understand it. Nevertheless, it prevents me from waging the battle that I should like to undertake."

Pausing, the judge eyed The Shadow closely. He saw the pallor of the wounded fighter's face.

"Your pain is great," declared the judge. "You must rest. Sleep will aid you, until I summon my own physician to—"

Estelle had returned in time to hear her father's words. She interrupted with a cry of alarm that halted Judge Benbrook's statements. The girl shook her head as she placed a bottle of pills upon the table, along with a glass of water.

"No, Father!" she exclaimed. "We cannot trust Doctor Lunden to preserve silence. I have often asked you to choose another physician. Your own condition has not improved under Doctor Lunden's treatments."

Judge Benbrook motioned for silence. The Shadow's lips had moved. In low, but steady tone the wounded fighter spoke:

"Telegraph to New York. Summon Doctor Rupert Sayre—"

The Shadow paused, closing his eyes; but both Estelle and her father nodded. They understood that Sayre must be The Shadow's own physician.

The Shadow's eyes opened; they met Judge Benbrook's gaze. At close range, The Shadow noted a largeness of the judge's pupils; a certain fixation in his stare.

Estelle was tipping three capsules from the medicine bottle. The Shadow reached forward with his right hand.

"Give me two," he requested. "One only for Judge Benbrook."

Estelle looked puzzled; but she followed the request. The Shadow swallowed each pill in turn, following with gulps of water from the glass which Estelle handed him. His head performed a slight nod, to indicate that he had made a correct supposition.

"These pills contain an opiate," declared The Shadow, looking toward Judge Benbrook. "As such, they will relieve my pain. They explain why your strength has failed you."

"You mean that I have been doped?" claimed Judge Benbrook. "That the increased dosages, given to me by Doctor Lunden, have been keeping me a semi-invalid?"

The Shadow nodded.

"Take only one," he repeated. "Ask Sayre about them when he comes tomorrow. He will reduce the dosage. Say nothing to your own physician."

JUDGE BENBROOK took a single pill and swallowed it. Watching The Shadow, he saw proof of the latter's statement. The Shadow's eyes had dulled; his eyelids closed. A relieved smile showed upon the thin lips. Judge Benbrook arose from his chair, faced his daughter with a triumphant gaze.

"He will sleep!" exclaimed the judge. "Soon, he will be well. Meanwhile, my malady will end; for this true friend has discovered its real cause. We shall handle Lunden wisely, Estelle. We shall keep him ignorant of the fact that we have learned his treachery."

Proudly, the old judge walked to the door of the room; turned to survey The Shadow, who was deep in a drowse. In imposing tone, Judge Benbrook spoke for himself and The Shadow.

"Together," he predicted, "we shall win this struggle! Truth shall prevail in Westford! When it does, crime will end!"

Those prophetic words must have reached The Shadow, just as he was sinking into a comfortable lethargy. Estelle Benbrook, watching beside the couch, saw thin lips form another smile.

CHAPTER XVII
THE BOMBSHELL

FIVE days had passed since the tempestuous night when The Shadow had found refuge in Judge Martin Benbrook's home. All had been quiet during those days.

Doctor Rupert Sayre had come from New York. During a brief visit, he had put two patients on the road to recovery. He had attended The Shadow's wound. He had reduced the opiate dosage that Judge Benbrook had unwittingly been taking. This, Sayre accomplished through a prescription of his own.

Outside of the judge's house, other matters had reached a settlement. The coroner had declared the death of Adam Woodstock to be suicide. His verdict had been based on definite evidence; the papers found in Woodstock's strongbox stood as clear proof that Woodstock had been the man "higher up" who hired Beezer Dorsch to slay Prescott Dunson.

The coroner was an honest official, though an unimportant one. He did not belong to Stephen Ruthley's ring; but he had been bluffed by the master crook's game.

Prescott Dunson had promised to reveal truth concerning corruption linked with crime. Apparently, all could be laid upon Woodstock. The dead contractor's own statement proved that he had swindled the city of Westford. All this evidence had been placed in the hands of Louis Wilderton.

The young district attorney had stated that he would force Woodstock's company to disgorge its half million of excess profit. The corporation was wealthy; it had promptly paid up without argument. Thus Mayor Elvin Marclot had received the fund in question; it was back in the city treasury. Money that did not belong there; but which would not stay long. Marclot was already looking for another fat corporation, headed by another of Woodstock's ilk; a man who would "play ball" and kick back the required graft in return for the contract.

One thing had caused trouble. The Shadow's presence at Woodstock's had made the coroner hesitate in his verdict of suicide. Director Borman had handled that; he had talked headquarters detectives into swearing that The Shadow had been entering the house when they trapped him. Hence, he could not be blamed for Woodstock's death. The crooks would have relished a decision that classed The Shadow as a murderer; but they preferred to have Woodstock's death pass as suicide.

None of the headquarters men had gained a good look at The Shadow; nor had Lieutenant Maclare or his bluecoats. Only the fake cops who formed the Flying Squadron knew who it was that they had fought. They testified that the intruder had been the mysterious man called Shaw. Thus it was decided that Shaw had served as go-between for Adam Woodstock and Beezer Dorsch.

Like Beezer, Shaw was wanted; and neither had

reappeared. Ruthley and his fellow crooks decided that The Shadow had gained his fill of Westford. Nevertheless, Lance Gillick expressed the view that The Shadow might someday return. Ruthley decided to take no chances. Through Borman, the master crook had arranged for members of the Flying Squadron to keep guard about his apartment house.

Ruthley did not know that The Shadow had found the secret entrance through the adjacent house; nevertheless, he wanted absolute security. The Shadow's path to Ruthley's was blocked, even if he should choose to use it.

Beezer Dorsch was hiding out in comfortable fashion at Lance Gillick's apartment. Popular belief had it that Beezer had fled Westford, the night of Dunson's death.

WHAT most concerned the quieted city on this particular day was a meeting of the Civic Club, the chief reform organization in Westford. That meeting was scheduled for late afternoon, in the club's own headquarters. When the hour arrived, the place was thronged. The chairman was Stephen Ruthley himself.

Standing on the rostrum, Ruthley beamed at the audience. In dulcet tones, he commended the city officials for their successful war against crime and graft. There were plaudits from the crowd; bows from Mayor Marclot and Director Borman, who were seated on the platform behind Ruthley. Finally, Ruthley's tone became sorrowful; he began a eulogy for Prescott Dunson.

"We must not forget one man who stood for a cause," droned Ruthley. "That man was Prescott Dunson! Though he had not fully gained our support, we were prepared to give it, in return for his promise to end corruption. I believe that our present district attorney"—Ruthley turned to Wilderton, who was seated nearby—"would have stepped aside for Prescott Dunson. As it is, Dunson's work has been completed. He was a martyr to the cause of reform!

"Fearing Dunson, the man who was behind corruption overstepped his bounds. I refer to Adam Woodstock, who hired murderers to do his evil bidding. Woodstock himself weakened under the strain. His suicide was the result. It has cleared the atmosphere. All is well in Westford.

"We can carry on as we have in the past, our courage strengthened by the noble example that Prescott Dunson set for us. Someone must hold the office that Dunson sought. I can think of no one better than Louis Wilderton, the present incumbent. I call upon you for unanimous support—"

Stephen Ruthley halted, disturbed by a commotion at the rear of the auditorium. His words were drowned. Men were rising to cheer an unexpected arrival, a man whose entry came as a bombshell to Stephen Ruthley.

Striding down the center aisle, step firm and carriage erect, came a man with keen face and flowing hair. Like a crusader from the past, his very appearance awoke thunderous applause. Wildly, the reformers were cheering Judge Martin Benbrook.

As the judge reached the platform, Ruthley stepped aside, bowing and smiling; for he knew that he must side with enthusiasm. As the judge stepped forward, a hush fell upon the audience. In brief words, the elderly jurist announced his purpose.

"I have come," he declared firmly, "to announce my return to public life. I intend to be a candidate for the office of district attorney!"

The crowd went wild again. Judge Benbrook waited for the enthusiasm to end. Stephen Ruthley retained his forced smile. Mayor Marclot and Director Borman restrained their nervousness. As the hubbub ended, the judge added:

"I hold high regard for the present district attorney." He turned toward Wilderton as he spoke. "Yet I feel that he has been handicapped through adverse conditions. My experience on the bench will enable me to carry through thoroughly the functions of the office. As my foremost assistant, I shall need Louis Wilderton."

Roars of approval. Wilderton was on his feet; shaking away from Ruthley, the young county prosecutor sprang forward and clutched Judge Benbrook's hand. The pact was sealed; Ruthley's hopes were spiked. As champion of reform, his part was to uphold such accord.

When new silence came, Judge Benbrook began a speech. His statements were mild at first; gradually, they carried veiled accusation.

"The death of Prescott Dunson was the cause of my decision," the judge told the reformers. "He promised to reveal the truth of crime and corruption. He promised to drive them forever from Westford. Have we proof that Dunson's hopes have been fully accomplished? No! You would like to hear the reason; therefore, I shall give it.

"There is laxity in our city government." The judge paused to let his words carry home. "If it had functioned to its full, crime and corruption would never have gained a foothold. Where were our police, when they allowed murderers to infest this city? What happened with our higher officials, when they permitted such contracts as Adam Woodstock's to be signed?"

The words were indictments of Mayor Marclot and Director Borman. The two officials winced; looked uneasy as they shifted in their chairs. Judge Benbrook drove home a final statement.

"As district attorney," he announced, "I shall make a full inquiry into every department of our administration! I know that our honest officials will welcome such investigation. They were elected on a reform ticket. I trust that they have stood by their pledges and done their utmost to further good government."

Cleverly, the old judge had softened his impeachment. His words gave Marclot and Borman a chance to regain their tottering favor. Both were too jittery to see the opportunity; but Ruthley was quick to grasp it.

Smiling in his best fashion, the master crook started a new round of applause, lifting his hands to bring the audience to its feet. He managed a nod to Borman, who nudged Mayor Marclot. The two came up, joined enthusiastically in the tribute to Judge Benbrook.

OFF in the judge's own home, The Shadow was seated in the parlor, listening to a radio hookup that brought Judge Benbrook's voice to his ears. The meeting of the Civic Club was being broadcast throughout Westford. The tumults of applause told their own story of the reception that the judge had gained.

The Shadow turned off the radio; ascended the stairs to the second floor. Judge Benbrook had followed a course as outlined by The Shadow. It had brought results. Through the judge's cooperation, The Shadow had thrown confusion into the ranks of crime.

THE meeting had ended at the Civic Club. Mayor Marclot and Director Borman were the first to shake Judge Benbrook's hand, hoping thereby to prove that they were foremost of the honest officials whom he had mentioned. Stephen Ruthley pressed forward; commended the speech in flowery tones. As members of the audience thronged the platform, Marclot and Borman made an inconspicuous departure.

They headed for Ruthley's apartment. They were there when the boss arrived, to announce that he had left Judge Benbrook still surrounded by enthusiastic admirers. Ruthley stopped their questions with impatient gestures.

"I called Lance on the way back," he told them. "I asked him where the slipup was. Doc Lunden was supposed to keep the old judge on the shelf."

Marclot and Borman nodded, worried. "Something went sour," purred Ruthley, maintaining the pose that he could keep best when angered. "We'll have to find a way to amend the new situation."

"Before the old judge talks too much," put in Borman. "He nearly spilled the beans today, Steve."

"He knows more than he told," asserted Marclot, fearfully. "He is holding back real information; though how he gained it, I cannot guess."

"We can handle this," announced Ruthley, "through Lance Gillick. He provided the way by which we reached Doctor Lunden. That kept Judge Benbrook on the shelf for a long while. Lunden has failed us; but that was his fault, not Lance's.

"Remember, we have kept Lance in the clear. He had a clean bill of health; we have strengthened him by our policy of pinning crime on Beezer Dorsch. Lance will be here within an hour. I shall confer with him, alone. Meanwhile, keep up the front that you have used so well in the past."

Stephen Ruthley waved his hand in dismissal. Marclot and Borman steadied themselves, made their departure with new confidence. Ruthley had reassured them; they were positive that the big shot had picked the right way to stave off threatening disaster.

Ruthley watched his lieutenants depart. His smile was one of actual confidence.

Possibly, the master crook's smile would have vanished had he known that The Shadow was the motivating force behind Judge Benbrook's appearance from retirement. Ruthley would have been troubled further had he guessed that The Shadow had also foreseen that Lance Gillick was the one man upon whom the big shot could at present depend.

CHAPTER XVIII
LANCE FINDS THE ANSWER

SOON after Stephen Ruthley had broken the bad news to Mayor Marclot and Director Borman, a package was delivered at the home of Judge Martin Benbrook. Estelle received it; she knew that it was intended for The Shadow. The girl carried the package upstairs; she knocked at the door of a front room. A quiet voice told her to enter.

Dusk had fallen; the room was almost dark; but against the window, Estelle saw a cloaked figure. As the girl entered, The Shadow turned; he stepped toward Estelle and took the package. He laid it upon a chair and beckoned the girl to the window.

The Shadow drew two envelopes from his cloak. He gave them to Estelle; then told the girl, in whispered tone:

"These are for your father. He is to open the smaller envelope and read its contents. It will explain the nature of the evidence which I have placed in the larger envelope."

Estelle nodded; took the envelopes and hurried downstairs to meet her father. The judge was shaking hands on the front steps; he waved good-bye to the reformers and entered the house with Estelle. The girl gave him the envelopes; entering the parlor, the judge opened the smaller one and read its contents.

His eyes lighted. He crumpled The Shadow's note and tossed it into a fire that was burning in the fireplace. Looking about, he chose a music cabinet as a place to keep the larger envelope. He unlocked the cabinet, put the envelope in the lower drawer.

"It will be safe there," the judge told his daughter. "Later, I shall turn it over to Louis Wilderton and explain its contents. Perhaps"—the judge looked toward the stairway—"yes, I believe that I should confer with our friend upstairs, even though he explained matters quite completely in his message."

Before the judge could follow his plan to visit The Shadow, there was a ring at the front door. Thinking that members of the reform club had returned, the judge waited while Estelle answered the door. A moon-faced man entered, removing his hat to display a baldish head. He saw the judge and bobbed forward with an exclamation.

"Ah, Judge Benbrook!" ejaculated the arrival. "You have again gone contrary to my advice. I must insist that, as my patient, you refrain from new exertion—"

"Come, come," snorted Judge Benbrook. "You forget yourself, Doctor Lunden. I have paid you to make me a well man. You have succeeded. I need no more advice."

"But the medicine that you have taken—"

"Has proven beneficial. Let me see, Doctor; I recall that you once told me that my improvement would be remarkable. You stated that when my weary spells ended, I would be free to exert myself again."

"Provided that you kept on with the medicine," added Estelle, nodding toward her father. "That was what Doctor Lunden told you."

Lunden winced. He remembered that he had made such optimistic statements.

"Very well," he decided. "But I warn you, judge, if you experience another turn of illness, I cannot be held responsible."

UPSTAIRS, The Shadow was busy before a mirror. He had donned a new suit from the package that Estelle had brought him; the attire was garish, but it did not conflict with The Shadow's countenance. He had taken another object from the package: a small, flat makeup box. With deft hands, he had already altered his face.

The Shadow's new visage was long, blunt-nosed and coarse. He had filled his eyebrows so that they hung heavy, and gave him a permanent glower. The window was open; The Shadow heard a slam of the front door. He peered out into the dusk, to see Doctor Lunden making his departure. The Shadow's thick lips moved, as he whispered a significant laugh.

Placing a brace of automatics in holsters under his arms, The Shadow donned hat and cloak. He picked up a small handbag, carried it with him and went downstairs.

Judge Benbrook and his daughter had returned into the parlor. The Shadow heard Estelle laugh, as she congratulated her father on the way he had managed Lunden. The Shadow passed the doorway and made a silent exit. His course led out into the darkness, through the side door to which he had a key.

Doctor Lunden had walked away from the house. Had he glanced behind him, the physician might have suspected that someone was on his trail. That is, if Lunden had been keen enough to note a strangely flitting streak of blackness that occasionally glided beneath a lamp light. Few persons, however, had the keenness to detect such a silent token of a follower; and Lunden, at present, was too intent with his own thoughts even to suspect that his trail had been taken.

The physician reached the Club Adair. He entered, went to a table near the far door. He signaled to the headwaiter, who nodded.

Lunden was ushered through to the gaming room, which was doing business. The baldish physician eyed the roulette wheel eagerly; then curbed himself and went to the door of Lance Gillick's office. He knocked briskly. The door opened.

LANCE smiled sourly when he saw his visitor. The sallow-faced gambler beckoned Lunden into the office; closed the door and snarled unpleasantly.

"Well, croaker," he questioned, "how did you make out?"

"No luck, Lance," whined Lunden. "The judge won't listen to advice."

"No? All right, sawbones. That means you're through. No chance of any dough for you."

"But I owe you twenty thousand—"

"That's written off. I got orders tonight from—well, never mind who gave them. Anyway, your gambling debt is canceled. You don't get a bonus, that's all."

"Then I can leave town?"

"You'd better. You've bluffed the medico fake too long. If it hadn't been for me fixing things, they'd have questioned your phony license long ago."

Lunden seemed relieved to know that he was

getting out of his uncomfortable situation. He stepped toward the door; Lance stopped him.

"Just a minute," said Lance. "You've given me the real lowdown on that dope gag, haven't you?"

"I swear it, Lance!" returned Lunden. "Three tablets were the absolute maximum. More would be fatal; if Judge Benbrook died, the coroner would surely learn the cause of his death."

"Then the old boy simply got used to the big dose and shook it off?"

"That seems the only answer. He is still taking his prescription. With a man of his age, the drug habit is not easily formed. The effects of a drug that is regularly administered may be lost. Nevertheless, I could not risk a greater dosage."

"O.K. You've got your walking papers. Take them."

"But if anything happens to Judge Benbrook—"

"You won't be blamed for it. Anyway, you'll be on the lam. Better start tonight."

AS soon as Lunden had gone, Lance returned to a task on which he had been working. That was the wording of a telegram, addressed to a man named Roger Callister, otherwise "Trig" Callister. Lance had mentioned that individual to Police Director Borman. Tonight, in conference with Stephen Ruthley, Lance had again spoken of Trig.

In fact, Lance had just returned from Ruthley's, with instructions to bring Trig Callister back to Westford. Trig had been around a lot, just before crime's heaviest outbreak. He had left Westford prior to the night of Lieutenant Maclare's raid on the Mississippi Hotel. Lance had intended to bring him into town again; but had postponed that plan because it had seemed unnecessary.

Right now, Trig would prove most useful, chiefly because he had been absent from Westford during the recent episodes. That meant that Trig would have a clean slate when he returned.

Just as he was finding the right words for the telegram, Lance heard a knock at the door. He thrust the telegram into a drawer, called for the person to come in. The door opened and closed; Lance turned about in his swivel chair. His sallow lips emitted a pleased ejaculation. The man who had entered was Trig Callister himself.

Trig was long-faced and blunt-nosed. His eyes had an habitual glower; yet his manner had a certain smoothness that offset those characteristics. Though he bore a reputation as a killer, Trig was recognized chiefly as a smooth swindler—a confidence man who could handle the most wary dupes.

Apparently, Trig had just arrived in Westford. He was carrying a handbag that he planked on the desk. Lance pulled out the telegram, passed it to his visitor.

"How did you guess I wanted you here, Trig?" queried Lance. "I thought you were going to wait until you heard from me?"

"I didn't have to be a mindreader," returned Trig, in an even-toned voice. "I read the newspapers, Lance. I saw that things were hot in Westford. Later on, I learned that they had cooled."

"That's sensible," agreed Lance. "Still, what made you think I'd need you?"

"When I heard that Beezer Dorsch was on the lam," explained Trig. "He was your best torpedo, Lance. I knew that you would need somebody to pinch-hit for him."

"Beezer's still good," chuckled Lance, "but he has to lay low. I'm hiding him out, here in my apartment. Listen, though, Trig. Here's the lay."

"WE have to handle an old judge named Benbrook," explained Lance. "We thought he was a has-been, but he has started to kick up some trouble. We can't croak him; we can't snatch him. We have to coax him away for a while; long enough to make people lose confidence in him."

"Won't he make trouble when he comes back again?"

"We'll fix him, if he does. Once he's lost his stranglehold on these club reformers, they won't care so much about what happens to him. Here's the idea, Trig: You're to go and see Judge Benbrook; to talk him into going somewhere with you."

"Easy enough," decided Trig, promptly. "I know one dodge that will work. These old gazebos always fall for a request to come to Washington and give expert testimony before a Congressional committee."

A pleased gleam reflected itself from Lance's eyes.

"Try it with Benbrook," decided Lance. "Only you won't have to take him to Washington. We'll have a place all set near here, where you can sidetrack him."

Trig considered; then shook his head. "That won't work, Lance," he objected. "That is, not unless you let me handle it my own way."

"How do you mean?"

"Keep your bunch out of the picture. Let me bring in some workers of my own. They're smooth; they look like dudes. Only they can be plenty tough, in a pinch."

"All the better," chortled Lance. "This will be a perfect setup! We can stage the stunt tomorrow. Duck out of town tonight, Trig; stay somewhere under a phony name. Call in your outfit; stop back to see me tomorrow. We'll frame the deal just the way you want it."

Soon afterward, Trig Callister made his exit, carrying his handbag. Lance Gillick did not remain long in his office. He left the Club Adair, to pay another visit to Stephen Ruthley; to tell the boss of Trig Callister's timely arrival.

Lance regarded Trig as a "con man" deluxe. A good estimate, since Trig had duped Lance himself. Not for an instant did Lance even begin to suspect the true identity of Trig Callister.

Lance would have been astounded had he known that Trig was The Shadow.

Actually, there was no such person as Trig Callister. The Shadow had assumed that character some time ago, in order to contact Lance Gillick and gain preliminary facts concerning crookedness in Westford. Knowing that Lance might consider Trig useful at present, The Shadow had wisely assumed the role again.

Lance Gillick thought that he had gained an answer to a pressing problem. He was sure that his plan of handling Judge Benbrook, through Trig Callister, would appeal to Stephen Ruthley. The real answer behind Trig Callister's visit had eluded Lance; therefore, it would escape Ruthley also.

Tonight, Ruthley and Lance would discuss the final details of the game which they intended, making due allowance for Trig Callister's suggestions. Crooks were playing squarely into the hands of The Shadow.

CHAPTER XIX
THE NEW GAME

EARLY the next evening, Lance Gillick again received Trig Callister in his office. Still oblivious to The Shadow's disguise, Lance came immediately to business. He spread a road map on the desk; pointed out a route leading to a spot some ten miles from Westford.

"The house lies right here," stated Lance. "It's an old mansion, but a swell one, that's just been fixed up great. It was for rent, furnished. We took it."

The Shadow nodded, in Trig's style.

"You've got to bluff the judge into thinking it's your place," remarked Lance. "How will you pull that, Trig?"

"Easy," returned The Shadow, in a boastful tone that suited the part of Trig. "I'm a special government representative; at least, that's what I'll tell the judge. I've come from Washington to investigate conditions in Westford. I want the judge to go down there with me; to make a preliminary report."

"All right so far. Go on."

"We start out in my car, the judge and I. Then I suggest stopping at the house that I've rented near Westford. When we get there, I decide that we ought to prepare a long report. One of my outfit is a secretary, who can take down everything that the judge dictates."

"How long will that last?"

"A couple of days, at least. I'll be making fake long-distance calls to Washington, getting requests for more and more details in the reports. I can follow that by getting phony word that the committee meeting has been postponed."

"Good enough. How long will it take to move your outfit into the house? The place is empty, waiting for them."

The Shadow picked up Lance's telephone. He put in a call to a neighboring town. When he gained the connection, he gave terse instructions in Trig's style, naming the location of the house where he intended to take Judge Benbrook. Finished with the call, The Shadow reported tersely to Lance.

"They'll be there inside a half hour," stated The Shadow. "It will only take them a little while to get settled."

"Fine," declared Lance. "I'll order all the gorillas in town to get out there an hour later."

The Shadow's eyes glinted. In a gruff tone that suited Trig, he objected:

"You'll queer the dodge, Lance, if you shove in a crowd of tough-looking eggs. They won't fit with my high-class outfit."

"They won't go to the house," explained Lance. "They'll stay in a couple of cottages near there. They ought to be out of Westford anyway; and they'll keep a circle around the house, to look out for your bunch. You know how it is, Trig. We can't tell when some G-men are likely to barge into town."

THE SHADOW knew what was behind Lance's suave explanation. The gambler was acting under instructions from Stephen Ruthley. Though the boss had liked the idea of using Trig Callister, he was taking no chances. He wanted Lance, as his own ace, to control the situation.

The Shadow was not surprised by this turn of events; in fact, he had expected something of the sort.

"They'll pass you through, Trig," argued Lance. "What's more, they won't bother your inside crew. It's for your own good; and it leaves us ready to grab the judge, if we have to get him later on. Just give me the license number of your car; it won't even be stopped when it comes along the road."

The Shadow nodded his approval.

He wrote the license number on a sheet of paper, and handed it to Lance. The gambler picked up a copy of the Westford *Daily Banner*.

"See this?" he queried, pointing to a headline. "It says that the Civic Club will hold another meeting—a special one. The date hasn't been mentioned yet. The fellow who is going to set it is Steve Ruthley, the biggest reformer in Westford.

"I guess I told you before that Ruthley is playing a dodge with that reform racket. He's the big shot in this whole game. You'll probably meet him later, Trig. Anyway, as soon as you have stowed away Judge Benbrook, Ruthley is going to call the meeting for the next night."

"So the judge won't be there," remarked The Shadow, with a smile. "Good stuff, Lance! Only one trouble, though. Suppose the judge wants to see a copy of the day's newspaper, to know when the meeting is coming off?"

"That will be handled," returned Lance. "Ruthley can fix it to get hold of a fake copy of the newspaper; just like the regular edition, except that it will carry a phony story about the Civic Club meeting."

"Saying that the meeting won't be held for a while?"

"That's it. We'll deliver a fake copy of the paper, out at the house where you're staying with the judge."

"Better let me come in and get one."

"All right. Anyway you want it, Trig. Anyhow, that will satisfy the judge. He'll stay out there with you; and he'll never get to the meeting. With the judge out, Ruthley can swing that mob of reformers to suit himself."

The Shadow arose; he glanced at his watch and decided upon a visit to Judge Benbrook. Before starting, he suggested that Lance go out to the mansion and meet the inside outfit.

"Ask for Vincent," explained The Shadow. "Tell him who you are. He'll fix it so you can see me blow in with the old judge. I'll hoax him tonight, Lance. You can count on me."

TEN minutes later, The Shadow rang the doorbell of Judge Benbrook's house. Estelle answered; she stared at the unfamiliar face of Trig Callister. Adopting a smooth pose, The Shadow asked to see Judge Benbrook. While Estelle hesitated, the judge himself appeared in the lower hall.

"Come right in, sir," invited Benbrook. "My door is always open. I am Judge Martin Benbrook. Your name, sir?"

"Callister," replied The Shadow. "Roger Callister. I drove here from Washington, Judge, especially to see you."

The judge ushered The Shadow into the parlor and closed the door. Estelle remained in the hallway, troubled. She was suspicious of this visitor, whose smooth manner so contrasted with his hardened features. She wondered what The Shadow would think of Mr. Roger Callister.

Unfortunately, The Shadow was not in his room. Estelle had knocked at the door a short while before, only to find that he was absent.

Twenty minutes passed. The door of the parlor opened. Judge Benbrook came out; his face wore a beaming look.

"I am leaving for Washington, Estelle!" he exclaimed. "Mr. Callister wants me to address a Congressional committee, on the subject of civic reform. My return to activity seems to have caused national comment."

The judge started for the stairs, adding that he would pack his bag at once. Unable to stop him, Estelle turned to The Shadow.

"My father cannot leave here, Mr. Callister," protested the girl. "He has to speak at an important meeting that may be held tomorrow night."

"The judge told me that," responded The Shadow, in Trig's tone. "I assured him that he will be back for the meeting, whenever it is held. It is only a few hours' drive here from Washington."

"But if he leaves with you, tonight will—"

"He will have a good rest at a Washington hotel; and will be ready to meet the Congressional committee in the morning."

While Estelle was thinking of other possible objections, Judge Benbrook arrived from the second floor. He had packed a suitcase in rapid time; he was carrying the bag with him. The Shadow took the suitcase, bowed to Estelle, and conducted the judge out to the street. Estelle watched the two enter a large sedan and drive away.

LESS than a half hour later, the same sedan reached a dirt road in the country. After a few hundred yards, it turned between two gates and stopped in front of an old, but well-preserved, mansion. A coupé was parked beyond the house; it was Lance Gillick's car. The Shadow and the judge alighted; they entered the house and went up to the second floor.

There, a clean-cut young man met them. The Shadow introduced him as Mr. Vincent, added that the man was his private secretary. Vincent ushered them into a comfortable-looking study, where a portable typewriter stood unlimbered on a table.

"This should suit you admirably, Judge," remarked The Shadow, in Trig's tone. "Tomorrow, you can dictate full statements to Vincent. I shall call Washington, to tell them that you will meet the committee on a later date."

"A good plan, Mr. Callister," agreed the judge. "I can work better here than at home. I shall send a letter to my daughter, telling her not to be concerned about my absence."

"I can mail it for you, Judge. Don't worry about the Civic Club. We are close enough to Westford to get in there when the meeting is scheduled."

"We must remember to look for a notice in tomorrow's newspaper."

"I shall attend to that, Judge."

Leaving Benbrook with Vincent, The Shadow went from the study and closed the door behind him. Immediately, another door opened; Lance Gillick appeared and joined The Shadow with a grin. The two went downstairs. At the door, Lance whispered.

"Vincent stowed me in the next room," he told The Shadow. "I heard you hand the hokum to the judge. He fell for it just the way we wanted. Say—this fellow Vincent looks great! If the rest of your crew is as good as he is, you've got a swell setup!"

"They all know their business," remarked The Shadow. "I've used them on plenty of smooth jobs before this, Lance."

The Shadow's statement was correct, though not in the sense that Lance took it. The men whom The Shadow had brought to this house were his own agents, who had aided him often in his battles against crime. Beside Vincent, The Shadow had brought into the house three whom Lance had not seen: Marsland, Burke and Burbank.

A huge African servant appeared to unlock the door for The Shadow and Lance. The man's size brought a smile of approval from Lance; he would have liked to have the African as a bouncer in one of his tough gambling joints. He asked about the man when they stepped outside.

"His name is Jericho," said The Shadow. "He makes a good servant; and he comes in handy if a brawl starts."

Another man appeared outside the house; he was small, stoop-shouldered and wizen-faced. This fellow watched The Shadow walk along with Lance to the coupé; then the wizened-faced man sidled to the front door and knocked for Jericho to admit him. Both he and Jericho were aides of The Shadow also.

"That was Hawkeye," remarked The Shadow. "I told Vincent to keep him outside. He looks too much like a torpedo. He's too useful, though, to do without."

"What a setup," chuckled Lance, as he boarded the coupé. "This outfit of yours would be a good one to have waiting for The Shadow."

"If he comes here," replied The Shadow, in Trig's harsh fashion, "my crew will know it soon enough."

Lance drove away. The Shadow returned to his sedan and followed into Westford. The outside cordon was set; The Shadow saw signs of lurking men along the dirt road. They let both cars go through; for Lance had told them that Trig Callister was not to be stopped. He had given them the license number of the sedan that The Shadow was using.

LATER that same evening, Estelle Benbrook again knocked at the door on the second floor. She had not heard The Shadow come into the house; but she felt sure that he must have returned.

The door opened; The Shadow stepped out into the hall. He was wearing his black cloak and slouch hat. Estelle could not distinguish his face, except for the burning glow of his eyes.

In troubled tone, Estelle reported the details of her father's departure. She described Trig Callister as a man whose sincerity she doubted. The Shadow reassured the girl with quiet, low-toned speech. He told her not to worry until the next day. He added that he would see to it that no harm came to her father.

Remembering The Shadow's prowess, Estelle was satisfied.

Back in his room, The Shadow indulged in a whispered laugh that was scarcely audible. He had not told Estelle the facts concerning her father; because, although he knew the judge was safe, The Shadow did not believe that Estelle would think so. It was better that she should learn the details after The Shadow's present plan had progressed further.

The Shadow was correct in that opinion. He had chosen the course that offered the least difficulty, so far as Estelle was concerned. Nevertheless, there was a chance that the girl's ignorance of the situation might prove a stumbling block.

The Shadow was to encounter real evidence of that fact, before this episode was ended.

CHAPTER XX
THE LAW'S TURN

AT dusk, the next day, Lance Gillick was seated at his desk, drumming nervously. In front of him was a copy of the *Daily Banner*, effectively faked with a false paragraph that announced postponement of the Civic Club meeting. Actually, the meeting had been called for this very night, by Stephen Ruthley.

What troubled Lance was the fact that Trig Callister had not yet arrived. To Lance, that meant that something might be wrong at the country mansion. Lance stopped his drumming, to pick up the telephone. He intended to chance a call to Stephen Ruthley, though as a rule the boss objected to such mode of contact.

Before Lance could dial the number, the door of the office opened. Lance grinned as he saw Trig Callister.

"Wondered where you were, Trig," voiced the gambler. He picked up the faked newspaper. "Here's the newssheet, ready for you to take out to the judge. Is everything all jake?"

"Just the way we want it," replied The Shadow. "The judge is getting jittery, though. I'll have to hurry the newspaper out to him."

"Slide along then, Trig."

The Shadow paused, as he folded the newspaper and pocketed it. Lance noticed that Trig had his handbag with him. He supposed that Trig had forgotten to take it to the country, the night before.

"There were some cops out front when I came in," stated The Shadow. "They looked me over pretty closely, Lance."

"Some of Maclare's bunch," snorted Lance. "He always keeps a flatfoot near here. Sometimes two or three. He's still sore because he never pinned anything on me. He had to give me an alibi once; I guess he's never gotten over the shock."

"Maybe you'd better steer me out by the back way," suggested The Shadow. "The cops may be suspicious at seeing me come out so soon. I don't want to be slowed up by an argument with a couple of dumb harness bulls."

Lance nodded agreement. He opened the panel in the wall; urged The Shadow into the passage beyond it. They followed along the passage to its end. At the left was a large door that served as the only entrance to Lance's secret apartment, in an adjoining building. At the right was a stairway. Lance led The Shadow downward.

There they found a small entry, with a steel door beyond it. The entry was dim; it was guarded by a huge bruiser who was almost the size of Jericho. In fact, Lance had compared the huge African with this particular husky when he had viewed Jericho and admired the latter's bulk.

"Open the gate, Boscul," ordered Lance. "Lock it up as soon as Trig goes out."

"So long, Lance," remarked The Shadow. "Don't bother to wait. I'd better come in this way, though, when I come back."

"Give three quick raps. Then two slow ones. That's the signal, Trig."

With this information The Shadow was quite willing that Lance should wait around. The gambler, however, followed The Shadow's suggestion and went upstairs. That made it even better. While Boscul was still drawing back a series of big bolts, The Shadow laid his handbag on the floor. Tightening in a crouch, he prepared to spring.

THE lookout must have caught some sign of the attack that was to come. He spun suddenly from the door; his dull face lighted in a glare. Boscul gave a snarl just as The Shadow sprang forward. With hamlike hands, the big husky met The Shadow's onrush.

Boscul thought that he was dealing with Trig Callister. That, perhaps, gave him more courage than he would have shown against a cloaked attacker. Boscul beat back The Shadow's thrust before long fingers could gain the clutch they wanted. With a fierce cry, he hurled the limber attacker across the entry.

Fortunately, Lance Gillick was too faraway to hear that shout. The Shadow had enough to do, handling Boscul. He managed to ward off a punch that the big lookout swung in his direction. He followed with a quick jab that bobbed Boscul's head backward, even though it failed to stagger the huge fighter.

The two locked. Boscul's arms tightened like the grip of a python. He hoisted The Shadow from the floor, intent upon crushing the supposed Trig Callister into submission. Swinging one wrist free, The Shadow squeezed choking fingers about Boscul's throat. The fellow gurgled; relaxed his fierce grip.

From then on, it was The Shadow's fight. Gaining a footing, he beat off Boscul's clutch; drove the lookout across the floor with a series of slashing blows. Again, they grappled; this time, The Shadow clutched Boscul as he had gripped Haija in that fight at Ruthley's.

The husky's bulk was greater than that of the Japanese; but it did not save him from disaster. Like a mongoose overpowering a cobra, The Shadow whipped his giant antagonist headlong toward the steel door. Boscul crashed the barrier. He slumped to the stone floor.

Opening his handbag, The Shadow brought out his black garb. He donned cloak and hat, eyed Boscul while he added gloves to his attire. The husky was groggily trying to rise. The Shadow spilled him to one side and opened the door that Boscul had already unbolted. The door came inward; its outer surface showed only battered wood, not steel.

Viewed from the outside alley, that door excited no suspicion. Its steel-sheeted interior, however, made it immune to ordinary attack.

The alleyway was darkened. The Shadow was invisible as he edged into its space. Producing an automatic from its holster, he pointed the .45 upward, fired two quick shots in the air. Immediately afterward, he swung back into the entry, took quick concealment behind the opened door.

There was commotion in the alley. Pounding

from the darkness came half a dozen men; with them was Lieutenant James Maclare. The raiders were blue-uniformed police. Their presence was explained by Maclare's own shout.

"Keep going, men!" ordered the lieutenant. "I thought this tip-off was on the level! Those shots were the signal we were told to wait for! We'll have the goods on Lance Gillick this time!"

Opposition came, as the police surged into the doorway; but it was not long-lived. Boscul had found his feet; he tried to grapple with the foremost bluecoat. Another officer swung a nightstick; he clubbed the groggy lookout into insensibility. Maclare and his men dashed up the stairs, never stopping to look behind the opened door.

They found the passage to Lance's office; reaching the end of it, they saw a glimmer of light through the back of the painting. Maclare took one look through the peephole; then ripped through the canvas, followed by his squad.

SHRIEKS arose from the gaming room, where play had started for the night. Croupiers were trapped at the roulette wheel; money and chips scattered everywhere as the police rounded up snarling waiters and frightened customers.

The door of the office opened; Lance Gillick peered at the scene. He bobbed from sight, slamming the door. Maclare leaped for it, ordered officers to slash the barrier with axes. One of the bluecoats gave a sudden shout:

"There goes Lance!"

The gambler had opened the office panel, to reach the passage. The policeman had spied him through the ruined painting. Maclare sprang away from the office door, led the chase with a pair of bluecoats following. Lance reached the door of his apartment, yanked it open. Peering from the entry below, The Shadow saw another man spring out to join the gambler.

It was Beezer Dorsch. Lance had feared that the killer would be trapped. The police had passed the apartment door in order to raid the gambling joint, but their return was imminent. Lance's pressing thought was to make a getaway with Beezer.

The pair dashed down the stairway, just as revolvers blasted along the passage above. The Shadow dropped behind the door. He let the fugitives get past, then bobbed out to follow them. He could easily have halted the two rogues; but he had a reason for permitting their escape.

Dashing along the alleyway, Lance and Beezer ducked through an opening in time to avoid policemen coming from the front street. The Shadow was close behind the crooks; but the clatter of their own footsteps drowned the slight sounds of his pursuit. Lance and Beezer reached a garage; they rushed in and boarded a coupé.

By the time the coupé swung into sight, The Shadow was in a small roadster, much like the car that he had used in his last flight from the Flying Squadron. He took up the chase; within two blocks Lance and Beezer knew that they were being tagged.

With hamlike hands, the big husky met The Shadow's rush.

Recognizing that by the burst of speed that the coupé showed, The Shadow unlimbered an automatic and dispatched two quick shots after the coupé. Bullets whistled close enough for the crooks to guess who was on their trail.

"The Shadow!" snarled Lance, as he gripped the wheel of the coupé. "Lucky he didn't bag Trig Callister. He must have barged in before Boscul had time to lock the back door."

"Yeah," growled Beezer, "and he tipped off Maclare to raid your joint. We gotta shake him, Lance."

"You bet we have to! We don't want him to know where we're headed."

"Where's that?"

"To Ruthley's. Where else would be safe for you to hide out, Beezer?"

Again, Lance Gillick was playing into The Shadow's hands. In this pursuit, The Shadow could have overtaken the crooks as easily as he could have dropped them on the stairway. His plan, however, called for their getaway. He wanted them to be at Ruthley's later; for The Shadow intended an end to crime tonight.

WITHIN the next few blocks, The Shadow was prepared to slow his pursuit; to give Lance the very chance that the gambler wanted. Once in the clear, Lance would head for Ruthley's apartment house; duck from his car and take Beezer along with him, straight to the big shot's lair.

Oddly, luck was to trick The Shadow. Had he ended his pursuit a few blocks sooner, all would have gone well. However, during the last stretch, Lance Gillick became jittery. He started to express his worriment to Beezer; then stopped short as he saw a sign that read: "Century Garage."

"What a break!" ejaculated Lance. "Just the place for us in a pinch, Beezer!"

Beezer recognized the sign.

"Yeah!" he agreed. "It's the joint the boss told us about, in case we needed to use it. Head in there, Lance."

Lance spun the wheel, jerked the coupé suddenly from the street, straight into the open doorway of the garage. He shouted as he applied the brakes; a waiting garage man caught his words and yanked a lever. A door slid open at the far wall.

The Shadow reached the front; jamming the brakes of the roadster, he saw the thoroughfare. In that instant, he thought that the far door had been open when Lance entered the garage; for the coupé was speeding through it. To give a last zest to his pursuit, The Shadow swung his roadster into the garage, intending to drive clear through and follow the crooks a few blocks farther.

He realized his error, as he sped his car through the front doorway.

The rear door slid shut before The Shadow could reach it. Jamming the brakes, The Shadow shoved the gearshift lever into reverse. Again, he was too late. The front door slithered shut before The Shadow could back out through it.

Lights showed the garage devoid of cars. A stone-walled room some sixty feet square, it formed a sealed snare, once the doors had closed; for they were of metal. More ominous still were two small, boxlike rooms at each side of the empty garage. They were sheeted with metal; their closed doors were fronted with loopholes.

The tiny rooms were pillboxes—safe spots from which hidden sharpshooters could riddle anyone who occupied the center of the garage floor. Once the barrage began, it would spell instant doom for The Shadow!

CHAPTER XXI
THE SHADOW'S EXIT

IN a single instant, The Shadow sized his situation. Big doors had clanged; to leap from the roadster and attempt to open them would be the worst move possible. The Shadow knew that machine gunners were sequestered in the pillboxes, ready to begin their fire the moment that he bobbed into view.

Even the roadster offered but temporary safety. Bullets would spray it soon. Yet, for some reason, the opening hail had been delayed. Quick to note that fact, The Shadow looked for the answer; and found it. A glance from the side of the roadster enabled him to see a scudding man in overalls, making across the stone floor for the pillbox on the left.

It was the attendant who had pulled the levers to close the garage doors. The fellow was still inside the garage; the men in the pillbox were giving him time to join them. The door of the pillbox was moving open, ready to admit the scudding thug.

The Shadow had an automatic handy. He could have dropped the rowdy as he ran. Such a move would have been futile. If their pal fell, the men in the pillboxes would have no further need to delay their machine-gun fire.

Nor would The Shadow gain by blazing bullets into the doorway of the pill-box when it opened. Unless he clipped every occupant, the door would slam again. Even if he did wound that crew of sharpshooters, the men in the second pillbox would make up for it. Not for an instant did The Shadow forget that he lay between two bands of murderers.

Without reaching for the .45 that lay on the seat beside him, The Shadow staged a prompt surprise. His move was totally unexpected; for that reason, it left his enemies momentarily bewildered. The thug who was dashing for the pillbox had thirty feet to go. The Shadow resolved to block him off; to keep him in a spot of danger as bad as The Shadow's own predicament.

With his left hand, The Shadow jerked the roadster's wheel. He rammed the gear shift into low, with his right. His foot thrust the accelerator to the floor. The roadster leaped as if alive, skewed to the left and roared like a thunderbolt straight for the pillbox, just as the door of that tiny stronghold slid wide.

The Shadow passed the running thug in a split second. Jamming the brakes, he again yanked the wheel to the left. The roadster halted with a screech, squarely between the startled thug and the opened door of the pillbox.

Again, The Shadow pulled a surprise. As the man in overalls heeled about and dashed in the other direction, The Shadow let him go. Diving to the right, The Shadow banged the roadster's door outward, with his left hand; while his rightmost grabbed the automatic from the seat. In one continuous leap, he hurtled onward, straight through the opened door of the pillbox.

Two startled hoodlums, crouched in darkness, saw the cloaked avalanche whirl in upon them. Dropping their machine gun, they sprang to meet The Shadow. His right arm swished downward; the automatic smashed a thug's skull. As the fellow sprawled, The Shadow swung a side blow, clipped the second gunner and rolled him out through the door of the pillbox.

The first thug partly blocked the door. Stopping, The Shadow seized his shoulders and pitched his senseless body out beside the dazed man who had floundered on the step of the roadster. That done, The Shadow grabbed the handle of the door and clanged the barrier shut. Safe in the pillbox, he peered through the tiny loophole.

The Shadow had completely tricked the gunners in the far pillbox. His car had blocked their view of his rapid action. They learned what had happened too late to defeat it. Their knowledge came when the thug on the roadster's step suddenly grabbed his unconscious pal and dragged him out in front of the halted car.

It was stalemate: a trio of crooks in one pillbox; The Shadow in the other. The abandoned roadster made a barrier in between; but it meant nothing. The Shadow, like the crooks, had a machine gun and could fire through the open sides of the small car. Volleys would prove useless, however, for both The Shadow and his opponents were safely entrenched.

True, there were three men somewhere on the garage floor; two of them were now dragging a third toward the front door. The Shadow could have picked out those crooks and finished them; but they were unimportant. He needed some way to break this stalemate; to leave the pillbox and be on his way to other tasks. That was The Shadow's real dilemma.

Had crooks recognized the situation, they would have let matters remain as they were. They, however, disliked the condition for reasons of their own. They knew the identity of their foeman. They were incensed because they had let The Shadow nullify their advantage.

Hoarse shouts came from the far pillbox. The words were incoherent to The Shadow, due to the echoes from the barren walls. To the men who were in the open, the cries were understandable. One dropped the senseless man whom he was lugging, leaped for a wall and pulled a light switch. The garage was plunged into darkness.

ON the face of it, this move seemed merely a protection for the men who were still at large. Crooks naturally expected The Shadow to stay where he was. Instead, The Shadow found the handle of the pillbox door. He slid the door open, slowly and cautiously. His move was just in time.

The thug by the outer door had found another switch. He pulled it. The result was sensed immediately by The Shadow. His pillbox began a descent into the floor, lowering like an elevator. The smooth action was accompanied by the rhythmic hum of hidden machinery.

Had The Shadow still been behind a closed door, he could not have left the descending pillbox; for it went down into the floor so steadily that the delay of opening the door would have been fatal. However, The Shadow had already attended to the detail of opening the door. His quick brain caught the need for immediate action.

With both hands, he grabbed the edge of outside floor when it was just waist-high. With a long, forward leap from the floor of the descending pillbox, he shot headforemost through the closing space; performed a quick roll that brought his legs clear, just before the top of the pillbox doorway could trap them.

The pillbox stopped its descent with a sharp *click.* Reaching along the garage floor in the darkness, The Shadow found that the roof of the pillbox was coated with cement; that formed a perfect level with the floor. He knew that the other pillbox must operate in the same fashion; and the reason was obvious. With the pillboxes lowered into their pits, the garage floor would appear quite ordinary; and would therefore excite no suspicion when not in use as a trap.

Some crook had seen a smart way to render

The Shadow's capture of the pillbox worse than useless. The pull of the wall switch had turned the stronghold into a prison, as close-walled as a tomb. Harsh, gleeful cries amid the darkness told that men of crime were sure that their ruse had worked. A raucous voice called for lights.

Quickly, The Shadow rolled beneath the roadster. He lay there, face downward, clasping an automatic in each fist. The lights came on; crooks piled from their pillbox to join the others on the floor. Together, they surged to the wall beside the roadster; they tramped roughly on the leveled roof; they bent to shout jeers that they hoped The Shadow would hear within his tomb.

While thugs made merry, The Shadow prepared to end their revelry. The far side of the roadster was deserted, except for the one thug who lay unconscious. Three from the pillbox; two from the floor, had all assembled above the tight-sealed prison where they believed The Shadow trapped. Edging outward, The Shadow was almost ready to come to his feet, when an interruption sounded.

Someone was pounding at the front door of the garage. For beyond that heavy barrier came the shouted order:

"Open! In the name of the law!"

THE SHADOW abandoned his plan to surprise the clustered crooks who stood flat-footed by the wall. He had recognized the shouting voice. The tone was that of Lieutenant James Maclare. Half to his feet, The Shadow dropped low again; he edged beneath the roadster as crooks scurried from the wall.

He saw one man reach the door and yank a switch that controlled the far pillbox. It descended; the thug at the switchboard pulled a lever to open the rear door of the garage. Two crooks picked up the unconscious thug; the lights went out to cover their departure by the opened rear door. Only two remained, to pass as garage attendants when they admitted Maclare and his bluecoats to the innocent-looking garage.

The Shadow had new opportunity in the darkness. He took it. Rolling from beneath the roadster, he moved swiftly to the rear door. Crooks were away before he reached it; The Shadow slid through just as the door was closing.

The rear alley was darkened; groping, The Shadow found a passage that led through to the front street, between the garage and an empty store. He took this route; stopped just before he reached the front. Peering from the corner, The Shadow was witness to the next scene.

Lights were on again in the garage; the front door had been opened to admit Maclare. The lieutenant had made a brief inspection; he had called the thuggish attendants out front, to give them a brief quiz.

"Nobody came in here tonight?" demanded the police officer. "You're sure of it?"

"Nobody, Lieutenant," replied one of the thugs. "This garage is closed for repairs. We're storin' no cars, here, right now."

"Humph! Who does that roadster belong to, then?"

"It's my own car, Lieutenant."

"All right," decided Maclare. "The men we're after were reported riding in a coupé. Last place we spotted them was near here. We thought maybe they'd made it into your garage."

A siren sounded as Maclare finished. Two motorcycles chugged up; then a police car. Members of the Flying Squadron stepped to the street. An official car arrived. Director Kirk Borman alighted. He talked with Lieutenant Maclare.

"I'll take charge here," decided Borman. "Good work, Lieutenant! I heard about your surprise raid."

"I meant to notify you, Director," stated Maclare, "only we weren't sure of the tip-off—"

"I understand," put in Borman, brusquely. "Results are what count, Lieutenant. You gained them. That's all that matters. Better get back to your precinct. The Flying Squadron will find Lance Gillick."

MACLARE saluted; he departed with his bluecoats. The honest lieutenant was grim. For once, he had kept back facts that he might have given to the police director. The tip-off that Maclare had received had specified that no one, not even Director Borman, be informed beforehand. Rather than miss his opportunity to catch Lance Gillick red-handed, Maclare had agreed to the terms. He had trusted the mysterious voice that had come over the wire to his precinct office.

Director Borman went into the garage, while members of the Flying Squadron spread out to fake a search of the area. The Shadow saw chance of new encounter, which he wanted to avoid. In darkness, he whipped off his cloak and hat and folded them under his arm. Choosing a moment when no khaki-uniformed men were near, he walked out from his hiding place and approached Director Borman's car. He opened the door, tossed his garments into a corner of the rear seat.

The chauffeur turned about; saw only the features of Trig Callister. The Shadow whispered gruffly, stating that he wanted to see Director Borman. The chauffeur was one of Borman's trusted aides. He knew that the director had dealings with characters of Trig's sort. He motioned The Shadow into the car.

Kirk Borman returned soon afterward, a pleased smirk on his sharp-featured face. As he entered the car, The Shadow spoke again.

"I'm Trig Callister," he gruffed. "Say—did they get The Shadow?"

"He's where we want him," chuckled Borman. "Buried alive! We'll leave him there until he croaks! That won't be long; he's in an airtight spot."

The Shadow's disguised face was visible by the glow of a street lamp. To Borman, those features answered Lance Gillick's description of Trig. Nevertheless, Borman questioned suddenly:

"How did you get here?"

"I hopped on the back of Lance's coupé," returned The Shadow with a sight guffaw. "I was in a bad spot when that raid hit. A worse one, when The Shadow tagged Lance. I had to drop off to keep from getting hit when he busted loose with those gats of his. I was too busy to yank a rod of my own. It's tough holding on to the back of a coupé, going the speed Lance was driving that one."

The story clicked. Borman told the chauffeur to drive along. He was not suspicious when The Shadow questioned:

"How about Lance and Beezer? Did they make it to Ruthley's O.K.?"

"They did," acknowledged the police director. "That's where we are going at present."

"You'll have to drop me on the way," objected The Shadow. "When we get to the place where I parked my sedan. I've got to get out in the country and keep the old judge bluffed. Tell Lance I made my getaway. Everything is jake."

BORMAN nodded. Events had worked out better than he hoped. With Lance and Beezer in a safe hideout and Trig at large, all was well with men of crime. Maclare's surprise raid had made trouble. Borman was sure that it had been instigated by The Shadow. The Shadow's return had brought recompense, however; it had spelled the finish of the black-cloaked warrior, according to Borman's positive belief.

The Shadow spoke as they neared his parked sedan. Borman ordered the chauffeur to stop; he chuckled good-bye to Trig Callister. He saw his companion alight; but he did not notice the small bundle beneath Trig's arm. The Shadow was careful to keep his wadded cloak and hat away from the police director's view.

The Shadow whispered a prophetic laugh as he boarded his sedan. His plans had worked tonight. He had slipped the trap without losing too much time; and with that exploit, he had left crooks confident that they had bagged their greatest foeman.

That, in particular, was to The Shadow's liking. The greater the confidence among men of crime, the greater would be their consternation when The Shadow delivered the final stroke of his campaign.

CHAPTER XXII
ESTELLE'S DISCOVERY

DESPITE his quick departure from the toils of crooks, The Shadow had lost many valuable minutes. He had purposely clipped the time element to a minimum, that he might complete his campaign while his enemies were retarded. The episode at the garage trap had therefore been damaging to The Shadow's schedule.

One vital phase of The Shadow's game was a trip to the country mansion—there to meet Judge Benbrook and bring him back to town. That would be easy; as Trig Callister, The Shadow could pass the outer cordon of thugs without question. But it was necessary to have Judge Benbrook in Westford well before the time at which the meeting of the Civic Club was scheduled.

If all went well, The Shadow would have another bombshell waiting for Stephen Ruthley when the pretended reformer arrived at the meeting. All could still go well; but time was short. A speedy ride to the country and a rapid return trip had become essential.

Delay, however, had already caused one difficulty. Just when The Shadow was embarking on a free, swift course, trouble began without his knowledge. The place where it occurred was the one spot where it was least to be expected: in Judge Benbrook's own home. The person who provided the chance element was Estelle Benbrook.

The Shadow had foreseen that Estelle would be worried over her father's absence. The night before, he had mailed her a letter, written by the judge himself. Estelle had received the letter this morning; it had partly ended her worriment.

Later, though, Estelle had read the true item in the *Daily Banner*, stating that the Civic Club would meet tonight. She had prepared dinner for herself and her father, thinking surely that the judge would return.

Judge Benbrook had not returned. Ending a lone repast. Estelle experienced a great increase of alarm. There was only one person in whom she could confide her fears. That person was The Shadow. On the faint hope that The Shadow had entered the house while she was eating dinner, Estelle went upstairs to rap at the door on the second floor.

There was no response. Estelle's spirits sank. She felt hopeless and confused; for once, her usual self-confidence was gone. The girl pounded wildly upon The Shadow's door. At last, in desperation, she opened the door. She entered the room and turned on the light.

Hopeful that she might find some message from The Shadow, Estelle looked about the room.

She saw a bureau drawer that was slightly open. Peering into the drawer, Estelle glimpsed a flat box that she mistook for a writing case. Thinking that it might contain a notebook or some written memoranda, Estelle nervously drew the box from the drawer. She opened the box; stared with wide-opened eyes.

THE box was a makeup kit—one that showed signs of recent use. It explained to Estelle why The Shadow's face had seemed so masklike. The girl remembered that The Shadow could not have carried this makeup kit when he first came to the house. She realized that it must have come in the package that had been delivered long after his arrival.

Hastily, Estelle looked in the closet; there she saw a dark suit, with torn coat sleeve.

It struck Estelle that The Shadow must have received new clothes; certainly the package had been large enough and sufficiently heavy to contain a suit. But why had The Shadow needed the makeup outfit?

Estelle was intuitive; moreover, her mind was concerned with her father's disappearance. For the first time, she felt a sudden doubt of The Shadow, for she remembered that, last night, he had expressed but little concern over her father's disappearance. Her mind was strained to the point where she could connect only a few definite thoughts; in that state, Estelle pictured two persons: The Shadow and the man named Callister, who had induced her father to leave the house last night.

A horrified gasp came from Estelle's lips. Through a chance thought, inspired by her discovery of the makeup kit, the girl guessed the truth. The Shadow and Trig Callister were one!

Reasoning from a false assumption, Estelle concocted a theory that she promptly accepted as fact. She thought of The Shadow as a man of crime; one with a lone game, who had run into trouble the night that Prescott Dunson was slain. True, The Shadow had saved the girl's own life; but there were many crooks who might have been as gallant, under similar circumstances.

Perhaps The Shadow had foreseen how useful that rescue would prove. It had enabled him to avoid the law, by entering the house with Estelle. It had won Estelle's confidence; later, The Shadow had found sanctuary in this house. As Estelle saw it, he had pretended friendliness in order to gain her father's confidence, as well as his own.

Ready for some crooked game, The Shadow had come here as Callister. He had taken her father as a hostage. He had some reason to keep Judge Benbrook from Westford. It all seemed a scheme of double dealing, even though Estelle could not fathom its full purpose.

Firmly, Estelle resolved upon some move. While she tried to find some possible way of counteracting purposes which she thought were evil, the girl heard the doorbell ring. For a moment, her worries vanished; she almost dropped the theory that she had built up against The Shadow. Estelle was hopeful that her father was back; hurriedly, she dashed downstairs and opened the front door.

On the threshold stood Louis Wilderton.

THE district attorney was anxious-faced.

"Where is Judge Benbrook?" he inquired. "I must see him at once, Estelle."

"I don't know," gasped the girl. "What has happened, Louis?"

"Lieutenant Maclare has raided the Club Adair. This time, he found a gambling room in operation. He has pinned crime on Lance Gillick—"

"But Father? Where is my father?"

Estelle fairly shrieked the questions. Wilderton's eyes popped. He stammered: "Your—your father isn't here?"

"No," replied Estelle. "Something has happened to him, Louis!"

"Just before this important meeting?"

"No! It was last night! But it began before that. I have to tell you the whole story, Louis. There was a man who came here—a man cloaked in black—he was wounded—"

"When was this?"

"The night that Adam Woodstock committed suicide. That was the second time I saw him. That was the night that he was wounded—"

"You mean Shaw!"

Estelle nodded.

"You took him in here?" demanded Wilderton. "The man who was wanted as an accomplice of the murderer, Dorsch?"

"This man talked to Father," Estelle explained. "He convinced Father that he was not engaged in crime. He persuaded Father to come from retirement. He acted as a friend—until last night."

"And then?"

"He dropped his masquerade. He came here as another person, a man named Callister. He persuaded Father to leave with him for Washington. He wanted to keep Father away from here tonight."

Wilderton raised his hand to halt Estelle's excited utterances.

"You have told me enough," he said. "The man has two aliases. He calls himself Shaw; also Callister. He has abducted your father. This is a matter for the law, Estelle."

"You will notify Washington?"

"After I have talked with Director Borman. The local police should act first. Borman will send out the Flying Squadron, to see if your father is still somewhere in Westford."

Estelle started an objection. Again, Wilderton halted her. The girl tried to blurt out a fact that she had just remembered: the envelope that The Shadow had given her father. Her words were confused.

"This man left an envelope with Father," exclaimed Estelle. "One that contained some sort of evidence—"

"Evidence of what?" demanded Wilderton, hoarsely. "No crook would leave a trail behind him. We can come to that later, Estelle. The pressing matter is to see Director Borman."

"You can call him from here."

"No. I shall see him personally, and come back here later. I know where he is at present; both Director Borman and Mayor Marclot are at Stephen Ruthley's apartment."

DASHING down the steps, Wilderton jumped aboard his car and drove away. Estelle stood wearily at the door; then went back into the house. She decided to find the envelope herself. To obtain it, she needed a key to the music cabinet.

There were keys in a table drawer near the music cabinet. As she rummaged among them, finding none that she wanted, Estelle discovered a .32 revolver. It was a loaded weapon that her father had long ago put away and forgotten. Nervously, Estelle gripped the gun; she glanced toward the hallway.

The tension had given her unusual alertness. A sound reached Estelle's ears; it was a key, turning in the lock of the side door. Acting upon sudden inspiration, the girl hurried upstairs; there, she stepped into a side room and waited. Soon, her ears again caught a slight sound. It was the opening of the door to the upstairs front room—the chamber The Shadow had occupied—where Estelle had forgotten to turn out the lights.

The girl sprang from her hiding place; she saw the door wide open and reached the threshold. She saw a black-clad figure in the room. The Shadow had returned.

He was turned away from Estelle; he was removing his slouch hat and dropping the folds of his cloak. He spun about as Estelle delivered a sharp cry. Face revealed, The Shadow stared into the muzzle of the revolver that the judge's daughter held.

Estelle's cry ended; her grip on the .32 became firm. She was ready to pull the trigger if The Shadow made a move. Estelle Benbrook had gained proof of the treachery that she believed had been The Shadow's.

The face of The Shadow was that of Trig Callister.

CHAPTER XXIII
AMENDED STRATEGY

THE instant that he saw the leveled revolver, The Shadow recognized a situation as crucial as any that he had met in Westford. He had encountered dangers that seemed far greater; but this one carried the worst possible hazards.

Estelle showed by action that she knew how to manage a revolver; she had aimed the weapon straight for The Shadow's heart. The girl's frenzied expression showed that she had lost control of her wits. She was prepared to fire a steady series of bullets on any provocation, real or imaginary.

The Shadow realized the futility of explanations. With her acceptance of fallacies, instead of facts, Estelle might interpret any statement incorrectly. Mere mention of her father's name might drive her to the wild belief that The Shadow had killed the judge. One chance thought would be enough. Estelle would fire to kill.

For one full second, The Shadow met the girl's vengeful gaze. He realized that each succeeding second would increase the risk; that any moment might be his last. It was a time for astounding action; some deed as outlandish as Estelle's imaginary beliefs. Knowing it, The Shadow acted in accord.

His cloak was half from his shoulders, retained by his left hand. He was holding the slouch hat with his right. For a moment, The Shadow seemed to cower; as he shrank away, his body huddled lower.

The move lessened Estelle's vigilance for an instant; then, suspecting trickery, the girl became more frenzied. She stepped forward, thrusting the revolver ahead. Her finger tightened on the trigger.

Huddled, The Shadow spun about; he started a sidelong lunge for a corner of the room. Estelle sped the gun muzzle in the same direction; as the cloaked form faded floorward, she pressed the trigger and stabbed quick shots.

The cloak crumpled; the slouch hat bounced on the floor. As Estelle fired again, a lithe shape seemed to weave up toward her, as if conjured from space itself.

The Shadow had caught cloak collar and hat brim with both hands; he had shoved them away toward the corner, releasing them as Estelle fired. Reversing his spin, he was swinging back, free from the cloak before the fatal moment.

It was the skillful move of the matador, who whisks free from his cloak at the moment of the bull's onrush. The Shadow's twist was far more speedy and better timed than that of any bullfighter. He had to be away before bullets zimmed in his direction. He was away; and his long, returning lunge was below the line of Estelle's aim.

The girl did not have time to fire again. Sighting The Shadow, she tried to aim; his quick clutch caught her wrist and held it numbed. Estelle struggled, still managing to clutch the revolver. As she went backward toward the door, she heard a cry behind her. Arms other than The Shadow's clutched the girl's.

The Shadow plucked away the revolver as Estelle subsided. Looking up, the girl saw the person who had seized her. A happy gasp told her relief, as she viewed the whitened face of her father.

BENBROOK'S whole countenance was tinged with alarm.

Estelle began to sob. Judge Benbrook gazed anxiously toward The Shadow; he saw a smile upon the false lips of Trig Callister. The uncloaked fighter was unhurt. Satisfied on that point, the judge spoke to his daughter.

"You were mistaken, Estelle," he told the girl. "The Shadow is our friend. How you guessed that he came here as Trig Callister, I do not know—"

"I found the makeup box," sobbed Estelle. "I thought—I guessed—"

"Your guess was wrong, my dear." Estelle turned about, to see The Shadow regaining his cloak and hat. He donned the garments; his quiet whisper silenced Estelle as she tried to express her regrets for her mistaken action. Judge Benbrook delivered an interjection.

"You were going to see Stephen Ruthley as Trig Callister!" he exclaimed. "Have you changed the plan?"

"Yes," replied The Shadow. "I believe that Estelle has already disclosed my double identity."

"I have," admitted the girl. "Louis Wilderton was here. I told him my suspicions. He has gone to Ruthley's—to see Director Borman."

"Our hopes are ruined," groaned Judge Benbrook. "Estelle, this was arranged when The Shadow gave me that written message. I knew who he was when he came here as Trig Callister."

"You should have told me, Father."

"No. It was better not. Had we returned in time tonight, all would have been well. Tell me, Estelle"—the judge's tone was more anxious than ever—"did Wilderton take the envelope with him?"

Estelle shook her head. The Shadow delivered a whispered laugh that brought immediate encouragement to Judge Benbrook.

"We need new strategy," declared The Shadow. "Come downstairs. We must first obtain the envelope; then be on our way."

The judge and Estelle followed The Shadow downstairs. He had the key to the music cabinet; he unlocked it and tendered the sealed envelope to Judge Benbrook. Noting the clock on the mantel, The Shadow made quick calculation."

"We are leaving here at once," he stated. "You will both remain in a place of safety until you hear from me."

Judge Benbrook was puzzled. He could think of no safe spot in Westford. Nevertheless, he beckoned to Estelle; they followed The Shadow through the side door; thence to the rear street, where they entered The Shadow's sedan.

"Borman will come to the house," declared The Shadow, as he started the car. "To your house, Judge. Not finding you there, he will hurry to the country. My work lies there; since my part has become known."

"But you spoke of a place where Estelle would be safe," reminded Judge Benbrook. "One where you wanted me to wait until I heard from you."

"Here is the place."

The Shadow stopped the car in front of the first precinct station. A light was showing from Lieutenant Maclare's office. Judge Benbrook gained sudden understanding of The Shadow's plan. He stepped from the car with Estelle; then asked:

"How much shall I tell Maclare?"

"As much as is necessary," replied The Shadow. "He has already gained an inkling of matters in Westford. You will find him ready to follow any suggestion that you give him."

With that, The Shadow sped away, leaving Judge Benbrook and Estelle to treat with the one man in Westford who could command loyal forces that would fight for the law.

AT the time of The Shadow's departure, events were shaping elsewhere exactly as he predicted. Louis Wilderton had reached Stephen Ruthley's. There, the district attorney had just finished pouring out his news. Stephen Ruthley, his countenance imposing, was quick to deliver a denunciation.

"We owe you much, Wilderton," affirmed the pretended reformer. "I speak for Mayor Marclot and Director Borman, as well as for myself. Come, Borman!" he turned to the police director, who was sitting rigid, in a corner of the den. "You must act at once to find Judge Benbrook!"

"So I must!" exclaimed Borman, coming suddenly to life. "We'll scour the countryside with the Flying Squadron!"

Rising, Borman strode from the den. Mayor Marclot, also a stunned listener, came to his feet and followed. Ruthley purred a smooth comment to Wilderton, who had sunk into a chair, too

She was ready to pull the trigger if The Shadow made a move ...

strained to notice the alarm that had gripped Marclot and Borman.

"No need for Marclot to go also," declared Ruthley. "He should stay with us, to discuss matters. I shall call him back."

Leaving Wilderton, Ruthley overtook Marclot and Borman at the door of the apartment. The three went into a quick huddle. Ruthley, as usual, was the brains.

"Get over to the garage," he told Borman, tersely. "If that pillbox is empty, we'll know that Wilderton is right. If he is, head for Judge Benbrook's, to make sure they haven't rolled in there. The Shadow will be bringing the judge with him."

"Where next?" queried Borman. "Out to the house where we're keeping the judge?"

"Yes. Lance has already ducked out to call the cottage. He heard Wilderton's blab from behind the picture. Leave some of the squadron at the judge's house. Take the rest with you."

Borman hurried from the apartment. Ruthley purred calming words to Marclot. The mayor steadied.

"Keep Wilderton bluffed," reminded Ruthley. "He will prove useful to us. Remember, we have Lance and Beezer covering up. Borman will be back before it's time to go to the meeting at the Civic Club."

Marclot nodded, as they walked back through the hall. He made whispered comment:

CITY OF CRIME   65

Mayor Marclot managed to smile in pompous style, as he came back into Ruthley's den to resume the talk with Louis Wilderton. That smile was forced; but the one that wreathed Stephen Ruthley's lips was not. The master crook smiled with real relish.

Often before, Stephen Ruthley had seen his hunches come through. He was confident that another such result was due tonight. To Stephen Ruthley, The Shadow's finish was a settled matter.

CHAPTER XXIV
DOUBLE BATTLE

CREEPING men were closing inward through the darkness. They were the thugs whom Lance Gillick had sent from Westford, to keep a circled watch about the old mansion that had been Judge Benbrook's lodging overnight. Audible comments passed among these armed hoodlums.

Word passed along concerning Lance's call to the cottage. The cordon was to tighten; then drive in hard upon the smaller crew within the house. Crooks knew the identity of the men whom they were to attack. They were ready with a vengeance, these thugs, to deal with agents of The Shadow.

Some were keeping lookout for The Shadow himself. He had come and gone as Trig Callister; they had let the sedan ride through. None knew if Judge Benbrook had gone out on that last trip; there was a chance that he was still within the house. If so, The Shadow would be back. He would fare badly when he came.

First the agents; then The Shadow. As for Judge Benbrook, the finger had pointed toward him also. This was to be a massacre; beginning with a surprise attack upon the mansion that stood so silent within the very center of the creeping horde. The house, itself, was open to attack. Every window would offer entry for invading thugs.

The tightening process ceased. Evil fighters were ready for command. They were under the leadership of two whom Lance had deputed to such duty. Those two commanded more than a score of gorillas; the dregs of the scum who had so long been rampant in Westford. Some of the crew, in fact, had been members of the horde that had gunned for Lieutenant James Maclare. Brave through power of numbers, they had boasted their wish for another contact with The Shadow.

It was the moment when a command seemed imminent. Thugs waited for rasped orders. Suddenly, the stillness broke; but not with the expected commands. From somewhere, like a ghostly taunt, came a strident, mocking laugh through the darkness.

The laugh of The Shadow!

"You've got the swag, Steve? In case—"
"It's all in the file cabinet, with the papers. Forget it, Elvin. We've had the best break in the world! The Shadow slipped us; he thinks he got away with it. That puts him right into our hands—this time to stay!"

THE cloaked fighter had arrived. He had left his car a safe distance away; he had slipped through a net of enemies set to watch for him. He was in the circle itself; and hard upon his mockery came the proofs of his actual position.

Automatics tongued from blackness; stabbed flame picked out crouching hoodlums. As snarling fighters spun about, they heard yells from their crippled companions. The Shadow had first located thugs amid the darkness. His first shots counted.

"The Shadow! Get him!"

As a mobleader roared the command, thugs sought to obey. Twenty against one, they had their opportunity; they would spot The Shadow if he fired again. They did not realize the purpose of The Shadow's opening shots; they did not guess that he had withdrawn for the moment. Those shots had been a signal.

An instant later, floodlights glared from the beleaguered mansion. Crooks were bathed in the brilliance that came from upper windows. The Shadow had applied the very method that crooks had found so useful in the past. His agents had set up searchlights, ready to use them when the signal came.

Crooks were as bewildered as Maclare's bluecoats had been, that night at the Mississippi Hotel. Wildly, they turned toward the house. Remembering The Shadow's marksmanship, they fired for the floodlights. The brilliant orbs remained unshattered. These searchlights were equipped with bulletproof glass.

Rifles crackled from below the brilliance. The Shadow's agents were at the ground floor windows, clipping the savage hoodlums who fired back in vain. Like wild tribesmen, thugs started for the house, thinking to dislodge The Shadow's agents with wide-aimed bullets and curdling yells. The rifles crackled on, at close range.

Crooks sprawled; as they kicked up the earth, others broke. They dashed for the limits of the lighted ground, followed by steady shots. Reserves, the ones posted to watch for The Shadow, came up with encouraging shouts; for they were blanketed by night. They were met by another fire: The Shadow's own.

The attack was ended. Those thugs who could, went scattering into the night. The Shadow's strident laugh resounded; it added impetus to the speed of the survivors. It was a signal also; at the sound of the weird call, the searchlights were suddenly extinguished.

TO fleeing crooks, the darkness brought new dread.

Pursuers might be anywhere, everywhere. Each thug who fled fancied himself the only one who had escaped; for more than half the horde had sprawled upon the turf. The same had happened with the cluster of reserves; The Shadow had driven bullets into their very midst. Some thugs found cars; they sped away from beyond the cottages, heading away from the direction of Westford. The others took to the brush, making the best time that they could on foot.

The Shadow had classed these toughs as mass fighters only. They had behaved in typical fashion, once their attack had become a rout. New silence dominated the mansion; then, from a space in front, came a hoarse whisper. It was "Hawkeye"; he had come out to join The Shadow.

The cloaked chief answered. He gave Hawkeye new instructions. Hawkeye slid back to the house. Soon men came stealing outward through the darkness. They were The Shadow's agents, ready for new battle. The first had taken less time than the limit The Shadow had set.

Choosing the banks along the dirt road, The Shadow's agents waited. Their chief had gone somewhere ahead; again they listened for his signal. Lights appeared; police cars and motorcycles came in caravans all manned by the khaki-clad thugs who called themselves the Flying Squadron.

The Shadow waited until the last car was abreast of his position. Again, his strident laugh rang forth.

Cars halted at the startling cry. Automatics tongued an opening message. Fake cops wheeled about, aimed for the spot whence the shots had issued. Again, The Shadow was gone; but his agents took their cue. From the sheltering embankment, they ripped away with automatics, raking the whole line of the halted squadron.

Bullets winged tires, windshields. They found the occupants of cars. Khaki-clad men dived from their machines; left their motorcycles and scattered on foot. This time, floodlights were unneeded. The cars and motorcycles of the unsuspecting squadron were targets enough.

From the rear, The Shadow pummeled shots along the road. Uniformed crooks ran ahead, hoping to join the thugs who had once formed a vanished cordon. The Shadow's aides pursued; keeping along the banks, they harried the newly routed horde and drove them off into the darkness.

Those scattered men would not soon return. When they did, they would find their cars useless. Again, The Shadow and his half dozen agents had routed more than a score. The Shadow's agents held together; their task accomplished, they were returning to the house; to hold it in case enough enemies rallied to attempt invasion.

THERE was one car that had remained unscathed throughout the fray, for the simple reason that it had been left alone. This automobile had come up behind the others. It had stopped at the command of a man in back. It was Director Borman's official car. Borman had told his chauffeur to wait.

Fuming, Kirk Borman recognized all that had happened. The pick of his Flying Squadron had been ambushed. He wanted to get back to town again; to summon other details, particularly the group that he had left idle at Judge Benbrook's house. With a growl, Borman told the chauffeur to swing the car about.

The chauffeur obeyed; as he swung the big car past the verge of a ditch, blackness rose from the fringe of the headlights. The chauffeur alone saw it; he yanked a revolver and jabbed it from the window.

A slugging fist came through, swinging an automatic. The chauffeur's cap was bashed down over his head; the man tilted sidewise; he sprawled to the roadway as the door yanked open.

Kirk Borman made a leap for the front seat. A black-cloaked avalanche came in from space. Springing past the steering wheel, The Shadow met the fighting police director; gloved fingers found their hold on Borman's neck. The police director slumped to the floor by the rear seat.

The Shadow picked handcuffs from a pocket in a rear door. They were useful items in a police director's car; The Shadow had noted them when he had ridden with Borman, in the guise of Trig Callister. He put the bracelets on the director's wrists. Borman offered no struggle; he was still gasping for air.

Leaving Borman sprawled in back, The Shadow dropped behind the wheel. He stepped on the gas; shot the big car back toward town. The tires jounced along the bumpy road, while Borman bounced helplessly about in back, striking his head against the seat and the doors, experiencing new grogginess every time he started to recover.

One laugh of triumph from The Shadow's hidden lips; then the cloaked victor maintained silence. Sooner or later, he would meet roving units of the Flying Squadron. They would let him pass, recognizing the police director's car. The Shadow was traveling far ahead of any reports that would come from the battleground where he and his agents had dealt with thugs and false upholders of the law.

In effecting his capture of Kirk Borman, The Shadow had topped off a well-planned campaign. He had known that his presence would bring the police director to the scene outside of Westford. The Shadow had counted upon this capture as a final stroke.

Each strategic move had succeeded. Massed hordes vanquished, The Shadow was ready to meet Stephen Ruthley and his remaining lieutenants; to deal with them as effectively as he had with Kirk Borman.

CHAPTER XXV
WITHIN THE DEN

HALF an hour had passed since The Shadow's victory on the road. Stephen Ruthley was standing in the center of his luxurious den, eyeing Elvin Marclot and Louis Wilderton. The mayor and the district attorney both looked troubled; but with different reasons.

"Kirk Borman ought to be back soon," purred Ruthley, staring from a front window to study the lighted boulevard. "He's taken along all the men that he had posted here."

"Men we posted here?" queried Wilderton. "Why was that, Mr. Ruthley?"

"For the same reason that we should have had men at Judge Benbrook's," returned Ruthley. "Any honest man is in danger, living here in Westford. I requested guards; Borman gave them to me."

"He offered to guard Judge Benbrook's house," put in Marclot, taking Ruthley's cue. "But the judge wanted none."

"Director Borman should have insisted upon it," asserted Wilderton. "In spite of Judge Benbrook's protest."

"Do not blame the police for laxity," retorted Marclot. "If criminals were convicted in this town, we would have no need for the Flying Squadron!"

Wilderton winced at the reference to the inefficiency of the district attorney's office. Ruthley clapped the young prosecutor on the back, and smoothed his feelings with honeyed commendation.

"You have done well, Louis," asserted Ruthley. "Which reminds me. We must soon start to the meeting. If Judge Benbrook fails to arrive, we must do our utmost to preserve the fine spirit that he aroused. Unfortunately, his absence will bring adverse comment. He will no longer be acceptable as a candidate for district attorney's office."

"Too bad," remarked Marclot. "It cannot be helped, though. Many persons doubted that Judge Benbrook could stand the strain of reappearance in public life."

"We still have you, Louis," resumed Ruthley, addressing the district attorney. "You are the right man. Your support of Judge Benbrook won you many friends. We shall return to our original plan; your re-election."

Wilderton tried to look pleased, but he was too worried about the references to Judge Benbrook's absence. At last he decided that Ruthley was right. It would be impossible to depend upon the judge. Seeing Wilderton's change of expression, Ruthley strolled again to the window.

"Kirk is back!" he exclaimed. "I see his car outside. He must have returned while we were talking. I suppose the Flying Squadron is still out. I see a few of the precinct police on duty."

The appearance of bluecoats disturbed neither Ruthley nor Marclot. The apartment house was not in Lieutenant Maclare's precinct. As Ruthley stepped back from the window, the doorbell rang. Ruthley heard Haija in the hall. The boss stood waiting for Borman to appear.

Suddenly, Ruthley glowered; his glinting eyes denoted perplexity. Mayor Marclot looked in the same direction and gasped. Louis Wilderton came to his feet with a glad gasp.

Kirk Borman had entered, sober-faced and glum. With the police director was a man whom none expected. Borman's companion was Judge Martin Benbrook.

ERECT and firm of step, Judge Benbrook strode to the center of the room. While Ruthley and Marclot looked to Borman for an explanation, the judge drew a large envelope from his pocket. From it, he drew objects that made Stephen Ruthley gape.

"These are for you, Louis," stated the judge, to Wilderton. "You will recognize this, perhaps. It is a list of names that you gave to Stephen Ruthley. Turn it over, Louis."

Wilderton took the crumpled sheet of paper, turned it over and saw Woodstock's name and telephone number. Judge Benbrook commented dryly:

"Ask Ruthley if he recognizes his own handwriting."

A look of understanding dawned on Wilderton's owlish face. He blinked through his spectacles.

"What does this mean?" he exclaimed. "You called Woodstock, after I was here, Mr. Ruthley?"

Ruthley's glower had faded. The big shot was smoother than ever.

"I do not recall that I ever called Adam Woodstock," he began. "In fact, I scarcely knew the man by sight."

"Yet you visited him that same night," remarked Judge Benbrook, coldly, "and left your signature upon the blotter on his desk. Along with Woodstock's own signature."

From the envelope, the judge took the telltale blotter. He gave it to Wilderton, who recognized both signatures despite their reversed form. Smiling, Ruthley purred his protest.

"Why should I have signed my name in Woodstock's presence?" he questioned. "On what sort of document would I have placed it?"

"At the bottom of Woodstock's statement," accused Judge Benbrook, in tone of firm denunciation. "The sheet from which you clipped your signature later; after you had bluffed Woodstock into signing the statement himself. Take this paper, Wilderton!" The judge unfolded a sheet and gave it to the district attorney. "It is Wilderton's own stationery; but this sheet is of proper length. Compare it with the clipped statement that you filed in your office files and—"

Stephen Ruthley interrupted with a harsh challenge. He had no more need for smooth procedure. Judge Benbrook was an enemy who had to be eliminated; so was Louis Wilderton, now that the prosecutor's eyes had been opened. Ruthley shot his hand to his hip; he carried a gun there and he intended murder, expecting the support of Elvin Marclot and Kirk Borman.

The mayor was too dumbfounded to make a move; but Borman shot his hand to his own pocket, whipped out a revolver and covered Ruthley before the boss could pull his gun.

"THE game is up, Steve," croaked Borman, sourly. "You're wanted for the murder of Adam Woodstock. Marclot and I will have to tell all we know. Don't blame me for it. I'm not acting on my own."

Kirk Borman's words were suddenly explained. A burly man stepped into view from the hallway; he was in blue uniform; he carried a police revolver. The man was James Maclare; the grizzled police lieutenant wore a triumphant expression upon his weather-beaten face. He spoke to Borman; the police director lowered his gun and let Maclare take charge.

Behind Maclare came three policemen from his own precinct. He had brought them with him, and had left a squad outside. In that instant, Stephen Ruthley guessed the answer. The hand of The Shadow was behind this showdown. Ruthley needed no news of the battles that had finished thugs and mowed down the Flying Squadron. He was too concerned with his own Waterloo.

"The graft money is in the filing cabinet, Maclare," informed Borman through gritted teeth. "Millions of it! Ruthley bundled it all, in case we had to make a break from town. With the papers, too—"

"You double-crosser!" snarled Ruthley, "saving your own hide by squealing on the rest of us! I suppose The Shadow shoved you into this?"

Borman caught a glint in Ruthley's eye; one that he understood. The police director's hard lips formed a smile; he gave a nod to show that he was ready. Ruthley bawled a sudden order:

"All right, Lance!"

The picture on the wall ripped inward. Men from beyond cracked the fastening loose as they hit the frame with full force. Headlong into the room came

Lance Gillick and Beezer Dorsch. With them, they brought full proof of Stephen Ruthley's guilt.

Though other evidence stood as circumstantial, the presence of Beezer Dorsch, known murderer, in Ruthley's own apartment was a fact that would stand in any court. It showed Ruthley's complicity in every crime that had happened in Westford. It marked him as the big shot of the crime ring, beyond all denial.

IN that startling moment, however, no one thought of that important detail. Lance and Beezer were straightening, leveling revolvers that they knew how to use. Maclare and the three officers were wheeling toward them; intent on dealing with these enemies, they forgot Stephen Ruthley.

The big shot whipped out his revolver; at the same moment, Kirk Borman rallied with him. Honesty did not appeal to the police director. Ruthley had guessed that fact; was counting upon Borman to side with him, using the gun that Maclare had allowed Borman to bring along on promise that he would side with the law.

The Shadow had arranged all this; through Judge Benbrook, he had approved of Borman's cooperation. The judge, dropping helplessly toward the wall, gained sudden fear that The Shadow's strategy had failed. Lance and Beezer, breaking past the picture of Aramis, had equaled the odds of crime against the law.

Then came the finish. Police guns ripped. Lance and Beezer never had a chance against them. Maclare and his bluecoats beat the two crooks to the shot; sprawled them with a deluge of bullets before they could recover from their hasty entry.

Judge Benbrook cried a warning. Ruthley and Borman were coming to a counterthrust. The advantage that the police had gained was lost. Borman was aiming for Maclare; the director had gained the bulge on the sturdy police officer.

Death for Maclare—and the others, for Ruthley was a close second with his gun. Such was the intent of crooks; but their purpose never carried. Before a single gun could bark within the room, an automatic spoke from the blackened doorway where the full-length portrait had been.

There stood The Shadow. He had entered by the passage, to watch Lance and Beezer. He had let them crash through; but he was close behind them. He had spared the two, so that the law could have them. His battle was with another pair. First, the double traitor, Kirk Borman.

The Shadow's first shot was aimed for Borman; a spurt of flame delivered a bullet that found the crook's heart. Borman sagged to the floor, his gun unfired.

Stephen Ruthley performed the move that The Shadow expected. He forgot Maclare; swung to deal with his archfoe, The Shadow.

Two guns spoke at once. The Shadow, as he fired, wheeled away, beyond the edge of the doorway. He was on the move as he snapped the trigger. Ruthley's quick bullet shot inches wide. The master of crime never knew that his shot had missed.

For Ruthley had made no feint. Standing his ground, hoping to beat The Shadow's shot, he received what he had sought to deal. A withering bullet pierced the master crook's chest. Forward, with a long sprawl, Stephen Ruthley flattened to the floor.

THE handcuffs were on Mayor Elvin Marclot. His pompous pose gone, the last ace of the crime ring shivered as he eyed the bodies on the floor.

Lance Gillick, his evening clothes smeared with blood, lay sagged across the rough-clad form of Beezer Dorsch. Kirk Borman's face was rigid in death, scowling its last expression of treachery. Amid them lay Stephen Ruthley, his profile glaring along the tufted surface of an oriental rug.

Weakling of the lot, Elvin Marclot had survived, to do the task that The Shadow had offered Kirk Borman: to gain some leniency through a complete confession of all the crookedness in which he and others had aided Stephen Ruthley.

While Lieutenant Maclare and his loyal men stood stern and motionless, Judge Benbrook turned to Louis Wilderton. Calmly, the gray-haired jurist reminded the district attorney that the meeting hour had arrived. It was time for them to depart this scene and carry the news of real reform to honest men who had been Stephen Ruthley's dupes.

The space in the wall was blank. The Shadow had not returned to it. From somewhere off in the depths of the adjoining vacant house came a weird, mirthless laugh that might have echoed from another sphere of space. The eerie tone faded, bringing silence.

That laugh was The Shadow's final triumph.

It marked the end of another life-risking battle against crime, and at the same time it presaged greater difficulties ahead. The Shadow, who escaped death a million times, was to face a new kind of death, and a new kind of crime, in *Death by Proxy,* matching his wits against the wits of a master villain, and stacking his two guns against the arms of dozens of hirelings. A strange menace hung over an ancient family home; death struck with uncanny regularity. Into this scene of fear and danger The Shadow must enter; here he must fight anew that justice would not be misled; that criminals get their deserved punishment—death, real death, not *Death by Proxy.*

THE END

INTERLUDE by Will Murray

For this volume we've selected two striking Shadow stories from the late 1930s, one in which The Shadow resorts to a perplexing variety of alternate identities to battle crime, and another where in his true identity of Kent Allard, he encounters supercrime.

While the Dark Avenger used New York and New Jersey as his base of operations, he often ranged the country crushing crime wherever he uncovered it. Early in his career, in the shattering *Gangdom's Doom,* The Shadow tamed Chicago, the acknowledged crime capital of the U.S. during that decade. Other cities cried out for his brand of singular justice.

City of Crime takes him to the fictitious city of Westford, whose municipal government has been infiltrated by organized crime. Walter Gibson provided no clues that enable us to deduce the real-life analogue that inspired the municipality of Westford—if such existed. It might have been any of a number of crime-ridden cities of that Depression era—Kansas City, Jersey City, Newark, Cincinnati, Cicero, or some other midsized metropolis.

But why not name the city in question? The usual pulp editorial reason was that unconvicted rogue lawmakers or corrupt city goverment officials might sue—or at least make things difficult for any magazines displayed on the newsstands of their fair city that might offend them.

City of Crime was written during that period when Gibson and his editor were searching for new kinds of Shadow stories that deviated from the familar formulas that had catapulted *The Shadow Magazine* into pulp bestsellerdom. Up until this point in his crime-fighting career, the Master Avenger battled criminals of all stripes from his natural element—the shadows. Here, he steps forward to operate in the half-light of semi-recognizability. This is the beginning of a risky new approach to contending with criminals, which will lead to other, more open anticrime campaigns in the future.

It's also a taboo breaker. Street & Smith magazines were loathe to paint either police or politicians as unsavory. This was a departure from that pristine portrait of America. Nor was the Mafia ever a factor in The Shadow's war against the Underworld.

Shadow editor John L. Nanovic explained the reasoning behind this: "We didn't make foreigners, Italians, Irish, Jewish—any of them—villains. We would have gotten a terrific response from those nationalities. That was a safety thing. We never made crooks in a way that would offend any race or nation. That was basic."

Walter Gibson recalled that this edict came from Street & Smith's ever-vigilant business manager, Henry W. Ralston, who early in Gibson's long career writing The Shadow, told him, "Make all of our crooks, good first-class American crooks. There's plenty of American crooks; nobody's going to scream about that. So let's do it."

Submitted in February, 1936 as "Killer's Vengeance," *City of Crime* was first published in the October 1, 1936 issue of *The Shadow Magazine.* It's a fast-moving yarn limited to a single locale for maximum dramatic impact, and an example of a kind of plot that has been dubbed a "Shadow on the run" story.

By contrast, *Shadow Over Alcatraz* took the Master of Darkness from Denver to San Francisco in pursuit of the mysterious supercriminal known only as Zanigew, ending in a shattering climax at Alcatraz Island.

A former military stockade, Alcatraz was made over into a Federal Prison in 1934, with new tool-proof iron bars, metal detectors, tear gas traps, and other design elements calculated to make it impregnable. And escape proof.

In the federal government's relentless war on crime, nothing symbolized the brutal retribution that awaited captured public enemies better than the island prison in San Francisco Bay. Otherwise known as "The Rock," Alcatraz was considered escape proof. It was here that two of the greatest felons of the 1930s, Al "Scarface" Capone and George "Machine Gun" Kelly Barnes, served hard time for their brutal crimes.

Capone had been the

The citadel at Fort Alcatraz in 1908

INTERLUDE

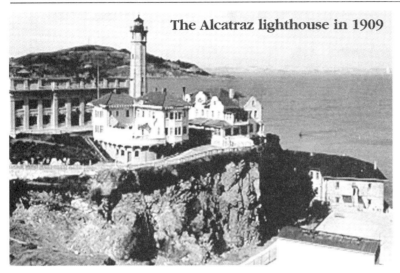

The Alcatraz lighthouse in 1909

virtually invincible mob boss of all Chicago until the IRS nailed him for tax evasion in 1934. Sentenced to Alcatraz, he later died in a Miami prison in 1947, a broken man.

"Machine Gun" Kelly was the gangster popularly credited with inventing the slang term for FBI agents that launched a thousand pulp stories when, upon being caught by government agents without a weapon on him in September 1933, he threw up his hands in surrender and cried, "Don't shoot, G-Men! Don't shoot, G-Men!"

Less sensational accounts say that Kelley's wife Kathryn actually originated the term when she turned to the captured Kelly to complain, "These G-Men won't ever leave us alone."

The spur-of-the-moment coinage caught on, and was further popularized by the 1935 Jimmy Cagney smash film, *"G" Men.* Soon, pulp publishers were issuing magazines like *G-Men* and *Ace G-Man,* giving *The Shadow* a run for its money. Walter Gibson retaliated by making Secret Service agent Vic Marquette a member of the F.B.I.

The immediate trigger for this tale may have been *Alcatraz Island,* a B picture starring John Litel and Ann Sheridan released in November 1937. It was the first Hollywood movie filmed on the grounds of Alcatraz Prison.

Gibson of course never visited the prison. His knowledge of the place no doubt came from careful research combined newsreel footage.

Professor Moriarty, as visualized by Sidney Paget in *The Strand*

Shadow Over Alcatraz enjoys one of the finest reputations in the entire series—and deservedly so. Few Shadow villains were as powerful and audacious as the grotesque Zanigew. When Gibson referred to him as a Napoleon of Crime with criminal connections in London, he was evoking a prior Napoleon of Crime, Professor James Moriarty, Sherlock Holmes' arch nemesis and (following in the literary footsteps of Nick Carter's recurring adversary, Dr. Quartz) the second supercriminal in popular fiction.

Gibson was a big fan of Arthur Conan Doyle's stories, and met the world famous author in New York in 1922. Both were friends with Houdini.

"I used to ride in Hansom cabs when I was a kid," recalled Gibson, who was born in 1897. "But it wasn't 'til later that I began reading the Sherlock Holmes stories. And it was something in the nostalgia that made me like them. Today, a lot of these readers are coming along, and they like [The Shadow] because of the time element."

Pay attention to these hints as you read *Shadow Over Alcatraz,* and see if you don't agree that Walter Gibson was doing a riff on Moriarity via Zanigew.

The enduring interest in Sherlock Holmes mirrors the continued popularity of The Shadow. In fact, some have seen the Master of Darkness as a latter-day Holmes. In the popular imagination, they share a similar cool intellectual approach to crime-solving that suggests a game of chess as much as a dangerous undertaking. Both possessed similar predatory features. One could easily imagine The Shadow swapping his slouch hat and cloak for a deerstalker cap and Inverness cape and successfully impersonating Holmes in his own Baker Street digs!

Submitted in February 1938 as "Empire of Crime," *Shadow Over Alcatraz* ran in the December 1, 1938 issue.

Crime and supercrime! These sizzling stories have it all. •

Shadow Over Alcatraz

A crime emperor of the future is buried with his vicious exploits of the past—by The Shadow!

A Complete Book-length Novel from the Private Annals of The Shadow, as told to

Maxwell Grant

CHAPTER I
CRIME'S CHANCE

THE banquet was over. Affable men in evening clothes were strolling out into the hotel lobby, shaking hands as they said good night. Not a large crowd, but they represented wealth. That was one reason why they had banqueted at this hotel, the swankiest in Denver.

A little group remained at the door of the banquet room. Center of the cluster was a wheezy, stoopish man whose frail body seemed ill-proportioned, especially to the old-fashioned dress suit that he was wearing.

He had the eye, the air of a fanatic. His voice rose to a hoarse pitch, as quiet-mannered men tried to humor him.

"You are all crazy, here in Denver!" wheezed the frail man. "I tell you that my invention was *not* at fault! Atmospheric conditions ruined the demonstration!"

"We understand, Lanyon." Someone clapped a friendly hand upon the frail man's shoulders. "But you'd better try it elsewhere. Afterward, we may be interested."

"That's right," urged another of the group. "You're tired, Lanyon. Over-strained. You'd better go up to your room. Don't forget that you're leaving on the midnight limited."

They conducted the frail man to an elevator. Once he was aboard, with the door shut behind him, the members of the group showed relief. Their handshakes were a form of congratulation, as they parted in the lobby.

A hotel guest, standing near the desk, had observed the scene. He turned to question the clerk:

"Who was the old nut?"

"Harvey Lanyon," replied the clerk, with a grin. "Calls himself the Rainmaker. Thinks that a machine he's invented will end droughts. But he hasn't been able to sell the idea."

Four men were lugging a bulky burden from the banquet room, out through a side door of the lobby. The object looked like a large aquarium, for it was oblong shaped and its sides were large panes of glass.

The clerk pointed out that the glass walls were misty on the inside. "That's all old Lanyon ever gets," he chuckled. "A lot of fog. No wonder he's foggy in the bean! Unless he's a fake, which some people claim he is."

"If he gets fog, though," remarked the guest, "maybe he can bring rain. What's his system, anyway?"

"He explodes some little puffballs inside the glass box," explained the clerk. "He says that if an aviator dropped a lot of big ones a couple of miles up, they would produce clouds, and that would mean rain."

A tall man, immaculate in well-fitted evening clothes, had strolled from the banquet room. He paused to light a cigarette, while he watched a crew put Lanyon's rain demonstrator aboard a truck.

There was something hawklike about the tall man's features, that went with the keenness of his gaze. His face, however, was impassive as he stepped toward an elevator. It had the inflexible mold of a stony Aztec god. "Kent Allard," identified the clerk, in a whisper. "The famous aviator! They say he just happened to stop off in Denver during a transcontinental hop. But I've got a hunch he wanted to get a look at Lanyon's goofy invention."

HIGH in a tenth-floor room, frail Harvey Lanyon was staring from a window, glowering at the famous "mile-high" tower patterned after the campanile in Venice. That sight didn't make Lanyon feel any better.

It simply made him mutter again his argument regarding atmospheric pressure. After all, Denver had an altitude of approximately one mile above sea level. Maybe that *was* why his tiny puffballs had produced nothing more than mist inside the glass box.

Lanyon was forgetting arguments that he had used in other cities. In Galveston, he had blamed salt air from the Gulf of Mexico. In Tulsa, he had said that the experiment had been made too soon after a settling dust storm.

Why couldn't these Denver financiers recognize the truth? Lanyon's device certainly produced fog. In turn, fog meant clouds. From clouds would come rain.

Still scowling, Lanyon remembered the midnight limited. He began to pack his suitcase. In it, he placed a metal box large enough that it could have held three volumes of an encyclopedia. That box was loaded with a few dozen of the inventor's precious puffballs.

There was a sucking sound from a corner of the room. Lanyon didn't notice it, nor did he observe what happened along the floor. Particles of dust stirring; they whisked into a hole drilled in the baseboard.

Nor did Lanyon recognize that this room was tight-closed, the locks of the windows jammed in place; edges of carpet were poked tight beneath two doors—one leading to the corridor, the other to a connecting room.

A vacuum device was sucking away air. Its suction was strong enough to overcome any air that might enter through keyholes and smaller apertures.

As Lanyon started to close the suitcase, he felt his head swim. He steadied himself against a chair. He thought it was just another of the sickening spells that he had experienced, like many persons unused to the high altitude of Denver.

This time, there was an added cause. The suction pipe was thinning atmosphere that was already too rare to suit Harvey Lanyon.

The "Rainmaker's" ears were thrumming, but his hearing remained acute. Despite the vertigo that gripped him, he suddenly tilted his head. He was hearing a sound that he could actually notice, for he remembered it from twice before.

Once in Galveston; again in Tulsa; the muffled buzz of a wireless set, somewhere close by; signals coming through in a code that made no sense. Lanyon knew Morse, and he recognized that the call must be a secret message, like the others had been.

Head tilted lower, Lanyon listened for the signature. There it was! The same that he had previously heard, but quite as mysterious as the message. For the signature wasn't even a name. It was just a curious succession of dashes and dots, that came in uniform procession.

Two dashes—three dots—two dashes—three dots—two dashes—three dots—two dashes.

Harvey Lanyon lifted his head, gripped by instinctive alarm. Crawly wiggles of black came before his eyes. The room was spinning; so were the lights of Denver, shining, through the window. Then came a *click;* a puff of reviving air. Viselike arms caught Lanyon, settled him in a chair.

Lanyon steadied, to recognize Kent Allard. The tall, hawk-faced rescuer had come through the connecting doorway. He had unlocked the door just in time to give Lanyon needed air.

NODDING in response to Lanyon's grateful mutters, Allard located the sound of the vacuum pipe. He stepped across the room, stooped beside it. He waited, timing the sucking sound by the long hand of a stopwatch.

Five minutes ticked by. Allard's left hand showed an odd shake. His right went to his forehead. Somehow, the air was thinning again, although he had left the door open from the adjoining room, with a window raised beyond it.

The stopwatch slid into Allard's pocket as he came to his feet. His head swam as he whirled about. His eyes seemed to catch mere snatches of the grotesque scene before him.

There, on hands and knees beside the suitcase, was Harvey Lanyon, a wild light in his dull-gray eyes. The Rainmaker's lips were parted in a crazy grin, but his extended tongue stopped the hiss that should have come from the panting breaths that he sucked between his teeth.

Beyond Lanyon was the connecting door, tight shut. Lanyon, himself, had closed it, less than a minute after Allard had placed him in the chair.

Mistrust had replaced gratitude, the moment that Lanyon revived. The crack-brained inventor hadn't guessed that Allard was here to help him. Befuddled over the radio message with its mysterious dash-dot signature, Lanyon had done the worst thing possible.

Shutting off needed air, the Rainmaker had done more than nullify Allard's work. Steady minutes had cut down the air pressure to a point below where it had been when Allard entered!

Not only that; Lanyon, in his half-demented state, was blocking Allard further. From the suitcase, the Rainmaker had tugged a small revolver. With sheer nerve sustaining him, he was keeping Allard covered.

Lanyon mouthed an order. It was to the effect that a move by Allard would mean immediate death. Despite his own dizziness, Allard waited coolly. The suck of the vacuum pipe had suddenly become the factor on which he depended.

It was plain that Lanyon didn't know the situation. Soon, the Rainmaker would do a fade-out, while Allard, accustomed to high altitudes, could certainly outlast him.

Timing his breathing, Allard became steadier. His hawkish gaze was fixed upon Lanyon's wild eyes. The inventor's tongue was drawn in again; his wheezy breathing was as loud as the sucking of the vacuum pipe, but Lanyon was satisfied, so long as Allard did not stir.

Lanyon's head swayed. His hand, too, was wavering. Seeing those symptoms, Allard gave a sudden lunge from the wall. Lanyon saw it, tried to steady. The very effort floored him. He coiled; in flattening, he tried to tug the gun trigger.

Allard stopped that effort. Rolling the frail Rainmaker a dozen feet across the floor, he saw the revolver scud from Lanyon's grasp. Rising, Allard clutched the chair where the suitcase lay. All he needed was a few moments to shake off the exhaustion from his hard charge.

Those moments were not given.

There was a muffled puff from the chair. The suitcase ripped apart. Bursting open, the steel box flung its heavy lid straight to Allard's jaw. Taking a long sprawl backward, the hawk-faced aviator stretched senseless near the window.

The decreased air pressure had exploded the thin-shelled puffballs. The lot had gone in a single puff.

A CURIOUS, smoky mist enveloped the room above the motionless forms of Allard and Lanyon. It thinned as the vacuum pipe sucked the atmosphere. Wisps of man-made fog remained, however, when the harsh suck of the pipe came to an abrupt halt.

The door from the corridor opened cautiously. Two husky men poked into sight, adjusting hand-

The suitcase ripped apart. Bursting open, the steel box flung its heavy lid straight to Allard's jaw.

kerchief masks across their eyes. They exchanged mutters when they saw two bodies instead of one.

Drawing a revolver, one of the invader's leveled it toward Allard. The other stopped him with a harsh snarl.

"Whatta you want to do?" he demanded. "Make more noise? There was enough already, from that funny puff we heard!"

The first man pocketed his gun. His companion saw the connecting door, tried it and discovered that it was unlocked. He nudged his thumb toward Allard, with the comment:

"The guy belongs in the next room. That's where we'll leave him."

They hoisted Allard's senseless form, carried it to a bed in the adjoining room. Returning, the pair locked the connecting door. While one was gathering up the debris from Lanyon's suitcase, the other screwed a perfect-fitting plug into the vacuum pipe.

Lanyon's frail body was nothing of a burden for those huskies. They lugged the unconscious Rainmaker out through the corridor and down an obscure stairway, that brought them to an alley.

A truck was waiting there, its motor throbbing. The men put Lanyon in it, stretching him on a mattress. The Rainmaker's huge, coffin-shaped tank was already in the truck. Lanyon's captors opened the lid and lowered the Rainmaker inside, mattress with him.

"A setup!" chuckled one of Lanyon's captors, as the pair clambered into the front of the truck. "Just like the chief said it would be. They'll think that Lanyon took the midnight limited, like he was supposed to."

"Except for the guy we left upstairs," gruffed the other husky, as he pocketed his mask. "Suppose he makes a squawk?"

"They'll think he's goofy, if he does. The chief has fixed things to make it look like Lanyon is still hopping around trying to peddle his invention. So we can forget the guy—"

The rest was drowned by the truck's rumble. Abductors were on their way, their job completed. Crime's chance, postponed in Galveston and Tulsa, had come at last in Denver.

Nonetheless, these lesser lights of crime had missed an opportunity that their chief would have regarded as far more important than the capture of the Rainmaker, Harvey Lanyon.

With a single well-placed bullet, they could have disposed of crimeland's greatest foe, a mysterious being known as The Shadow, who alone was capable of gaining the trail of Harvey Lanyon and whatever lay beyond it.

For Kent Allard, regarded by those crooks as unimportant, was none other than The Shadow!

CHAPTER II
CALL OF CRIME

THE pilot of the transcontinental plane was feeling rather proud. He had flown many notables over the Sierras, but the fact had never impressed him as anything to talk about.

They were passengers; that was all. But the man who was on the ship tonight was more than a passenger.

He was Kent Allard.

The pilot turned his head away to hide a pleased grin, for Allard was seated beside him, enjoying special privileges. Maybe Allard was thinking it funny, watching someone else handle the controls.

Funny, even, to have anyone else in the same plane with him, for Kent Allard was noted as an intrepid master of long, lone hops.

What also impressed the pilot was the odd accident that Allard had experienced, back in Denver. Entering his hotel room, he had tripped over a telephone cord in the dark and cracked his jaw against a radiator. He'd been unconscious when they found him, and a physician had advised him to finish his trip to the coast in a passenger plane, instead of flying his own ship.

That was the way it went. A real ace like Allard could crack up half a dozen ships and come out without a scratch. But a place like a hotel room was different. It offered chances of really getting hurt.

Bad weather tonight. Coming into San Francisco wasn't much fun, during this season. The beam was working, though, and the pilot would soon be following it right into the airport. Meanwhile, there would be radio reports.

Suddenly, the pilot nudged Allard, "Listen! There it is again!"

The same signal that had come before. The sort that the pilot had heard a few days ago, over Denver. Last night, also, and tonight, only a half hour ago.

The stuff that the government wanted pilots to pick up and report: those crazy calls that always started with the same dash-dot identification.

Allard was jotting it down, in dashes and dots. There it stood, in a single line:

—...—...—...—

More was coming through in curious, irregular code, that seemed to register some fanciful thoughts on the part of the dispatcher. It was tricky, the sort of stuff that no one could decipher.

Allard was copying it, the pilot observed, and that was something of a help. It wouldn't matter, though, if a thousand people put those messages on paper.

They were always garbled, always varied. Sometimes words had been made out of them, but even then, the messages had no sense. Sort of a code within a code, as the pilot had been told.

The message ended. Following it, the identification arrived—the same as before, with its doubles of dashes, its triplets of dots. This time, the pilot wasn't watching Allard. Thereby, he missed the unusual.

As he marked those dashes and dots, Kent Allard let spaces come at intervals between them:

—.. .- —. .. —. . .—

Thus broken into letters, the line spelled a name, which Allard's pencil wrote in capital letters, almost as though his hand inscribed the name from habit:

ZANIGEW

Those letters represented the usual international code. The name, at least, was translatable, although no one but The Shadow had cracked it apart. Everyone else had simply regarded it as a mere identification, because of the regularity in which the dashes and dots occurred. Then, again, they had been most concerned with trying to decode the actual messages.

ZANIGEW!

There were times, in the past, when The Shadow had heard the name spoken. Certain crooks had mentioned it, in the same hushed tone that they used when referring to The Shadow. To them, Zanigew was also a mysterious being.

There had been periods, during The Shadow's many campaigns against crime, when an unseen hand had seemingly stirred from far beneath the surface. There were depths below the underworld and it was there that Zanigew began his machinations.

One question, however, had always remained unanswered. Even The Shadow had been unable to learn if such a person as Zanigew existed. That name, spoken by the lips of dying crooks, could have been no more than a myth.

Until one week ago.

That marked the beginning of the strange wireless signals with the label that The Shadow knew for Zanigew's. The government had tried to locate the unlicensed senders, but without success. Direction finders had led investigators to barren spots.

Zanigew's broadcasting apparatus, though powerful, was evidently of a portable sort. He, or his agents, had ways of decamping without a trace.

The Shadow had left that quest to others, while he took a different trail.

Right now, unnoticed by the pilot of the big plane, Allard's hand was building a complicated pyramid of letters that looked like a mystic abracadabra. Zigzagging lines between those letters, he gave potential meanings to dots and dashes in the body of Zanigew's message.

There were other portions of the message that The Shadow crossed off, for a definite reason. He had detected a slight change of speed in their transmission, a common characteristic in all of Zanigew's messages.

That had been a clue for Zanigew's own listeners, and The Shadow had caught its significance. Those speedier transmissions, the parts that most persons would regard as highly important, were dummy letters introduced to complicate the code.

Another pyramid was building up from Allard's pencil. This message would soon be cracked to perfection. In the first that he had deciphered, The Shadow had made out the name of Galveston. The second had given him Tulsa, and a date.

By that time, The Shadow had seen a link to Harvey Lanyon. In solving a third message, he had worked with that name and had gained Denver, the day, and the hour. Ill luck had allowed Lanyon's abduction, but The Shadow intended to remedy that misfortune.

The new message stood decoded. Out of its many jumbled letters, The Shadow had the kernel:

DANSELL FRISCO FOURTH TWENTY TWO HQ

The name "Dansell" meant much to The Shadow. He had heard of James Dansell, a chemist and inventor, who rated highly within the War Department. Dansell posed as a retired manufacturer, but his actual work was creating improvements in various forms of armament.

Dansell traveled much along the Pacific coast, hence "Frisco" indicated that Zanigew had located him in San Francisco, where the inventor had a penthouse residence. From "fourth," The Shadow knew that Zanigew had reference to this very day—not the fourth of the month, but Wednesday, the fourth day of the present week.

The word "twenty-two" was an hour, figured on a scale of twenty-four; namely ten o'clock. Looking for the significance in the letters "HQ," The Shadow could interpret only the abbreviation "headquarters," signifying that Zanigew had himself dispatched the message. The symbol "HQ" had been in previous messages.

The transport plane was looming down toward the San Francisco airport, which cast its brilliant lights high through a slight drizzle. The clock on the broad instrument panel showed half past eight, Pacific Time.

The Shadow calculated a forty-minute trip to Dansell's penthouse. He could arrive there almost a full hour before the time mentioned in Zanigew's message.

Busy with his landing, the pilot did not hear the whispered tone that came from the unmoving lips of Kent Allard. It was like an echo, that sibilant throb of mirth; a mere shadow of a laugh, if such could be.

The laugh of The Shadow!

CHAPTER III
FOG COMES TO 'FRISCO

A BEEFY man was standing in a tiny entry thumbing a nickel-plated watch that showed five minutes of nine. Behind him was the open door of a small elevator. Glowing distant in the drizzle, the man could see the twenty-two-foot dial of the great clock in the Ferry Building tower.

Five minutes of nine. The elevator man snorted. For once, his old watch was right. That wouldn't save the old turnip, though. Tomorrow, he was going to chuck it in the Bay and buy himself a swell gold ticker, with a chain to match.

After tomorrow, he wouldn't be running this private elevator on an all-night shift between the street and the penthouse. His pocket was full of cash; he could feel it crunch everytime he poked it.

Five hundred dollars, with a duplicate amount to come. All he had to do was to ignore calls from the penthouse, and swear, if questioned later, that there had been no signals. There was another duty, also; but that was part of his regular job.

The operator was to admit no one to the elevator, except those persons who belonged in the penthouse. At present, all such persons were up there.

Poking his nose out from the entry, the operator looked upward toward the penthouse lights. Odd, he couldn't see them; odder still, the reason why. Fog was shrouding in from the roof of the building next door, wrapping all about the penthouse. That wasn't the case with other tall buildings, close by, nor the Ferry tower.

Shrugging, the elevator man went back into his entry. Maybe fogs didn't come with drizzles; maybe they did. Anyway, he'd keep his trap shut regarding it, the same as with anything else that happened here tonight.

HIGH up in the penthouse, a sallow, rat-eyed man was crouched on the window seat of a living room, watching that fog wreathe closer. It was thicker than ordinary fog, and already it had formed an impenetrable blanket.

That pleased the rat-eyed croucher. Too many buildings loomed close to this one: skyscrapers with windows that remained lighted at night, spots from which people could see what happened in the penthouse.

There was a radio close by. Eagerly, the man thumbed to the lowest number on the dial. He tuned the instrument to a slight pitch. Faintly, a wireless call came through, a series of double dashes and triple dots. The sallow man's leer became a prefect match for his ugly eyes.

Zanigew's call.

A voice boomed from somewhere in the penthouse. It roared a name in an angry tone:

"Querlon! Where are you?"

Instantly, the sallow man changed manner. His eyes opened into a simple, placid stare. His lips dropped their leer, becoming solemn, almost nervous. His voice had a plaintive tone as he called back:

"Yes, Mr. Dansell! I'm here, in the living room! I'm coming out there right away—"

Heavy footsteps interrupted. Into the living room strode James Dansell, a burly man with a heavy, thickset face. He was brandishing a big envelope. It crinkled as he shoved his fist inside, to show that the envelope was empty.

"Who got into my private files?" demanded Dansell. "Who even had a right inside the room where they are kept?"

"Why I—I—" Querlon's stammer was almost a giveaway. "How should I know sir?"

"Because you, as my secretary, knew what this envelope contained!" stormed Dansell. "My formulas, my correspondence! All are items that meant nothing when separated, but everything when together.

"And you, Querlon"—Dansell was closer—"are the only man who even knew the purpose of my latest experiments. You have known it for weeks, for months! And now!"

Dansell flung the envelope to the floor, to grab Querlon by the shoulder. Dragging the sallow secretary to the wall, the burly man began to shove the button that would bring the elevator, while he shouted:

"Freeman! Jerome! I want both of you!"

There were other buttons, to signal the servants, and Dansell began to jab them, in case his shouts were not heard. A very bull in strength, he had Querlon's arms pinned in back of him, toward the left, so that the fellow could hardly budge.

A clock on the mantel was striking nine, its tinkles scarcely audible through Dansell's shouting and the clatter of the arriving servants.

Querlon, however, caught the tone. With a gasp, he twisted his head and managed to dart a look at a watch that was on his wrist. Despite his predicament, his eyes took on their rattish squint.

The wristwatch also showed the hour, but not the same as Dansell's clock. Querlon's timepiece pointed to exactly ten o'clock.

THE servants had arrived. Jerome and Freeman were brawny fellows, of Dansell's own type. They were the sort who could worry an admission of guilt from a human rat like Querlon. Whatever glee the secretary felt, he temporarily forgot it when Dansell pitched him hard across the floor into the clutches of the servants.

French windows flung open. A wave of fog poured inward.... With that swirl came sweatered figures, revolvers glittering from their fists.

Querlon spilled so violently that his wristwatch ripped loose and sailed ahead of him, while loose change, keys, pencils, and other articles clattered from his pockets. Hauled to his feet, Querlon was twisted about in Dansell's direction, to answer accusations.

Despite that first taste of rough treatment, Querlon managed to gather his wits. Staring past Dansell, the secretary saw something that pleased him. Head tilting back, he emitted a snarly chuckle.

The utterance was no signal, but it produced the same result. French windows flung open. A wave of fog poured inward, like thick soup from an over-tilted bowl. With that swirl came sweatered figures, revolvers glittering from their fists.

They overwhelmed Dansell, clubbed him to submission with short-slugged blows. Past those attackers came others, surging for the servants. Flinging Querlon aside, Freeman and Jerome grabbed chairs to use as cudgels.

There was no chance to use those improvised weapons. Their foemen were upon them, pushing them back against the wall with gun muzzles, growling threats that savored of death. The servants let the chairs drop, raised their hands submissively, to stare stolidly at the stunned form of James Dansell.

From a corner crawled Querlon, drawing a stubby revolver that had been shoved tightly into his hip pocket. With an apish grin, the crooked secretary was taking matters over in behalf of the master that he really served.

That master was Zanigew!

CHAPTER IV
UNFINISHED CRIME

MERE minutes had given victory to criminals. Men from the fog were in full control, awaiting Querlon's orders. The briskness with which the secretary gave them was proof that the present situation had been foreseen.

Querlon ordered Dansell's prompt removal. The burly man was carried to the roof terrace edge; there, he was shoved out into space. The carriers followed him, managing in some strange fashion to bridge the space to the roof of the building opposite.

Looking at Jerome and Freeman, Querlon saw perplexity on their faces. It was nothing to the expressions that they soon would show. As yet, the secretary was not quite ready.

He swung the windows shut to hold out the heavy fog. There was another reason also, as Querlon's grimace told. Closed windows would prevent certain sounds from reaching the outdoor world that was so completely lost from sight.

Querlon tuned the radio higher. Still carrying his gun, he used his left hand to pick up various articles that had spilled from his pocket. He had gathered some of them, when he heard an expected sound.

It was Zanigew's call, flashing again, rapid and imperative, over the air. Querlon faced promptly toward the center of the room.

Four men were covering Freeman and Jerome. The gunners knew what Zanigew's signal meant; they were waiting for Querlon to corroborate it. The rattish man pointed his gun hand upward, preparing for the downward sweep that would order the squad to fire.

Something clanged from beyond the living room's wide door. Querlon's hand remained poised, his eyes took on a startled glaze. Gunners shifted to look with him. They saw the opened door of an elevator, a bulky operator moving clumsily from it.

Halfway to the living room, that figure took a forward sprawl. The man's thud told that he had been senseless all the while. Someone had been supporting him, shoving the stunned man forward. Above the flopped form stood a shape in black.

Diving for cover, Querlon yelled as he pumped his gun toward the cloaked foeman who had materialized as amazingly as the fog. It was his own excitement that caused Querlon to fire wide, but the fellow thought that he was shooting through a substanceless target.

So did the four men who composed the gun squad, until they heard the chill challenge of a mocking laugh. With it arrived a cloaked fighter, who had no regard for the scattered bullets that sprayed from Querlon's shaky gun.

Crooks knew those eyes that blazed from beneath a slouch hat brim.

The eyes of The Shadow!

THE black-cloaked fighter was almost in their midst. They flung themselves upon him, two taking hurried aim, the other pair resorting to the slugging tactics that had served so well with Dansell. Guns roared from the milling cluster, while gun hands slashed downward.

Perhaps that concerted effort would have floored The Shadow, had no aid come with it. He was supported, however, by two allies who acted as rapidly as his opponents. Jerome from one corner, Freeman from another—the two were flinging themselves upon the gunners, hoping to impede their attack.

Querlon scrambled for the windows to yank them inward. Over his shoulder, he saw figures fling apart. One sweatered man was prone and silent, dead; two others were grappling individually with Freeman and Jerome. The last had lost his gun, but he was clutching for The Shadow's throat.

Headlong, Querlon went straight through the window. Shots sounded from beyond, whistling inward above the secretary's head. Jerome and Freeman tried to drag their opponents toward the sides of the room. The Shadow flung his adversary to the floor.

Amid the gunshots came a sharp *zing-zing* from the radio. Double-dash—triple dot—double-dash—Zanigew's signal!

Maddened thugs broke from Dansell's servants, making for the window as the outside gunshots ceased. The Shadow sent his own opponent rolling; from hands and knees, he tongued shots at the escaping crooks.

One man blocked those bullets and lost his life. As he flattened short of the window, the other rushed across the terrace, and leaped into space like Querlon!

Up like a wild rabbit came the thug who had battled The Shadow. He didn't seem to realize that Zanigew's call had ended. The servants tried to halt him; closing behind the fellow, they prevented The Shadow's fire. With a sweep, The Shadow reached them, thrusting a long arm forward to club the last crook's skull.

Just then, the fugitive squirmed free with the lurch of a leaping fish. Out from clutching fists, away from beneath The Shadow's sledging gun hand, over the terrace's low wall, into—nothingness!

Whatever had saved Querlon and the others, it was no longer there when the last crook dived. His elated shout turned to a trailing shriek, as he plunged between the wide-spaced buildings.

From the window, The Shadow heard the sharp crack of a skull upon cement, muffled partly by the distance. That last fugitive had overtimed his stay.

Fog was vanishing, as the swift drizzle flayed it. The Shadow caught one glimpse of a dangling object whipping over the parapet of the opposite roof. It was a rod supporting the end of a double-wire track.

That told how the invaders had arrived. They had thrust a long, thin pole across from the other roof, to hook the cross-rod on two studs that projected from the terrace. Querlon, probably, had first placed those studs as future supports for the wire track.

Fog, provided by Harvey Lanyon's mist-producing puffballs, had been the cover for that action as well as the passage of the men who had come later. At Zanigew's bidding, crooks had used one man's invention to abduct another captive that Zanigew needed.

A truck was rumbling far below, out of sight beyond the next building. Pursuit was useless. Dansell's captors had made a quick trip downward and were on their way. The Shadow turned to the servants, and shot quick-hissed questions that they answered as best they could.

They knew that James Dansell had developed some new and valuable creation, but they had no idea what it might be. All that they could furnish were the details of Querlon's treachery. They told how Dansell had ordered them to seize the fellow.

SPYING Querlon's wristwatch, The Shadow picked it up. It was still ticking, and the time it gave brought a reflective laugh from The Shadow's lips. He found a new interpretation for the term "HQ" in Zanigew's message.

It had reference to the time of the attack. It meant that Zanigew's followers were to operate on the same time as headquarters. Evidently, Zanigew's headquarters lay east of the Sierras, in the zone of Mountain Time, not Pacific.

That time was an hour earlier. Ten o'clock, to Zanigew and Querlon, was only nine o'clock in San Francisco. The careful secretary had kept his own watch an hour ahead, to avoid any mistake.

Another object glimmered from the floor. It was a key, that neither Jerome nor Freeman recognized. A key from Querlon's pocket; a large, flat key bearing the number 308.

Pocketing the clue, The Shadow told Jerome to try the telephone. Jerome did, only to find it out of order. It was a simple matter, however, for him to summon the police. The Shadow pointed him to the window. Looking out, Jerome saw lights below.

Persons had heard the landing of the last thug. Officers had found the body. They were wondering, too, about reported gunfire, for they were flashing their lights up into the fog-cleared space.

Ordering Jerome to hold his call for one full minute, The Shadow beckoned Freeman to the elevator. They rode down to the entry; there, The Shadow told the servant to wait. Hardly had The Shadow stepped from the entry, before Freeman heard shouts.

Officers arrived, blinking flashlights as they came, to find Freeman staring dumbly toward the street. It took them half a dozen seconds to rouse the servant into speech. Even then, the fellow blinked.

To Freeman, it seemed that The Shadow had vanished like a ghost into the San Francisco drizzle!

CHAPTER V
ZANIGEW REWARDS

A LARGE, flat key bearing the number 308. A hand tapping that key against a windowsill, while a face peered through the pane into the darkness of another Frisco night.

That hand was not The Shadow's, nor was the face. The key was not the one that he had found at Dansell's. It was a duplicate of that key.

The man at the window was Querlon.

The rat-faced traitor had much to grin about. He was in a secure hideout—a room in a small, obscure San Francisco hotel. He was registered under another name; there didn't seem a chance that anyone could trace him.

A two-day hunt had been under way for Querlon. He was wanted for complicity in the abduction of James Dansell.

Querlon knew all about the search, although he hadn't once ventured from the room to buy a newspaper. His information had come from the radio set, which, at this moment, was supplying soft music from a corner of the squalid room.

To all appearances, the place was just a plain room. Even the proprietor of the hotel considered it as such, except for the fact that it was taken on a permanent lease which stipulated that no one should visit it, except when requested.

The original occupant had been Zanigew, himself. That accounted for the way the room was tricked.

The door, for instance, looked like a battered thing of wood. It was wood, on its two surfaces, but between those layers was a sheet of steel. Windows, too, had metal beneath their frames. It was impossible to open them, and they were fitted with bulletproof glass.

The room had other secrets, which an ordinary visitor would never suspect. That was why Querlon, in using it rather frequently, had treated the place in a matter-of-fact fashion.

For instance, the room had two keys, and it was Querlon's practice to leave both of them at the hotel desk, where they were placed in a box numbered "308."

Two keys had been there the other night. So Querlon had asked for one and left the other. The second key didn't matter. No one could open the door with it, once Querlon was inside the room, because there were bolts as well as a keyhole in which he could keep his key.

There was a fact, however, that Querlon did not remember, and another that he did not know.

Several days ago, he had carried away one of those downstairs keys and it had remained, forgotten, in his vest pocket. Meanwhile, the hotel clerk, noting only one key in the box, had ordered a duplicate, which had been placed in the box before Querlon's return.

Which meant that there were three such keys in existence, although Querlon supposed that there were only two. The third key was in the possession of The Shadow, as a clue that might eventually enable him to find the hideout.

NEWS was coming over the radio, from a local station. News that was no news. James Dansell was still untraced. Federal men were scouring the Pacific coast. But to no avail.

They had asked a famous aviator, Kent Allard, to fly one of the scouting seaplanes, carrying Feds with him. So far, Allard had not agreed to do so. Querlon snorted a laugh. It wouldn't matter if they brought in all the Navy planes from present maneuvers in the Pacific.

Zanigew could never be located by air.

There was something, though, along the coast that was important to Zanigew; but no one, not even The Shadow, would ever suspect it, until too late.

Querlon was one of the privileged few who knew about it. Leaving the window and stooping in the center of the dimly lighted room, he lifted a trap that was perfectly fitted in the floor.

There was a cubical cavity beneath. From it, Querlon drew a chart that showed a large-scale stretch of shoreline. On a promontory stood a large dot. The map was also marked with various names.

There was a pleased snicker from Querlon's lips, as they formed an avid smile. Querlon knew all the answers concerning Zanigew. That was one of the terms that he had asked in taking service with the master crook. Zanigew had granted the request.

First, Querlon knew why Zanigew had snatched Harvey Lanyon, the Rainmaker, along with the man's invention that could produce fog, if not rain. The device had, of course, been used in the capture of Dansell, but that was only a preliminary matter.

Thought of Lanyon brought another chuckle to Querlon, because the public had not yet learned that the Rainmaker was missing.

Next, Querlon knew why Zanigew abducted James Dansell. That was to acquire another invention, along with the originator; to use both, later. It was a known fact that Dansell had been kidnapped, but even the War Department had no idea what his new invention was.

Outside of Dansell, only two persons did know all about it. One was Zanigew; the other, Querlon.

As for Zanigew's next move, Querlon was again the only privileged person who knew what it would be. To keep his agreement with Querlon, Zanigew had left the chart in the secret cavity, with a message explaining it.

The message had said to destroy both. Querlon had destroyed the message, but not the chart. He was too wise to do both deeds. While he held the chart, Querlon had evidence regarding Zanigew. That, in his opinion, made him smarter than his chief.

It wouldn't be long before Querlon would leave this hideout. Zanigew had ordered him to stay in Frisco in case he happened to be needed for special duty. When Zanigew knew the way was clear, he would order Querlon on the move.

Meanwhile, Querlon was entirely safe.

As he folded the chart and pocketed it, Querlon observed a small switch in the floor cavity. He had pressed that switch when he arrived at the hideout. Zanigew had ordered it, as a final precaution.

"It will mean death"—Querlon could remember Zanigew's own words—"to anyone who attempts to open door or window, once you are within the room."

Buzzing sounds were coming from the radio. Querlon's intent ear heard Zanigew's dash-dot call. The first signal from the master crook since the affray at Dansell's penthouse!

It was for Querlon, that summons, though it carried no message. It meant that the way was clear; that Querlon could start out to join his chief.

More than that, it meant reward. Zanigew had promised Querlon that he would receive his proper due for the services that he had rendered!

Closing the floor cavity, Querlon turned off the radio. He sneaked to the door; pausing there, he worked a rod that controlled the transom. It looked like battered wood, that transom, but it split into two halves when Querlon pressed the rod.

Each half was hinged at the top. They spread like an inverted V, revealing metal plates as linings for each section. Those sheets were polished, bright as mirrors. One inward, the other outward, Querlon used them as reflectors to view the hall.

He was safe here even with the transom sections open, for between them remained a vertical sheet of bulletproof glass, fixed permanently above the door.

The gloomy hallway looked deserted; nevertheless, Querlon cocked his head in wary fashion, utilizing the mirrors above him to get angled views of every doorway along the line. He saw streaks of blackness; one seemed longer than the others. Stretched across the floor, it came up against the wall and ended in a grotesque silhouette.

That shaded patch did not waver, it was nothing but a shadow. It reminded Querlon, though, of a living Shadow that he had met not long ago. Nervously, the crook closed the halves of the transom.

He decided to take no chances going through that hall. It was the only stretch where he could not count upon Zanigew's protection. Once outside, Querlon expected men to cover his journey.

Drawing a revolver with his right hand, Querlon slid back the bolts with his left. He steadied as he turned the key in the lock. Tightening his grip upon his revolver, he leveled it straight ahead.

Turning the knob, Querlon gave the door a hard, quick yank inward.

Things happened with split-second speed, so rapidly that three occurrences could well have been classed as one, except that results showed otherwise.

A black-cloaked figure, looming in the hallway, turned its approach into an amazing spin that carried it into a side doorway. It was The Shadow taking cover in his rapid style, as prelude to a coming gun thrust.

Querlon's revolver spoke, zinging a bullet through emptiness that should have contained a black-cloaked target. But Querlon's gunshot was a puny thing amid the horrendous roar that drowned it.

The floor of the hideout blasted upward with a spreading sheet of flame. The explosion shook the whole hotel, as it hurled away the top of the little third-floor wing that housed Room 308. Even the steel window frames were twisted, the bulletproof panes puffed outward.

For old masonry and the roof above it had given with the blast.

AIR piled along the hallway in hurricane style. Walls and doorways shuddered as from an earthquake. The Shadow was flattened, with chunks of brick tumbling about him, but the top of the doorway diverted falling debris.

Along with the driven air went a scorching sweep of flame, carrying a fire-clad figure with it. The flame sucked backward, vanished, but chunks of blaze remained along the hallway.

The Shadow sniffed the odor of seared flesh. It came from the human torch that had whizzed past him. The floor had steadied when The Shadow reached the thing that had once been alive. He saw the limbless remains of Querlon's body.

Among the few patches of a much-burned clothing, The Shadow saw a burning paper. He snuffed the flame, but most of the sheet crumpled into ashes. What remained was a mere corner, upon which The Shadow traced a few inches of charted coastline.

The promontory, with its dot, was missing. But the unburned fragment bore a name that The Shadow recognized as that of a small bay far north of San Francisco. Keeping that clue, The Shadow moved toward the blast-tilted stairway at the other end of the hall.

Zanigew's promises to Querlon had been kept. Death had come to the person who opened the hideout door once the switch was set. Zanigew, too, had given suitable reward to a double-dyed traitor who knew too much.

Had Querlon known that the switch produced a current that made the door control a hidden bomb, he would have tried his best to give out facts regarding Zanigew. What he had failed to do in life, Querlon had managed partially through death.

The Shadow had gained a further trail. Tomorrow, Kent Allard would join the sea patrol!

CHAPTER VI
CRIME MOVES AHEAD

THE old lighthouse formed a giant finger shafting eighty feet upward from the low rocks of Point Sonola. When viewed from the sea, dawn gave the structure a reddened tinge, matching the beauty of an Oriental minaret.

Behind the lighthouse was the stretch where the point narrowed and flattened into sandy ground no better than shoal. Then came the tiny houses of the little fishing village, against a background of tree-studded cliffs.

Only from the sky itself did the lighthouse look as it appeared upon a map—a large dot centered in the curlicued shore line of the point.

Without the lighthouse, the scene was quite different. It was the view that Fay Tretter gained, when she leaned her bare elbows upon the sill and looked out from one of the wide windows that surrounded her. She was looking from beneath the dome of the lighthouse; from a room that had once contained a beacon, but which had been transformed to an observation post.

Fay lived here with her father, Glade Tretter; but he wasn't a lighthouse keeper. Tretter was an inventor who had chosen the abandoned lighthouse for certain scientific experiments.

Turning from the window, Fay looked about and shook her head. She had thought it fun when she first came here, but lighthouse-keeping wasn't the light housekeeping that she had expected.

Thought of the pun made her laugh, however. She had considered it a good one when she first made it, and it still seemed a real jest, even if her father had failed to smile when he heard it.

Fay's dad had always been too serious. He was stubborn, too. That was why he kept the living quarters at the bottom of the lighthouse, along with his equipment, but insisted on making the beacon room his office.

When Tretter came to the top, he stayed there, and sometimes demanded that lunch be brought to him. He seemed to think that running from top to bottom of a lighthouse and back again, was no more of a trip than going down to the cellar.

Worst of all, he kept the office untidy. Things were as bad as ever this morning. That was why Fay forgot the dawn view and began to clear papers from the flimsy table that served as Tretter's desk.

Fay didn't realize how charming she looked in her simple half-sleeved house dress, with the morning sunlight filtering through her ruffled auburn hair.

There was another person, also, who failed to appreciate the girl's beauty. Glade Tretter bobbed his head into sight from the lighthouse steps, uttering a crackling cry of anger.

Spry despite his huddled frame, white hair and wizened face, Tretter sprang across the room and wrested the papers from Fay's hands. The moment that he had clutched them to his chest, the old man's anger faded.

"I am sorry, Fay," he wheezed. "But those letters—"

"I know," nodded the girl—"the ones from Professor Barreau. But I didn't read them."

"That is good," approved Tretter. He began to sort the papers, to find the letters that were among them. "Fay, I believe that Barreau is a schemer."

Wearily, Fay shook her head. Her father had often argued that point before. Yet Barreau, as she remembered, had advanced funds that enabled Tretter to conduct his present experiments.

"Barreau thinks that he can frighten me!" Tretter mumbled, as he pushed the letters into the drawer of the table. "Yes, frighten me, by the things he writes in his letters!

"That is because he is like the others. A pretended friend! A man who has loaned me money, with no security to lull me, he is like the rest of

The floor of the hideout blasted upward with a spreading sheet of flame. Walls and doorways shuddered as from an earthquake.

them! He wants my invention!"

Fay had turned away. She was fluffing the pillow in the easy chair beside the window. Her father's talk worried her. Everyone seemed to want Tretter's invention, but no one ever came to take it. She was wondering the best way to humor her father when Tretter suddenly solved the difficulty himself.

"Fog!" he screeched happily, "Fine fog! Thick fog! Look at it, Fay!"

THE girl looked from a window that fronted on the ocean. She saw deep blue, with clear sky above it. She was alarmed for the moment, thinking that her father had become crazed. Hurriedly, she turned toward him.

Tretter gave the last letter a thrust that slid it away out of sight into the table. He slammed the drawer shut and pointed shoreward. Staring from the window on that side, Fay saw the fog that he had mentioned.

It was a thick, smoky mist that smothered the trees upon the cliff. It had a yellowish tinge among its cloudy billows, but that wasn't all that struck Fay as strange.

"Look, dad!" exclaimed the girl, half-awed. "That fog is coming from the land against a sea breeze! It can't be fog! It must be smoke from a forest fire!"

"At this season?" queried Tretter. "Bah! It's fog, I tell you! The finest fog that I have ever seen!"

Moving toward the stairs, Tretter stated that he was going below. He told Fay to watch, and to call down to him as soon as the fog completely enveloped the lighthouse.

Leaning on the stout metal rail beyond the window ledge, Fay watched the fog, entranced. It must be fog, for she could not sniff the odor of smoke. Its behavior, though, was as curious as its appearance.

The fog was moving above the fishing hamlet as if some controlling power forced it to avoid those few shacks. The creeping mist settled, however, when it reached the sands halfway out the point.

Despite the wind, the thick mass crawled toward the lighthouse, and pouring over it came new floods of soupish-yellow, like a Niagara of mist. From the shore, Fay saw a circling flank of haze that settled to the water, girding the fishing village.

Beyond was the clear blue of distant Marbu Bay, entirely unshrouded. Fay couldn't understand why the fog was keeping itself to such narrow bounds. She felt a shuddery sensation when she saw the eerie mist surround the lighthouse.

More was coming, like a slow-motion cascade. It was piling up, higher, higher, almost to the window from which Fay gazed. Yet Marbu Bay was as blue as ever, except for tints of white. Those whitish streaks weren't fog; they were choppy waves. A squall had lashed the bay.

That sharp breeze produced another effect, when it arrived closer. It jolted the fog that covered the water beside the fishing village, making it writhe like a yellow monster. The fog wallowed, seemed to buckle. Much of it caved downward and was driven against the cliffs.

The squall was gone. The monstrous mass billowed anew. It was writhing all about the lighthouse, up to the windows themselves. All seemed unreal to Fay; she could hear a harsh, chugging sound out in the fog.

It was coming closer, that sound, like a motor launch. It halted; Fay heard splashing sounds below. She was startled, suddenly, to see the fog above the windows forming a solid blanket that isolated her in the tower.

Coils of fog writhed through the windows, wavering about Fay like monstrous tentacles. Billows followed, engulfing the observation room, hiding even the table from Fay's sight.

The girl shrilled a call down the stairs. There was no answer from her father.

GRIPPED by a panic, Fay took to the stairs and followed the spiral descent that traced the inner wall of the lighthouse. Looking up through the narrow central circle, she could see fog drifting downward. It had become a grimy brown instead of yellow, for the thick mass had partly blotted the sun's rays.

Hideous gloom was present at the bottom of the stairs. Gasping, Fay looked for her father. She saw a squattish machine: her father's invention. It was a fog-breaker, the apparatus with which Tretter experimented. He hadn't started the motors, but a hose ran out through the open door, indicating that Tretter had gone outside the lighthouse.

Groping through the fog, Fay found the end of the hose. It was attached to another device that had long pipes poking up into the air, like the arms of a water sprinkler. Once that device began to revolve, it could dispel the fog.

Tretter had waited for Fay's call, because he wanted the fog as thick and high as possible. But he hadn't heard his daughter's shout. He was lying beside the bug-like sprinkler, as motionless as the thing's long air pipes.

Fay didn't realize what had overcome her father. She thought that her own gasps came from her hard run down the steps. She turned to go back into the lighthouse and start the fog-clearer. Just inside the door, she stumbled.

There was no scent noticeable in the air. Fay's sensation was more like suffocation, though she still could breathe. She seemed to be slowly fainting, her thoughts drifting far away.

Eyes still open, the girl saw the shapes that appeared suddenly from the fog. They were things like men, but with bulky long-snouted heads. Grotesque creatures that might have been created by the fog itself.

Her head tilted sideways, Fay saw the creatures lift her father from the ground. Then, other hands jarred her shoulders. She rolled as she was lifted, to stare straight into one of those gargoylish faces.

With that, Fay's senses faded. Like her father, the girl had become an unconscious victim that weird abductors were carrying away through thick brown fog!

CHAPTER VII
FORGOTTEN VICTIMS

KENT ALLARD banked his seaplane above Marbu bay, to swing back southward along the coast. His action brought puzzlement from a man who sat in the open cockpit beside him.

That man was Vic Marquette, a Federal agent, who had been sent along as Allard's observer. The F.B.I. man had thought that they were going farther up the coast. Then, suddenly, understanding showed upon Vic's mustached face.

Allard had kept along the cliff line, and had therefore cut in behind a long promontory that had a lighthouse at the end of it. The aviator was going back to take a look at Point Sonola.

It never occurred to Marquette that Marbu Bay had been Allard's actual objective, as indicated by the corner of a charred map. The Fed thought that they were simply another scouting party, hoping for some slight trace of the captors of James Dansell.

As the plane sped low above the point, Marquette noted a tiny fishing village just beneath. They went past the lighthouse; it looked totally deserted. As a result, Marquette expected Allard to continue on his way.

Instead, the aviator banked around the lighthouse and dipped toward a cove beside the fishing shacks.

Marquette wanted to put in an objection. Fishermen would know nothing. Certainly no kidnapper would be foolish enough to keep Dansell in so open a place as a lighthouse. But Vic's manner took a sudden change when he saw Allard reach out and make pointing stabs with his forefinger.

From the dipping plane, Marquette saw odd sights that he hadn't noted before. Clothes were flapping wildly from a line, like signal flags. The woman who should be tending them was hunched on the steps of her shack.

There was another person in an oddly huddled position—a man whose boat was half pushed from the shore. His boots were in the water; he was flopped across the gunwale. Near him, Marquette saw a dog lying with its feet up in the air.

The plane hit the surface and taxied into shallow, unruffled water. Soon, Allard and Marquette were studying the victims that they had seen from the air.

Man, woman and dog were either unconscious or dead. Moreover, they proved to be merely the visible victims. Moving from shack to shack, Allard and Marquette rapped on doors. When no answers came, they shoved inside.

The twenty-odd inhabitants of the fishing village all had that same deathlike appearance. There were animals—dogs and cats—in the same condition. Parrots and canaries were also stretched out, claws upward in their cages.

The only life that could be seen was in a fish globe, where melancholy goldfish stared vacantly from the glass.

RETURNING to the plane, Allard sent out a radio report, then rejoined Marquette on the shore. While they discussed their strange discovery, Allard glanced occasionally toward the cliffs, then off along the water past the lighthouse.

From this low level, his keen eye noted traces of a dispelled haze. Its yellowish tinge might have passed unnoticed, except for the fact that the ocean had a sea-green color. On a clear day like this, the ocean's proper trend was blue.

Within an hour, planes arrived bringing physicians. After first examinations of the victims, the doctors were inclined to judge them dead—until they came upon a child who showed distinct traces of life.

By the time the child was resuscitated, hope was found for others. All through that afternoon the recovery continued. By sunset, weak-eyed victims were telling a story that for a while showed no variance.

The way that most of them put it was that they had awakened to find themselves asleep. By that they meant that they had been overcome by something soon after they opened their eyes.

The witness who finally cracked the enigma was the fisherman who had been crouched across his boat.

He had more to tell. The trouble had come with fog. There had been fog above him and along the water when he had gone to his boat; but none by the shore itself. He had been slow pushing off, because he waited for the fog to lift. Instead, it had rolled in on him from the direction of Marbu Bay.

The Shadow heard a sound ... wheeled, just as a massive dripping shape lunged across the sill.

He had seen the fog cover the shacks. While he was watching it, he went to sleep.

Physicians belittled the fog theory. They had a better one. There had been a recent epidemic of dead fish off the Pacific coast, not an uncommon occurrence with certain species. When questioned, the villagers admitted that they had eaten fish that might have been tainted with the disease.

That could have accounted for their own

malady. None of them had suffered serious effects from their strange sleep. One physician remained to keep the patients under observation. The other doctors flew ashore.

Marquette was anxious to be on his way and told Allard so. The aviator reminded him that it was nearly dark; that tomorrow they could resume their journey from the point. The Fed agreed with the idea.

"By the way"—Allard was speaking in the even, quiet tone that had impressed Marquette—"I understand that persons are living in the lighthouse."

"They *were,*" corrected Marquette. "Some old chap and his daughter. But the fishermen think they must have left yesterday."

"You have been over to the lighthouse?"

"Yes. The place is nailed up tight. Whoever picked it as a spot for a vacation must have given it up as a bad idea."

NIGHT settled, illumined by starlight. Seen from the fishing hamlet, the lighthouse became a tall, vague-shaped sentinel against the sea. Planning another start at dawn, Allard and Marquette retired early, using an empty shack as their bunkhouse, sleeping in blankets that they had brought from the plane.

Marquette was drowsing, when a sudden thought occurred to him. He questioned in the darkness:

"Say—do canaries eat fish?"

Allard doubted that they did.

"Maybe the doctors missed something then," grunted Vic. "The canaries were knocked out, too. Remember?"

Allard remembered. He decided that they could talk it over in the morning. Marquette agreed, and went to sleep.

A soft laugh stirred the darkness. Perhaps Vic had caught that thought from Allard. He had been considering that factor ever since the doctors propounded their theory of toxic poisoning.

Other sounds followed the whispered laugh. A bag clicked open. A cloak swished in darkness. There was motion toward the door of the shack. Slight noises that Marquette would not have noted, had he been awake.

Close against the night-hidden rocks, a blackened figure moved from the shack. No one could have seen that cloaked form. Nor was its progress heard, for the muffled beat of the surf made a louder noise.

Kent Allard had become The Shadow. He had donned his guise of black so that, if seen, no one would recognize him as Allard.

There were times when a flashlight blinked, but its beam was always close the ground, its sparkle obscured by folds of The Shadow's cloak. The only twinkles in the night were those that came from distant stars.

Crossing the connecting neck of land, The Shadow arrived at the lighthouse. From his gloved fist, the flash flicked a beam no larger than the nail heads which it illuminated, one by one.

The door was boarded shut, as Marquette had said; but the nails were rusted, except for tiny edges. It hadn't occurred to Marquette what those signs meant. Rusty nails had been used to give the false impression to any casual visitor, that the lighthouse had been long closed; but the scratches showed that the nailing was recent.

Finding a slight space between the door and its frame, The Shadow inserted a small jimmy. Working in complete darkness, he pried the boarding, muffling the screech of nails by keeping his body close to the door.

There was a smothered rip as a board gave. Later, another yielded. Pried partly outward, the boarded door was reluctant to budge farther. That was unnecessary. The space, several inches when fully forced, was sufficient.

A rubbing sound occurred; released, the door jolted shut, to be stopped before it thumped. Blackness was less apparent against the outside surface.

The Shadow had entered the old lighthouse, scene of Zanigew's most recent crime.

CHAPTER VIII
THE THIRD TRAIL

SLOW, silent minutes proved the lighthouse to be empty. That high, hollow interior was an elongated sound box. The slightest stir, below or above, would certainly produce some sort of echo.

No longer obscured, The Shadow's flashlight darted long, thin licks along the lower level.

Discoveries were immediate.

The floor had been used as living quarters, as articles of old furniture proved, although many belongings had been removed. There was a space, too, that had served another purpose.

Approaching that spot, The Shadow saw floor bolts long enough to have clamped some heavy object. He assumed that some machine had been fitted to the lighthouse floor.

There were crates and boxes stacked in the corner. One crate, by itself, had a partly padded interior, as though some other piece of equipment had been stowed in it. Everything pointed to a rapid removal, wherein persons had wasted no time in extra packing.

None of the boxes offered identification, until The Shadow came upon one express company's label. The box lacked a lid. Looking for the missing portion, The Shadow happened to notice the heavy-boarded door.

Three braces were nailed across the inside of that barrier, to reinforce it. Each looked like a board from the box lid, put to a new purpose. The nails that held those braces were short and actually rusted. It was an easy task to pry them loose.

As The Shadow expected, portions of dim letters appeared on sides that had been against the door. Piecing the three boards, he read the name: "Glade Tretter." The address was that of a small town a few miles in from the coast.

Glade Tretter!

Acquainted with every phase of aviation, The Shadow promptly remembered the name. Tretter was an inventor who for many years had talked of fog control. He had ridiculed the fog-breaking devices that others had designed for airports.

Those, Tretter said, could merely thin the fogs in a small area. His idea had been to dispel fog entirely. He had called his own invention by the grandiose title of the "fog-destroyer," but—like Lanyon's rainmaking device, its tests had not come up to specifications.

Tretter had disappeared after that failure. This was where he had come, to make new experiments. From Tretter's present disappearance, a complete one, The Shadow reasoned that he must have perfected the fog-destroyer.

The links in the chain were obvious. This was Zanigew's work.

Zanigew had captured Harvey Lanyon, taking over a device that created fog. He had used Lanyon's invention to abduct James Dansell.

It followed that Dansell's secret invention must be a form of gas that produced stupor instead of death; a vapor particularly potent when induced into a moisture-laden atmosphere. Lanyon's fog. Dansell's gas had been coupled to overpower Glade Tretter and seize his invention, also.

Today's fog had probably been dispelled by breezes whipping in from the Pacific; but in the future, such mist could be dispersed by using the fog-breaker. Moreover, Zanigew had deeper purpose for acquiring the last-named invention.

Tretter's fog-breaker was the only device that could serve as a weapon against the double-barreled power that Zanigew had gained through Lanyon and Dansell!

MORE clues were needed. None was on the ground level. The Shadow focused the flashlight toward the stairs. He followed the spiral ascent, hoping that he might make new discoveries at the top.

Reaching the tower, The Shadow kept the flashlight low. It was beaming on a scarred table, when it suddenly flicked off. The Shadow's keen ears had detected an evasive sound, different from the murmur of the surf.

Listening at the stairs, The Shadow could catch no further echoes. He had barricaded the door from within; there was no likelihood that anyone could have entered. Turning about, The Shadow again played the flashlight toward the table.

This time, the beam was spotted.

Two hands had grasped the metal rail on the sill of the sea window. Over the ledge loomed the wide shoulders of an apish being, with a block-like head between them.

The creature had scaled the tapering outside wall of the lighthouse!

Again The Shadow heard a sound; this time, he located its direction. He wheeled, just as a massive dripping shape lunged across the sill. Ham-like hands at the end of long arms were quick and powerful in their grip.

Those hands clamped The Shadow before he could pull a gun. Flung clear across the observation room, he was clutched by a grappler who had the strength of a gorilla.

That fight was the most terrific hand-to-hand conflict The Shadow had ever experienced.

The advantage of darkness, his skill at trick ju jitsu holds, seemed nothing compared to the power of this human monstrosity that Zanigew had sent here. The apish man had made a two-mile swim from the mainland; he had scaled an eighty-foot tower with a steady climb.

Those feats had merely whetted his appetite for battle. He was flinging The Shadow from wall to wall, bounding upon him before he could recover.

The black-cloaked fighter's only counter was to break those falls; to wriggle partly clear of the hands that threw him. Otherwise, a single fling could have splattered The Shadow's brains upon a window ledge.

Hurled into another sprawl, The Shadow took the table with him. Though half-numbed, his hands clutched a table leg as he passed. Hitting the wall back first, The Shadow sledged a terrific overhand stroke.

The table clouted the ape-man's chest. The force drove his massive bulk against a window.

Though human, the monster used gorilla tactics. The Shadow had a bludgeon, so he wanted one too. Clutching the window rail, the creature ripped it from its stone fastenings as easily as a child might pluck a buttercup.

Flaying the rod in The Shadow's direction, the ape-man made another mighty lunge. Not trusting the frail table, The Shadow flung it as a temporary stop, while he took a sidelong dive through the darkness.

His opponent brushed away the table as it came. He lashed the rod hard for The Shadow's head. It wasn't luck that saved the skull beneath the cloaked hat. The Shadow had used strategy in his dive.

Making for the stairway, he had dropped below the floor level to avoid the swinging rod. Its end slashed a scant half inch above The Shadow's head.

The ape-man must have known why he missed. Recovering, he started a swing straight downward. A muffled roar came from The Shadow's cloak; an upward tongue of fire with it. The Shadow had brought an automatic into action.

THE bullet jarred the ape-man's arm, wavering his blow sideward. Stung by the wound, he flung his whole bulk upon The Shadow, flattening the latter's gun hand.

The two were wrestling on the steep spiral steps, The Shadow trying to use the automatic, the ape-man attempting a new swing with the arm that had been deflected, unweakened, by the bullet.

Heaving shoulders betrayed the start of a vicious side stroke. From beside the rail, The Shadow ducked inward, burrowing upward beneath the monster's half-raised, lurching form. The steel rod smote the slender iron rail, ripping its posts from their fastenings. Carried by his own impetus, the ape-man rolled across The Shadow, halfway into the space that he had broken.

Wasting no time with his gun, The Shadow threw his whole weight against the teetering monster. The "thing" grabbed for posts and caught them as it went over the edge. This time, the monster's own huge weight was against it.

The posts ripped loose. Sliding over the edge, The Shadow met a void. His hands caught an unloosened post above. Thanks to his lesser weight, the upright held. Swinging like a human pendulum, The Shadow heard a smashing thud eighty feet below.

Echoes were still reverberating, hollow in the darkness when The Shadow rolled safely upon the stairs. Final silence told that Zanigew's superhuman emissary had not survived the hideous plunge.

Crawling up to the tower, The Shadow found his flashlight, glowing beside the wall. His hand was shaky at first, but it steadied as he played the beam. He knew that Zanigew had sent the monstrous climber to search for something that Tretter's abductors had overlooked; to destroy some final shred of evidence that might provide a newer trail.

The flashlight found the overturned table. One leg was broken from it, the drawer was halfway out. Pulling the drawer clear, The Shadow saw that it was completely empty; but his ears caught the crinkle of paper.

Reaching into the space where the drawer had been, he drew out a crumpled letter. He read scrawled, blotty penmanship:

> Dear Tretter: This is my last warning. Come to Topoma, as I ordered, or I shall take measures to bring you there. Obey at once!
> Barreau

Topoma was a town in eastern Idaho. The name Barreau was familiar to The Shadow. It could only be Eugene Barreau, of whom the world had heard much but knew little.

Barreau was an electrical wizard long believed dead. Rumor, though unproven, had labeled him a person who held disdain toward all mankind. Whatever the case, Barreau was certainly an amazing genius, whose enmity might be unpleasant to experience.

A low laugh drew whispered echoes from the tower, mingling with the moan of the incessant surf below. That mirth was almost prophecy.

Through a visit to Eugene Barreau, The Shadow could foresee a meeting with Zanigew, master brain of scientific crime!

CHAPTER IX
BANISHED BARRIERS

THE town of Topoma wasn't far from beaten paths of travel. Nor was it difficult for strangers to lead the natives into conversation. The Shadow learned that the next evening, when he sat in the old-fashioned lobby of the frame-built Topoma Hotel.

He bore little resemblance to Kent Allard, this chance visitor. Although his features had a hawkish aspect, they were of fuller mold. He looked the part that he was playing. The Shadow was posing as an adventurous Easterner who wanted wide-open life in surroundings more rugged than those of the usual dude ranch.

Discussion of that problem produced the very fact The Shadow wanted. Another Easterner had taken over a ranch close to Topoma. Unfortunately, it was a ranch no longer.

"There's an old professor owns it," explained a native, "but he's dug himself in like a prairie dog! 'Tain't a ranch no more, the way he's rigged it."

The Shadow was interested. More details came. The old professor—that was the only name the natives knew him by—had fitted up the ranch with a lot of wireless equipment. He had posted the premises, warning off all trespassers; but even that had not been sufficient.

"Sheepdogs are smart," observed a native, "but they can't read. That's why a couple of 'em ran afoul of trouble. There was Carber's big dog, the one with the silver-mounted collar. He was fried, when we saw him through the fence.

"Yes, stranger. He was fried, with all the hair burned offn him! Layin' b'tween a couple o' them posts a few rods inside the fence. Wa'n't no wires there, though, as fur as we could see. The professor sent a chap to settle up with Carber, like he had with the others who had like complaints."

Gabfests ended early in Topoma. It was only nine o'clock by the lobby clock when the hawk-faced stranger found himself alone. The Shadow's watch showed eight, for it was on Pacific Time, whereas Topoma was in the zone of Mountain Time.

Correcting his watch as he strolled out from the lobby, The Shadow strolled to the deserted railway station. That, perhaps, was the last that the natives would see of the stranger who asked few questions, but who learned much.

Bringing a briefcase from beneath the station platform, The Shadow enveloped himself in a black cloak. Slouch hat upon his head, flexible briefcase girded beneath his cloak, he shifted a brace of automatics as he set out for Barreau's ranch.

AN hour later, The Shadow was looking through the fence that the natives had mentioned. It was high, with a sharp-picketed top, but it was not electrified. Scaling it, The Shadow advanced a short distance, then used his flashlight.

The low-focused beam showed one of the posts that the informant had mentioned. It looked like a robot, squatty, with rounded top for a head. Shifting to the left, The Shadow came upon another similar contrivance some fifty feet away.

These posts, set amid the trees, formed a cordon around the ranch house. Closer, probably, than any other person had ventured, The Shadow could hear a faint hum. The purpose of the posts was plain. They were an invention of Barreau's; sending posts that sent an actual current through the air.

Widening the flashlight's beam, The Shadow held the torch in his left hand. Taking a half dollar, he flipped it on a long toss between the posts, following it with the flashlight. The light wasn't necessary. The coin, itself, showed the result.

Sparks flew, turning the half dollar into a tiny meteorite as it scaled through that stretch of space. Current enough to kill a man instantly, as it had finished the sheepdogs.

Pointing the flashlight to the ground, The Shadow had the ray half narrowed when a snarling creature sprang from a hollow beside him. With an odd yelp, it dashed away in the direction of the posts.

It was a startled coyote, heading for the doom that had overtaken the sheepdogs. The Shadow expected its fur to burst with sparks. Instead, the coyote loped through the invisible barrier. Soon, its howl came back faintly from the dark.

Silence; then the stir of The Shadow's repressed laugh. Crouching beside the hollow, he began to stow his guns, his flashlight and other objects into the flexible brief case. That process done, he buried the case beneath a rock.

Dead sheepdogs—live coyotes.

No riddle to The Shadow. The sheepdogs had worn collars. The electric barrier operated only when something metallic came within its path. That was why The Shadow was ridding himself of all metal, from belt buckle to tips of shoe laces.

He made no attempt to toss guns and flashlight past the posts. It was preferable to risk an unarmed excursion. There might be hidden posts, many of them, closer to the ranch house.

INVISIBLE in the darkness, The Shadow took a devious route forward. Soon, he reached a clearing, to see the dim lights of a sprawling ranch house. There were other buildings about the premises; they looked like toolhouses except for one larger structure that had windows.

That building was squatty; from it, The Shadow could hear the *whir* of dynamos. From high above, he could detect another buzz. Looking upward, he saw four metal towers that formed the corners of an imaginary square. Steel needles, fifty feet in height, constructed like wireless towers. Their hum told that they were sheltering Barreau's ranch house with a rooflike current as potent as the invisible ground barrier.

Reaching the sprawling central structure, The Shadow saw a reason for its dim lights. Windows were open, but they were equipped with heavy hinged screens, laid between double sets of bars. It was apparent that those screens must be electrified. Insulated hinges indicated that wires ran through from the wall.

To touch any screen would mean death— except for one proviso.

Electrified in ordinary fashion, a screen could not kill, unless the person who encountered it also contacted another object. That fact urged The Shadow to a daring move.

With a short dash, he neared a window, ending his run with a high, upward leap. His hands caught outer bars near the top of the screen. His rubber-tipped canvas shoes found a toe hold just below. Clinging in catlike fashion, The Shadow jerked his shoulders backward, again and again.

A fastening gave. The barred frame swung outward on its heavy hinge. The Shadow loosed his hold, taking a long, hard tumble outward and away. Sweeping above his sprawling form, the screened frame thwacked the house wall.

The Shadow had launched clear of that fatal contact, missing death by less than half a foot.

The frame swung halfway back, wavered in leisurely fashion above The Shadow's head. Crouched in darkness, the cloaked invader waited to make sure that the screen's thump had not been heard. Satisfied on that point, he essayed the entry of the open window—a ticklish problem in itself, with the menace of the frame beside his shoulder. The thing seemed undecided whether to flap open or shut. It was perfectly hinged; despite its weight, it could respond to the trifling breezes that stirred about the ranch house.

Picking an instant when the frame wavered outward, The Shadow vaulted for the sill. He sensed that the fickle frame had reversed its course, but he ignored it, for an instant of hesitancy would be positive death.

Clinging in catlike fashion, The Shadow jerked his shoulders backward, again and again.

Diving across the sill, The Shadow rolled as he hit the floor, doubling his feet beneath him. Face upward, he saw the screen clack shut, as if drawn by the suction of his own whizzing flight. The fastening caught, holding the frame as it had originally been placed.

RISING, The Shadow saw that he had landed in a small bedroom, dimly lighted by a glow that came through an open door at the rear. There was another door, straight across the room but it was closed.

Easing that door open, The Shadow looked into a living room, saw a tall dark-haired man bending over a drafting board that rested on a broad table.

The man's back was toward The Shadow; beside him was an open drawer, from which his hand brought drafting instruments. The man was Eugene Barreau, the human spider who occupied the center of an electrified web.

Perhaps it was chance that caused Barreau to turn suddenly about. The Shadow glimpsed an elongated face, with hooked nose, tiny eyes that betrayed a suspicious glitter. Though he did not see The Shadow, Barreau noted that the door was ajar.

With a sharp ejaculation, Barreau came to his feet, whipping his hand from the table drawer. His fist displayed a stubby revolver.

The Shadow might have beaten the shot, by making a prompt surge. Instead, he wheeled farther into the darkened bedroom, for he had sensed a purpose in Barreau's exclamation. The Shadow's hunch was right: Barreau expected aid, and it was on its way.

A husky man in a white jacket was pouncing into the bedroom from a rear room, in answer to Barreau's call. He did no more than glimpse The Shadow as a vague shape in black that faded, smokelike, into the bedroom's gloom. Charging blindly, the fellow placed himself at instant disadvantage. Marking the white jacket in the darkness, The Shadow caught the attacker with a stranglehold.

From the living room doorway, Barreau saw the lash of the white shoulders; thought for the moment that his man had the upper hand. The professor hissed encouragement:

"Excellent, Cresham! Hold him until I—"

Jabbing across the threshold as he spoke, Barreau was met suddenly by the hurtling body of Cresham. Hoisting the husky like a sack of feathers, The Shadow had flung him straight for Barreau. Only a spinning dive saved the professor; his hurried twist carried him out into the living room.

With a speedy whip that only a rattlesnake could have matched, Barreau was aiming for the doorway; but the moments that he had lost were too many. Across the senseless form of Cresham came an avalanche of black, with gloved hands shooting forward.

One fist took Barreau's gun wrist, bending it with a force that numbed the professor's trigger finger. The other caught Barreau's throat in a clutch that prevented outcry.

Backed half across the drawing board, Barreau could see a face above him, for The Shadow's slouch hat had tipped back. Barreau caught the bore of eyes that drilled him with their burn. Madly, he rallied, writhing like a serpent in an effort to loosen from The Shadow's clutch.

That struggle failed. Barreau sprawled limp upon the table. As The Shadow's fingers relaxed from the professor's throat, Barreau gasped a breath; then, before the hand could grip again he gulped a single word.

Though his tome was no louder than a gargle, he mouthed that word with defiant fury. It was a name—one that The Shadow had heard in long-stringed dots and dashes, but never before from human lips:

"Zanigew!"

CHAPTER X
THE UNKNOWN SHADOW

UTTERANCE of the name "Zanigew" might have been Barreau's proclamation of his own identity; but The Shadow sensed a different significance. Shifting the professor into a chair, The Shadow waited until Barreau's eyes had opened.

Staring into the muzzle of his own revolver, the professor knew that fight was useless. He began to eye The Shadow as a figure, rather than a face. A slow enlightenment dawned on Barreau.

"I thought you were Zanigew," he said, apologetically—"the one man that I have learned to fear—"

Someone was knocking at the front door of the room. The Shadow whispered for Barreau to answer. The professor called:

"Who is it?"

"Hilgard," replied a muffled voice. "Ready for duty in the dynamo room."

"Very well. Go on duty."

By the time that Hilgard's footsteps had faded, The Shadow was spreading the crinkled note that he had found in the lighthouse. He showed it to Barreau, who gave a solemn nod.

"This places me in a bad light," declared the professor. "From reading it, you might have believed me to be Zanigew. It looks like an actual threat.

"This is merely the final note that I sent to Tretter. The others were pleas. I wanted him to come here, to be safe from Zanigew. But Tretter was too stubborn. I had no way to bring him here; such was mere pretense on my part. But it is plain that Zanigew had a way to seize him."

The Shadow suggested that Barreau tell his entire story. The professor willingly agreed. He launched into a tale that was simple, but awesome in its truth.

For years, Barreau had been regarded as a misanthropist who hated the entire world. That was untrue. Barreau's only contempt was for the ways wherein men fought with one another, bringing misery to millions.

He had retired, resolved to create some invention that would protect innocent persons against the horrors of warfare. Barreau had found success, through creating powerful sending apparatus that dispatched electrical currents through the air.

"Those towers," he explained, "are like the ground posts, but tremendously amplified. They protect me against air attacks. Any plane striking that force would crash."

"And its occupants?" inquired The Shadow. "Would they be electrocuted?"

"Not immediately," replied Barreau. "The current would first stifle the motor. Diving toward the center of the electrical field, increased amperage would be encountered. That would mean electrocution, unless the gasoline tanks exploded first."

"In that case"—Barreau was solemn, for the horror of the thing was to his dislike—"there would be nothing left of the plane's occupants."

RESUMING his narration, Barreau told of a message he had received from Zanigew. In it, the mastermind had openly declared his ambitions. He intended to become an emperor of crime. He had gotten facts regarding Barreau's invention, and saw that he could use it for his own protection.

Believing Barreau to be a kindred spirit because of the false stories circulated regarding the professor, Zanigew had considered a direct offer to be the best procedure. There, Zanigew had guessed wrong.

Barreau's answer had been to put his electrical barriers in immediate operation as his own protection against Zanigew. Since then, the dynamos had never once been halted. For months, Barreau had kept Zanigew at bay.

Not forgetting the human element, Barreau kept tabs on the dozen men who served him, shifting them frequently so that each could watch the others. Any treachery would be immediately discovered. Even the dynamos were sealed so that no one could harm them.

"The dynamos could be stopped," admitted Barreau, "but only for a few minutes. The man on duty is searched by others, and he remains unarmed while they guard outside."

"Meanwhile," questioned The Shadow, "have you heard any more from Zanigew?"

"No word at all," replied Barreau. "Yet I am positive that he is hereabouts, although the men that I sent to the town have reported nothing suspicious."

The Shadow mentioned Harvey Lanyon. Professor Barreau had never heard of the Rainmaker. He had read accounts, however, concerning the abduction of James Dansell. Those had increased his fears for Glade Tretter, with whom he had regularly corresponded.

Zanigew must have known of those letters, but had let them pass. Finding one letter missing among the papers brought from the lighthouse, Zanigew had sent the ape-man to look for it.

The theory that Zanigew was nearby seemed a sound one to The Shadow. He already knew that Zanigew's headquarters were east of the belt that used Pacific Time. Probably Zanigew, on the move, had circled close to this Idaho ranch. His next thrust would be here. The thing to do was to provide a stroke against Zanigew before he could find a flaw in Barreau's armor.

Deciding to start at once, The Shadow returned the revolver to Barreau. Together, they carried Cresham into the bedroom and placed him on the bed. Barreau's servant was groggy from his jolt, but otherwise unhurt.

Back in the study, Barreau reached for a telephone.

"I shall tell Hilgard to stop the dynamos," he said, "for a five-minute test. That will be ample for your departure—"

He stopped, his head tilted. His keen ear had noted something; it wasn't a sound, but the absence of one.

"The dynamos!" exclaimed Barreau, hoarsely. "They have already stopped!"

A rifle cracked. That shot was The Shadow's. . . . His aim was perfect.

THE SHADOW swung toward a window. He saw a screen that had been an inky-black against the background of night. But it was black no longer; it was a muggy-brown, tinged with yellow.

Fancifully, the screen seemed to shift with the swirl of jaundiced outside air. The creeping mass was Lanyon's fog, laden with Dansell's poison gas, pouring in past the electrical barriers. Zanigew had already started his thrust to capture Eugene Barreau!

The swirl was proof that the master crook had found a subtle use for Tretter's fog-breaker. He was using that machine at low speed, making it serve as a slow driving force behind the fog; not as an eliminator of the artificial mist.

With his snaring of Barreau, Zanigew had promise of capturing another victim; one whose presence here he did not suspect. His snare was closing in upon The Shadow!

Before The Shadow could proclaim the menace to Barreau, the long-faced professor had reached the door. He was thinking of the dynamos, not the fog, which he hadn't noticed. Speeding after Barreau, The Shadow saw him press a button beside a screened door. Operating from the house current, the door opened.

Once past the thick-meshed screen, Barreau was engulfed by the soupish fog. Heedless of danger, The Shadow dashed to overtake him. Barreau took a sprawl over a prone guard, who lay senseless, his rifle beside him.

From hands and knees, Barreau jabbed his revolver toward the squatty building that housed the dynamo plant. Hilgard was stepping from the open door wearing a gas mask that marked him as the traitor. He was reaching for a rifle that another unconscious guard had dropped.

Seeing Barreau, Hilgard ducked back. The professor's revolver popped in rapid fashion, its spurts taking an orange tinge within the fog.

The range was too long for that stumpy weapon, and Barreau spoiled his own aim by trying to bound forward as he fired. Hilgard hopped into the dynamo house, yanking the pine door shut behind him.

A rifle crackled.

That shot was The Shadow's. He had picked up the rifle dropped by the guard at the front door. His aim was perfect. The pine door splintered, then heaved outward, flung by the weight of a body that came twisting to the ground.

The Shadow had picked off Hilgard, through the slight opening of the door before it had closed completely. The man was a grotesque sight as he kicked the ground, clawing at his gas mask. His writhing ended a moment later.

Vengeance on the traitor was not The Shadow's only purpose. The black-cloaked marksman had hoped to reach the dynamo plant, obtain the gas mask, and start the power. That move was impossible, for a reason that The Shadow now saw.

Professor Barreau had fallen, about overcome by the sleep-producing fog. Such a quick result proved that The Shadow could not cover the hundred yards to the dynamo plant without succumbing also.

There was some life in Barreau, for he tried to rise on hands and knees. Acting on another inspiration, The Shadow sprang for the professor and hauled him back into the ranch house. Once inside, The Shadow pressed the button that shut the screen door.

Fog was oozing through the mesh windows, the screens yielding gas to which The Shadow must soon succumb. His plight would be worse than Barreau's, who was wanted by Zanigew as a consulting expert to team with Lanyon, Dansell and Tretter. The verdict for The Shadow would be death, once he was recognized.

DROPPING Barreau into a chair, The Shadow stumbled to a fireplace that was stuffed with paper and kindling. Fumbling with his cloak, he pulled it loose, along with the slouch hat and gloves. Lighting the paper in the fireplace, he flung his garments upon the blaze.

In the hems of the cloak were separate powders that could be mixed into an explosive. Hardly had the cloak caught fire, when it took a sudden puff. It was gone into smoke, the slouch hat with it, while the kindling continued a short-lived blaze.

Remembering Cresham, by this time gassed in the bedroom, The Shadow looked for another white coat. He found one in a closet. Peeling off Barreau's smoking jacket, The Shadow placed the white coat on the professor.

Barreau's eyes opened feebly. He saw The Shadow donning the smoking jacket. Barreau understood. The Shadow was staging a double-edged ruse. He was going to pass himself as Barreau, letting the professor appear to be just another prisoner.

Zanigew had never met Barreau. The only man who could later expose the deception would be Hilgard; but the traitor was dead. None of Barreau's faithful men, like Cresham, would talk. As Barreau, The Shadow might produce results when all became prisoners in Zanigew's domain.

The gas took Barreau. To The Shadow, the next few minutes were a nightmarish strain. Facing a mirror in the closet, he swayed as he clawed away the putty-like makeup that was on his face. Out from the built-up guise came the gaunt countenance of Kent Allard, a face that Zanigew could believe to be that of Eugene Barreau.

There were clumping sounds outside the ranch house. Monstrous men broke through the screen door, their gas-masked faces giving them the appearance of creatures from another planet. They saw Allard toppling toward them, screeching like a madman:

"Out of here! Away from my premises!"

They took him for Barreau, as he tumbled into their arms. The last victim had taken the gas sleep.

Soon, Zanigew's hordes had dismantled Barreau's equipment, including the sectional towers. They hauled the apparatus to trucks that awaited on a dirt road. In those same trucks they piled their prisoners, including the white-coated figure of the real Professor Barreau.

One prisoner, however, was treated with more care. The Shadow, his identity unguessed, was placed in the rear of a large sedan.

The Shadow had become Professor Eugene Barreau.

CHAPTER XI
ZANIGEW

"THIS way, Professor—"

The words droned like a monotone from space. They drilled deep into the whirl that formed The Shadow's thoughts. His senses began to snap into place.

Hearing had come first. Sight was next. The Shadow saw that he was in a square room with a low ceiling, facing a man whose drab, expressionless face marked him as a servant.

His sense of touch returning, The Shadow felt himself supported by arms on each side. He could move his head; by shifting his gaze, he saw that his supporters were drab men like the one who faced him.

Human machines, long-trained to obedience by their master, Zanigew!

In one rush, The Shadow's memory had come back. He knew these men for captors who had previously worn snoutish gas masks. He realized that his deception had worked.

They believed The Shadow to be Eugene Barreau.

Numbly, as though fighting off the restraining clutches of many cobwebs, The Shadow moved forward through a door that was pointed out to him. He paused long enough to sweep his hand across his forehead, fighting off the last trend of dizziness.

During that short halt, The Shadow's one thought concerned time. He was trying to estimate how long he had been prisoner.

"Two days, Professor—"

It was the drab-faced man who spoke in answer to The Shadow's unworded question. The effect was startling; despite himself, The Shadow stared at the fellow.

Could Zanigew have learned the secret of reading thoughts, and passed it to his followers? If so, all chance for pretense was gone, unless The Shadow could gather his scattered impressions and control them!

Then reason came suddenly to The Shadow's assistance. It wasn't a matter of telepathy. The fellow had simply watched the prisoner's expression and had given an answer to a probable question. It was likely that everyone who came out of the gas-induced sleep would first wonder how long they had been under.

The procession was moving along a vaulted, rough-hewn corridor, a veritable burrow driven through solid rock. As they made turns and went by side corridors, The Shadow could hear the occasional beating of waves.

Zanigew's stronghold was on the Pacific coast.

Evidently, crime's overlord had abandoned his more easterly headquarters, no longer needing it after his capture of Professor Barreau.

All along the route, The Shadow observed that the passages were lighted by evenly spaced bulbs screwed in the rock above. Set deep, those incandescents produced an indirect lighting that made the corridors seem a line of glowing patches.

Had The Shadow come here as an unsuspected visitant, he could have found many lurking spots, with or without his garb of black. Those places were useless, at present. The Shadow's only course was to continue his bold pretense of being Barreau.

Stopping at a metal door, The Shadow's captors pounded for entry. The door slid aside, actuated by a concealed mechanism. The prisoner was pushed into a roundish grotto that seemed like the interior of a half-dome. There was a grind as the door slid shut, cutting off any retreat.

Alone, The Shadow advanced toward a figure seated at a table. Dim light improved as he approached. He saw that the figure faced him and there could be no question regarding the man's identity.

The supposed Eugene Barreau had been brought for an audience with Zanigew!

IGNORING the prisoner's arrival. Zanigew kept studying a chart that was spread upon a table in front of him. Despite that down-turned gaze, The Shadow was able to form some impression of the master crook's appearance.

At present, Zanigew's face seemed all forehead, wide, bulky, as if crammed with an oversized brain. Forming a mental picture of what lay beneath the forehead, The Shadow found his visualization

almost exact, when Zanigew suddenly tilted his head upward to look at the prisoner.

From the forehead, The Shadow had gauged overhanging brows. Zanigew had them. His eyebrows were thin streaks along a bony protuberance; so extended that he was forced to put his head backward to get a full view of the captive.

Zanigew's temples were wide, but below them, his face tapered sharply into concave cheeks that made skull-like hollows. The curves broadened at the line of his straight, tight lips, to produce a square jaw as bony as his forehead, though not quite so wide.

Piercing eyes were the only portion of his face that showed life, but their brilliance was not human. They appeared as ruddy garnets set in the eye sockets of a skull. There was no blink of eyelids to prove their reality; but the intensity of their stare declared the existence of an evil brain behind them.

Otherwise, Zanigew's face could have been described only as a Napoleonic death's-head!

Listlessly, The Shadow met Zanigew's stare, then let his own gaze drift away. He wanted to give the impression that he could not bear the hypnotic glint, and he succeeded. From the corner of his eye, The Shadow saw a contemptuous smile come to Zanigew's lips.

Strange, that smile; as inhuman as the man himself: a downward grimace at the corners of the mouth, produced entirely by a tightening of Zanigew's lower lip.

Zanigew was pleased. He believed that he had gained another prisoner who feared him. He regarded the submission of Professor Barreau as a thing accomplished.

Rising from the table, Zanigew revealed a tall, muscular frame. Its solidity produced an appearance of thinness that was incorrect. With his unusual height aiding the illusion, Zanigew looked at least thirty pounds less than his actual weight.

Others might have regarded him as a creature of nerve, rather than power. Not so The Shadow. In Zanigew, he saw a latent strength that would render him formidable in combat. He could picture him outmatching a creature as dangerous as the ape-man that Zanigew had sent to the lighthouse.

Zanigew was superhuman: an evil master who could force obedience by brain or brawn. In producing submission from others, he apparently used whichever was their own specialty, to prove himself completely superior.

Mentality had been Zanigew's choice with the pretended Eugene Barreau. He pointed a commanding finger toward The Shadow, who let his eyes focus dully upon it. As Zanigew's hand swung slowly, The Shadow's gaze followed, to a door at the side of the grotto.

Words grated from Zanigew's lips:
"Go there!"

The Shadow obeyed. Reaching the door, he stopped stupidly. There was a gritted laugh from Zanigew, as the skull-faced man arrived to open the door. His finger pointed The Shadow through.

Three hapless men were seated at tables. The Shadow recognized Harvey Lanyon; knew that the others must be James Dansell and Glade Tretter. There was a fourth space, to which Zanigew pointed. Silently, The Shadow seated himself, to find papers and plans that concerned Barreau's electrical devices.

"We need improvements, Professor," rasped Zanigew. "The list on the table states what I require. Begin your work!"

ZANIGEW'S eyes glared about the room. The others went back to their own tasks. Stepping about, Zanigew looked over their shoulders. He passed Tretter and Dansell, came to Lanyon.

The Rainmaker must have sensed Zanigew's scowl. Springing about, Lanyon screeched wildly:
"I won't go ahead! You are asking what I cannot do—the impossible! I cannot do it!"

"You mean," grated Zanigew, "that you *will* not do it! We shall change all that!"

Long fingers gave a sharp snap. Figures sprang from dark niches in the wall. Three huskies seized Lanyon, suppressing his wild struggles. Zanigew rasped orders, the Rainmaker was hauled away.

"There will be torture," remarked Zanigew, dryly. "Perhaps Lanyon can stand it; perhaps not. It will change his mind; possibly his body also. Sometimes men work better when crippled physically. We shall see, tomorrow."

Zanigew waited until the guards returned. When they had taken their posts again, the skull-faced overlord turned toward his grotto. From the doorway, the ruby eyes surveyed the submissive prisoners working steadily at their desks.

The sound that came from Zanigew's lips could not have been called a laugh. It was a metallic utterance that blended with the *clang* of the closing door.

CHAPTER XII
THE TORTURE CELL

IN assigning work to Professor Barreau, Zanigew had tossed himself a boomerang. The Napoleonic crook had given The Shadow the one opportunity he needed to completely play the part of the electrical wizard.

During the hours that followed, The Shadow familiarized himself with every detail of Barreau's plans; and with that knowledge gained, he fulfilled Zanigew's requirements as well.

The master crook simply wanted ways to set up the electrical barrier over an oval area, instead of a circle. Any technician could work out those details, after studying Barreau's diagrams.

There was significance in the specifications given by Zanigew. He wanted an oval barrier five hundred and fifty feet in length, with a cross measurement of seventy feet. He also required two high sending posts, instead of four, spaced three hundred feet apart.

One question was: Could two such towers transmit an effectual barrier against air attacks?

The Shadow found out that they could. Barreau's four-tower arrangement had been an optional one.

While The Shadow worked, he was conscious of furtive stares that came from Glade Tretter. The man from the lighthouse knew the real Eugene Barreau and was puzzled by the presence of a substitute.

Tretter's silence, his evasion of the return glances, gave indication of his final opinion. He decided that the fake Barreau was a spy placed here by Zanigew to learn if Tretter had ever actually met the electrical wizard. That suited The Shadow.

It was curious, how things could be understood in this tense atmosphere without expressing them in words.

Besides divining Tretter's thoughts, The Shadow realized that Zanigew must have talked with the other inventors, as he would probably do with The Shadow, later. It was plain, too, what Zanigew must have told them.

Many lives depended upon these important prisoners. Zanigew was sparing others, as long as the inventors behaved. The Shadow had caught a flash of that, from rebuking looks that Dansell and Tretter had given Lanyon at the time the Rainmaker kicked over the traces.

A dull gong brought an end to labors. It was evident that The Shadow had been conducted here during the middle of working hours, for his toil had been comparatively short. Marched back to his cell, he found a meal awaiting him. When he had completed it, a guard closed the door from the outside. Bolts grated; the cell's lone light was extinguished.

DURING his dinner, The Shadow had studied what little there was to see in the small room. It had a window that opened onto complete darkness. The window was about three feet high, two feet in width. It had two upright bars, dividing it into three spaces, each about seven inches across.

Groping to the window, The Shadow tested the bars. They were solid steel, firmly fixed, so strong that even Zanigew's dead ape-man could not have bent them. That fact did not deter The Shadow. He had another procedure in mind.

Thrusting one arm through the central sector, The Shadow turned his head sideways and poked it through. Bars grazed his ears; when he turned his head, they became a sort of collar. He was wedging outward, drawing his other shoulder.

Below, his hand gripped rock. The Shadow tugged. It was a tight squeeze for his body, but he seemed to elongate as he drew his chest in. His hips slid past. His tall form teetered outward.

There was deep space below. That was one reason why Zanigew had probably regarded the bars as sufficient. To The Shadow, those depths were no menace. The wrench that his hands gave brought his legs through with a force that might have pitched him headlong, had he not been prepared for it. His feet turned, hooking the bars.

Doubling, The Shadow clutched rock with his lower hand, reached his upper hand to a bar. His feet wiggled clear. Probing the darkness, he worked his way downward, gaining finger and toe grips in the rock.

This space was a deep fissure in the ground. From above, The Shadow could feel cold air filtering down into the subterranean stronghold. Probably the surface was camouflaged, to keep out daylight and to escape the notice of chance observers.

At least, The Shadow was free within Zanigew's domain. He intended to make the most of that temporary liberty.

From his limited observations of Zanigew's honeycombed citadel, The Shadow knew that it had several levels, with numerous air passages. He was seeking one of the unbarred outlets that must certainly be along this fissure. During his descent, he probed to left and right, occasionally encountering barred openings that seemed like cell windows.

Not wanting those, The Shadow worked along the rocky wall until he finally came to a crevice, set at an angle. Squeezing through, he worked past rough rock, until he saw a corridor light gleaming ahead.

Then began a prolonged journey through a maze of passages that always seemed to trend downward. Doorways were few. The Shadow was away from the level of the cell rooms. Nevertheless, he continued the downward route.

The Shadow had chosen a special goal: Lanyon's torture room.

Again obeying a subtle impulse, The Shadow was confident that the torture chamber must be the deepest of these man-chiseled caverns. Something in Zanigew's manner—a gesture of his motioning hand, at the time of Lanyon's seizure—had indicated that.

Of all prisoners who needed aid, Lanyon's demand was the most imperative.

Turning a sharp corner, The Shadow saw a final slope ahead. It was a curious passage, this one, for although its sides widened, its path did not. The reason was a huge split in the rock, at the left. Where the passage leveled, that crevasse widened like a letter "V," until the path on the right became nothing more than a catwalk.

Where the path narrowed to a mere two-foot ledge, The Shadow saw a solitary doorway. The door itself was open, as the last light showed. Beyond, the walk blended into absolute darkness, for the rest of the passage was unusable.

Reaching the doorway, The Shadow heard the mutter of an ugly voice. Peering down a short decline, he saw a cell infused by a ghastly greenish light. There, stretched on a crude-shaped rack, lay Harvey Lanyon.

THE Rainmaker's ankles and wrists were bound with fetters attached to chains that ran over pulleys. All led to a metal drum beyond the rack. Above the drum was a crude clock, with swinging pendulum. As The Shadow watched, the clock's long hand—its only hand—marked a quarter hour.

With a sharp *click,* the chains tightened one link farther. There was a harsh chuckle from beside the rack. The Shadow noted the man who gave it—a rough-clad fellow with a bulldog jaw, who was obviously one of Zanigew's henchmen.

"Remember me, Lanyon?" gloated the tormentor, staring at the Rainmaker's scared face. "I'm Elthar, the fellow you fired. I'm the guy that sold your crackpot invention for you, to Zanigew!

"I never did like you, Lanyon! That's why I came down to see how you were making out. Not hurt much, just yet, huh? Don't worry, you will be, after a few more hours on this rack!"

A few more hours—and every fifteen minutes meant a *click* of the chain. That thought told The Shadow that Elthar was correct. The man gave a thrust of his bulldog chin, turned about to come from the torture cell. Needing immediate concealment, The Shadow found it by working farther along the catwalk. The ledge became so narrow, that he could only keep his balance by clutching the rocky wall.

At that moment, The Shadow's left foot dislodged a tiny fragment of stone. It dropped into the abyss; after a prolonged fall it struck the bottom, sending up a faint clatter from rocks beneath. Elthar heard that sound as he shouldered through the doorway.

A frightened look swept the fellow's rough face, proof that he had made this trip without orders. He glanced in The Shadow's direction, saw nothing in the blackness.

Looking the opposite way, Elthar saw no one in the rising passage. He was hasty, however, when he closed the door. His fingers fumbled the bolt, failing to shove it tight.

Hurriedly, Elthar took to the passage. Meanwhile, The Shadow was moving out from hiding. Once at the door, he found it unnecessary to touch the bolt. The Shadow merely shoved the door inward, closing it behind him.

A few seconds later, the haunted face of Harvey Lanyon was staring upward at a countenance that showed sympathy, instead of gloating. His eyes had a trace of disbelief, that suddenly faded.

In one glad gasp, Lanyon gave greeting to The Shadow.

CHAPTER XIII
DOUBLE DEATH

RECOGNITION gripped Harvey Lanyon.

That night in Denver—the man from the other room—his own mistake; all flashed to his tormented brain. With those thoughts came the rattle of a ratchet. The Shadow had found the device that loosened the chains.

Lanyon sat up. The chains clattered as he rubbed his numbed limbs. So far, his torture had been mental. He had felt the strain from the stretched chains, but the physical effects had not been serious. Dawn was the coming time when his joints would have begun to crack.

Doubly apologetic, Lanyon spoke regrets of his actions in Denver, also the stupidity with which he had today defied Zanigew. But Lanyon had real excuses for his latter action.

"I have been here long," he explained. "Zanigew has told me more than the others. He plans crime such as has never before been known; an empire of evil that will stretch throughout the world!"

When The Shadow asked for more details, Lanyon couldn't supply them. Zanigew had been hazy on most matters. One point, however, had impressed the Rainmaker.

"There was a word," he recalled, "that I had never heard before. Zanigew mentioned it, and I took it for a name. The word was 'Unaga'—yes, I am sure that was it."

A quick sparkle came to The Shadow's eyes, but he wasted no time in commenting on the name. He wanted to learn what else Lanyon knew. He asked if the Rainmaker had learned the location of this headquarters. Lanyon had.

"We are near Puget Sound," he declared. "I was awake when I was brought here in a boat that was low-built, like an old rumrunner."

The Shadow asked for details of the stronghold. Lanyon was able to supply a few. The honeycombs were high in a cliff above the Sound. There were several levels, and the highest one housed Zanigew's radio sending station.

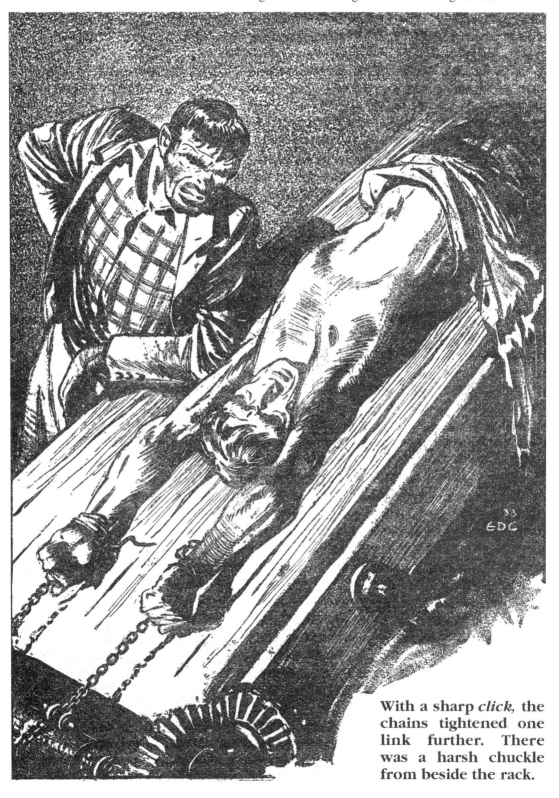

With a sharp *click*, the chains tightened one link further. There was a harsh chuckle from beside the rack.

"No calls have gone out from here, though," stated Lanyon. "Zanigew said so. He wanted me to feel less hopeful, so that I would accede to the request he made today."

"Which was—"

"That I design special mist bombs, to operate from rockets. He wants to project them in more rapid sequence."

"You will design them."

Lanyon didn't oppose The Shadow's quiet statement. The Rainmaker had previously realized his folly. In a pinch, Zanigew could design such bombs himself. It was preferable for Lanyon to submit, and thus avoid torture.

Furthermore, Lanyon admitted a fact that The Shadow had already guessed; namely, that Zanigew was holding many prisoners upon whom he could show wrath, since they were not as necessary as the inventors.

"He plans to use them, though," asserted Lanyon. "As slaves, perhaps, for he is merciless. At least he has spared their lives, and intends to continue that policy."

That fitted with The Shadow's own analysis of Zanigew. Crime's emperor had huge ambitions, that would require many followers. It would be easier for him to sign up prisoners few by few, than to depend upon the lengthy process of finding recruits.

Nevertheless, a criminal Napoleon would need generals. Just where and how Zanigew intended to obtain men of that caliber was another problem. The Shadow, however, could foresee the answer. It meant definitely that the sooner Zanigew could be crushed, the better it would be for the world.

The one-handed clock clicked another quarter hour. The Shadow ended his chat with Lanyon by motioning the Rainmaker back on the rack. Slackening the chains, The Shadow curled the extra links beneath Lanyon's legs and arms.

"The chains will be taut by dawn," he told the victim, "but not enough to mean torture. Zanigew will believe that you have borne up well. Continue the deceit—"

There was an abrupt finish to his statement, as The Shadow whipped toward the door. His twist was too late. A man stood there, leveling a revolver. It was Elthar; he had remembered the unshoved bolt.

MURDEROUS desire flickered on the man's bulldog features. Had The Shadow budged, Elthar would have gladly pumped away. But The Shadow forestalled gunfire, by going immediately into a part that suited Barreau.

He acted as the professor might have—cowering, raising his arms. His eyes looked hunted, fearful—enough so to suit Elthar. The fellow saw a better chance than murder. He took The Shadow for Barreau and decided that he could win favor by bringing this prisoner back to Zanigew. That prospect had an added touch that pleased Elthar. It would mean torture for a second victim.

In guttural tone, Elthar ordered The Shadow to approach. Still cowering, the prisoner came up the rough steps; Elthar could see him tremble. Shifting within the doorway, Elthar motioned The Shadow through. Shakily, the prisoner went past.

Then, it came: a stroke produced with whippet speed.

With a whirl about, The Shadow took Elthar, gun and all. He flung the fellow in a somersault half through the doorway keeping the gun for himself. Flattening, Elthar hit the narrow ledge and came to his feet wild-eyed.

A choking hand took his throat, shook him with the fierce play of a terrier's teeth. All the while, The Shadow kept Elthar covered, but did not fire. There were ways in which the fellow could be useful; contrarily, his disappearance might bring complications.

The Shadow's hand relaxed. Elthar subsided on the ledge. His snarling manner was gone; he raised his head hopelessly, as he looked along the passage. Then, before The Shadow could spy his face, Elthar shouted a name:

"Jollian!"

The Shadow wheeled. He saw a man dashing down the sloping corridor in response to Elthar's shout. Another of Zanigew's crew, aiming a gun as he came. Knowing the alarm that gunshots could produce, The Shadow didn't accept the duel.

Instead, he hauled Elthar upward, as a shield. Jollian slackened, crept closer, with a dart-eyed method of watching for signs of The Shadow's gun. Closer still, he tensed for a spring. The Shadow was ready for it. As Jollian lunged, Elthar's figure, pushed by The Shadow, took a forward plunge to flatten the rescuer.

Jollian didn't lose his gun. He pumped away as he sprawled. The side step that The Shadow made along the very fringe of the ledge was dangerous. It saved him from the shots, however, and a quick-footed twist brought him inward toward the wall.

He wouldn't quite reach Jollian. Recovering, Elthar blocked him. Shoved back toward the abyss, The Shadow had to take a sideward dive. As he went, he stabbed a shot at Jollian, attempting to halt the fellow's regained aim.

Jollian slumped. It was up to Elthar. Leering, he lunged upon The Shadow, expecting to batter the prone fighter's head against the rock. No time to aim—The Shadow's gun had doubled beneath him. But his feet were free.

Strong legs supplied a scissors motion that

clipped Elthar's lurch. That crisis didn't allow for subtle tactics. The Shadow gave all the power he had. Elthar took a sideways hurtle over the edge of the cleft.

A wail sickened into the distance. Up came the hollow sound of a splashing crash. Rocks, in shallow water, had received Elthar for his final lodging, sixty-odd feet below.

RISING, The Shadow took a look at Jollian.

The fellow was in a bad way, coughing inarticulate words. He was trying to call for aid, and it was coming. The Shadow could hear the clatter of men arriving from above. Visualizing a certain possibility, The Shadow took to his hiding spot at the deep end of the catwalk.

Three brutish men arrived. They lifted Jollian, heard the words he gulped. As The Shadow hoped, Jollian began with Elthar, gesturing toward the pit as he spoke.

"I found Elthar!" gasped Jollian. "He—he was—here—"

A final cough—Jollian slumped dead. Listeners constructed their own version of the story; false, but logical.

"Elthar, huh?" grunted one. "Used to work for Lanyon. Come to help the guy. I guess. It was good that Jollian got him."

They entered the cell, found that Lanyon's chains were loose. Tightening them, the crew came out. One bolted the door, while the others picked up Jollian's body again.

When they were gone, The Shadow drew the bolt. Lanyon breathed gratefully at his return. Again the chains were loosened; then The Shadow continued on his way, leaving a bolted door behind him.

The wrong story had gone back to Zanigew: the right one for The Shadow. Enough had been accomplished for tonight. Retracing his precarious course, The Shadow scaled the inside of the rocky fissure and squeezed back into his cell.

Prying a loose stone from a lower corner, The Shadow buried Elthar's gun beneath it. Stretching upon the cell's frail cot, he was again Eugene Barreau, asleep until the morrow.

CHAPTER XIV
THE SHADOW'S MESSAGE

THE next day, Zanigew held a short chat with The Shadow, alias Eugene Barreau. The skull-faced overlord was tight-lipped; the few facts that he mentioned were generalities that The Shadow had heard from Harvey Lanyon.

Zanigew intended tremendous conquests. He expected cooperation. Those who supplied it would be favored. Those who refused it would find torture. That applied to the many prisoners who had been taken along with the inventors.

"Such persons," remarked Zanigew, casually, "as Tretter's daughter. Have you ever met her, Barreau?"

The Shadow shifted uneasily, pulling his gaze away from Zanigew's. Apparently, Barreau didn't want to answer, and Zanigew did not insist. His grated laugh showed that he was pleased enough to see how his presence gave Barreau the jitters.

All day, the inventors continued the tasks ordered by Zanigew. Lanyon kept hunched at his desk, feigning the effects of pain from his overnight ordeal. Tretter, warier than ever, made no glances toward the pretended Barreau.

Most of the work was mere routine, except for a task that Zanigew had given Dansell. The burly chemist didn't like the assignment but he went through with it, remembering what had happened to Lanyon.

By tonight, The Shadow felt sure, something important would be due. These rocky caves on the shores of Puget Sound could not possibly represent the center of Zanigew's coming domain. The Shadow had a definite idea regarding the mastermind's next step; and the word "Unaga" was concerned in it.

When the inventors were put away for the night, The Shadow promptly started a new expedition from his window, taking Elthar's captured revolver with him. This time, he picked an upward course, seeking some higher opening in the rocky fissure.

He found one—a tighter squeeze—but it brought him to a level thirty feet above the cell rooms. Nearing a passage, The Shadow watched a pacing guard go by, then took an upward slope. As on the night before, he came to a final door; but this one was not a torture chamber, nor did it have an abyss beside it.

The door was a heavy barrier that completely blocked the passage. The Shadow knew that it must mean Zanigew's broadcasting room.

Despite its weight, the door yielded easily. The Shadow looked into a room fitted with wireless equipment. There were large crates, ready to receive the apparatus should Zanigew order it packed.

A squatty operator was seated at a table, earphones clamped to his head. He was receiving messages, not sending them.

Stacked on a filing pin beside him were previous messages that he had sent for Zanigew. Dust streaked the surface of the top paper. Those messages were ones that had been dispatched from the old headquarters, which had moved about in several states east of the Sierra Mountains.

Behind the operator's back, The Shadow reached a large packing box that was tilted on its side. Stepping past it, he eased inside and kept watch through a crack in the bottom.

THINGS happened soon. A metal-covered trapdoor opened in the ceiling. A man pushed a ladder downward and descended. The light showed his face: big-jawed, with a cheek marked by a scar.

The newcomer gave a grunt when he saw that the radio operator had not noticed his arrival. He poked the operator's shoulder. The fellow spun from the table, yanking off the earphones.

"You ought not to be listenin' when you're alone," growled 'Scarface,' "Any guy could do a sneak in here!"

"Yeah?" snapped the operator. "Who for instance?"

"Some mug like that bird Elthar, who got his last night. Maybe there's more of 'em in the outfit."

A telephone buzzed; with it, a light glowed. The radioman answered the call.

"From the chief," he told Scarface. "A message is coming up."

"Which means we'll probably have to get goin'," snapped the other. "Give me a lift with them batteries."

The two ascended the ladder, jogging the trapdoor as they dragged the batteries through. The trapdoor fell into place. Alone in the room, The Shadow could have made for the table, but he waited in his hiding place. He remembered that a message was coming up.

It came. A stupid-faced man brought it. Seeing no sign of the operator, he left the message on the table and departed. Once the door was shut, The Shadow edged out to the table.

The message was brief. It consisted of three jumbled words, each of five letters. There were two five-letter spaces in between:

DJVKA——-HGBWQ——-RVYJS

Those words, The Shadow knew could only be deciphered by a complicated process of pyramided letters, linking code with code. The spaces—as with Zanigew's other messages—were to be filled with dummy letters, which would be ignored by those who received the message.

Plucking a pencil from the desk, The Shadow introduced letters of his own, copying the exact style of the others. The completed message read:

DJVKA XXUNA HGBWQ GAXSX RVYJS

Below the message was written notation, evidently in Zanigew's hand. It stated:

Hold for six hours. Send from new location.

Creasing the lower edge, The Shadow tore it cleanly. Copying the ornate style of Zanigew's penmanship, he wrote:

Urgent! Send at once!

The trapdoor was opening. The Shadow slid out of sight behind the packing box as the radio operator reappeared with his scar-faced pal. The operator saw the message.

"Funny!" he remarked. "The chief filled in the dummy words. He must be in a hurry. He wants me to broadcast this from here."

"Better phone him," urged Scarface. "If you shoot the thing from here, we may get spotted."

"What if they do put direction finders on us? The chief sent word we're leaving here tonight."

"Yeah. But it's high tide right now. The chief don't want to get started until it's low tide."

The wireless operator snorted.

"The chief figures things for himself," he reminded. "That leaves you out. Why should I call him, and get called down? These are his orders, aren't they?"

TURNING to the table, the operator clicked his key. Zanigew's message, plus The Shadow's additions, was flashed across the air. Scarface waited, while the message was sent. At the finish came the double-dashes and triple-dots that identified Zanigew to his absent followers.

Hardly had the final call been sent, when the telephone buzzed. The operator answered, began to stammer answers to fast-put questions. In the middle of the conversation, an alarm bell clanged.

The trapdoor yanked open. Men poked their heads into sight. Scarface yanked a gun, looking about as if he expected trouble at his elbow. The door from the lower passage whipped wide. Armed guards were on the threshold.

Zanigew must have heard the message through a special hookup. He knew that something was wrong in the broadcast room. This was the first spot that would be searched; but The Shadow didn't allow time for a hunt to begin.

Coming up like a figure on a spring, he hurled the packing box straight for the scar-faced man. The fellow staggered backward with a howl, shooting everywhere except where The Shadow was.

The men at the trapdoor spotted what happened. Before they could fire, they were ducking for cover, The Shadow's revolver spitting bullets in their direction. Hard upon those quick shots, The Shadow whirled to meet the guards from the lower door.

They hadn't time to fire, before he was with them, slugging crisscrossed blows that sent them to the corners of the room. When they managed to shoot, their only target was the door that he had slammed behind him.

Bullets clanged steel. With snarls, the thwarted crooks yanked the door open, to begin pursuit.

The Shadow had reached a turn in the passage; but though foemen failed to see him, there was something that they heard. That was the taunt of a trailing laugh, that worried them almost to a point of indecision.

Dropping the part of Barreau, The Shadow was declaring himself to Zanigew's hordes. He knew that his battle challenge would aid him in the coming fray. Against tremendous odds, The Shadow had only one sure course.

That was to become The Shadow! The fact that he, the greatest of all crime's foes, had penetrated to this stronghold, could shatter the trust that crooks gave to Zanigew.

His gun half-emptied, that fierce laugh might become The Shadow's only weapon, in the lair where Zanigew ruled!

CHAPTER XV
THE BLACK TOMB

SWIFT in his driving tactics, The Shadow had given opponents but little time to glimpse his face. There was still a chance that he could reach the outlet that afforded a route to his cell.

That accomplished, Zanigew's men would scour the stronghold, only to find that The Shadow had vanished as evasively as his laugh. Again, the intrepid fighter could pass himself as Eugene Barreau.

Ill chance prevented that move.

Rounding a turn, The Shadow saw the fissure that led to the outlet. Between him and the cloven side passage were four of Zanigew's men. The fire that The Shadow opened proved more effective than he planned.

When one of the motley blockers tumbled, the others didn't trust their heels. Instead of running down the main passage, they dived into the obscure splits that The Shadow wanted as his own route!

Behind rough-hewn walls, deep in darkness, the foemen had a fort that they could use to good advantage. It would take long battle to suppress them, and by that time, Zanigew's entire horde would be present. The Shadow had to deviate from his original plan.

Snatching the fresh revolver that the crippled foeman had dropped, The Shadow continued a downward route, following the lighted passages. He paused at the next turn to jab back warning shots at pursuers who had come from the wireless room.

Speeding ahead, The Shadow looked for possible ways to get back to his cell. None was available. He was on the very level of the cell rooms, but that did not help. To unbolt the door of his own cell would be a giveaway.

In that moment, he seized upon another plan: to yank open other cell doors and release prisoners who could aid him. An excellent process, had he found time to accomplish it. But it chanced that this corridor was strongly guarded.

Someone barked a harsh order. There was a clatter at the end of the passage. The Shadow saw a metal shield swing into position, a machine gun muzzle poking from its center. Men were behind that shelter, ready to put the gun in action. Using the few remaining seconds, The Shadow reached a side passage and hurdled from sight, just as the machine gun began to rip.

Away from the direction that he wanted, The Shadow was deep in the underground maze. The few doorways were strange ones. There were many passages to choose, but most of them rang with the shouts of arriving foemen. The Shadow had reached a crossroads; only one passage was available. He took it.

Sighted as he hurried up a slope, The Shadow became a target for a dozen guns. Hurried shots were wide; the greatest danger was from bullets that ricocheted off the walls. One slug struck The Shadow's neck; but its strength was spent. He brushed away the hot, mushroomed metal as it slid toward his collar.

Then the sloped ceiling intervened. Shots were muffled, far behind, when The Shadow reached a fork where two passages curved in opposite directions. Not wasting time in choice, The Shadow took the channel to the left.

Passing a bend, he came to the end of the passage. It stopped at a big door that was wide open, a pair of armed men coming from the room beyond. Their guns roared with The Shadow's, but his shots were the only ones aimed accurately. The gunners slumped away as The Shadow emptied his gun.

ON the threshold, The Shadow was met by a huge guard who launched from the room, aiming a revolver. The gun tongued, but The Shadow was past it, slugging for its owner. The giant didn't mind the slashing gun blow that glanced from his head. Dropping his own weapon, he clamped mammoth paws for The Shadow's throat.

Twin of the ape-man in the lighthouse, this fellow intended to bash The Shadow into submission. In this setting, under these circumstances,

The Shadow was better able to size his foe. He gained a throat hold first, twisting as he made it. Soon, he was lashing about the room, flaying his big adversary like a puppet.

This was the storeroom where Zanigew kept the captured inventions. The fighters rolled against a table where Lanyon's mist bombs were stacked in a box that looked like an egg crate. They nearly overturned a tank containing Dansell's sleep gas.

They wallowed finally against a pedestal on which Barreau's electrical projector was mounted. It was there that The Shadow sent the giant in a long fling across the storeroom. Panting, The Shadow clutched for the apparatus beside him. His hand encountered a loose lever.

Ripping the rod loose, he whacked the apparatus itself. He was smashing coils, tubes that would be impossible to replace for weeks to come. Even from Barreau's plans, Zanigew would not be able to repair this damage.

One of the captured inventions—probably the machine that Zanigew regarded most important—would no longer he useful to the thief who had acquired it!

Given a few minutes more, The Shadow would have completely demolished the device. He was forced to stint his damage, because pursuers were shouting from the final passage. The Shadow sprang for the door, to close it. He was blocked suddenly by the giant guard, who shoved up from the floor with a snarl that told he was ready for more action.

The Shadow settled him with a long swing of the steel lever; but the brief delay was costly. Enemies were at the doorway. It was too late to keep them out. Ducking to an inner corner, The Shadow was away from aiming guns long enough to provide a counterthrust.

Grabbing the crate of fog bombs, he chucked it for the guns and faces that poked suddenly from beside the door.

The scattering missiles didn't explode; they needed lessened air pressure to go off in that sudden fashion. Some of them cracked, however, and gave fizzy puffs that literally spurted mist about the room. Men were dropping back, hands across their eyes, before they realized that the stuff wouldn't hurt.

By that time, the room was clouded. In the haze, The Shadow scooped the guard's gun from the floor and broke through the throng at the doorway.

Shooting ahead of him, he saw foemen duck as he came from the shroud of mist. Small wonder, for they couldn't tell whether one man or a battalion was headed for them.

Clear again, The Shadow reached the forked junction and took the passage to the right. Zanigew's reserves were coming; there was a whole horde at The Shadow's heels. New passages were few, but all led downward, giving hope that The Shadow might find a lower exit that would enable him to reach his cell.

Such hope was over when he came suddenly upon the lowermost passage in the stronghold, the burrow that ended in a deep abyss outside the torture room!

A run along the level—The Shadow was at the pit itself. Yells came in a deluge behind him. Guns were spurting, telling that he was spotted. No time to reach the torture chamber and use it as a fort. The place for The Shadow's stand was the edge of the abyss.

He flung about. Mighty mockery shivered from his lips. With that defiance The Shadow leveled his revolver. Sight of it, coupled with the fierce, unearthly mirth, put fear into their rat-sized souls. Though ten against one, they didn't care to battle. Each felt that the first who fired would be a prompt recipient of a bullet.

Not one of the band realized that The Shadow's gun had been emptied in that final fusillade outside the storeroom!

HOLDING his ground, The Shadow motioned for the tribe to drop their guns.

They began to obey, one by one, until a repetition of the laugh produced a panic in which weapons clattered like hailstones. The Shadow was motioning them back, and they were obeying his order to retreat!

At last, The Shadow moved. Boldly, coolly, he intended to approach those scattered guns and arm himself. After that, he could march Zanigew's own men ahead of him, as shields against other attackers. Only The Shadow could have managed such a daring ruse!

But there was another person in this subterranean den, whose keen brain could guess that strategy.

There was a sudden shift among the retreating crew. Shaky men were flung aside by powerful impatient hands. Out from the group came a solitary foe to challenge The Shadow's path.

Zanigew!

In his fist the master crook held a revolver, and the gun was fully loaded. Evil glared from his ruby eyes, deep in their skullish sockets. Again, his tight lips had the grimace that was Zanigew's closest effort to a smile.

Zanigew knew that if The Shadow had a single bullet, he would use it. This was the trapped fighter's chance to win the struggle, by rendering his opponents leaderless.

But The Shadow did not fire.

Steadily, Zanigew moved forward, until he had the range he wanted. His men were over their fright; they were crouching up behind him, reaching for their guns. The Shadow, in turn, had retreated close to the fringe of the crevasse.

Zanigew's finger tightened on its trigger.

Death seemed a certainty for The Shadow. Rather than accept it from Zanigew's gun, he took a desperate course. Spinning, he clamped his hands above his head and dived into the abyss!

Zanigew zinged a bullet through the space where The Shadow had been.

Other revolvers added a belated tumult, drowning the echoes that came from the depths. With the cessation of gunfire, Zanigew supplied his metallic laugh.

What matter, if The Shadow had managed to prolong his life for a few seconds?

That pit had been sounded. At no spot had it shown water more than a foot in depth. Zanigew remembered Elthar's fate: Death on the shallow rocks that filled the entire bottom of the abyss.

The same fate for The Shadow. The pit was a blackened tomb that held a new, and more important, victim. That thought pleased Zanigew. His men, too, showed their relish of the situation.

Zanigew saw many grins as he ordered his men to march above and prepare for prompt departure from the stronghold.

CHAPTER XVI
THE BROKEN TRAIL

A MAN was seated at a table, his back to the door of a small, square room. Beside him was a radio set; at the wall in front of him, a switchboard. On the table, a sheet of paper, which the man was studying beneath a lamplight.

From a maze of letters, the man picked two words separated by one that he disregarded. They were odd words, that other persons had supposed to be in code:

XXUNA GAXSX

Writing those words as one, the man crossed out every letter X. His result was the simple statement of a single word, with a letter for its signature:

UNAGA S.

Putting the earphones to his head, the man pressed a plug into the switchboard. He dialed a number, waited for the reply, then said in a matter-of-fact tone:

"Burbank speaking."

A voice came across the wire. Burbank gave methodical information, the word "Unaga" forming part of his discourse. When he had finished, he hung up the earphones and went back to other duties.

Elsewhere, a young man soon made a hurried exit from a hotel lobby and hailed a cab. Soon, he was riding posthaste along the steep streets of San Francisco. Reaching a big building, he went up to an office and spoke to the girl at an information desk.

"My name is Vincent," he announced. "I must see Mr. Marquette at once! Tell him it's Harry Vincent."

Three minutes later, Vic Marquette was staring across a desk listening to the story that Harry Vincent gave him. To Marquette, this clean-cut visitor was an old friend, and an important one. For Vic Marquette had long connected Harry Vincent with that mysterious being known as The Shadow.

"It's an F.B.I. job, all right," agreed Marquette. "Tracing those crazy messages with the dash-dot signature is important, because it may have something to do with the kidnapping of James Dansell. But according to direction finders, that last message came from Puget Sound, and not from out in the Pacific."

"That doesn't hurt the facts," declared Harry. "I don't say that the message was sent from the steamship *Unaga*. I'm simply stating that the ship was mentioned."

Marquette had a copy of the message on his desk. The name *Unaga* was in it, right enough, and he noticed how the letter "X" had spaced it. He also saw the letter "S," all by itself, and thought immediately of The Shadow.

The steamship *Unaga*, Marquette recalled, was a large coastwise vessel that had taken a shipload of settlers to Alaska. She was returning southward, and had last been reported at Seattle.

Vic got busy on the telephone. After a hectic thirty minutes, he had accomplished a great deal. He reached for his hat when he hung up.

"They picked up the *Unaga*," he told Harry. "Everything's all right on board her, except that she got a shortwave call a while ago, asking her position. She's about four hundred miles north of 'Frisco, and I'm flying out to visit her. You can come along."

THREE hours later, a sleek seaplane dropped beside the long hull of the Unaga. The ocean was calm, so it was an easy matter for the plane's passengers to board the eighteen-thousand-ton steamer. After a short chat with the skipper, Marquette signaled for the seaplane to return to Frisco.

Harry Vincent watched the plane take off and disappear beyond a distant, low-lying mist that marked the California coast. He was still staring at the skyscape, when Marquette rejoined him.

"There's only one thing that's funny on this boat," announced the Fed. "That's the cargo that was taken on at Seattle."

"What was it?" queried Harry.

"That's the funniest part," replied Marquette. "All sorts of fancy canned goods and bottled stuff. Particularly, the last part. Most of the bottled goods was champagne."

It sounded odd to Harry. He remarked that champagne was produced in California, which made it superfluous as an import.

"This isn't domestic stuff," stated Marquette. "It's French champagne—the real McCoy! Why it came by way of Seattle beats me! Let's go down and look it over."

Vic didn't intend to sample the champagne. He merely wanted to learn if the cargo was as stated. He and Harry found the champagne, along with the fancy canned goods. There were other foodstuffs, staples that had also been loaded at Seattle.

A seaman had come with them. Marquette asked him about large stacks of boxes that were deep in the hold. They had also been loaded at Seattle and they were marked "FURNITURE," a statement that roused Marquette's doubts.

He and Harry hefted a box. It was very heavy. Marquette pried it open, gave a sudden whoop.

"Look at this, Vincent! Rifles—dozens of them! Say—maybe those other boxes hold machine guns! They look big enough—"

There was a gruff voice that interrupted. Marquette gave Harry a shove that sent him sprawling between two crates. Turning, Vic raised his hands. So did the seaman with him.

Two rough-dressed men had crawled from the other side of the hold. They looked like stowaways, but they hadn't boarded the *Unaga* just for an ocean trip. Each man held a businesslike revolver.

One of the pair evidently recognized Marquette.

"Keep 'em up, Fed!" he said. "You and this sailor Vincent."

The armed lurkers had heard Marquette speak to Harry, and had only seen the seaman with Vic. A bad slip on their part, for Harry overheard it. Creeping around behind the boxes, The Shadow's agent popped out suddenly.

His crisp words meant business: "Drop those guns!"

The toughs obeyed. Vic and Harry marched their prisoners up to the deck, with the sailor bringing along the discarded hardware. Cross-examination brought no responses from the men. They didn't want to talk.

"One thing," Marquette told the captain of the *Unaga*. "It means your crew is O.K., because if any of them had been approached and bribed, these stowaways wouldn't have been needed."

The captain agreed. He excused himself, to return to the bridge. Fog had been creeping out from shore; the *Unaga* was heading into it. Harry, watching the prisoners, saw them exchange wise grins. Marquette was about to march the men to a cabin.

"Wait a minute," suggested Harry, looking along the deck. "I've got an idea these fellows saw something they liked."

Marquette stared blankly.

"What could they have looked at?" he queried. "Outside of the fog?"

"Take a look at the fog!"

HARRY made that suggestion suddenly. The fog bank had just caught his full attention. It was a thick swirl of mist, writhing like smoke, a monster rising from the surface of the deep.

That fog was yellow, its color insidious!

"Say, maybe"—Marquette gulped, as he remembered something—"maybe that's the same sort of fog that hit the fishing village! The place where I went with Kent Allard!"

The fog had blanketed the *Unaga*. Bells were clanging, men shouting along the deck. There was something choking in the mist, that made Marquette stagger toward the rail. He kept his gun on the prisoners. It wasn't necessary. They were coughing also, but they still had their grins.

Reaching the rail, Harry grabbed for Marquette just as the man slid helpless to the deck. It was hitting Harry too, that poison-laden fog, but he managed to hold out a little longer. The engines had stopped their thrumming; from spots that the fog obscured, Harry could hear men fall to the deck.

Then out from the dense mist came invaders. They were in small boats, men with gas masks over their faces. Through a chance swirl in the fog, Harry saw the ship they came from—a low rakish vessel that had lurked in waiting for the *Unaga*.

With that last glimpse, Harry Vincent rolled unconscious beside the overpowered figure of Vic Marquette.

CHAPTER XVII
HIGH TIDE

A SEAPLANE skimmed the waters of Puget Sound and taxied into the shelter of a cove flanked by high cliffs. Ahead, its occupants saw a stretch of steep beach. They landed.

Looking upward, they saw a path that wormed its way among the rocks.

"We'd better take it," suggested the observer. "That shack we saw on the cliff is located about where the direction finders showed."

The pilot agreed. The two men started to scale

the cliff. Halfway up the path, they paused. Plain against the rocks, they signaled to a small boat a mile away. Men in the boat had already seen the plane; they started chugging a course toward the cove.

Resuming their climb, the aviators failed to glance below. They were too eager to investigate the shack at the top. They expected results, and they were due to find them. That shack was the entrance to Zanigew's deserted stronghold.

There was a sight below that might have interested the climbers. Out from a crevice in the rock crawled a slow-moving figure. Painfully, the tall creeper drew himself across a ledge. His foot struck a loose stone, sent it bouncing down the route that he had used.

Clatter faded; finally, the stone gave a faint splash.

The man from the crevice was The Shadow. He blinked at sight of daylight, then looked toward the water's edge. It was high tide again, which meant that he had lain in darkness many hours.

For it had been high tide when The Shadow took his dive into the abyss. He had heard that fact mentioned; it was why he had made a move which Zanigew had regarded as suicide.

The pit, as The Shadow had hoped, was a tidal basin. Elthar's plunge had been at low tide, The Shadow's at high. His dive had ended in water deep enough to prevent a crush upon the submerged rocks.

Long hours of waiting; then, when the tide had lowered, The Shadow had sought an outlet with it. That had been his greatest ordeal. He had been sucked beneath rocks; had swum underwater, through low-arched channels. At times, unruly currents had battered him against jagged surfaces.

Lost in a labyrinth worse than Zanigew's underground passages, The Shadow had been long delayed. The finish of his trip had been a battle against the incoming tide, until he had crawled up into a slanted fissure clear of the water.

There, his strength entirely spent, he had taken needed rest. After that, an upward crawl had brought sight of daylight; with it, a hum that The Shadow had recognized as coming from a plane.

He was looking now at that plane, silent in the cove. Yet he could still hear a chugging beyond a low-sloping point just past the cliff. It meant an approaching boat, summoned by a signal from the aviator.

Would that boat mean rescue?

The Shadow wasn't certain. It could mean rescue for the aviators, if they were marooned among the cliffs, for they had already signaled the boat. But it might mean otherwise to The Shadow, if these were persons who served Zanigew.

In his present dilemma, The Shadow was trusting no one but himself.

Weary, weaponless, he was at least confident that he still could fly a plane. The winged ship in the cove was like a magnet to him. Rising shakily, The Shadow steadied as he neared the water. Splashing into the tiny wavelets, he climbed onto the seaplane.

THE motor roared with a suddenness that riveted the men, on the heights.

Their frantic shouts were puny against that drone. Men gawked from the motorboat, as it rounded the point. Then, a thing of speed and power, the seaplane was lifting out into the Sound. It took off like a creature released from bondage.

Easing up on the controls at an altitude of five thousand feet, The Shadow soon learned that this plane belonged to friends. He found written orders, regarding the search for the source of the mysterious wireless signals. He discovered that the ship had a two-way radio.

Under certain circumstances, The Shadow might have returned to pick up the men who belonged in the ship. There was a reason, however, that caused him to forgo that deed.

Among the latest orders were instructions to report any word from the steamship *Unaga*, mysteriously vanished off the coast of California.

The Shadow resolved that he would be doing the aviators the greatest possible favor, if he did not return for them. He had a mission to perform and preferred it to be a one-man expedition. Aides were superfluous in a meeting with Zanigew's hordes on their own ground. The Shadow had at least demonstrated that he could survive a lone battle against them.

The Shadow had definitely linked the *Unaga* with Zanigew's plans. As Barreau, The Shadow had been assigned the task of arranging electrical barriers for an area that resembled the lines of a steamship. Lanyon's mention of the *Unaga* made the whole thing definite.

Later, however, The Shadow had seen to it that Zanigew, no matter how he fared, would lack the protection of Barreau's electrical devices. The master crook had unquestionably captured the *Unaga*, but his only way to keep the ship out of trouble would be to hide it in an artificial fog.

Establishing radio contact with heads of the searching party, The Shadow coolly reported the plane by number and awaited a reply. He had found a small locker packed with sandwiches and a thermos bottle containing coffee. He was downing those supplies while he listened.

There were revolvers, too, in the plane. They would come handy against Zanigew. The Shadow was examining one of the weapons, when a return call came. He placed the gun down, while he took the message.

Instructions were to complete the search near Puget Sound. Other planes were scouting for the *Unaga.*

The Shadow asked for complete weather reports. He wanted specific details regarding fog in any area. Detailed word came back, with mention of a small but dense fog directly south of the spot where the *Unaga* had last been reported.

To The Shadow, that fog meant the *Unaga* itself. Probably other aviators had watched the mist, hoping that the steamer might poke its bow in sight. It wouldn't occur to them that the fog itself could be a veil that moved with the *Unaga.*

Rough calculation indicated that The Shadow's plane might overtake the creeping fog about a hundred miles northwest of San Francisco. Darkness, however, might prove a troublesome element when it came. Clear starlight could show the yellowish fog, when once The Shadow neared it; but he couldn't leave too much to chance.

Foreseeing certain moves by Zanigew, The Shadow decided upon added measures, for emergency.

Coding words by one of his own intricate systems, The Shadow announced them as a message that he had picked up. He subtly added that they had been signed in the dash-dot fashion. He knew that such a message would be given to hundreds of experts who were trying to crack Zanigew's codes.

Burbank, The Shadow's contact man, had connections with certain of those code experts. Once The Shadow's agent saw the message, he would recognize its real origin. Burbank would decipher it, and follow its orders to the smallest detail.

As for the code experts, they would remain quite as puzzled as if the message had actually been dispatched by the unknown Zanigew.

One minor problem concerned The Shadow. It was the matter of Zanigew's rakish rumrunner that had taken crime's emperor to his capture of the *Unaga.* That craft had not been reported from any source. The obvious inference was that Zanigew had sunk it, since it was no longer needed.

Only the *Unaga* counted. That ship was the floating nucleus of Zanigew's rising empire. A Napoleon of crime, the mastermind had plans which surpassed ordinary belief. Yet, to The Shadow, they were obvious; for he had analyzed the processes of Zanigew's gigantic brain.

Mere hours separated Zanigew from a long-sought goal that he would seek despite the lack of his electrical barrier. Risen from depths, The Shadow intended to drop from the sky, again the lone challenger who could thwart his super foe's great scheme.

The same fog that shrouded the *Unaga* would hide The Shadow, once he landed within its fringes. Then to deal with Zanigew!

It was high tide for The Shadow's hopes!

CHAPTER XVIII
CRIME RULES ANEW

THE steamship *Unaga* formed the exact center of a tiny fog working steadily south. That mist was yellowish, ominous, and other ships avoided it. The fog seemed ruled by the speed of a light but steady breeze, for off on the horizon, a small schooner was keeping pace with it.

That, however, was purely a chance occurrence. Zanigew was holding the *Unaga* to a speed of a few knots, simply to avoid attention. A fast-driving fog would be too peculiar to pass unreported by the occasional planes that droned overhead.

Those planes puzzled the crew of the little sailing ship; but they didn't perplex Zanigew. He knew that they were searching for the *Unaga,* and he didn't like it. In the best cabin that the steamer boasted, Zanigew was storming at the men who served him as electricians.

Fearfully, they had made final admission that they could not repair Barreau's electrical equipment.

Suddenly, Zanigew raised his massive head. Rage was gone from his ruddy eyes. He grated an order in a tone that promised solution of the problem.

"Bring Barreau's men!" Zanigew commanded. "All of them! Here, to this cabin!"

Dubious henchmen went to bring the prisoners. They could see no useful purpose in the mandate. It was common knowledge that none of Barreau's workers shared the inventor's secrets. Hilgard, the spy, had been unable, with all his treachery, to learn any such details.

In fact, Barreau had seemed so clever in the past, that none of Zanigew's men had been surprised when he proved to be The Shadow. Even Zanigew had accepted the obvious; but his mind had taken a sudden change.

When the prisoners stood lined up in the cabin, Zanigew moved from man to man, studying each face. All were silent, stolid. They had realized, soon after their capture, that Zanigew was practical as well as merciless. Their lives were safe as long as they might prove useful. It would be folly, therefore to be sullen or defiant. Resignation was their common attitude.

Without a word, Zanigew clamped a viselike grip on one man's shoulder. In metallic tone, he ordered his men to remove the others. When all were gone Zanigew pointed the lone prisoner to a chair. He eyed the man's longish features, tiny eyes, the conspicuous high-bridged nose. Then:

"You are clever!" declared Zanigew in clanging tone, "I admire cleverness, Professor Barreau."

The hook-nosed man could not restrain a flinch.

"No fear." Zanigew's voice lacked malice. "It does not matter whether you, or The Shadow, decided on the ruse. You worked together, and you did well.

"You even saved me trouble in disposing of Hilgard. I dislike traitors even when they serve me. Once, Barreau, I made you a fair offer. It still stands. Come!"

ZANIGEW led Barreau to a lower cabin, where the damaged electrical apparatus was on display. He asked the professor how soon it could be repaired. Barreau shook his head at sight of ruined tubes and coils.

"Impossible!" he said at last. "These cannot be replaced."

"But, perhaps"—Zanigew's voice was harsh—"you may be able to adapt substitute materials? We have a great deal of electrical equipment on board."

"I can try."

Barreau's tone was almost hopeful, as though he had become suddenly willing to serve Zanigew. Ruddy eyes drew the professor's gaze in a powerful, hypnotic manner. Barreau stared despite himself, and he stared too long.

"As I thought!" came the clanging tone. "You are playing safe, Professor. Clever of you, to say that you can try! When a man so speaks, it means that he can succeed!"

Barreau started to stammer his doubts. He was shaking off Zanigew's influence; but he had already botched matters. Barreau had almost admitted a fact that The Shadow had not known.

Though essential for long-range protection, Barreau's special devices were not needed in producing electrical barriers. He could do a good enough job to protect the area close about the *Unaga* with ordinary equipment.

There was a sharp snap from Zanigew's fingers. Two of his husky followers appeared. The skull-faced overlord gave a three-word order:

"Bring the girl!"

A few minutes later, Fay Tretter arrived in the cabin. Zanigew's sharp eyes spotted recognition between her and Barreau. Again his fingers snapped, this time in repetition. It was a coded signal.

Leering followers brought in a heavy chair fitted with clamps. Fay was placed in the device. Her ankles, wrists, and neck were shackled in the chair. Next came a boxlike cover that fitted over the chair and its occupant, exactly to shape.

The cover was equipped with panes of glass set in square frames. Each panel was studded with round chunks of metal that looked like bolt heads. A cord was plugged into a socket; the chair began to hum.

You have heard of the 'Spanish Maiden'," said Zanigew, to Barreau. "An old-fashioned torture device that brings death when it is closed, thanks to the spikes that line its interior.

"This is my adaptation of the Spanish Maiden: instead of spikes, it contains needle points set deep in the steel studs. The current"—Zanigew's tone clanged solemnly—"is pushing those needles inward. Their motion is slow, almost imperceptible.

"But in about two hours"—there was evil anticipation in the voice—"those needles will penetrate! The torture will be far more exquisite than that of the Spanish Maiden! You will hear screams, for there are airholes in the box. You will see the victim's agony—"

Barreau interrupted with a cry. He was gesticulating toward his own equipment. Zanigew waited. Barreau's words became coherent.

"More than two hours!" he pleaded. "Longer—say fifteen minutes longer—"

"Two hours only!"

BARREAU went feverish. He was shouting to Zanigew's men, telling them the things they needed. They moved briskly, for Zanigew's eyes commanded them. Barreau gulped that he could use assistants; his own men, preferably. Zanigew produced them promptly.

All the while that Barreau labored, he fought off two huge mental hazards. One was the buzz of the motor that controlled the needle-lined box. The other was a clock that ticked from the cabin wall, marking off the terrible minutes.

At the end of an hour and three quarters, crackles came from Barreau's machine. He turned to Zanigew, all the while a spectator, and gave an eager nod. Zanigew shook his head, pointed to the deck. Barreau turned off his apparatus, ordered the men outside with it.

Posts were already placed along the rail of the *Unaga;* two skeleton towers were planted in the deck. Barreau shouted for men to wire up the posts. He sent others scrambling like monkeys to the tops of the towers. It took ten minutes before the hookup was complete. Barreau yanked a lever.

Sharp crackles broke into a buzzing rhythm, from the towers as well as the posts. Barreau sank sobbing to the deck; then recovered, to stagger to the cabin. Zanigew was already there, pointing to the switch. A man tugged it.

Carefully, two others lifted the cover that encased the chair. Jutting needle points plucked Fay's dress, ripping long runners in it, as the girl shrank tightly in the chair. Her arm quivered as a line of needles scratched it. The result was slight, but Zanigew tongued a fierce-toned disapproval at his men.

He was keeping his promise to Barreau and was anxious that it be entirely fulfilled. For Zanigew could give reward as well as punishment. He was elated, as he listened to the hum of the electrical barriers; further pleased, when he suddenly caught the drone of a plane somewhere beyond the cloud bank that covered the *Unaga*.

Had Zanigew known the identity of that plane's pilot, his lips, for once, might have shown a full smile.

High in the dark, The Shadow was turning down the seaplane's motors. He had sighted the mist he wanted; had finally identified its yellowness against the sea's darkened surface.

Distant, beneath the starlight, was a tiny patch of white, a schooner's sail, that formed a contrast to the fog's ocher hue. Banking around the fog area, The Shadow saw its oval shape. He knew that the *Unaga* was the core.

Cutting down the motor further, The Shadow dived the plane for the fog's fringe. A coasting finish along the mist-clad water would bring him alongside the hidden steamer. The fog's mass seemed to rise in greeting. The motor coughed in answer.

Instantly, The Shadow took the warning. He was flinging himself from the plane before he realized why he was bailing out. The motor was choking ahead of him, deeper into the fog. Here was an emergency unexpected; but The Shadow had instinctively prepared for it. He was girded with a harness that had a parachute attached to it.

AS The Shadow's hand tugged the cord, an explosion rocketed above the water, deep toward the center of the fog. Flames were tinged a dull orange, lost in the muddy mist. That was the finish of The Shadow's borrowed plane.

Water below. The Shadow had drifted from the moving fog. The ocean gripped him; he was flinging away the parachute's folds. He pulled the harness from his shoulders and floated free, sustained by a lifebelt tight about his waist.

Barreau was the answer. The Shadow could picture many possible ways by which Zanigew could have forced the professor to new feats of wizardry. For the plane's own fate told that the electrical barriers were in actual operation.

First the motors halt, as Barreau had described. Then the explosion of the gas tanks. Death for a hapless pilot either in the blast or by electrocution. Barreau had specified that climax. But The Shadow had avoided it. He had bailed out far enough from the current's strongest field.

Life for The Shadow: that, at least remained. But despite The Shadow's survival, Zanigew was continuing toward his goal. The creeping fog was gone, a low bank of yellow, far toward the horizon.

Left in the *Unaga*'s wake, The Shadow was a speck in the Pacific!

CHAPTER XIX
ZANIGEW'S GOAL

A HALF-GLOOM filled Zanigew's palatial cabin. It was the effect of sunlight filtering through the fog. Though murky, the glow lacked being sickly yellow, for Zanigew was no longer pouring gas into the fog.

The master crook had a better protection: that steady wave of current that the towers flung forth into the air, making the fog a deadly hazard for any who approached.

Before Zanigew stood two prisoners men who had been captured with the *Unaga*. Crime's overlord was interviewing Vic Marquette and Harry Vincent.

"You are fortunate," announced the skull-faced criminal. "The sleep that I gave you was swift, but not prolonged. I needed this vessel's crew to work for me. Enough of them have been persuaded to do so.

"The rest have joined my other prisoners below. Since you two were passengers, I have decided that you shall be my guests, along with other privileged persons."

There was something in Zanigew's tone that added a different reason for his leniency. The master crook was moving to some triumph. He wanted the appreciation of certain spectators. Marquette was one; as a member of the F.B.I., he would be properly awed by the magnitude of Zanigew's methods.

Harry Vincent was in the same class. Zanigew had identified him as Marquette's companion. However they had happened to fly out to the *Unaga*, both had come on the same mission. In his role of host, Zanigew was willing to allow them equal privilege.

The prisoners were marched out to the deck. They arrived at the vessel's stern, to join a small group of persons who gazed askance at Zanigew's approach. Politely, but with his unassuming smile, Zanigew introduced the newcomers to the company.

Harvey Lanyon, James Dansell—those names were instantly recognized by Harry and Vic. They had never heard of Glade Tretter and his daughter,

Fay. But the name of Eugene Barreau awakened recollections.

"These gentlemen," said Zanigew, indicating the inventors, "have collaborated with me. In justice to their integrity—or should I say their folly?—have helped me against their will. Nevertheless, the results are the same."

He turned, pointing forward. Harry saw squatty, wide-mouthed objects that looked like trench mortars. As he watched, they gave mighty belchings. Bomblike missiles sped up into the grimy fog, to puff spreading clouds of white that added thickness to the mist.

"Lanyon's invention," remarked Zanigew. "Those puffs induce moisture. They bring fog"—he looked contemptuously at Lanyon—"instead of rain. You have my gratitude, Fog-maker!"

Lanyon winced at the backhanded compliment. Ignoring him, Zanigew pointed to large tanks beside the mortars.

"Dansell's contribution," he rasped. "The sleep gas! Intended to make warfare less horrible. We tried the gas in Lanyon's bombs, but the process was wasteful. It works better with the fog-breakers supplied by my good friend Tretter."

The fog-breakers reminded Harry of huge grass sprinklers. They were revolving slowly, sending out jets of air, for the fog whipped away from them. Men were fixing pipes from the gas tanks to the sprinklers.

"When those pipes are opened," stated Zanigew, "the gas will be carried with the air jets. That gas mixes readily with fog. You will not be troubled from it, here on deck. Its effects carry farther, off into the fog itself."

Zanigew was starting forward. He paused, turned about to give a mock bow.

"My final compliments to Barreau," he declared. "The buzz you hear, about and above you, come from his electrical barriers. I find the sound quite pleasant."

THEY watched Zanigew's great, rangy figure stride toward the bridge. His departure brought relief, but it was only temporary. In hushed tones, the spectators began to compare opinions.

Chances for escape were nil. Zanigew's guards patrolled the decks, heavily armed. Crew members were about, but Zanigew had carefully culled them from the lot that he had captured with the *Unaga*. The ones that he had chosen to man the vessel were a submissive-looking lot; and there were not many of them.

True, they might rally in case mutiny proved possible; but it would take a strong cause to urge them. As for the prisoners below, it would be a hard job to release them unless it could be accomplished without Zanigew's knowledge. That, in turn, seemed quite impossible.

Silent, Harry Vincent thought of The Shadow. He felt that his chief could swing the tide. The Shadow was a human spark who could set off tremendous blasts, once he entered into action. But there had been no sign of The Shadow; no trace of him.

For once, Harry felt an overwhelming fear that The Shadow must be dead. In a fair duel with Zanigew, Harry would have staked anything on The Shadow's victory. But Zanigew was master of many competent followers. Trapped by such a horde, even The Shadow might have found no escape.

Whispers buzzed among the inventors. They were talking of ways to offset Zanigew's power. Guards drew closer, suspicion in their gaze. Marquette spoke suddenly, giving a cue to end the chatter. Changing the subject, Vic remarked:

"Guess we're heading west. Zanigew has got to be going somewhere. He likes trouble. Maybe he's picked China."

Others disagreed. They thought the course was south. All were looking upward, hoping for some glimpse of the sun, when they heard the *clang* of a signal bell.

A moment later, they noticed the absence of the incessant buzz that had marked the progress of the *Unaga*. It was Lanyon who exclaimed, delightedly:

"The electrical barrier is ended!"

All glanced toward Barreau. He was very pale. His eyes went toward Fay, who smiled bravely. Chokingly, Barreau addressed the girl.

"It's not my fault," he gasped. "I did my best! Nothing should have happened! Zanigew may listen—"

Something produced a twilight upon the deck. It was like a wide cloud, blocking the filtered sunlight. Harry looked upward; he thought he saw a blimp in the mist. Had some strange thing of the air descended to halt the protective current?

No. The buzz had resumed, in response to another signal bell. Barreau sighed relief. The halt of the current, its resumption, had been at Zanigew's order.

"A test, perhaps," muttered Barreau. "Like the ones I used to make."

The brief incident produced silence. All were wondering what it signified. The *Unaga* was nosing onward; men had suddenly become busy along the decks. There was a hiss, as the fog-breaking sprinklers began to revolve more rapidly. Zanigew's men yanked levers at the sides of pipes.

Yellowish gas jetted clear of the deck. The fog seemed to scoop the vapor greedily. The mortars were at work shooting puffy bombs in quick succession, thickening the mist, helping it to absorb the gas.

The deck had become an oasis in a vast desert of fog. The fog-breakers were working at full speed, to get the gas away. That, in turn, meant that the surrounding atmosphere was saturating rapidly with the sleep-bringing vapor.

Zanigew's men were donning gas masks. It looked as if they were ready for some raid upon the *Unaga*.

Harry wondered if he had seen a ship back there in the thickness. Maybe the fog produced reflected shapes. He looked at Vic Marquette, saw puzzlement as great as his own. Then both became as tense as those about them.

The *Unaga* was almost halted. A shiver shook the vessel, as the bow grazed some object that they could not see. It occurred to Harry that they must have reached a pier. His guess was right, as he learned a moment later when Fay Tretter gave a cry:

"Look!"

High in the fog, where the girl was pointing, reared a weird, unexpected sight. It was like some medieval castle, transported to modern times and planted in mid-ocean. A mammoth citadel, yellowed by the gas-laden fog.

Then from Vic Marquette came the utterance that told them where they were. Vic's tone was hollowed by an awed recollection of a place that he had seen before.

One word was all Vic spoke:

"Alcatraz!"

CHAPTER XX
THE ROCK FALLS

OUT from the fog—"The Rock"!

Alcatraz, the fortress-prison in San Francisco Bay! A Gibraltar against attack—a Devil's Island which allowed no escape. Entombed alive within its walls were men whose criminal talents were the greatest in America, perhaps in all the world.

Men that the government had segregated in one spot where they could be controlled; for, on Alcatraz, big shot criminals became rank-and-file prisoners. Unable to stir up mutiny in such surroundings, even masterminds became impotent in the confines of The Rock.

Yet that system had one flaw.

Except for the few prisoners who had become "stir bugs," the occupants of Alcatraz still possessed their scheming brains. In effect, The Rock was more than a prison. It was a repository for criminal genius: the abode of public enemies.

Zanigew needed generals to aid him in Napoleonic achievements. He could have culled the country, finding only few. Big shots, active and at large, might have scorned the chance to play second fiddle, even to Zanigew.

Here, in Alcatraz, Zanigew had found many instead of few. The law, itself, had gathered them, ready for the taking—men who would gladly accept Zanigew's own conditions, when they recognized him as their liberator.

Until this moment, the magnitude of Zanigew's dream had occurred to no one except The Shadow. He, by sheer deduction, had finally foreseen Zanigew's goal. That was the portent of The Shadow's message to Burbank: to see that The Rock was guarded.

The advice had not been followed. The authorities were to blame, not Burbank. They had ignored the warning that had reached them. Alcatraz, of all strongholds, could certainly protect itself.

Against ordinary onslaught, perhaps; but Zanigew's measures were irresistible.

Fog was burying the prison citadel; the mist had taken a curiously lopsided shape. Controlling the fog-breakers from the bridge, Zanigew was speeding their spurts on the port side of the steamer. On that side, around Alcatraz itself, the fog was yellow-dyed. It was seeping into the fortress.

Electrical barriers no longer crackled from the port rail. Those on the starboard side were buzzing amid whitish fog. So were the high towers, that laid their invisible cordon in a huge, inverted bowl above both Alcatraz and the *Unaga*.

Onto the pier poured Zanigew's shock troops, wearing their ghoulish gas masks. They had rifles but they did not need to use them. Harry and the other spectators could see stumbling defenders, who sagged before attackers reached them.

Dansell's sleep gas was doing its quick work.

Masked men reached the yellow-stained citadel. Alarms were clanging; rifles talked in answer. There was a chatter of machine guns; the wave of invaders suddenly receded toward the *Unaga*. Zanigew's reserves were lugging up their own machine guns, to offset those inside the fortress.

The clatter faded. Gas had reached the men who guarded the portals. Zanigew's horde surged forward. Again there were rifle shots, more and more muffled. Clanging alarms had faded. Zanigew ordered a telephone cable to be dragged into the fog, so that he could keep constant contact with his advancing warriors.

A whine, far overhead. Another, that ended in an explosion high above. At last, The Shadow's advice had been accepted. Alarms from Alcatraz had told that the place was beleaguered.

Big guns were shooting for The Rock, from Mare Island, in San Pablo Bay. Under that barrage, marines were coming from the Navy yard. More bursts resounded; but Zanigew was not perturbed.

Those shells were shattering when they reached the invisible barrier. If motorboats arrived, they would find that their engines halted. Venturing marines would sizzle, should they approach too close.

There was a chance, however, that the current might lack full intensity on the other side of Alcatraz Island. Zanigew had made allowance for that fact by planning his raid as a swift one. He was talking over the telephone, urging prompt reports. Expected word came back.

ZANIGEW clanged a signal. The poison gas was cut off. The fog began to whiten. Harry and the watchers beside him knew that the attackers must have subdued the few defenders who had not succumbed from the sleep gas.

Oblivious to the increasing burst of Navy shells, Zanigew studied the color of the haze. It suited him. He rasped a command, then hung up the telephone. Arms folded, he gazed triumphantly from the bridge, as if surveying a field of conquest.

Out from the citadel came a few of the attackers, pulling the gas masks from their heads. They sniffed the air, felt no ill effects. They turned about and shouted. From within the walls came a long, exultant yell, throated by many voices.

Next, running men, a mass of them, poured for the pier, hailing the *Unaga* as they came. Men, all clad alike in prison costume. Invaders had unlocked the cells; the prisoners were free. On the bridge, they saw Zanigew. Hundreds of voices rose in tribute to crime's emperor.

Lifting one folded arm, Zanigew made pointing gestures with his forefinger. Certain prisoners understood; they grated orders at the others. Men shifted into squads, each with a commander. In turn, those groups clambered aboard the *Unaga*.

Vic Marquette gave an awed gasp close to Harry's ear.

"He must have gotten word inside!" voiced Vic, in reference to Zanigew. "It got to the ones he wanted! Look at the way they're organized!"

Harry nodded. He was thinking of the men left on Alcatraz. Fortunately the defenders had made only a brief resistance. Probably only a few of them had died. Zanigew, in his accustomed fashion, had spared the rest, because he regarded them as harmless.

That, at least, was a helpful factor. But Harry realized that there might be times when Zanigew would order wholesale slaughter, if convictions made it worth while. That thought was something of a premonition. Harry was about to see such a deed enacted.

Counting the squads, Marquette calculated the released prisoners at a total of three hundred, about seventy short of the full quota imprisoned on Alcatraz. The invaders had probably rejected some, at Zanigew's order, leaving behind those who were ill or otherwise unfit for use.

All were aboard, and Zanigew's shock troops were following from the pier. Above, the bursting shells were producing a display of mighty pyrotechnics that sent visible brilliance through the thickish fog.

Suddenly, the posts on the port side began to buzz. Zanigew was starting the full current, restoring the completed barrier. The *Unaga* had become immune to any flank attack. The ship was in motion, swinging from the pier.

The fog went with it, drawn closer, for the air sprinklers had slowed their whirl. The ship swung about; from the stern, Harry and his companions could see the heights of Alcatraz fading in the fog.

The screaming of shells no longer sounded overhead. Instead, it was coming from behind the *Unaga,* accompanied by thunderous crashes. No longer protected by the arched electrical barrier, Alcatraz was receiving the effects of the bombardment.

That soon would cease. When the moving fog had drawn clear with the *Unaga,* viewers of the silent citadel would know the truth. Impregnable Alcatraz had been conquered!

Zanigew had proven master of The Rock!

CHAPTER XXI
ZANIGEW DECREES

IT looked like Old Home Week aboard the *Unaga,* as the ship veered its five-hundred-and-fifty-foot length through San Francisco Bay. Prisoners upon the deck were dancing all about; whacking the backs of others and shaking hands with pals.

Some were starting up to the bridge to voice their thanks to Zanigew. He stopped them with a gesture. Leaning to a microphone, he rasped words that became a thunderous command, when amplified by a loudspeaker.

"Order!" commanded Zanigew. "Form your squads! Watch straight ahead!"

All obeyed, including the little group of actual prisoners huddled at the stern. Harry heard an awed voice—Fay's—close beside him.

"What will be next?" inquired the girl. "What else can happen, after all that we have witnessed?"

Harry racked his brain. A recollection flashed: The thing that he had seen in the fog before reaching Alcatraz. Its bulk, he remembered, had reminded him of a blimp, but that was because he had believed that they were far out at sea.

"The Golden Gate Bridge!"

Harry voiced the words in an excited tone. Vic Marquette took up the theme.

"That's why the barriers were cut off!" exclaimed Vic. "So nobody would know that we were sneaking up on The Rock! They took us for a fog; that was all. But now—"

A stray bomb burst above the *Unaga*. It was Fay Tretter who sighed a terrified understanding.

"Zanigew can't afford to cut off the currents," expressed the girl. "We shall have a sample of his ruthless ways. That is why he told us to look ahead."

Despite herself, Fay could not turn away; nor could the others. They felt that they were about to see a cataclysm that would never be forgotten. While such thoughts were flashing in their minds, the horror came.

Something stretched across the fog bank. It was the bridge above the Golden Gate, two hundred feet above the channel, its long span spreading off into the mist. For a mere instant, the bridge was a darkish mass. Then it caught the barrier current.

With a horrendous crackle, the whole bridge became a mass of sparkling fireworks. Its cables seemed to quiver from the juice that whipped along the forty-two-hundred-foot span, climbing to the high towers that supported it.

An uncanny effect was produced by the increase of the current, as the *Unaga* came closer below. It seemed that the electricity crawled to the tops of those seven-hundred-and-forty-foot towers.

A few seconds later, the *Unaga* was squarely below the bridge. The current was at its full intensity. From all along the bridge came sharp explosions, accompanied by bursts of light. They looked like popping firecrackers, when seen from the steamer's stern.

Fay's gasp was audible, despite the mammoth crackling, that still shook the bridge.

"Those can't be bombs!"

"No." Harry's tone was grim. "They were automobiles! Their gas tanks exploded!"

Fay's fists clenched. It was she who had said that Zanigew would prove ruthless. She hadn't realized how true her words would be. From the number of explosions, she could estimate deaths at hundreds.

THEY were past the bridge, now. The mighty structure had stood the test without harm. The sparks receded, the crackles faded down to their usual hum. For a few minutes, Harry and Fay could imagine that they saw a glowing shape back in the fog, representing the red-hot metal of the bridge.

That might have been imagination. But the voice that suddenly drilled their ears was no fantasy. Zanigew had come to join them.

"My thanks!" he told them, in his metallic tone. "You formed an appreciative group of spectators. Having witnessed my power, you may be more willing to continue in my service."

His words were addressed to the inventors, but he included Harry and Fay, along with Vic Marquette. For a while, there was silence; then Barreau questioned suddenly:

"The other prisoners?"

"They shall be treated well," assured Zanigew, "and given a chance to serve me, also. But let us consider your own status, since that of others depends upon it.

"Which will you be, Professor? My prisoner or my guest?"

Barreau accepted the inevitable. He agreed to serve Zanigew. Tretter followed with the same decision, for he was concerned over Fay's safety. Lanyon capitulated, but Dansell shook his head.

"A majority is sufficient," decided Zanigew, indulgently. "You may all remain free, within reasonable limitations, except Dansell. Take him below"—this was to two guards—"and place him there with the other prisoners."

While Dansell was being led to the hold, Zanigew gave a parting bow to the others. He remarked that he could not neglect his new guests, three hundred in number. With that, he strode away.

Two groups separated at the stern. One included the three inventors, all trying to excuse themselves for having sworn fealty to Zanigew. In the other cluster were Harry, Vic and Fay.

"Zanigew just about ignored us," declared Harry. "We can still take a chance on some kind of attempt to escape, and argue ourselves out of it if we fluke."

"Unless he comes back," put in Vic, sourly, "and makes us give our oath. It will be curtains, if we try anything after that."

"Whatever we do," insisted Fay, in an undertone, "we've got to leave father and the others out of it. They've given their word to Zanigew."

All agreed that prompt action would be needed. They could wait until dusk, but no later. Zanigew might remember them, before this night was over. There was another factor that occurred to Vic Marquette. He put it logically to the others.

"The shore authorities must be wise to Zanigew by this time," declared Vic. "Which means that his fog is a giveaway. But once he runs into a real fog, he can do a sneak. After that, he might bob up anywhere, with nobody to spot him."

GRADUALLY, the three hatched their plan. There was only one point of suitable attack. That was the ship's bridge, where the controls were located. Once they were there, they could shut off most of Zanigew's devices.

Fog bombs could still be puffed into the atmosphere; but the poison gas could not be utilized, for Zanigew was using the air sprinklers to pump it. Those sprinklers were controlled from the bridge.

The same applied to the electrical barriers. Whoever held the bridge could end them. But the capture of that vital spot would be no easy task. Every approach was held by Zanigew's guards, and their ample number was never lessened.

Behind the bridge was the superstructure, which boasted two large funnels. A few guards were lounging on the roof of the upper deck, covering the space around the funnels; but their main job seemed to be that of watching events below. As Harry gazed, he saw that one guard was looking at the people near the stern.

Turning, Harry leaned his elbows on the rail, whispering for the others to do the same. With Vic on one side, Fay on the other, and all three apparently staring at the sea, Harry undertoned his plan. His comrades agreed that it was feasible, although the hazards were so numerous that it seemed almost certain of failure.

"I'm for it, anyway," decided Harry. "If we pass it up, we'll all regret it—worse than if we tried and took the consequences. How about it—are you game?"

Vic and Fay supplied affirmative responses. By mutual agreement, they decided to forget the matter until dusk. The less they thought about it, the better. Zanigew seemed to have an uncanny faculty for ferreting out persons who schemed against him.

Fay walked over to talk with her father regarding other subjects. Vic Marquette strolled forward with no apparent purpose. Harry Vincent alone remained at the stern, staring back into the following fog that seemed to rise from the Pacific's bosom.

Harry was thinking of The Shadow. Could his chief be present, any strategy might work; even the wild plan that Harry had himself propounded. As it stood, the coming attempt would be no more than a last defiant gesture against Zanigew.

With The Shadow, anything was possible, could he but reach the spot where his hand was needed. But the *Unaga* was one place where arrival was impossible, while the electrical barriers functioned.

Such was Harry's complete conviction, and it eliminated any prospect of assistance from The Shadow.

Even if The Shadow still lived!

CHAPTER XXII
THE SHADOW RETURNS

A RATTLETRAP car stopped at the north end of the Golden Gate Bridge, flagged down before it could cross the span. A pair of marines looked over the hawk-faced driver, then made a search of the car's interior. The driver asked what was up. One marine was obliging enough to tell him.

"Some mystery ship came in and out with the fog," he explained. "It tried to demolish the bridge. The word went out though, quick enough to save the people."

"The people?"

"Yeah. The ones that stalled their cars on the bridge. They got excited, some of them. But the center lanes were clear. Other cars went through and picked them up."

The hawkish driver looked puzzled. The marine explained that the abandoned cars had gone up in smoke, from explosions of their gas tanks. As he motioned for the driver to be on his way, the marine pointed out to Alcatraz Island.

"Take a look at The Rock," he suggested. "That's where the trouble started! They had a jail-break there—a big one!"

Crossing the bridge, The Shadow looked toward Alcatraz. Men were climbing about the fortress, piling up debris from shattered walls. From what the marine had told him, The Shadow could picture all the details.

The warning about Alcatraz had not been heeded. But when trouble actually swept the rocky island, the authorities had remembered the word they had received. There had been a second order: to clear all traffic from the Golden Gate Bridge. They had done that in a hurry.

A grim laugh trailed from The Shadow's lips. Zanigew had performed in the style that The Shadow expected. He had sneaked the *Unaga* under the bridge the first time, but had bombarded it with electric current while outward bound.

Somewhere off in the Pacific, crime's emperor was moving away in search of actual fog to absorb the oval-shaped shroud that represented the *Unaga.* A few hours of precious day remained. Time, even yet, to overtake the master foe before darkness aided him.

Getting back to 'Frisco had been a slow process for The Shadow. Dawn had brought him luck, for he had been sighted by a fishing schooner. The sailing craft had heard the seaplane explode and had heaved to for the night. Close by, it had picked up The Shadow.

Then had come delay as irksome as the long exposure in the water. Lacking breeze, the schooner had taken hours to come ashore in a little bay many miles north of the Golden Gate. The Shadow had taken a ten-mile hike before he reached a hamlet where a car could be hired.

The Shadow made an incongruous sight, when he reached the hotel where he still was registered as Kent Allard. The doorman gaped at the ramshackle dust-streaked car and its occupant, attired in rough, ill-fitting clothes.

The desk clerk, however, smiled when he recognized Allard. He decided that the aviator must have made a forced landing, and experienced difficulty getting back to town.

Upon reaching his room, The Shadow called Burbank. He held an important conversation with his contact man. His first questions concerned an autogiro. Burbank replied that it was at the 'Frisco airport. He said that Miles Crofton, The Shadow's private pilot, was still busy with the alterations, but that they would be completed within an hour.

That news pleased The Shadow. He had other orders for Burbank. Stupendous orders that would have produced amazement from any other listener. Burbank received them in his usual manner. Methodically, he acknowledged with:

"Instructions received."

HIS call finished, The Shadow had time to change his attire. When dressed, he still appeared as Kent Allard, but the bag that he packed carried evidence of The Shadow.

In that suitcase, Allard stowed a brace of automatics. He added a black cloak and slouch hat that he had brought in a secret compartment in a trunk. Carrying the bag, Allard went down to the street and had the doorman call a cab.

Southward past the city limits, the taxi followed the Bayshore Highway to Mills Field, the Municipal Airport. An autogiro was standing near a hangar, with a man who looked like a mechanic tinkering about it.

The giro was the newest style of ship, completely wingless, capable of making remarkable descents. There had been a curious throng about it a while ago, but they had left. Miles Crofton, who had flown the autogiro here, had given them to understand that the ship would not fly again that afternoon.

Allard's voice brought Crofton from the cockpit. A slight twinge of disappointment showed on Crofton's face. He was in The Shadow's service, and had hoped that his chief would fly the ship today. Instead, The Shadow had assigned the job to Kent Allard.

Acquainted with Allard, Crofton supposed that he was another of The Shadow's agents. Crofton always identified The Shadow as a globe-trotting, big-game-hunting millionaire named Lamont Cranston; never as Kent Allard. Preserving the

MILES CROFTON

secret of his actual identity was important to The Shadow, even with his most trusted agents.

Allard asked about the gas tank, Crofton indicated a lever.

"Greased to a fare-you-well!" he stated. "One yank, you could dump a hundred gallons in a jiffy!"

"And the cockpit?"

"Double insulated." Crofton thwacked his hand on the thick-rubbered edge. "All set for the takeoff."

Allard was aboard. Stepping back, Crofton watched the giro's big blades spin. They were running slowly, when a man from a hangar arrived suddenly beside Crofton.

"Say!" he exclaimed. "You ought to hear what just came over the radio! About a fog bank sighted off the coast! They've ordered the whole—"

The rest was drowned in a huge roar from the autogiro. Blades whirled like lashing arms of a maddened monster. The ship gave a forward, upward jolt; rose, as if hoisted by a spring, into a takeoff that was almost vertical.

Heading due west, Allard saw the foam-lined shore of the Pacific. Reaching outside the cockpit, he drew in wires that he hooked to a radio. Soon, he was hearing the very news that the man had started to tell Crofton, but with further details. More reports were promised over the air. Allard would not need them.

Burbank had followed instructions. This time, the authorities did not doubt the value of the mysterious tip-off relayed to them from The Shadow. There had been a long-distance call to Washington, with a prompt reply.

There was only one place that the news could not possibly reach. That was aboard the steamship *Unaga*. With his electrical barriers keeping up their steady pulsations, Zanigew was unable to obtain any facts by wireless.

THE big-bladed autogiro was swift. The ability of such ships to throttle down gave a false idea that they lacked speed. Such wasn't the case with The Shadow's autogiro. It was whipping westward at a speed of one hundred and twenty miles an hour.

Two miles a minute was a pace that would soon overtake the slow-steaming *Unaga*. An hour passed; the sun was low against the horizon, where Allard could see streaks of smoke, at intervals. Nearer, however, was a sight that pleased him more:

An oval cloud of low, flattish fog upon the water. A darkish mass, for at that lower level, the sun had already set. That cloud bank was The Shadow's goal, its exact center the target for his autogiro.

Detaching the radio wires, Allard flung them from the cockpit. Setting the controls, he reached for the bag beside him. Out came garments of black; beneath his cloak he placed the automatics, tight in their holsters.

Kent Allard had become The Shadow. From his hidden lips issued a whispered laugh that spoke of challenge and adventure. Equipped for the coming test, The Shadow was again ready to meet Zanigew and his criminal horde.

Five thousand feet above the oval fog, The Shadow cut off the motor. He yanked the lever, dumping the entire contents of the gas tank. Crouched in the insulated cockpit, The Shadow guided the autogiro downward.

Big blades were doing their work above. Motorless, they served the ship as a wing, restraining it like a parachute. Silent as the approaching night, The Shadow was descending toward his goal.

CHAPTER XXIII
THE LONG CHANCE

CLOSE by the superstructure of the *Unaga*, three huddled persons crouched beneath lighted windows. The fog was dark about them, bringing a pall to the steamer's decks. This was the dusk that three venturers had awaited.

Early dusk, while strong daylight still flushed the surrounding surface of the Pacific. Dusk as good as night, so long as they kept clear of the lighted windows which marked the great dining saloon of the *Unaga*.

Inside was merriment, fast turning into an orgy. Zanigew was entertaining three hundred guests. Caviar and other delicacies were quite to their taste, as was the champagne. In one grand banquet, the three hundred were forgetting the simple fare of Alcatraz.

Harry Vincent took a quick peek through a window, then turned suddenly to the two persons beside him.

"They're bringing in more iced champagne," he whispered. "Get started—quick!"

Fay Tretter stepped over toward the rail; her figure showed dimly against the fog. As she moved along, she hummed a tune that attracted the attention of a guard.

Vic Marquette was sneaking along below the level of the windows. The guard didn't see him. The fellow was too interested in Fay. He approached her.

"Whatta you doing here?" growled the guard. "You're supposed to be back at the stern!"

Fay laughed, lightly.

"The view's better here," she remarked. "That's why I came forward."

"The view?" demanded the guard. "There ain't no view! Say"—he poked his face close to Fay's—"maybe you came forward to say hello to me. Huh?"

"Maybe—"

As Fay spoke, Vic hurtled across the deck. He took the guard in a hand tackle as Fay whisked aside. Floundering, the fellow tried to pull his gun. He got it halfway from his pocket as Vic swung him beneath the windows. Harry Vincent piled in to aid.

From the dining saloon came the loud pops of champagne bottles, opening a dozen at a time. Amid that imitation barrage, the guard's gun went off. Its muffled shot sounded like part of the celebration.

The hand dropped, with its gun. The muzzle had been poked against the guard's own ribs. Marquette grabbed up the weapon, pointed Fay ahead of him. The girl met another guard further along the deck.

This time, Marquette supplied a hard slug with the captured gun. Popping bottles weren't needed to cover the only sound that occurred; the guard's slump to the deck.

Two such victories didn't mean that the rest would be easy. On the contrary, they foretold coming difficulties. More guards would be along; usually, they came in pairs. Once actual battle started, time would be short and precious.

Taking the second guard's gun, Harry started toward an upper deck. Marquette dropped to a companionway, ready in case of trouble. Fay went back toward the stern, to bring word if searchers came from that direction. By this time, there was a chance that the conspirators had been missed.

A LITTLE ladder gave Harry access to a space beside the funnels. He took that route; rising on hands and knees, he looked around. A shout came from below; it was answered almost at Harry's side. A flashlight glimmered. With a spring, two lurking men pounced for Harry.

Never could he have stopped both of them, but he aimed for one, hoping that luck might halt the other. Harry fired; so did his adversary. Since both were sidestepping, the shots missed. As they locked, Harry expected a revolver jab from the second opponent.

Instead, he was conscious of a shot from below. He heard the fellow drop to the roof of the deck. Vic Marquette had seen the attackers and had dropped one—the right one.

Harry expected to win his grapple with the other. The fellow was stubborn, but Harry was bending him toward the roof edge. The flashlight lay on the planking between them; its glow showed their bending faces, as each strained for a finishing hold.

With a jerk, Harry started the man headlong. One foot moving forward, Harry made a false step on the flashlight. Losing his hold, he rolled frantically for cover. A gun flashed just above his ear. Harry groped for his own revolver and couldn't find it.

Shots came from below. Marquette was trapped; but he was holding off his attackers. He couldn't help Harry. In fact, Harry couldn't aid himself. For other men were piling upon him, all with guns and flashlights.

They recognized Harry as he tried to rise. Their snarls told that they had orders to kill in an emergency such as this. A pleasure, from their viewpoint. Gun muzzles jabbed toward Harry's face, a semicircle of steel that met him every way he looked. Shoving his chin up, Harry expected the death shots. Eyes toward the foggy sky, he gave an amazed gasp.

The foemen heard it, along with another sound; a crackle from the high current that the big towers sent into the air. It was roaring louder, downward. Killers couldn't miss this sight. Holding Harry pressed with their muzzles, they let him view what was about to happen.

Another plane, enmeshed in Zanigew's snare, was due to explode within the next few seconds. But that ship didn't burst. Crackles ripped louder; suddenly they supplied a flash of vivid light.

A mass of brilliance was shaped in the fog, so vaguely that Harry thought it must be a meteor dropping upon the *Unaga*. Then the thing took on the outline of an airplane—but with one curious feature. It seemed to be flinging away the blazing sparks that clustered it.

Settling straight between the two funnels, the plane resolved into an autogiro. The flayed sparks were explained; they had been whipped away by the revolving blades. The ship hadn't exploded, because its gas tank was empty.

The Shadow!

He, alone, could have brought that ship to this strange landing. Harry knew that, as the autogiro jolted squarely on its wheels. But Harry remembered the potency of the protective current. Barreau had admitted that it would electrify anyone whose plane did not explode.

Harry's captors knew it, also. They spat contemptuous snarls toward the contrivance that loomed beside them. Oddly, their tones were answered—by a laugh! A shivering challenge that awoke hope in Harry Vincent!

He saw The Shadow rising from the open cockpit protected by the rubber interior. That one spot had been immune to the crackling currents. The Shadow was here, prepared for battle!

HARRY dived, hoping to escape the muzzles about him, frantically trying to grab up his own gun, half a dozen feet away. Neither his sprawl nor his weapon were needed. Surrounding men had forgotten him. All were wheeling to fire at The Shadow.

It was impossible for Harry to get into the fight soon enough to halt their shots. But there was another battler already primed for action. That fighter was The Shadow himself. His big automatics poked over the cockpit's side; they spoke in alternate bursts, timed to split-second swiftness.

Hot lead poured into the clustered group of guards. Too late, did they try to spring apart. That attempt only injured the aim of the few who were able to scramble. Two seconds later, they were sprawling like the first men that The Shadow clipped.

Wild bullets from sagging guns rattled the sides of the autogiro, well distant from the occupant. With a vaulting spring, a black-cloaked figure came from the plane, to land beside Harry Vincent.

Instantly, that shape had blended with the dark background of a funnel. Ready for new battle, The Shadow was in the shrouding gloom that he preferred.

Again, The Shadow's laugh! Sardonic, fierce in its weird crescendo, it was a challenge to all comers, Zanigew included!

CHAPTER XXIV
BROKEN BATTLE

BEFORE Harry had a chance to state facts to The Shadow, his cloaked chief turned in the direction of the bridge. The Shadow had picked it as the one logical spot where Zanigew would have the controls. Moreover, The Shadow remembered details of the plans that he had drawn up while passing as Barreau.

Those plans had indicated a control room placed approximately where a ship's bridge would be.

Shots brought The Shadow to a temporary halt. They were not closeby; they were from below. He leaned from the edge to pick off marksmen who were after Vic Marquette. In that thick haze-formed dusk, the only visible targets were spurting guns, but they proved sufficient for The Shadow.

As his adversaries took to cover, Marquette found opportunity to reach the roof of the upper deck, bringing Fay with him. Glimmering a flashlight, The Shadow showed plenty of guns lying about. Eagerly, the others gathered them.

With a quick order to Harry, The Shadow started on his way, intending to reach the bridge alone. It was a crafty move, for when he passed the funnel, he ran the gamut of playing lights. By leaving the others behind him, The Shadow put them in a spot of comparative safety, where they could keep up a misleading fire.

Groping forward, The Shadow neared the bridge. Crouching low, he could see armed guards ahead of him. They were looking past the funnel, trying to gauge what was going on there. Firing was spasmodic. Harry and Vic were holding their ammunition in reserve, while Fay arranged other guns in readiness.

Men on the decks beneath had learned who the troublemakers were. They thought that they had the trio boxed. A cautious advance would be the easiest way to force them out. A few men had reported seeing the sparking autogiro when it descended, but they hadn't made out just what the plane was.

They agreed that no living person could have arrived in it; and that seemed sufficient. The only men who could have given an exact report were those who lay flat above the upper deck.

There had been talk, though, of The Shadow's laugh!

That seemed incredible; too fantastic to report to Zanigew. It was bait that drew lurking men along the hunt, but to the wrong spot. Zanigew's murderous men were being drawn into the ambush that Harry and Vic controlled.

Something whimpered high above the *Unaga,* then exploded. The sound was repeated, but it was ignored by Zanigew's horde. They had become at ease beneath the sheltering electrical barriers. Their upward creep continued.

Then swift fury struck the guards close to the bridge. Out of their very midst rose blackness that launched into the glow of their flashlights. A two-fisted fury, with big guns in each hand. Slugging down the first men that blocked him, The Shadow made for the others, both guns at aim.

No quarter was asked or given. But The Shadow's guns were the ones that brought results. Each .45 delivered stabs like knife thrusts, dropping men from rails and stairways. Some dived to miss those devastating shots. Others, waiting too long, made vain efforts to clip The Shadow as they fell.

His tactics were too swift for them, until one marksman, hanging to a rail, put a last-minute shot toward The Shadow's shoulder. The black-cloaked fighter staggered, just as the man lost his grip and tumbled to the deck beneath.

Mouthing that he had clipped The Shadow, the marksman breathed his last. There was no one close to learn the news; a fortunate fact, for it would have produced a renewed attack on the part of the crooks.

THOUGH his wound was not serious, The Shadow felt its crippling effect. He wavered as he yanked open the door to the bridge. Then, with a renewed burst of strength, he launched upon two men within. They had no guns, for Zanigew had copied Barreau's system of keeping all armed men outside the control room.

They had weapons, though, in the form of big wrenches; and The Shadow's guns were emptied. Dropping one automatic, he used the other as a cudgel, to fight back from a corner just inside the door.

Harry and Vic were too busy, sniping at sneaky foemen, to realize The Shadow's plight. It was Fay who noted the finish of the shooting near the bridge. Grabbing a loaded gun, she made her way forward. Nearing the bridge, she jabbed two shots at men who were creeping for the steps.

Fay's aim was good. The two men stumbled. Others dropped back, thinking the blasts were from The Shadow. Fay saw the swinging door of the bridge, snatched a glance inside.

The Shadow was locked with his last adversary. One man already lay on the floor. Fay gave a grateful gasp as The Shadow's weighty gun descended. His last opponent fell.

Then Fay turned about again, to send another warning shot below. She didn't look to see The

Shadow, on the floor beside the men that he had felled. He came up, groping, crawling, fumbling for the levers that he wanted. It was a slow-motion process, in these last minutes when success seemed sure!

Above, new whimpers sounded from the fog. Whines, with occasional bursts.

THOSE sounds were heard by Zanigew, as he sat at the head table in the dining saloon, overlooking the food-gorging throng from Alcatraz. They were enjoying food in plenty, and drink with it. All of which pleased Zanigew.

What did it matter if fools had learned that this fog held the secret of the missing *Unaga*?

None could harm Zanigew. He ruled supreme! When greater fog received the lesser, he would vanish. One by one, he would add new boats to his flotilla. His empire would be everywhere!

Zanigew arose. His metallic voice pierced the great room, as he called for silence.

Revelry ceased. Out of three hundred faces, Zanigew was picking men of his choice. He beckoned them; they came to his table, his future generals. All was silence when Zanigew spoke.

"Every man shall serve me," declared crime's emperor. "I have already proven my power as the world's master of crime. They call you public enemies"—his lips took on their down-turned smile—"and the term is a good one. Public enemies are my private friends!"

Cheers that rose from the listeners drowned a few distant shots that Zanigew might otherwise have heard.

"London!" Zanigew held up a fist, clutching its fingers as though he had the British capital in his grasp. "A city of fog! Made to our order! We shall creep up the Thames, when the time is ripe, and spread crime everywhere!

"The Bank of England will be ours, thanks to my poison gas that mingles with the fog. All of you will aid me in the sack of London. These men beside me"—he gestured toward the chosen henchmen—"will lead picked squadrons to the attack."

Arms lifted, Zanigew quelled the new enthusiasm. He was coming closer home, in describing his globe-girdling tour of crime.

"New York has fog," he reminded. "We shall wait longer, perhaps for our attack there; but it will be worthwhile. Another victory; more wealth to fill our coffers!

"And after that"—his tone rasped high with confidence—"I hope to make use of other new inventions. To plan crime unheard of on this planet. To use crime as the mighty weapon that shall rule the world!"

Zanigew halted, one fist raised. A man had staggered into the great room, a smoking revolver in his fist. He fell half across the table beside Zanigew. Lifting him, Zanigew heard the name that the man's lips barely gasped:

"The Shadow!"

For a moment, Zanigew's eyes flashed disbelief. His ears could hear a sound that told him all was well: the buzz of his electrical barriers. Then, as Zanigew listened to make sure the sound was undisturbed, he noted its absence.

The Shadow had just pulled the controls on the ship's bridge!

Never had Zanigew been calmer. Letting the informant slump to the floor, he turned to the mighty band that faced him. Here were men who, singly, were worth a dozen of the followers upon whom he had so far depended.

Men who would rally to the battle cry that Zanigew intended to give; who were already armed with revolvers that their new master had brought from crates in the steamer's hold.

"There is one enemy," Zanigew told them, "who has caused many of you great trouble. He, alone, has actually tried to interfere with my great plans. That is why I lured him here today.

"He is actually aboard this ship. He has seized the controls and believes himself triumphant. He has not guessed that I allowed all that, to give you, my chosen guests, the privilege of ending his career."

Zanigew paused. Turning toward the door, he raised a pointing finger.

"Come!" he rasped. "I shall lead you to—The Shadow!"

THREE hundred men piled to their feet as one. Tables went spilling, bottles flung with them. Under the crystal chandeliers of the brilliantly lighted saloon, drawn revolvers flashed.

Springing to the curtained doorway, Zanigew waited for the yelling mass of murderous men to surge in his direction.

In that instant, Zanigew could picture The Shadow's fate: a crushed form of black, trampled beneath a vengeful stampede! He was glad that The Shadow had survived his former ordeal, to generously sacrifice himself to this occasion.

Amid the tumult, Zanigew did not hear the whine that came, with meteoric speed, in the direction of the *Unaga.*

A mighty crash took away a corner of the dining saloon.

The deluge of glass and woodwork was but an instantaneous prelude to the coming cataclysm. A titanic blast rocked the mammoth room, scattering men and furniture into a chaotic heap.

Every light was extinguished, but the effect of monstrous, scorching flames remained. Flattened among the curtains, Zanigew could hear howls and moans amid the air's reverberations. Eyes blinking, ears deafened, Zanigew could not realize what had happened.

Had he guessed the truth, his groans would have joined the others.

The thing that had struck the mid-structure of the *Unaga* was an explosive eight-inch shell!

CHAPTER XXV
THE FINAL TRIUMPH

ZANIGEW reached the deck, staggering until he struck the rail. Behind him were other men, masses of them, some reeling, others crawling. Quivering, plaintive creatures, many of them unscathed, but all rendered temporarily harmless by the effect of the mammoth concussion.

Men were struggling all along the deck. Crew members of the *Unaga,* called to sudden mutiny, were heaving Zanigew's followers down into the hold. Whirling fog-breakers had stopped, along with the electrical barriers. Coasting ahead of the fog, the *Unaga* was coming into the glow of sunset.

Zanigew turned toward the mortars, hoping to shoot more of the fog bombs. He saw crew members pitching the fragile missiles overboard, where they floated, useless. Then came the whine of a warning shell, just above the steamer's stern. Crew members scurried below.

They were on their way to release the prisoners! There was only one way for Zanigew to halt them. That was to reach the bridge, to deal with The Shadow in person.

Oddly, the route was open. Battle had carried below. No one wanted to go near the spot where The Shadow held control—no one except Zanigew. He reached the steps, sprang upward. Fay Tretter tried to stop him at the open door. Her gun was empty; Zanigew brushed aside the blow she gave with the bulletless weapon.

A gun ready in his fist, Zanigew saw The Shadow. The cloaked fighter's arm was already on the swing, bringing down a lever that he had wrenched loose from apparatus on the bridge. The iron bar clanged Zanigew's gun; even his strong fist could not hold it, after the numbing stroke.

Swinging his arm wide, Zanigew brushed the lever aside before The Shadow could attempt another blow. Crime's dethroned emperor locked with the being in black.

Fay watched that conflict, unable to give aid. The Shadow, already crippled, was battling a maddened monster of superhuman strength. The glow in those eyes of Zanigew's was ruddier than ever, his face more skullish, in the half-light from the thinning fog.

But Zanigew had lost his calm. Once driven to fury, he used brute tactics only. Skillfully, The Shadow was breaking off his choking thrusts, using the lever to aid his one-armed maneuvers.

Swinging against a window, Zanigew saw the deck. He twisted The Shadow toward the scene, rattled the harsh word:

"Look!"

Men from Alcatraz were on their feet, rallying in half-stunned fashion. Once they recuperated, they would take over battle as their own.

Death to The Shadow!

Zanigew did not voice those words, but the grit of his teeth told that he meant them. Into his ear came a whispered tone, sinister from The Shadow's lips.

"Look, Zanigew—beyond!"

Instinctively, Zanigew stared. For once, those odd eyes of his took on a bulge. It was light on the Pacific, for the fog had at last drifted clear of the *Unaga.* The ship, no longer hidden, was in the center of a gray flotilla that spread to the horizons.

Those vessels were the Pacific battle fleet!

Returning from maneuvers, the Navy had been ordered to surround the traveling fog. The facts that Burbank had revealed were sufficient to start the needed machinery. Observers had watched for a promised sight; an autogiro dropping into the fog bank.

To ascertain when the field was clear, they had fired test shots. Not while shells burst on the outskirts of the fog itself, but only when one landed, did they know the protective power was off. One shell had struck closer than intended. But its landing had been timely.

Through spyglasses, observers saw the decks of the *Unaga;* they made out the drab prison uniforms of the rallying horde. Zanigew had omitted the detail of providing new clothes for the men from Alcatraz. Recognized as rioters from The Rock, they were destined to meet new opposition.

GUNS opened fire from Navy ships. Shells bombarded the *Unaga*'s superstructure, to send men staggering from the shocks above their heads. Other missiles ripped the bow and stern of the *Unaga,* crippling the steamer without harming those below.

"Hell-divers" zipped downward in their planes, dropping smoke bombs on the decks, stifling the Alcatraz mob. Boatloads of bluejackets were heading for the stricken *Unaga.* She was settling lower in the water, for Zanigew's men had opened the stopcocks. Not knowing they were surrounded, they had decided to scuttle the ship and take to the small boats.

Amid all that, The Shadow took sudden advantage of Zanigew's doubled fury. He wrenched away, as the skull-faced fighter drove him toward the rear of the bridge. Clubbing cross-armed, he staggered Zanigew with a stroke of the steel rod that ended against his opponent's oversized head.

Then, locked again, the two reeled through the doorway. Zanigew was using all his massive strength in an attempt to hurl The Shadow down the steps. They were on the edge, The Shadow folding backward, when Fay sprang into the struggle.

She clutched The Shadow's cloak, pulling with all her strength. Her weight could not halt the coming fall, but it twisted the strugglers as they went. Instead of going backward, The Shadow was side by side with Zanigew.

Fay still gripped the cloak. It ripped from The Shadow's shoulders, and the last wrench was enough. The fighters were still turning as they cleared the ladder-like steps; they were plunging headlong. Zanigew beneath!

The massive head that had teemed with hopes of empire, was first to strike the deck. As The Shadow rolled clear, Zanigew's form stretched to its entire length and lay still. Fay looked down toward the skullish face. The deep-set eyes were closed. Upon the lips, Fay saw the fixed grimace that had once been Zanigew's smile.

Reaching The Shadow, the girl helped him halfway to his feet. He slid back, for the deck had taken a decided slope. Sinking steadily, the *Unaga* was almost awash. Fay looked up, hearing footsteps. Beside her arrived Harry Vincent and Vic Marquette.

They lifted The Shadow toward a boat that appeared near the lower rail, beckoning for Fay to follow.

She still held The Shadow's ripped cloak. Fay saw the slouch hat lying by the steps. She realized suddenly that The Shadow, whoever he was, had an identity to preserve. One last look at Zanigew's hideous face decided her next action. Fay spread the cloak over the crime emperor's stiffened form.

ACTUAL dusk had gathered as the little boat put off. It was the last from the *Unaga*, Fay learned. Bluejackets had gathered in the convicts from Alcatraz—some from the decks, others from the water, a few from the remnants of the wrecked dining saloon. Loaded aboard a cruiser, that drab throng were already headed back to the drabber walls of The Rock.

Fay's father and the other inventors were rescued, along with the many prisoners released by the rallied crew of the *Unaga*. If any live men remained aboard the sinking steamer, all were remnants of Zanigew's former force. Some of those shock troops were captured, others dead.

But probably some were missing. Hidden deep in the *Unaga*, they were one breed of rat that preferred not to desert a sinking ship. Perhaps their choice was best; for all were murderers who would pay due penalty, if taken by the law.

The small boat reached a waiting destroyer. In the darkness, Fay felt The Shadow raise himself as Harry and Vic began to help him from the boat. Once on the destroyer, he rested, leaning upon his unhurt arm.

Great searchlights were playing across the now-darkened waters. Those broad gleams showed the *Unaga* settling at the stern. With a shivering heave, the steamer thrust her bow above the surface; there was a surging gulp upon the ocean's surface as the *Unaga* sank from sight.

As the maelstrom ended its whirling, chunks of wreckage appeared amid the foam. Many eyes looked for human forms, but saw none. Those who had hidden deep in the hold were bound for the bottom with the vanished *Unaga*.

From the lips of a being beside her, Fay heard the solemn whisper of a mirthless laugh; a tone that spoke of justice, more than triumph. Its note, too, seemed to carry mention of a superfoe whose evil dreams were crushed.

Such was The Shadow's knell for Zanigew, whose empire of the future was buried with his vicious exploits of the past!

THE END

Coming in THE SHADOW Volume 17:

Ying Ko's shadow falls over Chinatown, unmasking ancient evils and strange disappearances. What is the sinister secret of

THE FATE JOSS

plus The Shadow and Myra Reldon investigate the mystery of

THE GOLDEN PAGODA

Only $12.95. Ask your bookseller to reserve your copy now!

THE MYSTERY OF THE VANISHING ARTIST by Anthony Tollin

George Rozen's dynamic cover paintings were an integral factor in The Shadow's success. His tenure as *The Shadow Magazine*'s regular cover artist began with the eighth issue when he inherited the assignment from his twin brother Jerome (whose paintings graced the covers of four 1931-32 issues).

George Jerome Rozen (1895-1974) was raised in Flagstaff, Arizona, where the twins first studied art with cartoonist Jimmy Swinnerton ("the father of the American comic strip"). After serving as a Signal Corps telegrapher during the First World War, George studied illustration at the Chicago Institute of Art (where his brother was already an instructor). During much of his pulp career, George lived on Shadow Lane in East Williston, N.Y. The street, formerly part of Will Rogers' Long Island estate, was named in honor of the artist who was one of its first residents.

George Rozen was abruptly fired in early 1939, though he later returned to *The Shadow Magazine*, first from 1941-43 and again from 1948-49 His initial run ended with the cover for *The Vindicator* (March 15, 1939) which appeared just three months after *Shadow Over Alcatraz* went off sale. George moved on to Thrilling Publications, where he turned out hundreds of superb covers for *Phantom Detective, The Ghost, Rio Kid, Masked Rider, Range Riders* and a variety of aviation pulps including *Air War, Sky Fighters* and *Lone Eagle*.

The reasons for Rozen's abrupt termination have been lost to the shadows of time. Jerome Rozen refused to discuss it, explaining that hurtful accusations were made that deeply upset George. Rozen's successor, Graves Gladney, was initially ordered to simulate George's style, and recalled that "though they fired Rozen summarily, they evidently retained fond memories of him."

Street & Smith Publications was undergoing a major reorganization at the time, following the arrival of Allen Grammer as the company's new president. Art directors William "Pop" Hines, Bill Lawlor and Heighton James had recently departed, and covers for *The Shadow Magazine* were being supervised by a new art director named Sniffen. A number of rejected *Shadow* covers by Rozen and Gladney were later reworked for other S&S pulps including *Crime Busters, Clues* and *Mystery*.

George Rozen's initial cover for *Shadow Over Alcatraz* pictured the Dark Avenger releasing a carrier pigeon in front of the prison's famous lighthouse. However, no pigeon appears in the published novel, suggesting that revisions made to Walter Gibson's original story outline necessitated a second cover painting, with the pigeon replaced by a sea gull. (Harry Vincent later sent messages to The Shadow via carrier pigeon in *The Museum Murders*, while foes employed the birds in *The Chinese Disks, The Vampire Murders* and *The Magigals Mystery*).

No one knows whether George Rozen received a kill fee for his rejected *Shadow Over Alcatraz* cover. What is clear is that the artist revised his rejected *Shadow* painting and sold it to Munsey, a rival publisher. The reworked painting, featuring a Shadow lookalike and the Alcatraz lighthouse, was published on the December 17, 1938 edition of *Detective Fiction Weekly*, which appeared on newsstands within weeks of the publication of *Shadow Over Alcatraz*. It's not unlikely that many retailers simultaneously displayed the similar covers to the probable chagrin of S&S executives.

For our back cover, graphics wizard Michael Piper has altered the published image from *Detective Fiction Weekly* to simulate George Rozen's original Shadow painting. •

Shadow **cover artists Jerome (left) and George Rozen. A *Detective Fiction Weekly* cover (center) may have led to George Rozen's removal as *Shadow* cover artist.**

Walter B. Gibson (1897-1985) was born in Germantown, Pennsylvania. His first published feature, a puzzle titled "Enigma," appeared in *St. Nicholas Magazine* when Walter was only 8 years old. In 1912, Gibson's second published piece won a literary prize, presented by former President Howard Taft who expressed the hope that this would be the beginning of a great literary career. Building upon a lifelong fascination with magic and sleight of hand, Gibson later became a frequent contributor to magic magazines and worked briefly as a carnival magician. He joined the reporting staff of the *Philadelphia North American* after graduating from Colgate University in 1920, moved over to the *Philadelphia Public Ledger* the following year and was soon producing a huge volume of syndicated features for NEA and the Ledger Syndicate, while also ghosting books for magicians Houdini, Thurston and Blackstone.

A 1930 visit to Street & Smith's offices led to his being hired to write novels featuring The Shadow, the mysterious host of CBS' *Detective Story Program*. Originally intended as a quarterly, *The Shadow Magazine* was promoted to monthly publication when the first two issues sold out and, a year later, began the unique twice-a-month frequency it would enjoy for the next decade. Working on a battery of three typewriters. Gibson often wrote his *Shadow* novels in four or five days, averaging a million and a half words a year. He pounded out twenty-four *Shadow* novels during the final ten months of 1932, he eventually wrote 283 *Shadow* novels totalling some 15 million words.

Gibson also scripted the lead features for *Shadow Comics* and *Super-Magician Comics,* and organized a Philadelphia-based comic art shop utilizing former *Evening Ledger* artists. He also found time for radio, plotting and co-scripting *The Return of Nick Carter, Chick Carter, The Avenger, Frank Merriwell* and *Blackstone, the Magic Detective*. He wrote hundreds of true crime articles for magazines and scripted numerous commercial, industrial and political comic books, pioneering the use of comics as an educational tool. In his book *Man of Magic and Mystery: a Guide to the Work of Walter B. Gibson,* bibliographer J. Randolph Cox documents more than 30-million words published in 150 books, some 500 magazine stories and articles, more than 3000 syndicated newspaper features and hundreds of radio and comic scripts.

Walter hosted ABC's *Strange* and wrote scores of books on magic and psychic phenomena, many co-authored with his wife, Litzka Raymond Gibson. Walter also wrote five *Biff Brewster* juvenile adventure novels for Grosset and Dunlap (as "Andy Adams"), a *Vicki Barr, Air Stewardess* book and a *Cherry Ames, Nurse* story (as "Helen Wells"),

Rod Serling's *The Twilight Zone;* and such publishing staples as *Hoyle's Simplified Guide to the Popular Card Games* and *Fell's Official Guide to Knots and How to Tie Them.*

No one was happier than Gibson when The Shadow staged a revival in the sixties and seventies. Walter wrote *Return of The Shadow* in 1963 and three years later selected three vintage stories to appear in a hardcover anthology entitled *The Weird Adventures of The Shadow.* Several series of paperback and hardcover reprints followed and Walter wrote two new *Shadow* short stories, "The Riddle of the Rangoon Ruby" and "Blackmail Bay." A frequent guest at nostalgia, mystery, and comic conventions, Gibson attended the annual Pulpcon and Friends of Old-Time Radio conventions on a regular basis, always delighted to perform a few magic tricks and sign autographs as both Gibson and Grant, using his distinctive double-X signature. His last completed work of fiction, "The Batman Encounters—Gray Face," appeared as a text feature in the 500th issue of *Detective Comics.*

Walter Gibson died on December 6, 1985, a recently-begun *Shadow* novel sitting unfinished in his typewriter. "I always enjoyed writing the *Shadow* stories," he remarked to me a few years earlier. "There was never a time when I wasn't enjoying the story I was writing or looking forward to beginning the next one." Walter paused and then added, a touch of sadness in his voice, "I wish I was still writing the *Shadow* stories."

So do I, old friend. So do I.

—Anthony Tollin